mattie spyglass

and the Lady of My Soul

Shoba Sreenivasan

HOLYMOLYPRESS

HOLYMOLYPRESS

For more information visit www.holymolypress.com or www.mattiespylass.com

Sreenivasan, Shoba
Mattie Spyglass and the Lady of My Soul/Shoba Sreenivasan/HolyMoly Press
Cover illustrator: Dan Ungureanu
ISBN-13: 9780985360436
ISBN-10: 0985360437
Library of Congress Control Number: 2015952559
HolyMoly Press

Printed in the United States of America

CONTENTS

characters and terms

Key Characters

    Mattie O'Reilly: begins as an eleven-year-old from Hackensack, New Jersey, in 1968 who finds the Spyglass among her deceased father's archeological effects and is thrown onto the Path of the Virtuous

    Spyglass: a conniving ancient entity trapped in an ancient Babylonian archeological artifact who seeks to occupy a pure soul

    Geeta Raghavan: begins as the eleven-year-old friend of Mattie who recently emigrated from India. She is a bookworm, as well as a princess of gypsies, and is also thrown onto the Path of the Virtuous.

    Eddie Petersen: begins as the eleven-year-old friend of Mattie; his father is fighting in the Vietnam War. Eddie, who longs to be a soldier like his dad, is thrown onto the Path of the Virtuous as well.

    Herman Biddle (aka Dmitri Gneezy): an old wizard who was long in hiding as a furniture salesman at Sears. He is Uri Gneezy's twin brother.

L. Rufus Wigglesworth, PhD: aged sorcerer and professor of assyriology at Columbia University in New York; friend of Herman Biddle

Gilgamesh: the ancient king of Uruk. He is three-quarters god and one-quarter mortal and seeks his lost friend, Enkidu.

Uri Gneezy: the evil twin of Herman Biddle, now serpentine in form

Ashurnasirpal: once king of an ancient kingdom, now servant of Marduk. He now appears in the shape of a hairy, ugly bull beast and is the master of the tunnels beneath Kurnigi.

Other Characters (Alphabetical)

Abaddon: a rodent-faced satanic creature of the underworld, once a subject of the Beast when he was the mortal King Ashurnasirpal II

Ab-gal-lu: Captain of the Outlaws of Hell, or He Who Commands the Chariot of the Great Waters of the Underworld; from Sumerian (ab = water, gal = great, lu = man, a sage associated with water)

Abyss of Blackness: the amorphous land and sea of darkness below Kurnigi

Asaru-alim-nuna (aka Ancient Demon Gods): the forgotten mighty demon gods of old, consisting of the gods of death of antiquity, the cave gods, and the primeval sea shark-snake creatures of death

Austen Henry Layard (aka Sir Henry or Layard): fictionalized British archeologist, discoverer of the Tablets of Creation in Nineveh in the mid-1800s at a mound called Kouyunjik

Counselor: the advisor to the Prince of Demons. In his mortal form, he wrote a medieval treatise to advise those in power regarding how to keep it.

Crone: an ugly hag, once the holder of the Black Book of Magic, now servant to the Snake Uri Gneezy. She longs for her lost beauty.

Daughter of Tiamat (aka the Hidden Daughter or the Hidden Sister of Marduk): a female entity who holds the Tablet of Destiny of Light and has been lost to time

Dottie O'Reilly: Mattie's mother and a former a student of Dr. Wigglesworth. She left Columbia University after her husband perished and now works at Sears in Ladies' Hats Accessories.

Duke of Muscovy: a master of cruelty in the underworld who is also a member of the Brotherhood of Evil

Enkidu: Gilgamesh's friend and fellow warrior who was lost in the forest of Humawa

Four Terrors (aka Nergal, Namatar, Lamashutu, and Zaltu): old demon gods of destruction who form one part of the Asur-alim-nuna, the forgotten mighty ones

George Smith: fictionalized British clerk with a genius for deciphering cuneiform. In 1872 he translated the Babylonian story of the Great Flood (the Epic of Gilgamesh) from the tablets. He died in Nineveh on an expedition at age thirty-six.

Great Magician (aka Master Magician): a magician who holds the golden key to fame and fortune.

Great Spirit of Darkness: an entity even greater than Marduk as a force of darkness. Man's senses can only feel this being as the stillness of a black, bottomless pool or the coldness of death.

Great Spirit of Light: an entity even greater than Tiamat as a force of light. This being is spread across the universe, above where the minutest of glimpses of the sky of the world are seen by mortals in the form of stars and planets.

Great Spirit of the Universe: the controller of the Universe of Light and Darkness

Grim Reaper: the hooded figure of Death and the holder of Death's scythe

Hannu: ancient noble Egyptian seafarer in the Red Sea who sailed for treasures for the pharaohs 2,750 years before the Common Era/Before Christ (BCE/BC)

Humawa: the guardian of the Forest of Death, where the Grim Reaper lives under the dominion of the Beast Ashurnasirpal

Iron Knight: a man known as Goering; once second-in-command of Hitler's forces, now a servant to the Snake Gneezy

Keke: Stal's long-suffering mother, pious in the Georgian Orthodox Christian faith

Khan of the Huns: a bloodthirsty titan who now resides in the underworld and is a member of the Brotherhood of Evil

Lamashtu: one of the Four Terrors, the demon goddess of tribulation. Her evil fingers hold the unborn to be devoured. Hairy in body, she bares her teeth in a face shaped like a wolf and has feet with sharp, predatory talons.

Lev Nicolayvich: a wise old sorcerer and mentor of Wigglesworth who walks in light and resides as a mendicant (beggar) in old Russia

Marduk: the Dark Master of the underworld and holder of the Tablet of Destiny of Darkness. He is the son of Tiamat and the brother of the Hidden Sister.

Mesh-ki-ang-gasher: an ancestor of Gilgamesh who drowned in the Sea of Abyss but whose spirit gives strength to the warrior spear

Mrs. Elmwood: Mattie's fifth-grade teacher at Fairmount Grammar School in Hackensack, New Jersey

Muhra: conniving creatures of the underworld. Condemned to eternal life without bodies, they form the atmosphere of Kurnigi at its gates.

Namatar: one of the Four Terrors, a demon god of death and disease. His arms are covered with boils, and his face is half eaten.

Nanshe: an ancient Mesopotamian goddess of light and life

Nergal: one of the Four Terrors, a demon god of destruction with fiery locks about his head

Once-Noble One: a noble of an ancient land with two rivers that crossed it. After he betrayed his brother, he was reduced in his mortal life to a scavenger of the sea.

One of the Nile: an ancient female sea outlaw, with skin like black velvet, hazel tiger eyes, and hair in spikes embedded with sapphire beads

Outlaws of Hell: creatures so evil and two-faced that they are condemned as criminals and plunged into the sands of the Sea of the Abyss

Paddy O'Reilly, PhD: Mattie's father, who died mysteriously in Nineveh in 1957 while attempting to find the mysterious Eighth Tablet of Creation

Prince of Wallachia (aka Vlad): a bloody impaler and a member of the Brotherhood of Evil who lurks in the underworld

Rasputin: a charismatic monk in the time of Tsar Nicolas

Roanes: sluglike gray demons who live in the Sea of Abyss and take the form of beautiful sea-maidens to lure mortals to their deaths

Saghulhaza: the upholder of evil, the new title for Uri Gneezy

Sea of Abyss: an underwater void contained in the Abyss of Blackness

Sebitti (aka Seven Guardians of Marduk): seven monsters who are half demon, half mortal, male and female. Some have the faces of a raging wolf and dragon bodies; others are giants with scorpion bodies; and still others are huge creatures with fangs and human bodies.

Sergeant Petersen: Eddie's father, who is fighting deep in the jungles of Vietnam in 1968 in the Special Forces

Seven Bitter Widows: seven widows on shaggy gray mares. They are the holders of bloody shrouds of bitterness and are forever mourning their lost loves.

Seven Murderous Brides: brides who killed their grooms after they were forced into marriage. They are condemned to the Abyss.

Seven Sista: a wise old woman who was born in the slave days in the United States

Stal (aka Isoif, the Prince of Demons, and *Il Principe del Abyss*): once pockmarked boy and son of a Georgian cobbler and washerwoman, now a cruel tyrant of the underworld

ThaTha: Geeta's grandfather

Tiamat (aka Tiamet and Tiamut): the Mother Spirit, thrown into obscurity by her wicked son, Marduk

Trina: one of the wandering spirit children, once known by Stal in his boyhood. She is also Eddie's beloved.

Tsar Nicolas: a martyr who was the last emperor of Russia

Unclean One: a cruel servant of Stal, Prince of Demons. This creature rises from the Sea of Abyss with seven heads, ten horns, and a crown made of the bones of the blasphemous.

Unholy Trio (aka Tarnished Knights): a threesome who, when they lived in mortal form, were corrupt knights of early medieval Christendom but now reside in the Abyss. They are the high priests of the Abyss who read the Unholy Rites.

Utnaspishtim: in the story of the Great Flood, the old man who holds the secret to eternal life

Vengeful Spirits: souls tricked by Abaddon in mortal life. They are now trapped in the underworld and seek revenge against him.

Wandering Spirit Children: orphan souls caught in the underworld

Zaltu: one of the Four Terrors, the demon goddess of confusion. Her long gray locks of hair emit fogs of confusion.

Terms and Places (Alphabetical)

Assyriology: the study of ancient Mesopotamia; the Akkadian, Assyrian, and Babylonian languages; and the deciphering of cuneiform

Black Book of Magic: the book of dark magic held by Uri Gneezy

Boat of the West: a vessel that, in ancient Mesopotamian, Babylonian, and Sumerian myths, carries souls into the underworld

Book of Life: the story of humanity's creation

City of Condemned Spirits: a land deep beneath Kurnigi in the Corkscrew of Terror

Corkscrew of Terror: the horrific circle of terror within the bowels of Kurnigi

Cuneiform: the written language of the ancient Mesopotamians, appears in slashes

Death's scythe: an instrument to reap the souls of the living

Dup Shimati: the Babylonian tablets of destiny

Eighth Tablet of Creation: mysterious and dangerous tablet that Paddy O'Reilly seeks

Enuma Elish: the Babylonian tale of creation and also a chant used by Herman Biddle to invoke White Magic

Ettuku, Ekimu, Asag, Alu: the Four Terrors' incantation of protection, the names of evil spirits

Kurnigi (aka Land of Darkness): the underworld

Muktablu: term for "warrior"

Mushussu: a red snake, a symbol of the Dark Master Marduk

Nineveh: an ancient city of great wealth that was located in the kingdom of Iraq. It was settled possibly as early as 6,000 BCE near the rivers Tigris and Khors.

Ordinem Sanguis Draco: the Order of the Blood Dragon, Vlad's legion of the unliving

Path of the Virtuous: the mysterious, treacherous eight stones of suffering

Radix Malorum Cupiditas: a Latin phrase that translates to "the root of evil is desire"

Ša Nagba Īmuru: the story of He Who Saw the Deep

Seven Tablets: the Babylonian tale of creation

Sefer Yetzirah: the Book of Creation, also known as the Book of Formation, in Jewish mystical traditions

Space-Between-Two-Seconds: Herman Biddle's chant of protection

Spiritus Non Sancti: the Spirit of Darkness of the unsanctified and unpurified that is the underlying power for the Unholy Book

White Book of Magic: the book of magic of light held by Herman Biddle

Zi-ukkina Zi-azag: the incantation for the release of creatures from the Black Book of Magic

CHAPTER 1

the fourth stone of Bitterness

Mrs. Elmwood slapped the blackboard with her eraser to emphasize a point. Behind her was today's date, Thursday, October 31, 1968, followed by the quote of the day written in her loopy schoolteacher handwriting: "Learning is not attained by chance. It must be sought for with ardor and attended to with diligence. —Abigail Adams." She sternly stood in front of Mattie's fifth-grade class at Fairmount Grammar School in Hackensack, New Jersey, pointing at the quote with a finger dusty with chalk.

"Abigail Adams, wife of John Adams, second president of the United States. Mother of John Quincy Adams, sixth president." Mrs. Elmwood paused and added emphatically, "But most importantly a *devoted* reader."

She was the type of teacher who wanted everyone to read books all the time—and Mattie wasn't a reader.

Mrs. Elmwood had dark-brown hair pulled tightly back into a bun, heightening a broad white forehead that bulged out in a sort of half-moon shape. She wore thick black-framed glasses that sat on top of a beaked nose. Mrs. Elmwood wasn't what one might call pretty. Rather, she was prim. At least this was the way Mattie's mom described her. Then her mom would always add, "Beauty, Mattie, is in the eye of the beholder. Always remember that." Why she needed to do this Mattie couldn't tell you. But that's the way her mom was: telling her to remember all sorts of things that didn't make a lot of sense. Maybe it was because "prim" wasn't exactly a compliment, and Mattie's mom, who was pretty herself, didn't like to insult anyone. Who really knew? Just like when her mother would sigh and her eyes would pool up with tears as she held an old framed picture of Mattie's dead father, Paddy O'Reilly—chubby with frizzy red hair, a bushy orangey mustache, and glasses; wearing expedition gear and standing on a mound somewhere in a faraway land. "Deceased, Mattie," her mother, would always correct her. "Always remember that your father died on a very important archeological quest in Nineveh in the kingdom of Iraq." This had happened in 1957, right when Mattie was going to be born, so she didn't ever know her dad and couldn't really miss him like her mom did. So Mattie would just nod.

The wind blew through the windows into the classroom with a creepy howl. Fairmount Grammar School was old and creaky. Outside, the trees were shedding their leaves like tears. A branch scraped at the windowpane with a mournful sound. It was the perfect Halloween day, except for it being a school day. *Gosh! Couldn't Mrs. Elmwood just let us out early this once!* Mattie thought. But this wasn't Mrs. Elmwood's way. Mattie noticed that her friend Geeta (who was Indian from India and wore her hair in two black braids and always sat in the front of the class with her big glasses that magnified her eyes, like the brainy owl she was) had already finished copying the quote. Mattie glanced again at the blackboard. They were supposed to memorize it because "a quote a day keeps the dullness away," according to Mrs. Elmwood. Plus you got extra credit if you could recite all five at the end of the week. Not that Mattie ever had.

Mattie impatiently hit the back of her chair with her heels. She looked at the clock again. It was slooooowly tick-tick-ticking toward three—just ten more minutes! She thought about the costume she would wear tonight for trick-or-treating. On account of how she had red hair that was frizzy—and *highly unmanageable*, as her mother always said—she couldn't really wear it back in a bun and be a pilgrim lady, like her mom had wanted. Plus the pilgrim hat her mother, Dottie O'Reilly, had gotten from Ladies' Hats and Accessories at Sears (where she worked) looked more like a witch's hat on Mattie, what with her hair zigzagging underneath it. Mattie figured that she got the frizzy red hair from her dad, as her mom's shiny blond hair was smooth and behaved itself. The black-and-white dress her mother had her try on was way too tight. The pilgrim costume was something her mom had worn when she was Mattie's age, but her mom was skinny, and Mattie was…well, she was chubby (again, this seemed on account of her dead—*deceased*—dad, who had been chubby like her).

This was just as well, as Mattie was going to be a popcorn machine for Halloween, just like she wanted. A few weeks ago, she had taken a cardboard box that nice old Mr. Biddle had found in the basement of Sears, where he worked in the furniture department. Mr. Biddle had old-fashioned white whiskers that went up around his face, as well as sad blue eyes, and was real smart but never talked down to kids. He had helped Mattie pick out just the right size box. She had spent all month working on it at home: first wrapping the front and back of the box in aluminum foil, then gluing popped and unpopped corn onto it, cutting red knobs out of construction paper, making a slot for where you put the money in, and even getting some old pop-corn boxes to glue onto the sides. It had been a *lot* of work. She was going to wear gray tights so it would look like she had metal legs. Because the box was big enough, she could wear her coat underneath and be nice and toasty warm while trick-or-treating. Mattie had cut two holes on each side of the box where she could stick out her arms and one for her head on top. Last week, when she had proudly shown the finished popcorn machine to her friend Eddie—who lived across the street and was in the same fifth-grade class with her—he didn't seem too impressed.

"What's it supposed to be?" he had asked, squinting at the box.

This kind of made Mattie mad. Eddie knew exactly what her costume was and was just pretending not to see it. She figured Eddie was most likely jealous. When Mattie told him what it was, Eddie shrugged and said that a popcorn machine was something he'd already done when he was in the first grade, remember? So she was just copycatting him and not real well either. Mattie had gotten hot under the collar because it wasn't the same thing as Eddie's first-grade getup. This was *not* some made-up little-kid popcorn machine. Mattie's costume looked exactly like the *real* popcorn machine in the basement of Sears. You had to be really dumb if, like Eddie Petersen, you couldn't see that. Plus, Mattie had added, it was way better than always going as a Green Beret like Eddie had been doing since the third grade. Eddie's dad was in the Special Forces, leading a platoon somewhere deep in the jungles of Vietnam, and Eddie wanted to be just like him. Only he was eleven, just like Mattie. Eddie had yellow hair that stood up in a cowlick and lots of freckles splattered across his face. When he scowled to look like he meant business, he still didn't look like Special Forces on a special op, even in his soldier getup. But you couldn't tell Eddie that. But Mattie had, and Eddie got mad and stomped out of her house. When Mattie complained to her mom, she said, "Eddie misses his father terribly, Mattie." Mattie didn't think this was right; she didn't have a dad either but that didn't mean her mom would let her take hissy fits. Still, she did feel bad for Eddie, she knew he was always worried about his dad way out in the jungles fighting like he was.

"Trick-or-treating"—Mrs. Elmwood's voice shot through Mattie's thoughts, her brow scrunching over her sharp face—"can be dangerous." A few kids groaned. This was the same lecture they'd all heard over and over. Only Geeta seemed to be paying attention.

Someone yelled, "Can't we go?"

Mrs. Elmwood ignored the question and continued, ticking off the rules one by one with her fingers. "Do not eat any apples that you are given. They might have razor blades in them. Do not eat loose candy. *Do* go in groups, not alone. Do not stay out past eight p.m. Do not—" Then the bell rang.

All the kids jumped out of their seats to grab their coats and rushed past Mrs. Elmwood. Mattie was swept along with the crowd of kids who were pushing the big front door of Fairmount Grammar School open and bolting out onto the steps and into the street.

Fairmount Grammar School was a red-bricked, two-story building that fronted a treelined street in a neighborhood filled with large old houses. Some lucky kids actually lived in those homes and were going to be able to lickety-spilt get into their costumes and get the jump on the good Halloween candy! Mattie's house was at least fifteen minutes away. *Where are Geeta and Eddie?* she thought, her face flushed by the effects of the sheer excitement that Halloween offered. Then she spotted Eddie, who was whizzing past her. He had planned, "the mission," which was to get to as many houses as possible before it got too dark. Eddie had "reconned" the "terrain" and knew which houses gave the best candy. He shouted to Mattie, "Fifteen twenty hours at my house!" Eddie always gave military time, which was annoying because then you had to think of what that meant in regular-people time.

"Three twenty. Hoo. Hoo," Geeta said as she came up behind Mattie.

Mattie took another look at Geeta, who was wearing an owl costume, her small brown face with the big black glasses magnifying her eyes, which blinked above a beak. *How did Geeta get into her costume so quickly?* Mattie wondered. She couldn't have run home and back already. Geeta lived on Andersen Street, right next door to Eddie, and both of them lived across the street from Mattie.

Suddenly all sorts of kids sprouted around Mattie. Everyone was wearing Halloween costumes. Witches. Spiders. Ghosts. Ghouls. Goblins. They were ringing doorbells, running past her, loaded down with pillowcases filled with chocolate bars and candy corn and lollipops. Mattie looked down—she still had her school clothes on! *Run fast! Run fast!* she commanded herself. She had to get into her costume fast or there'd be no good candy left! But as much as she willed her legs to move, she remained in the same place. She hadn't gotten away from Fairmount Grammar School at all!

The sky behind the school dimmed into dusk as a large yellow moon rose above it. The trees bent as if a high wind were blowing them downward. They wailed as if in pain. Leaves fell off—red, yellow, orange like bright crystals. Then Mattie's popcorn machine fell from the sky and landed right on top of her. Her head popped out of it, as did her arms. Geeta flapped her wings, every second looking more and more like a real owl. Kids with blue and green monster faces, bulging eyes, and gnarled hands were springing up all over the place—right from the ground, it seemed. They snarled at Mattie with big red lips, the wax kind that you could chew. Then the lips melted as the kids' faces and bodies dissolved into puddles at Mattie's feet: blue, green, red wax. The big yellow moon melted right in the sky like a pat of butter. It dripped down over the red bricks of Fairmount Grammar School, and the buildings walls sizzled as if they were hot as a griddle.

All around her, witches, ghosts, goblins, spiders were screaming, "Trick or treat!" as they turned into puddles on the sidewalk. The ground was liquefying right beneath Mattie; everything around her was vanishing away. Even her! "Aaagh! Mattie yelled in fright. Her gray tights were oozing into a lava-like waxy substance onto the pavement until she had no legs. The cardboard popcorn box was floating on the oozy ground. She was getting hot; she felt the heat from the aluminum foil and heard the sharp sounds as kernels of corn popped. Her arms rotated desperately out of the box as she tried to escape the pull of the oozy rising pool. Soon Mattie would be nothing! She heard a hoot above her. There was Geeta flapping real owl wings and flying above her. She even had large owl talons: three in front and one sticking out in back as she hovered over Mattie.

"Help!" Mattie shouted.

Geeta tugged at Mattie's popcorn box with her owl feet but couldn't budge her. The landscape was lit with gloom: the weak, thawing moon threw long shadows upon the churning rising wax of dissolving trick-or-treaters; it was forming a river around Fairmount Grammar School. The sky was an ink black streaked with the yellow of the melted moon. A great wailing wind rose and flung Geeta right into the liquefying ground. She flapped her wings helplessly in the roiling river of wax. "Hoo! Hoo!" she hooted.

Soon Mattie, Geeta, and all the Fairmount Grammar School trick-or-treaters had been reduced to screaming, bobbing heads in the percolating torrent of molten wax. Above them appeared a strip of light that transformed into a bulging white moon of a forehead, and then below it emerged the familiar beaked nose and the glasses, large in the sky. It was a giant Mrs. Elmwood. Her face was set in grim lines as she intoned, "Trick-or-treating can be dangerous." Mrs. Elmwood turned green, the color seeping down first from her shiny forehead, over her glasses and nose, until her face was a shimmering lime color and scaly in texture. The scaly green dripped over her face while the shape changed, erasing her humanness, turning triangular, until there was nothing left of Mrs. Elmwood; there was only a huge hissing cobra head of a snake that shook in the sky. One blue eye and one emerald eye glittered.

Mattie tried to scream, "Geeta! It's the Snake!" But the words were caught in her throat. The Snake's mouth opened, and a large black forked tongue darted out and hit the black sky just like Mrs. Elmwood smacked the blackboard with her erasers. From the long black forked tongue, large glossy red apples dropped down. The apples split, and gleaming razor blades fell from them. The blades glinted against the dark sky then fell in a torrential fury onto the trick-or-treaters, who were quickly dissolving into goo. Only the heads of Mattie and Geeta bobbed up and down in the churning river of wax. The Snake in sky hissed, "Trick-or-treating can be dangerous!" The words whooshed in Mattie's ears as the molten wax pulled her and Geeta downward like water swirling into a drain.

𒀀𒌋𒉿𒇷𒄿

"Trick-or-treating can be dangerous!" Mattie screamed in terror.

Her eyes blinked against a blinding white light. The whoosh of the spinning giant Hourglass made a buzzing sound in her ears, and her legs hit its side. Realization flooded her consciousness. She had a body, and it wasn't in a popcorn box—she felt her legs dangling down and the rubbing of her green-checkered pants with the deep pockets against her thighs. One arm was jerked up; the other was free. The skirt her mom always made her wear over her pants was gone. Then her foot hit a head. *Geeta's.* Mattie sighed in relief. But when she looked down, all she saw was a whiteness that was bright and shining like glittering mounds of snow. At least she hadn't turned into goo melting into the ground. The bad news was she was still trapped in that giant Hourglass, spinning away. Whether she had really traveled to Mrs. Elmwood's fifth-grade class in Hackensack, New Jersey, in 1968, she couldn't say.

Nothing had been usual anymore, Mattie thought ruefully—especially time—since she had found that no-goodnik Spyglass and she, Geeta, Eddie, and Mr. Biddle were thrown onto the Path of the Virtuous to cross the eight stones. So much had changed since she had pulled the Spyglass out of that chest of her dad's stuff in the attic in her house in Hackensack and she had become the Mistress of the Spyglass.

Flashes of memory sped through her mind: how Eddie's dad, Sergeant Petersen, had led them through the jungles of Vietnam to find the Path—those magical glowing stones—and how only she, Geeta, Eddie, and Mr. Biddle could be on it. How Mr. Biddle had been a small boy in Russia and the brother of that horrible Snake Uri Gneezy; how she had golden skin and led her people, the lost souls of Nineveh, to freedom. Then there was that elfin old man with the large ears crisscrossed with blue veins who had said he would protect her, not to mention the beautiful Goddess, the Mother, who had called her "Daughter." And, oh, yeah, her mom had found her dad alive again backward in time, but now they were being held prisoners by the Snake and the Beast. And who could forget the awful events on the Third Stone of Anger, where Eddie had disappeared?

Now Mattie was again in the giant Hourglass with Geeta, spinning away from the Third Stone of Anger. Where were Mr. Biddle and Eddie? Where was Mattie's mom? The thought racked her heart with pain. *Mom!* She had to save her mom from that horrible Snake. Mattie struggled fruitlessly, dangling in the Hourglass. One arm was stretched up and stuck through the hole that separated the Hourglass into two parts. That upper part held all the sand, and Mattie felt the angry hold of the Spyglass clasped in the hand that was thrust up. *Spyglass! It's all your fault! Rat fink! Traitor!*

The Spyglass heard Mattie's words and bristled at their unfairness. *Traitor? No, stupid girl,* the Spyglass thought, as she was held in the sand in the other half of the Hourglass. *You are the traitor. To me. I gave you one of my precious gold bands. I saved you!* Spyglass had shuddered at the searing red orbs of Marduk, the Dark Master, which had penetrated through the Hourglass when they had been on the Third Stone. See where Mattie had taken her? Straight into the jaws of danger! But the Dark Master had been thwarted, at least momentarily, by the chaos that reigned as the demon gods had erupted from the underworld, gathering in power to defy him. The heat from the red orbs had spurred the Spyglass into action, precipitated by claustrophobic panic brought to the forefront of her memory: her burial in the hot sands of Nineveh.

Spyglass turned in her dual prisons: the metal tube that held her and now the Hourglass; she spun, and the sand turned colors: purple, yellow, orange. The colors were brittle sparks dissappearing into the blinding white light. Spyglass had mightily thrown her will against that of the pull of the Path of the Virtuous, vowing to having nothing more to do with this treacherous journey! Gale-force winds twisted the Hourglass, and try as she might, the Spyglass couldn't overcome the pull of the Buddhas and the strength of the blinding white light. Once again she resolved to crush Mattie's will—that force that resisted her—and take full possession of her soul.

Three bands of gold had been given to the Spyglass for her protection. By whom, when, or even why she didn't know. Only by giving Mattie one gold band to save her when she ate from the poisonous Tree in the Midst of the Garden on the First Stone had she acted with uncharacteristic selflessness. Now only two were left. Two bands of gold were all that stood between the Spyglass and utter annihilation. She needed to occupy a pure soul—and fast. She had easily tempted corrupt ones with the lure of extraordinary power, and through the eons, these dirty souls had left her imprisoned. If she could possess a pure soul, the Spyglass was confident that her memory would return—of who she was and how she had been imprisoned in the metal tube. More important, the location of where the Hidden Daughter of Tiamet lay would be revealed to her. Then the Spyglass would wrestle from the Hidden Daughter the Twin Tablet of Destiny.

But how? she wondered.

All these plans she had made again and again over the eons, failing in the end to be released from her metal prison. She had chosen Mattie as a pure soul, but the girl had turned out to be a headstrong fool who cast her away at every turn, right into the mouth of danger. Now what chance was there for her to secure her freedom on the treacherous Path of the Virtuous? What chance did she have when her fate was so dependent on this reckless girl who constantly thwarted her? A gray fog of despair silenced the Spyglass's thoughts.

Geeta's black braids flung about her face as the Hourglass spun higher and higher, away from the ground and into the pull of the Buddhas. Her head smacked against the bottom of the Hourglass. She realized Mattie's dangling legs were just above her, as she felt them hit her arms as she was tossed about the Hourglass. Geeta's eyes were shut against the searing white light. Thoughts whirled in her mind—as many, it seemed, as the very grains of sand in the Hourglass. How the gypsies had called her "Princess" in the frozen land of Siberia. How Rasputin, once called the Mad Monk, but now turned good, had himself had called her "Princess." How this journey of fate had thrown her backward in time and how that evil creature, Uri Gneezy, snake and man at once, servant of the Great Master of Darkness, Marduk, had been chasing them across the Stones. How they had met the kind Gilgamesh, the giant blue ancient king of Uruk, who called Eddie a warrior, *muktablu,* and how Eddie now wielded Death's Scythe in his living hands. How she and Mattie were trapped in this giant Hourglass, created by the Black Card of Time given to Geeta by Mr. Biddle. Geeta had seen Mr. Biddle and Dr. Wigglesworth pulled from the bloody battle between the Cossacks and the Russian peasants on the Third Stone and into the great light that was the Buddhas. But Eddie? Had she seen him below, engaged in the battle using Death's Scythe? And was that Gilgamesh, the king of Uruk, with him? Geeta felt the sharp premonitory stab of fear for Eddie. Then there was Mattie pushing the Hourglass to move against the light, screaming, "No! We have to stay here and find my mom. No!"

It seemed to Geeta that the more Mattie pushed, the more the Hourglass shook and moved into the light. *The illusive power of Maya,* the voice of Geeta's grandfather, ThaTha, rang in her mind. In her mind's eye, she saw his brown face lined with wisdom, the sacred trident-shaped marks upon his forehead, his head shaved with a small white pigtail sprouting from the middle, signifying his Brahmin caste. His eyes appeared rheumy with age as he sat in his dhoti, the white cotton robes he always wore, reciting his prayers. Geeta remembered sitting with him in Bombay when the priests—also in their dhotis, which barely covered their large bellies with saffron-colored string diagonally crossing their chests—would come to perform rites on holy days. Why priests were so well fed Geeta never understood, for it seemed to her that if their world was that of the spirit, shouldn't they avoid the lure of food? ThaTha had only smiled at her when she had said this. "Maya holds us all," he would say. Then she would ask him, "What is Maya?" ThaTha would give her the same puzzling answer: "That which is unreal has no existence and ceases to be." Maya…Geeta couldn't grasp it. When she said she still didn't understand, ThaTha would only add, "That which is real never ceases to be."

Still, the smell of the burning sandalwood incense, the offerings of fruits—mangoes, bananas to the gods, the coconut broken in half with its fleshy white skin embedded in the hard brown casing—and the mantras, the chants that followed, always made her feel peaceful. ThaTha had told her over and over her favorite tale, the story of the Song of the Lord, of how Arjuna had faltered on the battlefield, tried to avoid his duty, and how

Lord Krishna, disguised as his charioteer, had revealed himself. It was a poem that was not a poem at all but the story of how each soul had the duty to fight evil, to do good, to understand how to distinguish what was real from unreal. And then there were ThaTha's words on the Third Stone of Anger: *In the battlefield for the soul, whether there is to be eternal order or chaos in the cosmos, those who fight their dharma lose, not just for themselves but for all.*

What does that mean, ThaTha, now? Geeta wondered. Now that she and Mattie were imprisoned in this great giant Hourglass and plunging downward? How were they fighting their dharma? For it seemed to Geeta that the Path of the Virtuous set their fate, their journey, and it brooked no opposition.

The chant that had risen on the Third stone vibrated over and over in the air. The sound spun the Hourglass faster and faster into a starless, inky blackness. The blinding light was gone now. Mattie and Geeta both opened their eyes. The Hourglass was suspended in the sky and surrounded by hundreds of translucent Buddhas in saffron robes. Some had rolls of fat, so corpulent were they; others were gaunt, with ribs that protruded from their sides, their eyes hollow. Some were male; some were female. Some were chalk white, others black as obsidian. Others bore the brown color of tilled soil; while still others were pale yellow or bore a rusty reddish tint; those remaining had faces that were translucent. All were suspended in meditative poses, some with eyes that were shut and some with eyes wide open as they intoned:

> *Eight precious stones,*
> *Eight matters of the soul,*
> *Rise like the wind of wrath.*
> *Eight stones of suffering.*

Suddenly the Hourglass shot through the sky, the words of the Buddhas pushing it down toward a roiling mustard-colored sea that was choppy with iridescent pale-green waves. The Hourglass struck the churning sea, falling on its side. It bobbed up and down. The Buddhas in the sky were now very faint in form, glimmers of images burned into the air.

Mattie's arm jerked as the Spyglass, trapped in the other half of the Hourglass, shuddered. Mattie lay sideways. At the bottom of the Hourglass, Geeta steadied herself on her knees, pressed her palms against the slippery glass, and through her big owl glasses, stared at the strange shimmering sea. Geeta thought: this must be the Fourth Stone. Then her eyes widened. "Look!" she cried to Mattie.

𒀭𒈾𒆠 𒂍 𒀭𒈾 𒁉

Herman Biddle felt the relentless pull of the Path of the Virtuous lift him up from the Third Stone, along with Dr. Wigglesworth. Biddle's cape flew about him, turning colors— now purple, now cobalt blue, now the color of a steel-gray sea under gloomy skies. His boots were covered with a faint patina of dust, his pants tucked into them, as was his way on expeditions. Oh, what an expedition this had become: crossing the deadly Path of the Virtuous! Turning time asunder. Releasing the evil that lay dormant under the written and unwritten destiny of humanity. His long white hair flew back, while his long beard lay heavy upon his chest. Herman Biddle's light-blue eyes were shot with darts of fear and worry. He shut them tightly against the searing force of the rising wind. Now he was encircled by the darkness of his thoughts. The sky was torn asunder in vengeance against Marduk by the demon gods of destruction, pain, confusion, and conflict.

They were the Four Terrors: Nergal, god of destruction; Namtar, demon of tribulation, bearing dark winds of pain; Lamashtu, the long-haired demoness, with her gray locks spreading a fog of confusion; and Zaltu, goddess of conflict. Their cries were of vengeance against the Dark Master, who had imprisoned them in the tunnels beneath Kurnigi. Thus had the war between Marduk the Dark Master and the demon gods who called themselves the forgotten mighty ones, Asaru-alim-nuna, begun. There had been the battle in the sky: evil against evil. In the ensuing maelstrom, Biddle and Wigglesworth had been released from Marduk's terrible hold. Though Marduk couldn't penetrate the Hourglass that held Mattie and Geeta, as it was a creation of the White Book of Magic, the powers of light were fading, and this Biddle recognized, as surely did Marduk. Biddle tried but failed to grab Mattie and Geeta with his cape as the Hourglass that held them spun away. *Wigglesworth, how miserably we have failed in our task!* Biddle bemoaned. For below them on the Bloody Sunday Russian ground of 1905, in the Square before the Tsar's Winter Palace, the souls of the mortals had fallen to the underworld. Rasputin had perished, as had Tsar Nicolas. In the battle of dark against light, evil was now the victor. Biddle and Wigglesworth hadn't averted the evil of Bloody Sunday at all.

Again and again Biddle chastised himself for his cowardice, for his capitulation to ill-placed family loyalty. He should have killed Uri in cold blood, brother or not, before Uri Gneezy had risen in his serpentine power, before his soul had been given to Marduk and the dark forces of the Black Book of Magic. His heart was stabbed with pain for Eddie, who was impossibly wielding Death's scythe and sure to lose the battle against the pockmarked demon upon a dragon horse. Oh, what terrible events had Biddle unleashed for all in order to avoid his fate? Just before he plunged into the churning sea that was the Fourth Stone, he saw the round figure of Wigglesworth, his bald head and his eyes shut tight, his cape upon his shoulders, fluttering in wisps of light, tumbling toward him.

L. Rufus Wigglesworth's three chins shook against the vibrations that were the sounds of the Buddhas' chants as his hefty old body was pulled upward. He had hidden himself for one lifetime in that body, in the form of the esteemed chair of the department of assyriology at Columbia University in New York. On the surface he appeared to be an academician interested only in furthering the works of Sir Henry Layard and George Smith toward deciphering and interpreting the *Enuma elish,* the Babylonian Seven Tablets of Creation. He thought now of the plans and schemes he and Biddle had concocted to hold Paddy O'Reilly at bay from opening the Pandora's box that was the search for the Eighth Tablet of Creation. How they had traveled back and forth in time to undo the Gordian knots of evil, failing at each turn. How Sir Henry Layard, in their visits to the past, had pressed upon them for keeping in the future the writings that spoke of the underworld and the cruel King Ashurnasirpal, formed in the nightmares that had awakened him trembling with fear in his nineteenth-century expeditions to Nineveh. And how he and Biddle thought they had kept buried the malicious Spyglass, who held knowledge that was best left alone and who had been kept buried until Mattie had unearthed it and had thrown time into Chaos.

Wigglesworth shuddered as his pudgy figure flew with the contradictory lightness of a feather into the pull of the Buddhas. Asaru-alim-nuna, the forgotten mighty ones, now rose and tread the land, as the Moon Goddess prophecy had foretold. The Asaru-alim-nuna were the evil triumvirate of demons of destruction and death: demon gods of ancient times, the cave gods, and the primeval sea shark-snake creatures of death. This trio was the first to tempt man to relinquish free will and clasp the hand of evil. They, Asaru-alim-nuna, now rose again in sinister demonic power to shut out light. Wigglesworth knew well that the Path of the Virtuous was a terrifying one and doubly so for him, in the moribund mortal body he now wore, bearing the heavy burden of the Cape of Ša Nagba Īmuru. He Who Saw the Deep Ša Nagba Īmuru, beholder of the Mysteries and protector of the fate of the souls of the world. The cape was ancient beyond the reckoning of mortal man's time, as well as the thing of legends: of the gods of old who had worn it in the battles against evil, who had draped it over those who had died to save mankind. The Moon Goddess, it was said, had formed the first strands of the cape with her light for those ancient gods of light; had woven and infused into it were the Mysteries. It was soft and light and heavy and dark at once, for it held the fury of the seas and the tremors of the land, and woven into its threads was the story of the earth and of humanity's fragile existence and that of their souls, of the dualities of darkness and light. Too, it held a mystery within which was embedded the secret. The Cape of Ša Nagba Īmuru demanded much of the wearer. It was in substance bands of light that fell seemingly gentle as a soft, warm breeze upon Wigglesworth's shoulders.

In fact the cape was neither flimsy nor caressing but an entity of destiny as substantial as fate itself. The story of how

Wigglesworth had been pledged its protector was written in the hours when youth was his, in those many lifetimes ago, in those eons since Wigglesworth had held the White Book of Magic—when the division of light from darkness first began to dim, and goodness became more and more elusive to humanity upon the earth. Now he had realized his destiny: he was to be the wearer of the Cape of Ša Nagba Īmuru, whose eyes saw the Deep but whose lips could not form the words and speak what he saw. He was doomed to watch mortal man in his folly run headlong into peril. Such was the burden of the cape, that of knowledge of a seer. And the time for humanity was at an end, and too this meant that all that was good and light would fall if, in the final balance, the souls were tallied to darkness. These thoughts held L. Rufus Wigglesworth tightly as his body spun toward the sea.

"Look!" exclaimed Geeta, again pointing. For there was Professor Wigglesworth, plopping into the churning mustard-colored sea with light-green waves in a rather undignified manner: legs ups, arms fluttering. A strange cloak, at once cloth and light, was under him, keeping him buoyed over the choppy green waves. He looked like a fat bug on its back. Mattie turned her head; her shoulders hurt from the way the Spyglass was pulling at her arm, which was still stuck in the top half of the giant Hourglass.

"And there's Mr. Biddle!" Mattie cried out happily as he fell into the sea. Hope surged in her heart. Now that Mr. Biddle was here, maybe he could get her and Geeta unstuck from the Hourglass, and they could search for Mattie's mom.

"Mr. Biddle!" Mattie yelled. "We're here! Over here! Behind you!"

Geeta tapped hard on the Hourglass to get the attention of Biddle and Wigglesworth, who had fallen such that they faced away from the Hourglass. "Mr. Biddle! Dr. Wigglesworth!" she yelled as Mattie joined her.

Herman Biddle's cape floated around him; it was a wispy sea green color that almost blended with the choppy green waves upon the water. Was it water? For Herman Biddle saw that the substance was thick and oily. Beyond him Rufus Wigglesworth was on his back, kept afloat by the Cape of Ša Nagba Īmuru. Wigglesworth's thoughts ran to the martyr Tsar Nicolas, the gleaming blue of his uniform and the gossamer gold wings that showed him to be an angel over the sky of ancient Nineveh. He thought of Tsar Nicolas's pronouncement after Mattie's actions had thrown time into chaos: *Before the Book of Life can be written again, the Path of the Virtuous must be crossed.* The Path of the Virtuous couldn't be tread by those weak of will, nor could it be tread by those who wanted to thwart their own destiny. The Path of the Virtuous, the terrible Eight Stones—of which they were now on the fourth—must be tread to the end. *No*, he thought, *not must. If. If it could be traversed to the end.*

"Mr. Biddle!"

Herman Biddle heard Mattie's cry as he floated on the now mustard-colored substance. He immediately turned his body toward the sound. He saw the giant Hourglass, and trapped within the bottom half were Mattie and Geeta. His heart jumped with relief and fear at once. Mattie and Geeta were here. But Eddie? Where was Eddie?

"Try to keep the Hourglass steady!" he called, seeing how it was spinning slowly away from him under the pull of the sea.

Herman Biddle struggled against the yellow-brown sea toward the Hourglass. The sea was turning every more gelatinous in consistency. The green waves upon it were small slashes of movement but fierce in their strength. Biddle pulled his cape in order to escape the hold of the waves and soar upward. The waves slapped him back, small chastising hands that then pulled on him, pinning him in place.

The chants of the faint outlines of the Buddhas in the sky rang again as their forms slowly faded away.

Eight stones of suffering:
Fear, hate, anger, bitterness, envy, duplicity, greed, and despair.
Five stones remain.
If you can cross them,
You will find the Seer of Truth.

The Fourth Stone of Bitterness, Biddle thought, as the Buddhas disappeared. The Hourglass was now pulled farther and farther away from them under the ever-changing sea. The mustard sea and its lime-green waves hardened and crumbled. The waves turned brittle, and the Hourglass stopped rolling. The surface was now a web of cracked land. Freed from the grip of the waves, Biddle stood up quickly and shook his cape to lift him toward the Hourglass. Biddle felt its weight, for it held the White Book of Magic. In fact the cape held magic itself: the Cards of Time. Now with time in Chaos, that which had been set in the cards was uncertain; it changed as the sky and clouds did, reflecting the mercurial nature of destiny, of fate. The White Book of Magic was dimming as the balance between light and dark and good and evil was moving in the direction of Marduk and his dark forces. So the potency of Biddle's cape must have been ebbing, as he and Wigglesworth had feared. And now the cape—once protector—needed protection, vulnerable as it was to the penetration of evil.

The cape darkened into an indigo blue as it spread from Biddle's shoulders like a giant wing before lifting him. Just as his boots left the fissured yellow ground, the weight of the sky pressed him back down as the Hourglass rolled farther away.

Rufus Wigglesworth grunted as he stood up. His eyes widened as the visions that were moments in coming shook his heart with premonitions.

Seven chalk-colored wisps formed a ring in the sky. They grew and took shape: seven women riding upon seven shaggy gray mares. They wore black robes, and their hair was long and flowed behind them like streams of grief. Each woman held draped in her arms milk-white shrouds that were gruesomely stained with splashes of blood. The seven women's faces varied in color: that of the ploughed earth, the pale moon, the light brown of the sands of the desert, the pink of the dawn, the red-rock mountains, the black pebbles of the stream, and the yellow of a fading sun. They now formed a semicircle in the sky, their faces hollow and flat of expression, in striking contrast to their tawny-colored eyes, which glowed with bitterness. They raised their bloodied shrouds, and their doleful song fell in bitter droplets upon those on the ground.

> *In the gray, silent stream bed,*
> *Among the reeds and rushes we stay*
> *The decaying and the dead.*
> *In these melancholy waters,*
> *Where the loving heart is prey,*
> *Bare we our widows' faces, bitter and gray.*

O my lost love,
Weep do I for you!

The Seven Bitter Widows moaned a long sound of sorrow. Their voices raised in unison. The sound of the widows' mournful song rose, its notes of bitterness cutting through the souls of the listeners as each widow sang of her lost love, their words overlapping:

O my lost love!
Long do I for you!
Your hair coarse and black, eyes the brown of winter meadows
Your hands held the strength of mighty mountains
Your hair smooth and golden, eyes the color of the summer sky
Your face bore the scars of the warriors of the great forests
Your skin the color of a lemon before it has ripened
Your voice held the roar of the mighty ocean
Your passion burned like a ring of flames
O weep do I for you, my lost love! A thousand rising suns cannot lighten
the darkness of our spirit.

The splash of their words fell on Herman Biddle's face like small needles and stained his white hair and beard a sickly brownish yellow. Upon his tongue lay the bitter metallic taste of the Seven Widows' tears. And in his heart, Biddle felt the prick of a thousand sharp stabs of anguish. As the Hourglass rolled upon the ground, the widows' tears hit it and fell through it. Geeta's eyes were large with wonder at the sight, and her heart felt the stabs of pain as the tears struck her face. Then there was another feeling, an aching, as if her heart had been squeezed and pulled. Geeta heard Mattie whimper as the widows' song rose again.

Not for us is sunshine.
Not for us are the singing pines
Or the soft green meadows.

The gray mares whinnied, their high shaggy heads quivering in the sky. The bitterness from the widows' dirge seeped into Biddle like a slow poison. He felt the beats of the widows' heartache, of their sorrow and resentment at their fate. He saw the Hourglass beyond him, no more than thirty feet. How to help Mattie and Geeta? For this Fourth Stone was insidious in its hold.

Wigglesworth knew they must resist its pull, for bitterness once sown in the heart grew strong and bled the soul of its strength. The widows' elegy rose again in acrid notes.

For our loves are lost and beaten,
Taken from our bosoms,
Taken from our sides.
But cry alone we must.
Care not do others for our wails.
Care not do they for our bitter tales.

Then the Seven Widows threw down their shrouds, which formed into a thick rolling blanket of fog in the sky and fell slowly and heavily toward the ground. The fog enveloped the Hourglass, and a wind spun around it. Inside, Mattie and Geeta were buffeted by the force of the wind as it turned their vessel faster and faster until it blurred and disappeared into the fog.

Herman Biddle saw the torment of despair envelop the Hourglass and vanish with Mattie and Geeta. The moan of the Seven Widows was now a windstorm in the fog. Their lamentations were now no longer intelligible but sounded like the high wail of the wind. It was a woeful sound that pierced the ears of Biddle and Wigglesworth while the dense fog blinded them. Biddle faced the windstorm, fruitlessly trying to leap into the sky in the direction the Hourglass had disappeared. Then the widows' moans took form once more, took the shape of words, eerily echoing in the dense fog that had gathered on the ground.

> *Our loves' last garments, tattered and bloodied,*
> *In our arms, weak with sorrow, have we carried.*
> *Come you now to this stone, hardened with our tears.*
> *Now these shrouds shall fall upon you.*
> *Lose shall you, as did we, that which is precious,*
> *So your heart, as does ours, may beat agony and despair.*

The wind rose with the last notes of the widows' song. It lifted Biddle off the ground then tore his cape from him. Biddle first felt the shock and unreality of the loss, followed by the sudden realization that the cape had been torn from him. The cape rose in the wind just above him; Biddle's arms were outstretched. Within the dense fog, the cape glinted purple. Its folds were pitted with the yellow, caustic tears of the widows. As the cape fluttered up, Biddle lunged to grab it, his fingers just missing the cape's folds. The cape then rose into the fog. Biddle felt as if a knife had been plunged into his heart, and a moan, long and dark with despair, emitted from his lips.

Rufus Wigglesworth's eyes caught the violet glint of Biddle's cape as it fluttered away. He pushed his massive body slowly against the force of the wind of the widows toward Biddle. Herman Biddle's cape held the White Book of Magic. It couldn't be lost on this stone. *Biddle, keep fast…Do not yield to the bitter wind!* Rufus called to him in his mind. Wigglesworth felt the sour taste of the tears upon his lips. He could rise with the magic of the Cape of Ša Nagba Īmuru, as it was impervious to the widows' laments. Wigglesworth felt the beats of Herman Biddle's despair. Suddenly the cape appeared just inches beyond Biddle's grasping fingers, flitting so close to his touch.

I'll get the cape, Biddle. Don't touch it! Wigglesworth mentally called to Biddle.

Biddle's touch, tinged with desperation, would only shred the cape. Such was the malicious capriciousness of the Fourth Stone of Bitterness: to allure you with what is taken and then destroy it in front of your eyes. But Herman Biddle didn't heed his colleague, consumed as he was to recapture the cape. Instead he lunged up again, now grabbing the edge of his cape. As he did, the cape ripped. *No, Biddle! Your touch only threatens to tear the cape asunder!* Wigglesworth cried. Again Biddle was deaf to his words, for he held fast to the cape and pulled it toward him. Wigglesworth heard Biddle's soft moan as the cape fell to shreds at his touch. *The bitter wind plays you well,* Wigglesworth lamented as he saw his friend's outline within the fog, holding the tattered pieces of the cape in his hands. The dense fog rolled around and through Biddle until he disappeared.

What now? Now that the cape that held the White Book of Magic lay in tatters in the grieving hands of Herman Biddle? Wigglesworth whispered to himself the answer, "Ask me whence and upon what time the fury of the oceans might in darkness drown the land. Ask me when the thunder of the evil ones, Asaru-alim-nuna, rose from the blackness, stones shattering upon the earth."

"Now," Wigglesworth heard his voice. "It is now that they will drown the land in darkness."

The words fell weakly from his lips as the heavy fog encased him.

CHAPTER 2

song of the bewitching roanes

The Abyss of Blackness was a vortex formed not by the absence of light but by the presence of a force. The Abyss drew and twisted Eddie downward with the potency of a cyclone. No longer was his body that of an eleven-year-old but that of a tall, lean but muscular young man: a yellow-haired *muktablu* (warrior), though he had no armor to shield him, just Death's scythe. He had transformed on the Third Stone into a man when the notes of endless love that had played upon his heart through his lifetimes rang once more in his consciousness. Then he had unthinkingly plunged into the Abyss, as the warrior spirit of rescue had surged through his veins. Plunged had he without a thought to his safety into this universe of shadows that lay deep below Kurnigi, the Land of Darkness. The hell beneath hell. It condemned those doomed there to a pointless existence, an endless loop of power struggles—wins and losses—only to be repeated.

This was a story that had been told and retold through the eons. Its permutations were known to all who had been condemned there, and they all were forced to live it over and over: a song, a refrain, a joke heard and heard again until the very sounds of it made one retch. That was the unchanging, senseless, hellish existence of the Abyss. Until now. Until order had been shaken between light and dark and time plunged into Chaos. The reverberations of Mattie's actions on the First and Second Stones had been felt first faintly then stronger as they moved through Kurnigi then into the Abyss. Chaos had filtered down from Kurnigi into the Abyss. Consequently the unthinkable had now been introduced into the Abyss: change in a world where for eternity there had been only an endless repetition of the same notes of conflict and duplicity. And now a living being who, incredibly, held Death's scythe had plunged into its midst.

Eddie's thoughts ran fast and hard to this conclusion: he was dressed for battle. He felt the combat boots heavy on his feet and the weight of the combat flak jacket upon his chest. But the darkness was such that no intel could be gathered from his surroundings. All he knew was that the force of the Abyss was pulling him downward. Gilgamesh, the king of Uruk, had called it the "Abyss of Blackness" as Eddie had thrown himself into it, ignoring the king's warning. He had plunged into the Abyss in contradiction to everything his father would have warned him against: going into enemy territory without having reconned it first, without a plan and backup.

As the Abyss continued to pull Eddie downward, his fingers gripped Death's scythe. Though it was an instrument of death, the scythe now paradoxically vibrated with life. The blade, with its sharp lethal point, marked one as the maker of death, not a hapless victim of it. He sensed its power grow in the blackness and felt the evil weapon seek to spring from his hands. Eddie grasped it tighter with his living hands, quelling its rebellion and conveying to the scythe that he was its master.

Although Eddie's body was that of a man, his face still held the dew of youth, what with his yellow hair shooting up in the back in a cowlick, his freckles now the fading memories of boyhood. However, the square of his jaws spoke of manhood, and a fierceness shot through his eyes, which were now an emerald green surrounded by the light color of the sea sand. He was now a *muktablu*. A warrior. Destiny had changed his form from boy to young man. Though Eddie wouldn't know it, his face would stir the heartstrings of females with longing, for it was at once boyish and mannish and promised an innocent eternal devotion. But for one and one only: Trina. And this would be both a curse and blessing.

Trina. Trina.

These were the thoughts that filled his mind as he catapulted into the Abyss of Blackness. Though his eyes couldn't see what was before him, he felt her presence.

Trina. Trina.

His heart beat her name, etched as it was in his soul through lifetimes. Endless lives of love found and lost. This Eddie understood the way one understands the splintered stories of dreams, whose tales come in pieces: memories from past lives mixed in with the events of the present. Above all, he knew he must seize Trina from the demonic hands of the pockmarked Prince of Demons who had taken her upon his dragon horse; in fact it meant everything. No other mission—here he thought of his childish attempt at warriorhood—was paramount. Trina had to be rescued to be by his side. Then the strength of their love would guide him onward to overcome evil.

The sounds of a battle raging within the jungles of Vietnam struck Eddie's consciousness. They ran like a stream over rocks, garbling a man's words. Eddie quickly realized it was the commanding warrior voice of his father, Sergeant Petersen. They were only snatches of sounds, weak at first, then stronger and finally formed. *Abandon this mission. Escape the Abyss now before it's too late!*

For the first time in opposition to his father's counsel, Eddie thought back, *No, Dad.* For though his father was a warrior who had been battle hardened in Vietnam, he was wrong about this.

Eddie! He heard the underlying tones of anxiety in his father's voice. *Keep your guard up! Don't let your heart rule your head. Don't forget your mission: to cross the Path of the Virtuous.*

Eddie bristled at this, for he was well aware of the mission and needed no reminder. *I'm not a kid anymore, Dad.* His heart led him to jump into the Abyss of Blackness, for to find Trina and rescue her from the red-eyed pockmarked demon who held her was all that mattered. Without Trina, he was Samson shorn of his locks.

Eddie's thoughts ran fast to the events of the Third Stone of Anger: how he had thrust Death's scythe at the pockmarked demon upon the dragon horse. How the terrible demon had wielded his sword, the savage Sword of Shadows, at him again and again till he was filled with a searing pain. Then Trina came toward him, her eyes sorrowful, and behind him he heard the wails of the wandering spirit children and the soft cries of warning of Gilgamesh, who was struggling to stand. "*Muktablu!* I will… come." Flashes of memories filled Eddie: Trina bending over him, whispering, "You're hurt." Eddie's arms had been bloody and raw, his eyes blurred by pain. *Trina.* No harm could come to her; he couldn't bear it. He had felt his love for her surge and saw it reflected in her eyes and pound through his heart. It was then that he understood that his love for Trina was profound and enduring—that he had loved her throughout the ages.

Thus it was the awakening of that endless love that led kindred souls to find one another over and over in the sea of time and that had transformed Eddie from a boy to a young man. Trina's eyes reflected back this knowledge. Eddie had seen her change before him from a girl into a young woman—the one he had loved and lost through lifetimes. Trina's chestnut hair fell in long waves, framing her hauntingly beautiful oval face; her hazel eyes were fringed with long sable lashes, her lips full.

Then the terrible thing had happened: the arm of the pockmarked demon upon the dragon horse had grabbed Trina and held her tight. The pockmarked demon had cried, "I am Stal! Prince of Demons!" He then claimed Trina as his consort; she would be the princess for the Prince of Demons! Into Eddie's mind Trina spoke, held prisoner by Stal as they plunged into the Abyss of Blackness: *Muktablu, leave this place and save yourself.* But Eddie closed his mind to it. For all he saw was Trina grasped by Stal, and the sight was too unbearable. It was then he had lunged forward with Death's scythe and plunged into the Abyss of Blackness, where now the terrifying forces had pulled him into their maelstrom.

Sergeant Petersen's voice now shook with strength and warning. *Eddie, think with your mind, and beware of your heart, for it will deceive you.* Abruptly the sergeant's presence faded, and the blackness felt different. Eddie sensed it lift, though not fully. And the very material of the Abyss transformed. It felt like water but wasn't. The pull of the liquid was cold. Eddie struggled to see his surroundings and gauge the depth of the Abyss; it seemed to be a bottomless ocean. It was not, in fact, bottomless, for the body of this *muktablu*, a living being holding Death's scythe, was felt by those who lived at its base, sleeping creatures of the sea—now awakened—that had been pulled into the vortex of the Abyss of Blackness.

The scythe gathered energy in the dark substance that was pulling Eddie farther and farther downward. His body turned and twisted. His chest tightened. A sound, hypnotic and melancholy, rose. It was the call of the sea apparitions that inhabited the deep waters of the Abyss. Eddie struggled to keep his eyes open; the alluring vibrations filled his ears with a rhythm like that of waves upon a shore. His eyelids fluttered closed. Instinctively his body assumed an airborne position as he continued to fall into the depths of the malevolent sea. For that was what it was: filled with danger and the promise of destruction with underwater demon creatures of the Abyss that had been awakened once more.

𒀭𒌷 𒂍 𒀭𒌷 𒀸

Gilgamesh, the seventh king of ancient Uruk, had felt the rumbling of the ground beneath him upon the Third Stone when it had given way under the weight of evil. His long black ropes of hair and his beard of twisted braids had flung back against the force that rose on the earth. Now his blue face was a portrait of anguish. For the *muktablu,* who was still young though he had been thrown suddenly from boyhood to man, had run toward the spirit girl Trina for whom his young heart beat with love. Only moments ago the ground had split suddenly into a deep chasm: the Abyss of Blackness, into which the young *muktablu* had plunged—a black canyon from which a great force rose and pulled into it the demonic creatures that had been flying around this ground.

This soil was the frozen land of the living where man killed man on a day called Bloody Sunday. This, Gilgamesh didn't know, nor did he know of the Path of the Virtuous. He only knew that when the red-haired child with the evil amulet had destroyed the museum's Seven Tablets of Creation, in which Gilgamesh had been trapped, Chaos had churned.

Then it was that the red-haired girl, the brown owlet girl, and the yellow-haired boy whose bravery would show him to be a warrior had begun their journey into the menacing forest of Humawa. There the young *muktablu* had saved Gilgamesh, interrupting the Grim Reaper, and had pulled into his own living hands a weapon that reverberated with the rhythms of evil: Death's scythe. Then rose in Humawa's forest the wicked and cunning rodent-faced Abaddon, with his four-fingered hands that ended in long black nails. Abaddon once had been a prisoner within the folds of the Grim Reaper but was freed when the harbinger of death himself crumbled to dust when the young *muktablu* had grabbed the scythe. Still later, incredibly, came the destruction of Humawa himself, the lord of the forest, by the twin powers of the scythe and Gilgamesh's warrior spear. So it was that the spirits of the underworld had risen, with Death's scythe now in the hands of Eddie, the living *muktablu*.

On their journey toward Kurnigi, the Land of Darkness, Gilgamesh and Eddie had met the spirit girl Trina and the wandering spirit children. They had beseeched Gilgamesh and the young *muktablu* to help them traverse through Kurnigi, upon their journey of Seven Tears, which would set them free. To this Gilgamesh would have said no, for his quest was to find his lost brother, Enkidu, as well as to bring eternal life to the lost souls of his people of the kingdom of Uruk and to help the *muktablu* find the red-haired girl and the brown owlet, who were now trapped in Kurnigi. But the heart of the young *muktablu*, Gilgamesh realized, beat with the rhythms of first love for the beautiful spirit girl Trina. Her shiny chestnut-brown hair, her hazel eyes, and her lovely pale face had allured the young *muktablu* when he had agreed to help Trina and the other wandering spirit children.

Next they were flung into this cold land of conflict, where men on horses killed those on the ground, where the condemned dead had risen from Kurnigi, including the vengeful spirits who had been tricked by Abaddon for their souls when they had held mortal form. Abaddon's razor-sharp teeth then sank into the red-eyed Prince of Demons, whose hands showed they held Abaddon's evil black-and-blue thumbs. This demon rode a dragon horse and sliced the air with a mighty sword that left in its wake slashes of malice. This pockmarked, red-eyed demon had fought a giant serpent that hissed his revenge as it flew into an evil black book. Gilgamesh then had seen spirits appear in the sky in saffron robes—the Buddhas who called the chant of Eight Stones and pulled the young *muktablu* up. Then it was that Gilgamesh had felt sorrow at this sight of the *muktablu* moving up into the light of the Buddhas above. The young *muktablu* had been like Enkidu, a friend, a brother.

Still, as king of Uruk, Gilgamesh understood that each warrior had his own journey to travel, and he saw that the young *muktablu*'s journey lay with the spirits that had wrenched him up from the land. However, the young *muktablu* had thwarted the pull of the Buddhas, for his love for the spirit girl Trina was strong. He fought against the wind, slashing the scythe at the Prince of Demons, kicking against the force that drew him up. As the winds of the Buddhas had risen in strength, the young warrior's will had grown as well. The *muktablu* rolled his body down, broke the force of the sky spirits, and jumped to the ground. The light of the Buddhas dimmed and faded. Gilgamesh had grabbed the young *muktablu* as he tumbled down. His heart was at once glad and anguished, for the young *muktablu* sprang up to lunge at the

Prince of Demons, whose grip upon Trina was strong. With his other hand, this pockmarked prince called Stal then swung his weapon, the Sword of Shadows.

"Trina, grab my hand!" Gilgamesh had heard the young *muktablu* shout. As Gilgamesh had swung his spear, the spirit girl Trina had struggled against the tight grasp of Stal to reach the young *muktablu*. Then had come an immense and terrifying sound that shook the ten feet of Gilgamesh from head to toe. It was the unified cry of the many forms of the old demon gods, Asaru-alim-nuna, the forgotten mighty ones. With their broken forms—their giant bodies of scorpions, skeletons, and dragons— these forgotten demon gods triumphantly shouted, cracking the air: they would no longer be forgotten!

> *O Marduk, Dark Master, will you be no more?*
> *For our poison demon arrows*
> *Into mortal man's heart have struck,*
> *Filled with envy and greed,*
> *Filled with pride and need.*
> *So will it be war and vengeance,*
> *An endless dance of bloodshed,*
> *As man will hate the other,*
> *As man will kill his brother,*
> *And rule shall we Kurnigi,*
> *Land of Darkness and the Dead,*
> *Land of Misery and Dread!*

Gilgamesh's blue face had deepened in distress under the alarming prophecy of the mighty demons. Evil had grown more powerful, and humanity would suffer, for Gilgamesh knew there was always chaos before the victory. He also had shuddered at the sight of Marduk, the Dark Lord, the enemy of Mother Tiamat, who had appeared as red orbs in the sky then dimmed and disappeared over the Third Stone. Next the weight of the gathered evil ruptured the ground and formed a chasm. Gilgamesh had shivered with trepidation at the sight before him: the harrowing Abyss of Blackness. With a coldness that was like the steel of a knife, it lay underneath even the deepest bowels of Kurnigi and held an awfulness that silenced the soul. But whom it held as master of the Abyss wasn't known. The depth of this realm's malevolence was so malevolent that the Abyss lay even beyond the control of Marduk himself,

As the chasm had widened on the Third Stone, the demon gods of old were pulled downward, howling into the vast blackness of the Abyss. Right before Gilgamesh's eyes, the Prince of Demons, clutching Trina and riding a gigantic dragon horse, fell when the ground gave way and were instantly sucked into the blackness of the Abyss. The *muktablu* stumbled against the great reverberating boom of the earth at the precipice of the Abyss. Gilgamesh had shouted in alarm, "No, *muktablu!*" for he saw what the young warrior was about to do to save his love. "It is the Abyss of Blackness!" The *muktablu*, however, hadn't heeded Gilgamesh's warning. Instead he had called to his love, "Trina!" and hurled himself into the Abyss as it closed over him.

So it was that Gilgamesh now stood alone upon the desolate, frozen earth of the Third Stone as the Abyss of Blackness closed, his spear held aloft, his heart swelling in the agony of what to do. For Gilgamesh had heard the ancient tale and knew to fear the Abyss. He had heard it in Uruk in the tongue of old from the elderly, wise priestess Nana as she sat tall, her face crisscrossed with lines like a walnut, shadows cast upon it by the light of the fire, her black hair and red hair tied in a knot. *The Abyss is a darkness, Gilgamesh,* he recalled her saying, *so deep that man's senses can only feel it as the stillness of a black, bottomless pool. Its fingers are icier than even the coldness of death. No mortal survives the Abyss. Even those who are both mortal and god—like you, Gilgamesh—dare not enter the Abyss.*

Here Nana had whispered that this was why the people of Uruk had kept the endless fire lit: so the Abyss would be kept at bay and the Great Spirit of Darkness could not envelop them. She had whispered this to Gilgamesh when he was just a boy: "See how each night the Spirit of Darkness seeks to capture us. See how it is held back only by the Spirit of Light, for does not each night give way to the morning? And even in the blackness of the evening sky, has not Mother Tiamat given us the stars and moon to keep away despair? To know that light glitters strong behind the darkness?"

Nana also had told Gilgamesh that these Great Spirits—of darkness and of light—were too enormous to comprehend fully. Each one was spread across the universe, above where the minutest of glimpses of the sky of the light of the world were seen by mortal man in the form of stars and planets and the darkness that surrounded it. Then, one night when the winds had borne the disease that had decimated the people of Uruk, when it was clear that Gilgamesh must leave Uruk to find Utnapishtim and the leaf of eternal life, Nana had spoken a prophecy. Her face was twisted in braids of sadness as she whispered, "I see in the fire your story to come. How the Abyss will swallow you. And even you, Gilgamesh, king of Uruk—you who are three-quarters god and one-quarter mortal—will suffer the agonies of eternal imprisonment that await those who are interred in the Abyss of Blackness."

Sharp jabs of fear pierced Gilgamesh's heart as he remembered Nana's long-ago prophecy. He recalled his cowardice when he had left his warrior brother, Enkidu, defenseless to the terrors of the beast Ashurnasirpal and the agonies of Kurnigi. He felt the shame of it rise through him, thought of the braveness of the young *muktablu,* and knew that there was only one path open to him. In less than a thousandth of a second, the Abyss had transformed into the smallest sliver of a crack, and all that remained of the black chasm was a line narrower than the width of a thread. Into this Gilgamesh plunged the point of his golden warrior spear. This noble weapon had been crafted in ancient times by the gods and strengthened in power through the eons by the bravery of the purehearted. It had been forged of mighty metals by the six kings of Uruk before him, each emboldened by the valor of the warriors before them. The tip of the blade was a flame, a light green that now flickered within the microspace of the Abyss. It widened the Abyss into a long, thin black line that lifted from the ground and wrapped itself around the spear. The black thread then roped around Gilgamesh. His blue face twisted in agony as it pulled him downward, downward into the Abyss. Then all Gilgamesh knew was darkness.

𒂠𒆜 𒂖 𒂠𒆜 𒀪

A glimmering light illuminated the underwater landscape of the Sea of Abyss, at once luminescent, at once gloomy. It flickered first a green the color of jade, shot with gray streaks and relieved by flashes of colors: dark oranges, purples, and wild combinations of pink, yellow, and black that floated downward in infinite combinations of prisms, strange seaflakes that snowed down. The spirits condemned here had awakened to the vibrations of change that finally had descended to their depths from the surface of Kurnigi. Change had come to a land where there was an infinity of sameness, an existential void; Chaos had risen and shattered the vacuum. To this the creatures of the underwater world pulsated. Their forms were hidden by the dimness of the sea bottom; still, if one looked, their grotesque outlines could be seen. Sailors, their drowned mouths gaping wide, grasped for treasures that lay just out of reach of their hands. The chests were open with rusty riches spilling out. Then there were others whom the sea had taken and transformed—a multitude of creatures, some with long claws like crustaceans and human faces, others like sea anemones but with tendrils that sprung out and shot black liquid. Still others were both fish and fowl, strange birds that flew and swam at once. Others, with jaws that opened wide with sharp teeth, crawled upon the detritus of a hundred thousand sea wrecks. The seaweed elongated, their gray green shining, glinting from an eerie glow that came from within.

As Eddie tumbled to the bottom of the Sea of Abyss, the watery light cast long shadows like prophecies of doom over his face. He had maintained his airborne position: his knees to his chest, his eyes shut, his hands clasped over the handle of Death's scythe. He was indeed geared up for battle in the green camouflage battle dress of a foot soldier: a thick vest, an olive-green T-shirt and long pants, and combat boots. This outfit was intended for a land battle, and here within the Sea of Abyss, his garments only weighed him down. Creatures who were formless at first but then sprouted hands, if the extensions of these shapeless creatures could be called that, reached toward Eddie. The beasts surrounded Eddie as he fell. The sea bottom was littered with bones, broken spears, rusty cannons, and swords that still lay lodged in the chests of sailors, where they had been plunged. It was debris that spoke of war and vengeance.

Soon shapeless, murky, sluglike gray masses swam around Eddie, who stirred, groaning as one does in troubled slumber. From lipless smudged faces, their mesmerizing song rang through him, pulling him deeper and deeper into unconsciousness. Then the creatures, a dozen in number, reached toward his hands, and an oozing slime formed over them and between his fingers, trying to dislodge the scythe. As Eddie's fingers loosened, he uttered a garbled sound: a muffled cry from somewhere within the depths of his consciousness. Eddie's touch upon the scythe was faint; the creatures sang their cry again, death's call. The scythe vibrated in response, an answering call to the evil that beckoned it. Eddie's fingers encircled the handle of the scythe but no longer held it. The weapon moved up in the space between his fingers and the handle to escape the hands of the living. Eddie's lungs expanded, filling with the awful liquid in which he was immersed. Bubbles flew out of his mouth as he choked, awakening him.

Instinctively he grabbed the scythe. As his living fingers grasped the instrument of Death, his lungs immediately cleared, and strength surged again through his body, awakening him entirely. The weapon's energy enveloped him. Eddie stood in a defensive posture, his legs spread, the scythe up. Around him the seaweed rose, now dark and shining green whips that struck Eddie. He wielded the scythe, slashing at the seaweed, which retreated. He screamed a warrior cry—"*Aaaweee!*"—as he swung the scythe about, feeling, but not entirely seeing, the slug creatures that surrounded him. As the creatures pulled back, Eddie's eyes widened as they took shape before him. Instinctively he swung the scythe up as they surrounded him.

The creatures swam excitedly around him in a wide swath, circling him and clasping one another's hands. These sea beings have had many names in the mind of mortal man: mermaids, or

Roanes, in their benevolent form; underwater demons in their malevolent states. The gray, shapeless creatures took the form of a dozen beautiful maidens with hair that fell to their waists—hair the color of ripened persimmons that waved hypnotically about their faces. Their eyes were deep and fathomless, dark mysterious pools, yet bright and haunting. At the bottom, their bodies were those of seals, with the skin covering their torso but leaving bare the shoulders and sinewy arms. Eddie gasped at their loveliness. The Roanes smiled upon their find, this living *muktablu* whom they would capture and kill and from whom they would take Death's Scythe.

Eddie tightened his grip on the scythe as he swam, turning around and around in this strange circle within the sea. The Roanes could lure humans with their knowledge of the desires that rang in the hearts of their prey, for once they had been mortals who also had loved and lost. Mortals whose hearts had been filled with bitterness at the cruelty of love unrequited, unreturned. As they traveled the seas, they too had been lured by the Roanes' mournful songs and had fallen into the depths to their deaths in the Sea of Abyss. When mortal victims dropped into the waters, Roanes and other sea demons swarmed around them. They'd plunge their sharp teeth into the mortals in order to feel the warmth of human bodies before the pulse of life ebbed, in order to grab souls as they rose from their bodies and trap them alive within their fiendish waters. Then these mortals too would become sea demons, where they would roam the Sea of Abyss for eternity.

Eddie's heart was transparent in its longing. *Trina. Trina. Trina.* The memories of her face, her touch, her voice filled him—memories that were sensations more than thought, formed as they had been across lifetimes of endless love found and lost. The sea-maidens raised their voices, singing a song so lovely that it went straight to Eddie's heart. His arms grew heavy, his heart laden with dread, for the notes of the Roanes were filled with the weight of mourning, his grieving for his lost love. They were singing his song of heartbreak. Eddie felt each note, sharp as a blade, plunge into his heart. He moaned, and his head fell back. The alluring sea-maidens' voices raised in song, striking the notes of heartbreak again and again. Eddie felt each note as strongly as the beats of his own heart.

Then suddenly, faintly, he heard the voice of his father, in snatches: *Beware these sea spirits…Keep your heart closed, son.* But the voice of Sergeant Petersen was soon submerged by the song of the Roanes, who were now unclasping their hands as they moved toward him, breaking their circle to let another Roane in, as they sang:

Trina. Trina. Trina. Trina.

Eddie gasped. "Trina!"

For there, before him, was Trina, her body now like that of the Roanes with their seal forms but her bare arms and shoulders in human form. Her pale oval face with hazel eyes shot with green; the dark, shiny chestnut hair, now loose and about her—it all mesmerized Eddie. She reached out her arms, long and lovely, toward him. Eleven maiden Roanes with persimmon-colored hair swam about Eddie, forming a semicircle, the pressure of which pushed him forward toward Trina.

Trina swam around him, her eyes beseeching.

O my lost love!
Your hair the yellow of the shining sun,
Your eyes the green of the shimmering emerald sea,
Come you have at last!
Weep no more shall I my endless tears.

Mourn no more will my heart,
For our reunion nears!

Eddie's heart stirred with deep longing. All he wanted was to hold Trina, his lost love, gone from him lifetime after lifetime and now here, in this strange form. But *here*. *Here*. "Trina!" he cried out, moving to grasp her, but she swam away from him. A sharp pain stabbed his heart. He looked hurt as he cried out, "Come back!"

Trina then sang as she swam still farther away.

O my lost love,
I cannot come into your
Arms when you hold
The sharp and deadly scythe,
For it will shred me to pieces.

The Roane maidens gathered around Eddie as Trina swam farther and farther away from him. Mesmerized, he started toward her, but the more he tried to moved, the more the liquid held him in place. Eddie felt his heart would surely break now; it already was splintering in pain. "Trina, come back," he beseeched her. "Come back." Trina turned and looked at him, her eyes filled with love and longing. She stretched her arms toward him once more.

O my sweet love,
Drop you must the scythe
To the bottom of this sea.
Then we shall be together,
You and me.

The eleven Roane maidens with their reddish-orange locks that moved with the rhythms of the strange sea raised their arms toward him and pointed downward.

> *Drop you must the scythe*
> *To the bottom of this sea.*

Death's scythe vibrated in Eddie's hands. He looked at its sharp and deadly point. Then he looked up. Trina was swimming above him. Her arms stretched again toward him, her eyes soft and inviting. His thoughts were consumed by her. She swam again toward him, her arms out. Eddie reached his arms toward her, up above him, the watery light shining around her face, her seal body swimming gracefully just above him.

> *Drop you must the scythe*
> *To the bottom of this sea.*
> *Then shall we be together,*
> *You and me.*

The Roanes crooned their intoxicating song, their doleful notes of heartbreak. *Eddie,* he heard his father's faraway voice, *don't drop your weapon!* But these words were lost to the wrenching feeling of love lost. The pangs of love that leave the soul broken and in despair filled Eddie as Trina's form faded, her words whispering in his ears:

> *Drop you must the scythe,*
> *Before we can be together,*
> *You and me.*

Only his broken heart spoke to him, quelling the sounds of reason that counseled against so dangerous and foolish a move as to drop Death's scythe. Eddie cried, "No! Don't go!" to the disappearing form of the sea-maiden Trina. He knew he couldn't live without her. His fingers quickly unclasped the handle of the scythe. His chest immediately tightened against his combat vest, for no mortal could live within these death waters, at least not without the power of the scythe. The liquid of the Sea of Abyss filled his lungs almost instantly. Eddie gasped in pain; the agony of drowning seized his body as his knees gave way. His body curled at the bottom of the sea. There he lay, his heart beating its last notes. Vibrating, the scythe fell to his side. Other creatures that lived deep in the Sea of Abyss heard the scythe's notes and, like a magnet, were drawn toward it. The scythe's death notes rang throughout the floor of the sea, creating a clearing around it and Eddie. The Roanes, those conniving sea-maidens with the orange hair, formed around Eddie's writhing body, their greedy hands reaching toward the scythe. When the death sparks of the scythe shot forward, they moved back.

The Roanes swam quite a distance away; they didn't dare touch the scythe till the *muktablu* was no more. The sea-maiden Trina swam down to the bottom. Eddie's eyes opened, and he saw her. His hands reached up weakly. "Help me," he implored her. She extended her hands toward the handsome yellow-haired warrior. Across her face flitted greed, for when the *muktablu's* last breath was gasped, she would receive the spoils.

Eddie's eyes slowly shut as the sparks of the Death's scythe diminished. Then the lovely oval face of Trina disappeared to reveal the seal face of a Roane, its mouth open, displaying long jagged fangs plunging toward Eddie.

CHAPTER 3

saghulhaza: guardian of evil

Even through the depths of unconsciousness, Uri Gneezy recognized that it was heat rather than the familiar blasts of cold that struck his large, coiled serpent body. The Dark Master Marduk always had returned the Snake to the frozen Siberian ground, to the shack on the fringes of the gypsy encampment in the Russian land of his boyhood. In that place, in his mortal form, he had sought to learn the gypsies' tricks of black magic, but instead he had discovered true evil in the shape of the Crone.

Uri Gneezy's snake head burrowed farther into his coils in response to the lashes of heat. The Snake thought of how he had wrested from that ugly hag, the Crone, the Black Book of Magic and assumed the form of the giant serpent that resided within it. He had grown immensely in power. Still the Third Stone of Anger underscored that there was no loyalty among evildoers. There were only fragile alliances that broke when they no longer were expedient. The enemy of one's enemy was an enemy. The Snake's head shook as he recalled the moment when the duplicity of the odorous Beast—once the great, mighty King Ashurnasirpal—had been revealed. The Beast sought to capture the Spyglass for himself, and to that end, he had taken the creatures precious to the red-haired child who held the Spyglass. The red-haired girl had the protection of Herman Biddle. Upon the Third Stone of Anger, the Snake had again come so close to killing Biddle. *So very close.*

The Snake's head shook upon the coils where it lay. A faint hiss escaped its gruesome mouth as the slits that were his eyes opened slightly then quickly shut tight. His green shiny scales undulated to the lure of memories. It had been a long, tiresome game of trying to lay waste to Biddle, who thwarted him at every turn. Always Biddle. He with whom the Snake Uri Gneezy had once shared a womb in mortal form. *Brother. Twin brother.* The words produced a tremor of revulsion in the Snake, for he despised the weak, softhearted Dmitri, as he was called in their shared boyhood. The Snake had detested him even when each was formed in the womb. Gneezy had sought even then to rob his twin of sustenance; his embryonic fingers had tried to pierce this interloper in the womb, to stab the nascent heart so the creature would be born dead. But unfortunately for Gneezy, both were born alive.

Uri and Dmitri. From one mother but different as good is from evil, as darkness is from light. From their mother, Alexa, Uri had sought—but never could obtain—her complete attention. Right at the start of infancy, Uri felt Alexa's instinctive repulsion toward him. How her body arched away when she had to pick him up. How she murmured prayers over him. Then, in troubled realization, she had whispered, "Seed of evil," and Uri had heard her. His blue and green eyes had flickered with knowledge within his dark, sharp infant face. He saw too how

his mother's eyes held Uri with wariness but were filled with profound love when they beheld Dmitri. How she held Dmitri close
and placed kisses upon his head. The Snake's body moved in
bitterness at these hideous recollections.

Again a faint hiss flickered from the tips of the forked black
tongue at the remembrances of his short mortal life. Then there
was their father, the brutal Grigori, whose megalomania knew
no bounds. He considered himself a holder of special powers,
a seer, when all he was a lunatic. The family moved from one
hovel to another—from the frozen lands of Siberia to Sitka,
Alaska, then back, but were always chased out by villagers who
had grown weary of the bearlike Grigori and his ravings. In the
Russian village of Pokroyske, still in the time of Tsar Nicolas,
when the Orthodox Church was strong, Grigori was viewed as
a heretic. Though Alexa was quiet and pious, the entire Gneezy
family had been viewed with distrust.

The villagers had murmured of Uri, "Look at the little dark
one with the evil eyes—how strange they are! One blue. One
green. The eyes of the devil." And of Dmitri, they'd said, "See the
fair-haired one who looks like an angel. A devil and angel born
of one womb!"

They shuddered and yielded in broad swaths when Uri passed
them but felt pangs of guilt when they saw the beaten-down
Alexa and her fair-haired boy Dmitri wearing rags, starving and
freezing in the cold. Even so, the villagers shunned the whole
family. Grigori's wild moods and rants about Satan frightened
them—this Uri knew. He knew and saw that in fear there could
be power. Their father, Grigori, was wild and uncontained and
couldn't channel fear into control. This too Uri saw as a boy—
saw and took note. Claiming to be a prophet, Grigori brought
his family to the village of Pokroyske to seek the counsel of the

rising monk Rasputin, rumored to be mad himself, even then in the early years before he had the ear of Tsarina Alexandra. At this point, Uri should have been the Chosen One the Crone had prophesized about, and Dmitri should have been crushed to oblivion, but events had twisted victory away from him.

In the village of Pokroyske, Grigori had fallen dead in the Devil's Shallow, as should have Dmitri. However, time warped, and it was Dmitri who rose with White Magic. Dmitri fled, taking possession of the Spyglass and hiding it. And if he, Uri Gneezy, had clasped it as was his right, the Dark Master would had given him incredible dominion and power over the underworld. Then the Snake would have been reviled and feared, more so than now, as he was condemned to change from old man to serpent through endless travels back in time. Gneezy's snake body slowly unwound under these bitter thoughts. Herman Biddle, as Dmitri had called himself, was all that had stood in his way from full realization of the power and dominion over others that should be his. Biddle had become a wizard in possession of the White Book of Magic, thwarting Gneezy at every turn when his reach had come close to the holding the Spyglass—though he had held it once, and that was enough to imprint upon his bony palm the image of the Spyglass. Enough to allow him power over the Spyglass when again he seized it.

The Snake again rustled in his deep sleep. The Spyglass, it was said, held the knowledge of where the Hidden Sister lay. The Snake often had wondered how the Dark Master, Marduk, was the powerful demon god ruler of Kurnigi, even though Marduk himself couldn't grasp the Spyglass. The legends only told of how great the spell was that the reviled Tiamet had cast over the Spyglass to keep it away from Marduk's grasp. The mysterious powers of Tiamet were vaster than the Dark Master acknowledged, Gneezy realized. Marduk, who had struck into obscurity the worship of Tiamæt as the Great Mother; Marduk, who had overpowered the gods of old to take grasp of Kurnigi—despite all this, he was still only holder of *half* of humanity's Destiny. She who held the other Tablet of Destiny—the Daughter of Tiamæt, Marduk's sister—had been given the Book of Destiny that was light. This Hidden Sister, this Hidden Daughter of Tiamæt, had vanished eons ago, and the story of that disappearance was entangled inexplicably with the Spyglass. The mystery of the Hidden Sister, Gneezy knew, was more than what appeared on the surface—things of which the Dark Master surely knew but didn't share. Power lay in knowledge, for though the Snake was greedy for power, he also was shrewd and wisely realized that to probe the intrigue would only anger the Dark Master. The route to dominion, he knew, was through obedience to the Dark Master.

The Snake's coiled body stirred in slumber. During the periods when he awoke, his thoughts returned again and again to the mystery of the Dup Shimati, the Twin Books of Destiny, of the Hidden Sister, and the ever-elusive Spyglass. The mystery drew him. The Snake knew that Marduk, the Son of Tiamæt, had been given the book of darkness. Good and evil had been divided so that free will would be preserved for humanity: destiny wasn't set for man but set *by* man. The Dark Master sought to be the holder of the Daughter's Twin Book of Destiny—the book of light. To be the holder of both Books of Destiny meant possessing fully unleashed power. Then Marduk, by banishing free will, could harness the immense power of the energy that would be the collective souls of all of mankind. Therefore he would be the master of all souls. Gneezy knew there was an even greater power that Marduk sought: the Infinite Sky of Heaven.

Still man's free will held such power that Marduk could cull souls only from mortals who willingly gave it away. And for that the Dark Master had to use trickery forged by his legions of those who were once mortals but now were residents of Kurnigi. And he also had to keep the treacherous creatures who lived within the depths of Kurnigi under his power. Therefore he needed creatures like the Snake. The Snake knew there were other secrets that Marduk held: that with both Tablets of Destiny, Marduk would unleash infinite power; until then the Dark Master was not all-powerful. Marduk needed the Snake—wasn't it the Snake who could clasp the Spyglass, the imprint of which lay upon his palm? Though this made the Snake valuable to Marduk, it wasn't enough to release him from imprisonment in the shack. The Snake had yet to bring Marduk the Spyglass, as his attempts at grasping it were always thwarted. *Biddle.* The Snake's scales rippled. He knew the heartbeats of Herman Biddle as he knew his own. Gneezy should have been able to strangle Biddle—he who protected the red-haired girl who now held the Spyglass with White Magic imbued by Tiamæt, even though those powers were dim. Destroy Biddle, then into his hand the Spyglass would fall. But Uri Gneezy had failed again and again. For his failures, the lashes of the Dark Master had fallen upon him, each stroke deepening his hatred for Biddle. Gneezy longed for the destruction of Biddle; it was a primeval need that almost eclipsed his need for power. A lash of searing heat cut through the depths of his slumber. So strong was it that it splintered the sleep and thrust him immediately into full consciousness. His cobra head sprung up from the coils of his body.

Uri Gneezy's giant serpent form was transforming into snake and man. His cobra head wobbled above a thin neck and shoulders, around which a black cape—held by an eye, the all-seeing eye of the traitor—unfurled. Arms sprung from the Snake's ribbed and scaled torso. The rest of his body was that of a giant olive-green python pulsating with strength. Underneath the coils the serpent felt the rising heat of the ground under his scales and, within his cold reptilian body, a pulsing hatred for Biddle. Strangely, unlike the cold, which had felt like sharp daggers, the heat didn't harm him. The Snake's long black forked tongue struck the air and vibrated against it. His eyes, one green and one blue, scanned the land, each flashing in turn with surprise.

Gneezy's mind was sharp with curiosity at the new landscape where he found himself. It was dark, desolate, and flat in form. No trees, no mountains—just an endless dusky landscape of nothingness looming into infinity. The sky above was a foreboding dark red. No creatures were about. The place was heavy in its stillness. "Kurnigi," Gneezy hissed in realization. Kurnigi. The former lair of the Beast. Land of Darkness. The outer layer of hell, with layers of dread deep within. Kurnigi's surface was hot but not fiery. It was ground littered with trouble, a skin of anguish that covered the great horrors that lay beneath it in the form of dark tunnels and corkscrews of terror and beneath that the dreaded Abyss of Blackness.

The Snake uncoiled his giant body further, his blue and green eyes scrutinizing the dusky red sky. He swiveled his head and saw what was behind him: the massive, rusty, bloody gates to Kurnigi, open and guarded no more by the creatures that once were its gatekeepers. Chaos had opened the doors to Kurnigi when the living hand had clasped Death's scythe, when order had been turned asunder when the red-haired child had given souls belonging to darkness to the light. The Snake never had been allowed to take residence in Kurnigi, for this place was under the dominion of the Beast Ashurnasirpal. So it was

through his flights through time that the Snake had no kingdom he called his own, just the hovel that lay on the outskirts of
the Russian gypsy encampment. It was understood that Marduk
would elevate him once the Spyglass was captured; he would give
him some portion of Kurnigi to rule. But it hadn't happened.
Instead the Snake had been condemned to limbo. What was the
meaning of his awakening on the miserable, barren surface of
Kurnigi? Was the Dark Master punishing him for his failures?
Imprisoning him in this dusk of emptiness for eternity?

He raked the air with his bony fingers. The slight imprint
of the Spyglass upon his left palm pulsated. Around his palm
he first felt an unseen force, a pressure gathering. Quickly he
dropped his arm. The force rose in strength around him, trying to imprison him within its invisible walls. The Snake's cobra
head bobbed in alarm upon his thin neck. His arms thrust out
to push back the currents that eddied around him, tightening
him, much as his python body might wrap around its prey. As
Gneezy's serpent tongue lashed at the force, the energy grew
stronger, more intense in its paralyzing hold. Gneezy braced his
gigantic reptilian body against the invisible force pressing upon
him. His cobra head swiveled about and saw nothing. His great
serpentine body twisted futilely to escape the current.

The Snake's blue and green eyes glittered in anger as he spat
out, "What are you that holds me?"

Brother! Heed us! We are Muhra! We are Muhra. Hear us!

The Snake heard only a sound like the screech of a rising
wind. The Muhra were two-faced, conniving creatures of the
underworld who lay invisible at the gates and had awakened at
the sight of the imprint of the Spyglass upon the Snake's palm.

Among themselves they buzzed in anticipation. This Snake with a forked tongue had materialized with the imprint of the powerful talisman upon his palm. They gathered around the Snake, greedy with thoughts of capturing the Spyglass. Brother—surely such a creature as this was a brother to them, a creature whose thoughts in slumber had risen like heat from his cobra head: thoughts of dominance, glory, and control. These were things that the Snake wanted and that they understood. A creature who served the Dark Master yet held the imprint of the Spyglass. If the Spyglass were found and seized through this creature, they would be able to have form again. The hell of an eternity of invisibility was their punishment. The Muhra were a collective of those whose mortal souls had reached for glory, for attention at all costs. As humans, they had used others to forward their wants, but their egos now lay as air in Kurnigi. They once had held in thrall tens of thousands with their songs, their dances, their brilliance. These men and women had basked in mortal adulation but now faced eternity with no applause, no adoring eyes, no sycophants to keep their egos afloat. Only nothingness—never seen, never acknowledged. Those who resided on the surface of Kurnigi had quickly learned to become deaf to these Muhra, who formed the ether of Kurnigi.

It was a hell they bore poorly. And through the eons, they relished with a vengeance the one portal that had been given to them through which to experience form: through unsuspecting minds of those humans who didn't guard their dream gates. There they could take shape that was elusive and unreal. They kept this privilege as long as they brought Marduk the souls they entered. Through the doorway of nightmares, these beings cultivated in the minds of mortals desire for all-encompassing adulation and admiration for their beauty, their talents. The

Muhra had to plant the seed, grow it, and tantalize the mortal with fame and fortune. In mortal man these evil creatures of the ether, these Muhra of Kurnigi, had no shortage of those willing to trade everything for moments of earthly glory. Through these mortals who fell prey to them and sold their souls for the small, insignificant dance of reverence by others in their human lives, these beings brought into Kurnigi souls like themselves. For it was the shiny trinket of fleeting, mortal fame that was the currency they bartered with—an exchange they knew well, having fallen for it when they too had held mortal form.

Fame and riches fell into mortal hands, given by the very creatures they would soon become in death. Creatures who appeared in disguise, readily producing both praise and curses from their two-sided tongues. In mortals whose shallowness made them vulnerable to believing that human admiration for their songs, their dances, their talents meant something greater than what it was, these Muhra found their victims. The evil ether creatures of Kurnigi in nightly dreams would grow the egos of these souls, fattening them with falsehoods of their greatness, plumping them up until they were beyond redemption. Next the mortals would promise their souls to the Muhra upon the death of their bodies in exchange for the glitter of gold, for the shining lights of fame, for importance. Once the bargain was struck, their wishes for adulation would come to full realization upon earth. These mortals basking in idolization would grow to see themselves as superior to other mortals and thereby would be blinded to the truth that all souls are equal. These mortals would seal their fate; their souls sold to Muhra could never be retrieved. So it would be true as it was said, that a camel could more easily travel through the eye of a needle than these mortals could enter the gates of Heaven, so gigantic were their egos.

When their mortal casings withered, these mortals would find a cruel surprise: they had sold their souls for the paltry prize of less than a blink of time's adulation in exchange for an eternity of nothingness. Their bitterness was profound.

The Muhra spun around Uri Gneezy with a bewitching web of false promises.

Great and mighty
Snake of snakes will you be,
Ruler of the dusky earth and the fiery sea,
Demon of all hell.
But you must heed us well.

They swarmed around the Snake. He would be theirs to control. Marduk they knew to be a fickle master: giving and taking power. The Muhra understood duplicity, and so they feared the Dark Master. They saw how in the ancient fight for control of all of the underworld how Marduk had tricked the old demon gods, Asur-alim-nuna, and grabbed their power from them. But even the powerful could fall. See now how the old demons gods had escaped Kurnigi and the powers of the Dark Master Marduk were ebbing. The odorous Beast, when he was master of Kurnigi, had been deaf to their plight, impervious to their honeyed words. Now the Beast too was gone.

In this Chaos, they screeched, *we too shall gain form and escape the hold of Marduk!*

Here now stood this giant serpent creature, with scaly skin, with the head of a cobra, but the arms and torso of a man. But most important, the first several Muhra who had risen around the serpent had seen the faint imprint of the Spyglass upon his palm. The Snake would lead them to it. With the Spyglass they could escape Kurnigi. Words flew around the Snake and shocked him with small currents. These words they spoke with their invisible tongues, unctuous words that the Snake felt upon his scales as slight vibrations.

The Muhra's voices grew:

> *Serpent! Serpent! Seed not of the womb of prey!*
> *But born of the summer threshing*
> *Of iron and clay.*

Uri Gneezy's snake head quivered against the vibrations of the Muhra, which buzzed like a swarm of invisible mosquitoes. The Muhra knew he held bitterness and had heard his thoughts in his slumber.

> *Better than your brother.*
> *Equal to no other!*

These words entered the Snake's mind, their lure mesmerizing him.

> *Master will you be*
> *Of all Kurnigi!*
> *Heed us now,*
> *And we will show you how!*

Gneezy felt the hypnotic effect of the Muhra's incantations, his eyes shutting to their sedative power.

> *O mighty Mushussu!*
> *Red snake of glory!*

He shook his cobra head against their chants. He felt the warning pulsating heat of the black eye of the traitor upon his cape. It was a dangerous spell that these invisible beings, foes of Marduk, sought to cast upon him when they called him the Dark Master's name: *Mushussu*, the red snake. The Snake hissed against the lure of the Muhra. This was surely a test by Marduk of his loyalty. Were he to succumb, he would no doubt endure unknown agonies. *The Dark Master is watching*, the Snake thought. Uri Gneezy raised his serpentine body with all of his strength, sharply in opposition to the snare of the Muhra. He threw his long forked tongue out and slapped the air and hit the Muhra. Sparks flew, small thin needles of current.

"Keep back, fiends!" the Snake hissed. "Keep back!"

The Muhra fell back, stung at first by the rejection, then angered. Invisible they might have been, but who was this creature to slap them back? Layer upon layer of Muhra bristled at this affront to their egos. Doubt rose among them as to the importance of this creature. The Muhra buzzed among themselves, their thoughts flying quickly, all of it in the split of a second. The imprint of the Spyglass upon the Snake's palm was faint, almost as invisible as they were. Perhaps it wasn't even there, the Muhra muttered among themselves, for it was only the first of the Muhra who had come upon the Snake and had told of it. Other Muhra, who had come later upon the reptile, said they had seen nothing upon the Snake's palm. And those Muhra who had first sworn that the imprint of the Spyglass lay upon the left palm of the serpent now doubted themselves. They, more than anyone, knew the want of something could be so strong as to create illusions. So, the Muhra concluded, the Snake was nothing but another powerless creature condemned to Kurnigi. Fame and fortune had slid into their mortal hands such that their very presence had made the masses swoon. When they spoke, their words glittered like diamonds with wit! This newcomer to Kurnigi would learn what it meant to thwart the Muhra. They would teach this one that the Muhra weren't to be treated with disrespect. This ignorant *reptile* was nothing to them, only another stupid creature of evil. One among the many who had fallen into the Land of Darkness. They, on the other hand, were *Muhra*.

The Muhra churned to gather winds of energy. As their vibrations grew around Gneezy, he felt their rising displeasure. The current formed into impenetrable energy. The Snake threw back his head, straining against the Muhra's current. *The Black Book of Magic*, he thought. He needed dark magic to thwart the Muhra from imprisoning him. When he slapped the air with his tongue to release the Black Book of Magic, the Muhra's current hit him fast and hard. The Snake's forked tongue quickly receded into his mouth. Again and again the Muhra hurled bolts of energy at the reptile as they laughed at the creature's helplessness. The Snake's head wobbled on its thin neck, the black cape around it lying limply back. The Muhra struck the Snake with a bolt of current straight at its head. They saw with glee how the blue and green eyes shut in pain. Gneezy's bony arms flung out, and his hands slapped the air blindly. Then the Muhra hit the Snake's ribbed body, forcing him down. The Snake bent his head into the coils of his scaly body. His head rose, and the blue and green eyes opened and gleamed with anger. The Muhra felt the Snake's rage at his powerlessness, and a great roar of triumph rose within them.

> *Hoorah! Hoorah!*
> *Know you now, serpent, who we are?*
> *We are Muhra! Glorious Muhra!*

But in that roar of delight at their cleverness, the Muhra's strength ebbed. It ebbed enough to allow the Snake to spring forward and strike the air with his forked tongue. The Black Book of Magic appeared at the tongue's tip, flying out like a black crow, reptilian rather than avian, with an undulating cover of black scales that rippled with evil. The Black Book hovered protectively above its master, the Snake. Its covers were like large wings that cleaved the air that was the Muhra in two. The Muhra's force waned as they drew back in fear of being captured and subsequently trapped in the Black Book of Magic. They retreated to lie upon the ground near the rusty gates of Kurnigi.

The Muhra snarled from the corners: *Beware, Snake, for in the Muhra you now have an enemy.*

The Snake hissed a note of satisfaction that he had passed this first test of entrance into Kurnigi. He uncoiled as he sprung up into the sky: a giant gleaming green python. The Black Book of Magic ominously hovered above him. The Snake hit the book with his tongue, and from it two creatures flung out. One was the Iron Knight, and beyond him, growing like an ugly stain, was the Crone. The Snake's tongue struck the Black Book again as a command for it to hover silently in the dusky red sky, for he realized Kurnigi's tests were likely more in coming.

The Iron Knight scrambled up, the medals upon his breast glowing like embers from the heat of the land and rapidly melting into a liquid that ran down his tunic. Upon his forearm that band of hatred, the swastika, pulsated. Tightly cinched around his fat middle was a broad black belt that cut into his stomach. The Iron Knight was once known as Goering in his mortal form. He had remained clean-shaven, ruddy faced, blond, and pudgy even in the dark afterworld. With some dismay, the Iron Knight noted that he no longer wore the bright uniform of Tsar Nicolas's royal guard. He had received that uniform from the Snake on the Third Stone of Anger but had been returned to wearing the dress of the Nazis, stained now by the melted medals—an affront to his fastidiousness. He felt the Snake's green and blue eyes upon him.

"Master," the Iron Knight immediately said, standing straight at attention.

Then he bowed his head in deference to the giant Snake who hovered over him. For all his mortal adornments and titles—commander of the Third Reich, hero of the great First War, one of the noble race, the former president of the Reichstag, ace fighter pilot, recepient of the military honor known as "Blue Max"—he was now just a slave to the Snake.

The Snake heard these thoughts and inwardly sneered at the German's pompous notions. If the River of Time had run as one story, before the red-haired girl had turned time to Chaos, the Iron Knight's proud neck would have been snapped by a noose, his body burned and its ashes dumped into a can. The Iron Knight, of course, didn't know this, for Chaos had interrupted the flow of events, and now he was doomed to spend his afterworld in the Snake's scaly clasp. As Uri Gneezy's cobra head loomed over the Iron Knight, a small glint formed in the slits of his green and blue eyes. His tongue lashed the sky, and the Reichsmarschall's baton fell into his hands. He tossed it down to the Iron Knight. Gneezy knew well the affected pretensions of the Iron Knight and also knew he would be firmly under his control as long his ego was well fed.

The Iron Knight reached up and greedily caught the baton, his fat sausage fingers instinctively caressing it.

"Commander," the Snake said with a slight tilt of his head to show his feigned respect for the title.

The Iron Knight's chest puffed, for he saw the Snake's gesture, and he bowed again in response. The Iron Knight's hands held the Reichsmarschall's baton lovingly. It was a long tube of ivory, covered with gold and silver blades and embedded with gold snakes and scorpions. It was inlaid with rubies, emeralds, and diamonds. On each end of this baton was a black snake, entwined to form the symbol of the swastika. The Iron Knight looked around at the desolate landscape and the dusky red sky. He raised an eyebrow quizzically at the Snake. Suddenly he felt intense heat all around him. *Hell. Is this hell, though?* he wondered. *Even though there are no flames?*

"Master, what place is this?" he asked the Snake.

The Crone, who had crawled toward the Iron Knight, her face filled with trepidation, whispered, "Kurnigi."

Her repulsive face turned fearfully toward the open gates of Kurnigi. She smelled the evil that lay there, the sour smell of fear, the cloying sweetness of deception, blending with the salty smell of a dead sea felt the lurking presence of the Muhra. The Crone shuddered. Land of Darkness, where the Beast once had served as the Dark Master's lieutenant, where Marduk ruled supreme over all. The Crone held out her withered arms for the Iron Knight to help her up. She moaned, feeling the heat of Kurnigi as a pain that rose from the ground and infiltrated her lumpy body. Here the perception of pain increased a thousand-fold through her consciousness, as it did in those condemned to Kurnigi. Eons ago she had lost her true mortal form, although she had felt its sensations when she had possessed the Black Book of Magic. The Dark Master had risen to punish her for mistaking this miserable peasant boy Uri Gneezy for the Chosen One, rather than the creature who had shared the womb with him. Then that miserable cockroach Uri had struck her in half, seizing her small essence of self and thus enslaving her to him. In return, the Dark Master had given Uri the body of the huge python that lived in the Black Book of Magic, and the book itself was Uri Gneezy's to control.

The Snake's head tilted toward the Crone, whose stench—that sour smell of greed and duplicity, was heightened by the heat of Kurnigi. Even in the dusky light, the Crone's ugliness was vivid: pockmarks, puss oozing from eruptions on each side of a large, crooked nose; grizzly hair; a foul-smelling mouth in which one lone yellow tooth shook; and a chin from which sprung coarse gray hairs that wiggled like worms. The Crone's body was hunchbacked, and she wore soiled black robes that gave off the stink of death. The Snake knew that the curse of her ugliness was rivaled only by the beauty that once had been hers. It was a beauty so captivating that she could use it to extract souls for the Dark Master—until she had betrayed the Dark Master and was condemned to ugliness for eternity. Yes, somehow this sibyl had been given the Black Book of Magic, until it was torn from her hands for failing to capture the Spyglass and then was given to the Snake. This was all the Snake knew of the Crone's story, although he was certain there was more to it than that, and it was filled with treachery. The Crone had surely been a resident of Kurnigi at one time; the Snake saw this by the wary look of knowledge that flitted in her bulging eyes. And like all its creatures, she wasn't to be trusted.

"Save me from this torture!" the ugly old one begged the Snake.

The heat rising from the ground was unbearable. Here in Kurnigi there was no escaping the pain, even though the mortal body didn't exist, for the currency of the dark underworld was pain.

Uri Gneezy's tail swung around, and he grabbed the Crone. First he would extract from the hag what she knew of Kurnigi. Then he would get rid of the old woman.

"The tests of Kurnigi…what are they, Crone?" the Snake hissed, his head moving in palsied jerks as his black cape flew back from his thin neck.

"I can't think with your clasp upon me," the Crone whimpered, then added as an afterthought, "Master."

The Snake tightened his tail around her. His forked tongue struck and stung the hag's wrinkled face. "Try."

Flinching in pain, the Crone whined, "I don't know, Master. I've never been here until now."

The giant python tail lifted the Crone further aloft. The serpent tightened his clutch upon her. The Snake's green and blue eyes glittered with anger at this blatant lie, for the old one knew at once where she had landed.

"You, Crone," he hissed, "were once holder of the Black Book of Magic. You've read its spells."

"As have you, Master," sputtered the wily Crone, her face turning a bluish gray as the Snake squeezed her tighter and tighter. "As have you."

Yes, Kurnigi was known to her. Known too well. She had escaped from its unending terror through her wit. The Crone knew Marduk had kept knowledge from the Snake, for knowledge was power. Power from that knowledge was what the Crone possessed. She had traveled through the ages and picked up secrets from those who had fallen into Kurnigi through trickery and barter, talismans, spells, and dark chants. She had held all these secrets close to her wrinkled breast. She had made bargains with fallen fiends who had begged for relief from the misery of condemnation to hell—bargains, much as she had fostered with

Stal. In this way, when the Black Book of Magic had been given to her, the Crone's knowledge of the evil incantations she had gathered throughout the eons had blended with the book's dark sorcery and revealed to her layers of knowledge unknown to the Snake. The Crone felt the Snake's Black Eye upon her; she forced her thoughts to be still.

The Snake held his gaze upon the repugnant visage of the Crone, her gaping mouth emitting puffs of foul smells, her greasy body squirming in his tail. As he crossed his arms over his thin body, the clasp on his cape glowed. It was the black eye of the traitor, glowing ominously at the Crone. It sensed the old one's treacherous thoughts, though it didn't decipher them, and blazed to alert its master that a liar was about. Gneezy had seen her scurrying with that pockmarked one, the conspirator against him who now called himself the Prince of Demons. He who had betrayed him upon the Third Stone, who sneered at the Snake and called himself mighty. *Stal.* Steel, he had said he was. That traitor would be found and punished. Stal would be melted to nothing. The Snake hissed, incensed by the Stal and what he knew with certainty was the Crone's role in the traitor's rise.

The Iron Knight still stood at attention. His thick black boots fended off the heat of the field; his right foot unconsciously tapped in impatience for the show to begin. The Crone's punishment was coming, and he would delight in it, savor the terror of the victim as one does the aromas of a delicious dish before consuming it. Such were the pleasures he had developed when in his Nazi mortal form.

The Snake's tail constricted. The Crone whimpered. He lifted her body aloft and horizontal to his terrifying cobra face. The green and blue eyes pierced her with accusation as his forked tongue lashed her face again and again. The Crone let out a screech of pain.

The Snake hissed, "Crone. You have betrayed me."

She wheezed under the tightening hold of the Snake's tail. Still, the Crone, who over the eons considered herself skilled in deceit, believed the Snake could be persuaded away from these thoughts. "I am but an old, ugly woman with no power," she mewled. "How could I betray you?"

The clasp of the black eye of the traitor pulsed brightly in response. The Crone's yellow tooth quivered in her mouth at this sight. She dared not have any thoughts, for the Snake heard all. The Crone also knew that the serpent had read the Black Book of Magic with shallowness and that he didn't possess all its secrets—he never would. Though the Snake now enslaved her, if she gave him all her secrets, she would be utterly destroyed. Once the Crone regained her power- and she would, as she had over the many eons, she, she would grab back the Black Book of Magic—and more—so the Snake would be the servant and she the master. Though she was his servant, having lost the Black Book of Magic for failing to capture the Chosen One and thereby the Spyglass, the eons of her having been the book's mistress left her with knowledge, including skill in how to mask her thoughts, to cloak them so that what was heard wasn't what was thought. These thoughts were hidden as she willed herself to speak over them, gibberish that the Snake would hear as murmurings of pain. The serpent couldn't know what she had done on the Third Stone, how she had plotted to overthrow the Snake and wrest from him the Black Book of Magic. *Her book.* He couldn't know of the secret black magic of the thumbs of Abaddon, which had lay inert in her oily black robes and which she had given to Stal—those black and blue thumbs that had bored through Stal's forehead and quickly lodged in him and stretched him into manhood. Stal had called out to the mighty demon gods and received the Saber of Shadows on one side, the Sword of Deception on the other, and had been proclaimed by the conjuration of the spirits awakened within the blade and by the Asaru-alim-nuna to be the Prince of Demons.

The Snake heard the Crone's gibberish and knew she was covering her thoughts. A traitor she was, somehow plotting with the pockmarked one against him. He flung the Crone to the hot ground in disgust. The old one landed with a thud. The Crone whimpered piteously, though she knew it would have no effect on the heartless reptile. She saw how his gigantic serpentine body coiled upon the ground and didn't flinch at the heat. The Iron Knight sneered as he stood in sturdy black boots that repelled the heat—boots made for kicking. The Crone, sprawled on her back on the ground, struggled to rise. She saw that the pompous fat one, the so-called Iron Knight, was poised to beat her with his baton. His thick red fingers seemed to be itching to do so. A sadistic smile flitted across his lips.

One day, one day, fat one, the Crone thought, *I will crush you.* This thought escaped from the Crone's mind.

The Snake heard. "The Iron Knight isn't a traitor to me, as are you, Crone. It is he who will crush you."

The Crone caught this threat as she scuttled on her knees on the ground, her head up, the coarse grizzled hair wild about her panicked face. How to escape? How?

The old hag was useless to the Snake now that she was a traitor. He had to bury her in oblivion, and what better place to do so than Kurnigi? He would plunge her malodorous body into the hot ground, drill her down into the Corkscrew of Terror, where she would be imprisoned and forever harmless to him.

The Snake's triangular head loomed over the Crone, his forked black tongue slithering out of his mouth. The blue and green eyes gleamed, hard as stones. "Good-bye, Crone."

The tongue struck the Crone, the flat surfaces hard like a hammer, driving her body flat to the ground on her belly. Her arms and legs were splayed out. The hotness thoroughly invaded her consciousness. It traveled through the Crone, beads of sweat now forming an oily sheen on her face. She moaned in pain. The black lumpy mass of her body seemed to be on the verge of melting into the ground of Kurnigi. The Crone cried out in fright at the thought of being buried in the hot earth of the Land of Darkness for eternity.

She babbled her lies, rapidly shooting the words out to cover her deceptiveness. "No! Master, it wasn't me but the enemies of our master, Marduk! They who escaped from Kurnigi. It was they who gave the pockmarked cockroach power. It was they... the forgotten mighty demon gods of old."

The Snake hissed in displeasure at this attempt by the Crone to gain time by telling him what he already knew. His forked tongue sprung out and struck her again and again with lashes that were excruciatingly painful, driving her farther into the ground. Beyond her the Crone heard the soft, malicious pleasure rise from the Iron Knight's laugh.

The old one reached a long clawlike hand that ended in blackened nails to scratch the air. *Hot. Oh, the awful heat.* "Not me, Master Serpent! Not me but them!"

Searing heat rose through her body as she felt herself about to dissolve into the ground. The Crone had kept back the name of the forgotten mighty ones. She knew that if she called their forbidden name here in Kurnigi, the Dark Master would lay a terrifying banishment upon her. But there was no other way.

The Crone shouted, "Asaru-alim-nuna! Asaru-alim-nuna! Asaru-alim-nuna!"

𒀯𒊑 𒂊 𒀯𒊑 𒁹

Churning deep within the Abyss of Blackness were two of the evil triad of the Asaru-alim-nuna, the forgotten mighty ones: the demon gods of old and the cave gods. The third, the serpent-sharks, had disappeared with the Beast into the land of the living. Now their name had been called. They who had been cheated by Marduk when they had won dominion over Tiamat for him— yes, they would call the name, for the forgotten mighty ones knew that the power of light had diminished, that Tiamat was as forgotten as they had been. *Had been,* for they who had been held prisoner by the walls of tunnels beneath the Corkscrew of Terror had risen to the bloody land of the living when Chaos had splintered Kurnigi and then had been plunged into the Abyss of Blackness. They had been called. The sounds of the cry formed a pinprick of an opening within the Abyss of Blackness into which the Asaru-alim-nuna flew.

𒀯𒊑 𒂊 𒀯𒊑 𒁹

The Crone called again, "Asaru-alim-nuna! Asaru-alim-nuna! Asaru-alim-nuna! Asaru-alim-nuna!"

Dark winds rose from deep within the Black Abyss. The ground of Kurnigi rippled in response to the sound of "Asaru-alim-nuna," the name never to be uttered in the lair of the Dark Master. Asaru-alim-nuna lifted the skin of Kurnigi with the fierce force of a mushroom cloud of split atoms. Blackness exploded and streaked the red sky of Kurnigi. From it emerged the demon gods of destruction and tribulation and the demon goddesses of confusion and conflict. They rose and formed the morbid shapes that spoke of death and destruction: Nergal, with flames for hair that flew in fiery locks about his head; Namatar, with the stink of death and disease, his arms covered in boils, his face half eaten; Lamashtu, hairy in body, teeth bared in a wolf-shaped face, her evil fingers holding the unborn to be devoured, her feet of sharp predatory talons; and Zaltu, with her long gray locks flowing like a fog of confusion. They were the Four Terrors: Nergal, Namtar, Lamashtu, and Zaltu—one part of the forgotten mighty ones. The Four Terrors roared for their brethren:

Asaru-alim-nuna are we!
Rise, my brother fiends! Rise, my sister devils!
Winds of hell blow; rains of terror fall.
Cave gods, serpent sharks, demons of old,
It is you we call!

Asaru-alim-nuna were one of the triad of demon gods, used by Marduk to overcome Tiamet and then betrayed by him. Marduk had driven them into obscurity within the depths of the wall of tunnels beneath Kurnigi. So for eons no mortal man had uttered their names or given them sacrifices, for they feared not them but Marduk, who grew in power and names.

The Four Terrors spun in the sky of Kurnigi.

Chaos broke out and freed us.
Lifted were we to the land of the living,
Plunged into the Black Abyss,

Prisoners no more of the demon Marduk.
Mortal man's memory awakens to our deadly cries.
Marduk's servant calls us.
Asaru-alim-nuna! Asaru-alim-nuna!

The waves erupted under the power of the explosive force of the demons below, who were responding to the call of the Four Terrors. The old gods, thousands upon thousands, whose tales had been told again and again in ancient tongues, emerged— they for whom sacrifices in the form of the blood of man and beast had been offered. Then too came the cave gods. Although they were stick figures, they also held power, for they too had been given mortal souls as a sacrifice.

The Four Terrors called to the serpent sharks:

Mighty are we! Forgotten no more!
Rise, our serpent-shark brothers and sisters!

Still the serpent-sharks, the oldest of the demon gods, who held a deep and terrifying power over man, did not come. The Four Terrors registered their absence but knew that their weakest point always had been the primeval, wordless, inscrutable serpent-sharks. They also knew that these serpent-sharks had bound themselves with the Beast Ashurnasirpal upon the surface of the land of the living. They were mighty enough even without the serpent-sharks.

𒀭𒁇𒆠𒀭𒌋

"Aaargh!" cried the Crone, thrust up high by the wave of dirt that carried her upon its crest.

Her withered arms futilely reached into the air for something to grab. The Snake slithered fast on the ground and, turning his head, saw the old demon gods, volcanic in force, as they were thrown to the soil of Kurnigi. The Crone saw the Snake, just below the gigantic wave, spring to escape its clutches. The Snake jumped toward Black Book of Magic, which hovered in the sky; he also was no match for the tsunami of dirt upon which the Crone rode like a deranged witch rides a broom. The Iron Knight stumbled under the wave of earth.

Kurnigi shuddered, and with each shake of its dark and evil ground, demon gods of old emerged. They had been released from the hold of Marduk, who sought ownership of Kurnigi and vengeance against Marduk. They had flown into the land of mortals to battle Marduk and then had fallen deep into the Black Abyss. These demon gods were dreadful in their forms, reflecting the fears of ancient man: vipers, dragons, raging beasts, monsters cloaked in terror. All were demon gods once worshiped by early man; in the thousands they erupted from the Black Abyss below. After Chaos had been unleashed in the universe, the call from the surface of Kurnigi was enough to free them. Even the Black Abyss couldn't imprison them. They rose to exact revenge and seize the Tablet of Destiny of Darkness for themselves. So the challenge to battle by the forgotten mighty ones commenced—against Marduk, who had betrayed them when they had given him their strength to overcome the Mother Tiamet. Now the Dark One would learn who the real master was.

We will lay you asunder.
You will bow your head in submission to
Asaru-alim-nuna!

The Four Terrors flew about the red sky. The skin of Kurnigi was now defiled with the old demon gods, who were snarling and ready for battle. But the Dark Master was nowhere to be found. His orbs did not shine in the dusky crimson sky.

𒆜𒌋 𒂍 𒆜 𒁲

The Snake registered the silence of the Dark Master. Marduk was testing his strength; he knew this at once. He had to demonstrate that he could battle these demon gods if he wished to be given dominion over Kurnigi. Gneezy's python body sprung into the air, his scales gleaming green and his underbelly glistening black. He twisted aloft vertically into the shadowy red sky, above the crashing tidal wave of dirt brimming with demon gods of old and bearing the Crone. He soared high above Kurnigi's surface, which roiled with abominable creatures as they emerged from the dust. The demons' fierce cries shattered the menacing silence of Marduk. The Black Book of Magic, with its cover spread wide like the wings of a vulture, hovered just above Gneezy. His forked tongue rapidly struck the cover twice.

He hissed the incantation of release:

Zi-ukkina! Zi-azag! Zi-ukkina! Zi-azag!
Rise, souls of fright, creatures of once-mortal might!
Shuk-nat-mu-shi! Shuk-nat-mu-shi!

The Four Terrors heard his chants and laughed derisively; they were more powerful than the magic of Marduk's reptilian servant. They surrounded the Snake and the Black Book of Magic. The book that held dark magic would be theirs. It was a small tool but one well worth possessing toward weakening and overcoming Marduk. A powerful wind rose from their mouths and blew the serpent and the Black Book of Magic back.

The Snake's incantation grew loud. He writhed in the sky as his body entwined over the Black Book of Magic. His blue and green eyes glimmered against the rising intensity of the wind of the Four Terrors.

> *Zi-ukkina! Zi-azag!*
> *Souls of old, souls sold!*
> *With your poison tongues, spears, and swords!*
> *Whips and lashes and bodies bold!*
> *Full of wrath, rise and rage,*
> *Bel-matati!*

The Snake uncoiled quickly, letting the book free. At these last words of the incantation, the Black Book of Magic shuddered and grew enormous. The black-scaled cover opened and expanded into mighty wings, silent and fast as a predatory bird. The book sliced the wind of the Four Terrors in two, its underbelly holding the stained pages of the stories of eons of misery. From it dropped creatures who had been captured and thus were beholden to the Snake: those villagers from his boyhood village who had struck men dead and flung them into the Devil's Shallow—those Cossacks from the battlefield of the bloody Russian land who had fallen prey to the Snake's disguise as Tsar Nicolas. All were now slaves of the Snake.

The Cossacks rode out of the pages of the Black Book of Magic upon their powerful sable steeds with mighty hooves. They rode through the Four Terrors, jumping to the ground to battle the demon gods. These creatures bore ancient spears and clubs, their bodies covered in skins; avarice and cruelty lay as blood upon their faces. Others were beasts, boars with long snouts and sharp cloven hooves. Some had faces of wolves and bodies of man; others were like lizards with heads of men. These creatures had made pacts in their mortal forms and had found eternity in bodies that were neither beast nor man. The Iron Knight fell under their onslaught, his arms above this head, brandishing the Reichsmarschall's baton. The hooves of the mighty steeds of the Cossacks galloped past him, raising waves of dirt.

The Iron Knight felt the sting of his position: he, hero of the First War, to be crawling like an insect when a great battle was afoot! He struggled to get up, but yet again was thrown under dozens of hooves, beaten by the creatures that tumbled from the Black Book of Magic.

The Snake remained aloft in the air, his giant body writhing above the flying Black Book, which dropped creatures likes bombs upon the soil of Kurnigi. His tail reached down into a land that swarmed with battling creatures and pulled out the sputtering Iron Knight, his face bright red as he clutched the baton. The Snake's cobra head turned, and his black tongue flicked the Iron Knight's baton. From the baton uncoiled the snake swastikas that were upon each end. The small swastika snakes fell to the ground. They rose like a steam of small serpents then transformed into soldiers of the evil Third Reich, their eyes dead, their mouths set in cruel lines as tightly about their faces as their red and black swastikas were about their arm. They used their ruthless black boots to kick the demon creatures on the ground. Still others—their gray-green tunics torn, their faces set in grim determination to exterminate all in their path—raised their bloodied swords against the rising demons on the ground. Thousands upon thousands of the small black snakes, shaken from the Iron Knight's baton, grew into the Third Reich's soldiers and crashed against the Cossacks' horses.

The Snake dropped the Iron Knight. Swirling above the battle, the Snake called to the pompous Iron Knight's mind. *Supreme Commander! You must take charge of this battle.*

The Iron Knight's face flushed with excitement as he eagerly accepted the Snake's accolade: *Supreme Commander!*

The Iron Knight's rotund body, encased in a tight tunic, was suddenly bedecked again with medals. *Yes, Excellency,* he mentally replied to the Snake, who still hovered above him. He grabbed a large black steed and held aloft the Reichsmarschall's baton then struck the Cossack upon it, toppling the rider to the ground. In his hand, the baton turned into a large sword, its blade flashing with evil. *Night of long knives!* The Iron Knight's mind rang with pleasure at the memory of old mortal victories when the blood of traitors flowed upon the fatherland. This battle would be greater—and far bloodier—than all.

The Four Terrors flew about the chaos below, shrieking in delight. The Snake's creatures were only dead mortal souls who would be easily conquered, for they were demon gods. The Four Terrors jeered Marduk as they flew about the red sky over Kurnigi. *Cowardly demon! Bow your head in submission to Asaru-alim-nuna!*

Marduk's dark orbs still did not appear. The Asaru-alim-nuna took this for surrender. They laughed in triumph, seeing how the demon gods below were decimating the Snake's servants. The dead souls of evil who bore battle on behalf of the Snake were no match for the demon gods of old! For these she-devils and demons bore bloody teeth and sharp nails. Some took the forms of serpents and dragons, others of scorpions, still others of creatures of the water, slimy and foul of smell—some giant, some small. Some had bodies of wolves and the faces of the ancient mortal men and women who once had worshiped them. Others had narrow orange eyes embedded in large sharp faces of rodents and bodies of black steeds. Some had remains of twisted bones, while others were hollow-eyed ghouls with bloodied bodies. Some held spears and swords as they rode in chariots constructed of the bones of the sacrificed. Others held balls of fire; still others blew hurricane winds from their mouths. Some were scorpion and man—or woman—at once. Some changed in form from viper to dragon to shark to wolf. Some were the children of Medusa, with the hair of serpents writhing about their heads, their six-armed bodies clad in the dark bristly skin of boars. These released she-devils and demons were angry at their long captivity, at how Marduk had cheated them of mortal adulation.

Uri Gneezy twisted high above the ground and landed upon the flying Black Book of Magic. His giant python body lay upon the spine of the book, his torso up, his nails digging into the edges. The Black Book flapped its covers and flew silently under the wind of the Four Terrors but over the wreckage below. The Snake's cobra shook, his blue and green eyes flashing in disappointment as he saw how the demon scorpion gods stung the steeds of the Cossacks, who, as they fell, were trampled by the riders of the carriages of bones. The she-devils and he-devils hurled fire and winds. The Nazis, with their dead eyes, withered and smoldered on the ground. The ancient cruel warriors toppled one after another as the demon gods rolled over them. Everything that served the Snake was being annihlated. It was a defeat beyond defeat. The Snake's eyes caught the glimmer of a baton then saw that the Iron

Knight was still engaged in battle. He rode a black horse, its hooves flying deftly over the reaches of the she-devils and demon beasts, as he shouted commands to his fast-dwindling force. Shrieks of terror echoed across the sweltering landscape of Kurnigi as the demon gods tore the Snake's servants in half. And still the Dark Master did not appear. Had Marduk finally been overcome by the forgotten mighty ones? But this thought the Snake shunted aside. If he lost this battle, he would be relegated to the dust—like his lost army—upon the ground of Kurnigi.

The Snake guided the Black Book low then lashed his forked tongue at the demon gods on the ground. In retaliation, the snakes upon the heads of the children of Medusa sprung up and rained upon his body and bit him. The Snake felt their venom enter his body and paralyze him. His bony hands dug farther into the Black Book of Magic before his eyes rolled back in his head. Then unconsciousness seeped into him.

𒉺𒈦𒀭𒈦𒀸

Lying limply upon the Black Book of Magic, Uri Gneezy was under the effects of the venom of the small snakes, who plunged their tongues like needles into his body. His black cape fell to one side; the eye of the traitor that was its clasp was shut. The wrath of the Four Terrors was raised against this servant of Marduk who dared battle them. This creature who was once just a mortal would submit to them. They turned as one to unleash fire, wind, fog, and a rain of pestilence upon the Black Book of Magic, which held the serpent. The Black Book too would be theirs; soon they would tread upon the Dark Master's neck in triumph. The forgotten one would soon be Marduk.

The Four Terrors—Nergal, Namatar, Lamashutu, and Zaltu—spat fire, wind, fog, and pestilence at the Snake. The Black Book of Magic shuddered under the assault. The force of the powers of the Four Terrors hit the wings of the Black Book hard, making a tear in one of the covers, which was attached to the spine by just a thread. The fog carried pestilence, flying maggots, ants, and flies, all of which embedded themselves in the Black Book of Magic. Without its master to cry out an incantation, the Black Book of Magic was helpless. It turned downward into the chaos of the battle below. Lamashutu, hairy in body, her yellow fangs bared from her wolf-shaped face, saw her chance. She quickly threw down from her evil fingers the unborn, which she had planned to devour. Then those deadly fingers, long and ending in sharpened nails, reached up to clasp the Black Book of Magic for herself. But in this she was thwarted, for greed and mistrust rang loudly in the ears of the others of the Four Terrors. Who was she, this hairy wolf-woman, whose breath stank of those she devoured, to grab for herself the Black Book? And in one moment, the other three—Nergal in a fiery rage, Namatar with gale-force winds, and Zaltu with her long gray hair of swirling fog—lunged for the Black Book. As they crashed upon one another, the fog hit the fire, quelling it, and the wind hit the pestilence and swept it away. Lamashutu's greedy hands of death were shoved away from the Black Book of Magic as the Four Terrors swirled about in a cyclone of confusion.

As the Iron Knight brandished his baton, his face appeared ruddy with the energy of battle. The black steed upon which he rode trampled demon gods in the form of spiders and ants below him. He pulled the reins upon the black horse and thrust the animal up into the air, escaping the grasp of those who rode on flying chariots formed of skeletons. The Iron Knight's forces had been laid to waste; the landscape was littered with their bodies, which were quickly disappearing into dust as the demon gods on the ground screeched in victory. If the Snake didn't survive, what lay ahead for him but the same fate? The Iron Knight's horse again hit the ground hard, racing toward the Black Book of Magic, with its torn wing and the Snake lying limply upon it, spiraling downward. The Iron Knight quickly observed the enemy's four leaders caught above in a maelstrom. He rode fast under the falling Black Book of Magic until he was just underneath its giant wings, the torn one almost off.

The Iron Knight cried, "Awaken, Master!" He urged his black steed up into the air and cried to the unconscious Snake, "Awaken! Awaken, Master!"

He wielded the Reichsmarschall's baton to hit the underbelly of the Black Book of Magic. Sparks flew from the vibrations of the rod striking the Black Book. Evil beating evil. Uri Gneezy awakened to tremors that ran through the Black Book of Magic. As his cobra head shot up, he saw the Iron Knight riding below, his face puffed as he shouted and pointed upward. There the Snake saw the Four Terrors in a confusion about him. His tongue quickly hissed an incantation as his bony fingers grabbed the torn wing of the Black Book of Magic: "*Bel-matati ta-mel-aki!*" In milliseconds the Black Book was whole again.

The Four Terrors disengaged from one another and snarled:

> *Snake! Far not will you go! For we are master now!*
> *Vipers, dragons, raging beasts, monster demons,*
> *Rise and grab this serpent, now our servant!*

From below a great surge of the demon kin of the Four Terrors, monsters of beast and man, rose up, tearing the skin of Kurnigi. The Snake guided the Black Book toward the Iron Knight, and then his tail reached out to grab him off the black steed. Still the Black Book of Magic was sandwiched between foes below and enemies above. The book flapped its wings to no avail against the forces that surrounded it. Although the Snake was pummeled by the intensity of power above and below him, he held tightly to the Black Book of Magic. His tail grasped the Iron Knight, who sputtered in pain.

Nergal, Namatar, Lamashutu, and Zaltu, their faces wild in triumph, chanted derisively:

Marduk! Marduk!
Red orbs of cowardice!
Who shall toil and suffer now?

The question struck the air in echoes.

Who shall toil and suffer now?
Who shall toil and suffer now?
Who shall toil and suffer now?

Suddenly the red sky of Kurnigi split open to reveal a black vortex of energy. The blackness grew in strength, pulling the Four Terrors toward it. The Four Terrors countered with hurricane-strength winds formed from their mouths of destruction. The Black Book of Magic fluttered between the two foes: the Four Terrors above and their demon kin below. The blackness gave way as seven monsters—giant in form, male and female—burst forth. The demon gods below them sprung up to aid the Four Terrors then fell back at the sight that formed in the blackness above.

It was the Sebitti, the Seven Guardians of Marduk, warrior demons. They were fierce in appearance: some with faces of raging wolves and dragon bodies, others giants with scorpion bodies. Still others were fanged creatures with human bodies, wielding spears and spiked clubs. They blew from their mouths evil whirlwinds as their chants rose: *Imhullu asamsatu, imsuhhu saparziqqu!*

So began the raging war between the Sebitti, Marduk's Seven Guardians, and the forgotten demon gods, the Four Terrors. The Sebitti weren't full demons but half demons who held the weaknesses of mortals in their veins. They never had been worshiped, revered, and feared by mortal man, as had the Four Terrors and their demon kin below. The Four Terrors fought back in sequence so as not to quell one another: first with fog, then pestilence, and finally fire and wind. In this respect, as ancient demon gods, Nergal, Namatar, Lamashutu, and Zaltu had much power. The fog clouded the eyesight of the seven half-demon monsters, who blindly lunged forward as the pestilence flew at them, biting their bodies. Soon the flames engulfed them, and the Sebitti's screeching wails filled the sky as they tumbled toward the landscape of Kurnigi.

With his cobra head flat upon the spine of the Black Book of Magic, his eyes shifting from the ground to the sky, the Snake guided the book away from the falling giants. With a deafening thud, the Sebitti fell. There they lay upon the soil of Kurnigi, which was littered with the demon kin of the Four Terrors, enemies of Marduk. Quickly the ancient demon gods upon the land swarmed, some upon their chariots of bone, some upon steeds that were huge boars, and others upon feet that were the talons of birds. They wound their ropes around the Sebitti, who were writhing on the ground.

Relishing their conquest, the Four Terrors defied Marduk by taking one of his names.

Call us now Nibiru!
Seizers of the midst!
Conquers of Kurnigi!
Masters of the Sebitti!

The glee of the Four Terrors was abruptly broken by a thunderous sound. The words came forth, falling from the sky—sounds that formed into black wedge-shaped slashes. The faces of the Four Terrors twisted in pain as the slashes fell upon them with the strength of an earthquake rippling through the land.

The Black Book of Magic flew about haphazardly. The Snake Gneezy, clinging to its spine, felt the words as shocks reverberating through his body. The Iron Knight, clasped tightly in the Snake's tail, sputtered in agony. The words weren't mere sounds. They were the fifty names of Marduk. Fifty sounds of the awesome supernatural strength of the Dark Master: *asar-ri-asaru-tutu-zi-ukkin-na-zi-azg-aga-azag-mu-azag-shag-zu-z-z!* The ancient names burst forth from the falling cuneiform in thunderous sounds that fell upon one another and splintered the sky: *suh-ku-agi-zu-lum-mu-mu-um-mu-mu-lil-gish-kul-lugal-ab-pa-lugal-dur-mah-a-du-nun-na-lugal-dul-azag-ga-ni-bi-ru-be-el-matati-shag-gar-ea-bi-lu-lu-ne-be-ru!*

Below, upon the land of Kurnigi, the names of Marduk, the black cuneiform slashes, surrounded the Sebitti like armor. The slashes cut the demons' ropes, and the Sebitti were released. They jumped up, the cuneiform slashes falling away from them, and launched themselves like daggers toward the old demon gods, piercing their chests, faces, necks, and torsos. As these she-devils and he-devils cried out in pain, the Sebitti flew up toward the deep black vortex and formed a semicircle. The cuneiform slashes that were the name of Marduk continued their assault against the Four Terrors in the sky, until in defeat the Four Terrors spun downward to where their demon kin lay.

The blackness of the sky of Kurnigi gave way to the two glowing red orbs beneath the semicircle of the Sebitti. *Marduk.* Then the darkness was pierced by horns like a ram's, curved with spikes. Soon the Dark Master's head formed, with his hair and beard of long, writhing, black-and-orange vipers. Marduk showed his face in many forms: from that of a demon with an aquiline nose and narrow red eyes and a crown of daggers, to a dragon beast that spat fire, to a predatory bird with a giant beak dripping blood. Marduk now took the full form of a red goliath dragon with great black wings, dwarfing even the giant Sebitti, who stood at guard. Upon Marduk's dragon breast lay silver armor that held the Tablet of Destiny of Darkness.

The Four Terrors lifted their greedy eyes toward the Tablet of Destiny of Darkness. It would be theirs soon enough; one defeat was nothing to those who measure time in units of infinity.

Nergal, Namtar, Lamashtu, and Zaltu threatened:

> *Craven heart, blackened soul, demon foe,*
> *Son of Apsu! Born of Tiamat!*
> *Many things we know of, but hark this so:*
> *Creature mingled of sweet and salt water,*
> *Soar not in triumph.*
> *Find we shall the droplet that bears your slaughter!*

Their defiant chant filled the air. They proclaimed that Marduk wasn't almighty—as they were—but a lowly mortal born of the waters of the primeval Apsu and Tiamat. They hadn't called the Mother the defiled, powerless name of Tiamet, as ordained by Marduk, but as Tiamat, showing their disrespect for the Dark Master. And they spoke of the Dark Master's weakness: the droplet.

Enraged by the insolence of the Four Terrors, Marduk's scaled, leathery body glowed red with anger. His mouth opened and thundered:

> *You are but shadows in the sky,*
> *Phantoms from mortal man's misty past,*
> *Nothing but a weak and distant cry,*
> *While I am worshiped by names anew.*

The Sebitti, the Seven Guardians of Marduk, called the names that gave their master power—names that had grown and strengthened through worship by mortal man:

> *Devel, Deofol, Ha-satan-ba-al devar, Iblis,*
> *Azazel, Baphomet, Ba'al-zevuv, Beliar, Bheliar,*
> *Shaitan, Satan-el, Mastema,*
> *Satan, Devil, Lucifer!*

The chant rose like a drumbeat from the mouths of the Sebitti as they sang of Marduk's might:

> *Mighty holder of the Dark Tablet of Destiny,*
> *Speak we now of the great destroyer of Tiamet!*
> *Legal-dimmer-ankia is he who is the Mighty Dark Spirit!*
> *Lugal-ab-dubur is he who snatched the demon goddess's weapons!*
> *Lugal-dur-mah is he who is highest of all in darkness!*
> *Lugal-shu-anna is he who sits upon the mighty throne of evil!*

The Dark Master shot enormous flames from his dragon mouth—flames that glowed with a searing heat that never had been known before, even in Kurnigi.

The Four Terrors felt all the force of the Dark Master's rage as the flames enveloped them. They and their demon kin saw how the Dark Master's power had grown through the worship of mortals, while they had languished, forgotten. The flames soared and crashed, licking the land, covering it in a red blaze. Still the forgotten demons knew that Marduk's power had been forged when Chaos didn't rule Kurnigi, as it did now. For the Dark Master couldn't have held them imprisoned in the walls of the Corkscrew of Terror, had they not escaped? Nor could Marduk prevail when they had fought in the land of the living, for his powers were strong in the underworld but weak in the land of the living, where he still sought souls to enrich him and hoarded them like as a miser did gold coins. Nor could the Dark Master keep the Four Terrors in the Black Abyss; did they not emerge to the very surface of Kurnigi, called by the Crone, who was enslaved to the serpent and therefore Marduk? These thoughts ran through their minds and were transmitted to one another. The Four Terrors formed a tight cyclone of protection on the ground. They spun around and around, creating a wind that blurred their shapes and repelled Marduk's flames. The flames rose in response, surrounding the Four Terrors in a great conflagration.

The Four Terrors cried in defiance:

> *O Marduk, hear our vow.*
> *Pain of defeat, tears of sorrow,*
> *These shall be your morrow!*

The Four Terrors then invoked the names of evil spirits as protective incantations against the wrath of Marduk: *Ettuku, Ekimu, Asag, Alu!* As they did, their demon kin rose from the ground of Kurnigi into the cyclone as it deadened Marduk's flames to wispy smoke. Then they plunged downward to return to the Abyss of Blackness.

𒀭𒊩𒌋𒀭𒊩 𒀀

Kurnigi lay silent as a tomb. It was covered with a soft gray dust: all that remained of the evil souls the Snake had once taken from the land of the living. The Snake flew upon the Black Book of Magic, his tail still clasping the gasping, ruddy-faced Iron Knight. He circled just above the ground, uncertain what to do. The flames were gone. The Snake's blue and green eyes gleamed with terror as he beheld the dust that was all that was left of his forces. He had lost the battle with the forgotten mighty ones. What punishment now lay ahead for him? He shuddered at the thought. Bitterness suddenly formed in his chest. *Biddle.* All was lost because of him. Because of Biddle's continual thwarting of his grasping the Spyglass, he had felt nothing but the lashes of the Dark Master's displeasure. If the Snake were to survive this with power, he vowed, Biddle would be crushed finer than the dust that now lay below him.

Above him, the Sebitti, the Seven Guardians of Marduk, remained in the red sky. The dragon form of their Dark Master had disappeared.

The Sebitti sneered at the Snake flying below them in confusion upon the Black Book of Magic. Then one of the Sebitti showed that he held by his talons a large hideous winged creature, at once insect and bird. It had a featherless, beaked, red vulture head and a feathered black body that ended in an enormous dragonfly tail colored yellow, green, and black. The Sebitti released the vulture-insect creature from its grasp. The Snake was weak—he who had lost the battle to the Asaru-alim-nuna must be destroyed, and to their kin, the vulture-insect creature, the Black Book of Magic would be given.

The winged creature flew downward, straight toward the flying Black Book of Magic, which hovered just above the dust-covered ground of Kurnigi. The Snake Uri Gneezy, who lay prone upon the spine of the Black Book, shot his head up in surprise. The vulture-insect plunged its talons into him, shaking his reptilian body so that the Iron Knight fell from his tail. Uri Gneezy's cobra head flew about, his blue and green eyes upon the ground of Kurnigi, which was quickly receding from him under the bird's talons. Then the evil creature dropped the Snake.

The Snake writhed helplessly in the air. He heard the pounding drumbeat of the Sebitti as they struck their giant hands in a warlike rhythm. Then the vulture-insect flew downward, its black beak grabbing the serpent in the middle. Gneezy's thoughts turned to despair. Why did the master wish to destroy him? Did he not hold the imprint of the Spyglass upon his palm? Desperately the Snake turned his left palm up to display the mark, but Marduk was nowhere to be found. Gneezy felt the razor-sharp blade of the creature's beak cutting through his center.

The Sebitti chanted the song of the vulture's ascent:

Above the soil of darkness, flying over the skin of death,
Casts the vulture's shadow upon the serpent's head.
Cut will it the reptile, till it quivers like the dead.
Cut will it the python, with its razor beak and sharpened talons.

Then this bird of prey, this winner of the fray,
This writer of the Snake's tale of tragic
Will carry upon its morbid feathers the Black Book of Magic.

The Snake, hearing the chant, realized the Sebitti were heralding the vulture as the new master of the Black Book of Magic. This was how Gneezy was to be punished: destroyed for his failure to defend Kurnigi.

Uri Gneezy's body was clasped in the bird's deadly beak. He turned his cobra head upward and saw it: the creature's long, featherless neck was exposed. The serpent shot out his forked black tongue, its venomous tip hitting the creature's neck. Again and again, with each sting of the serpent's tongue, the poison culled from the dark magic of the Black Book penetrated the vulture's neck.

The creature screeched in agony, and in doing so, its beak opened and the Snake fell loose. The vulture spiraled downward, its multicolored dragonfly tail raising a dust of gray as it hit the ground. The Snake dropped to the ground as well and slithered rapidly toward the great creature; then he opened his mouth and swallowed it whole. The Black Book of Magic rose from the land and hovered over its master, the Snake Uri Gneezy. The Iron Knight, his face showing the ravages of fear, his tunic covered in the gray dust of Kurnigi, yelled out a cry of triumph for the Snake.

The Snake's body shuddered. Then the great black wings of the creature he had swallowed pierced through his scales. The serpent's tail changed to the dragonfly's colors of yellow, black, and green. Gneezy's blue and green eyes glistened in conquest as he spread his vulture wings and flew up. A lament rose in the air from the mouths of the Sebitti at the demise of their kin, the vulture-creature:

Saghulhaza! Saghulhaza! Saghulhaza!
Rise does he, strengthened with the sinews of the bird, insect, and snake.
Rise does he, the Saghulhaza. Smite shall he those who lie in his wake.

The Black Book of Magic flew toward Gneezy, the newly appointed Saghulhaza, and turned upside down so that its underbelly, the yellow-stained pages, fluttered with images of darkness, death, and cries of horror. The vibrations of fear surrounded the Snake and the Iron Knight then sucked them into its pages and vanished.

C H A P T E R 4

last séance for the master magician

On the rooftop of a Harlem brownstone, a stubby candle flickered upon a small round table around which four battered men sat. The obsidian night sky was offset by the lights of New York City. The Great Depression was in full force, a ghastly curse that had cast a grim shadow on the nation. A curse these four men had sought to reverse but to no avail. No amount of beseeching to the dark forces had lifted the darkness. No amount of cries and threats had brought gold back into their palms. So it was this Halloween, October 31, 1936, that they were seeking the Master Magician, a last desperate try. For this date marked the tenth anniversary of *his* death. Was he dead? Had he really been alive? Each of the four now had their doubts whether he had ever really been of flesh and blood. How could a man of flesh and blood survive being bound in rope and coffined in a box and plunged into ice-cold waters? Yet he had. Over and over. Double-jointed, they said. And here the four men each now silently laughed in derision at such a simple explanation of the impossible. The Master Magician had sold his soul to the Devil. That was the only explanation for his feats. And tonight they would wring from him the key to open chests full of riches for them. Their fingers itched with anticipation at the prospect.

The fact that the Master Magician had died on October 31, 1926, had meant less than nothing to them back then. But now it meant everything. And it was upon *his* rooftop that the four now gathered. They sat silently around the table, which moments earlier they had stolen from the magician's home, brought to this rooftop, and covered with a black cloth. Their hands were palm down, their fingers splayed out to touch one another's, their eyes fixed intently on the flickering flame. Each man was immersed in his thoughts. Now they waited. Their threadbare coats were no defense against the cold wind on this October New York night. The memory of heady times when money had flowed like rushing water into their coffers was the only thing that could distract them from the bitter reality of their vagabond lives.

The four had once held riches and wielded their power with heedless arrogance. These four had known each other through the rise and now in the fall. Their worn brown suits, their scuffed shoes, the stubble about their faces, the dirt embedded in their nails told another story now. Then they had money to throw away on theater plays, musicals, silent films, magic shows. With amused eyes they had watched the Master Magician's tricks and feats of escape. They had watched his shows from select tables reserved especially for them. They had done so smoking their cigars, drinking the finest whiskey, eating meals with elaborate carelessness—course upon course, just one portion of which would now pay for an entire week's sustenance. Also at their tables were their mistresses, empty-headed buxom blondes and brunettes, flashy showgirls whose laughter was too loud, whose touch was filled with the truth of how it had been bought.

This was what money did—it bought you anything you wished and made you superior to the mass of humanity. These four men had grown rich so quickly. Stocks bought and sold at a dizzying pace. Mansions on Long Island, townhomes in Manhattan, parties into the dawn. Wives from the proper set, mistresses from the improper. Until they had grown so rich so fast that it was difficult to keep an account of how much they were worth. They once had been magicians too, of a sort. They didn't pull rabbits out of hats, but they pulled out money. Masters of Wall Street. Emperors of stocks, purveyors of steel, of oil, of grain. They had held the secret magic of making money from nothing.

Until it all fell from them in an instant.

In the flame's flicker, the four men held the same hope: that they would be rich once more. The Master Magician, they had been told, had possessed a key that had opened not only the chains that bound him but also the doors to fame and fortune. And did not the Magician in his mortal life fulfill all his wants: treasures galore, fame as the Magician of all Magicians? This key he had taken with him to the beyond. These former kings of Wall Street had heard this secret just this night from a man who had said he had seen and touched the key. He had told them this secret in the grimy alleyway that they, like many of the city's vagabonds, called home. In a corner of filth, that man had lain, just an hour ago, gasping for his last breath through the wispy beard around his chapped and bloody lips. His skeletal body shivered against the cold of impending death as delirium set upon him. The four men had seen this before; death frequently came to the corridors of poverty. It came with the same indignity that destitution gave their living bodies. They'd turned to leave, to let the dying man have his small privacy in the throes of death. But the sick man had beseeched them to stay. And in spurts, the story came out: his claim to have been the Master Magician's assistant and how the Magician had used a key to open the doors to his fame and fortune. A key given when the Master had called to the dark forces that had given him his fame and fortune.

The dying man had screamed for this key. "Mine! Mine!" he'd cried. "He must give it to me so I may be rich again!"

Desperation swept aside any skepticism in the four as to the man's credibility. Any means to return to fortune. *Any.* The dying man coughed. Bloody spittle formed upon his lips. His words were low. The four men squatted, and one lifted the dying one's greasy head. His breath was fetid and sour.

"Phantom Magician…tenth year…Master's passing," he uttered, the words formed painfully. "Séance tonight."

In the dank, dark alley in that city within the land of the living, the man's frame trembled as death's quakes racked his body. Bloody drool formed a ghastly rivulet from the corner of his lips and gathered within his grizzly beard.

The four ragged men knelt around him. The dying man spoke again, his voice so low that they had to lower their heads. His breath now came in gasps. The widow, he whispered, had said, "No more after this night."—ten years was more than enough to have waited for the Master Magician's return. The widow was an unbeliever, the dying man's spittle gathered at the corners of his mouth as his anger rose, she was not serious in her attempts to to contact the Master Magician from the spirit world on the death anniversary. The dying man bitterly accused the widow of spoiling the séances of past Halloweens, barring him from entry, and poisoning the dark chants with her spirit of disbelief. He said that the Magician's widow had abandoned the Harlem brownstone and fled to the

West to keep him from the death anniversary séance. But he knew the Master Magician would never appear in a strange home in the West. He felt certain that on this last attempt the Master Magician's spirit would appear at here in Harlem. But the man also knew that without her petition to the afterworld, the Master Magician wouldn't cross over. But if he were there, upon the rooftop of the Magician's old home, he might grab his spirit first, before the widow did, and take the key for himself. The dying one begged the four men to take him to the rooftop of the Master Magician's home. In a small bedroom, he said, hidden in a closet, was a stub of a candle, a dirty round table, and a soiled black cloth. These were what the Master himself had used—accoutrements shunned by the widow and now believed by the dying man to be the core of the force of the chant to the dark spirits. These items must be taken up to the rooftop, he wheezed.

"Lift me, take me...I will share the fortune of the key with you." The dying man's body had shuddered. "As the bell rings midnight...the circle of hands must not break. Call him...call... the Master Magician."

Before they could lift the man, his throat rattled the dry notes of death, and his eyes snapped wide open at horrors unseen: fingers reaching toward him from the dark ground below, plunging into his eyes before taking his spirit. The tremble of the earth beneath the alleyway rose through the dead man's body as his corpse was flung upward then thrown down.

𒀸𒅖𒁹𒅖𒀸𒁁

Mattie scrunched her eyes shut against the whirling sand. Her right arm remained painfully stretched through the hole and into the other half of the Hourglass, where her fingers tightly grasped the Spyglass. Her body moved as if it was a pendulum as she was flung back and forth within the spinning Hourglass. In fact the Spyglass held Mattie, rather than the other way around. *Creepy, rat-fink Spyglass!* Mattie thought again and again of how the Spyglass had betrayed her. How the Spyglass pretended to be her friend but was a two-faced fink. And now Eddie was gone somewhere with Gilgamesh, that nice king of Uruk. Mr. Biddle and Dr. Wigglesworth also were gone, and her mom and dad were somewhere with the flying frog. Below her, she heard Geeta pounding the side of the Hourglass. What would Eddie call her parents? *Missing in action.* A great pain stabbed Mattie's heart, and a tear rolled down her cheek. She wasn't made for this kind of thing; it hurt too much to find and lose people like the Path was always doing to them. She was *supposedly* Mistress of the Spyglass. And also she'd had her own people in Nineveh, way back when she had found them the Tree of Moreh, and everyone had flown up like glittering fireflies into its beautiful shiny branches with glowing blue fruit. Mattie felt these thoughts flying in her head and hitting against one another, much like the sand hit the glass sides. It was because of her that time was mixed up. "Chaos," she had heard Mr. Biddle say. Mattie sighed. All her fault.

Eddie was off on his own somewhere, and Geeta was too much of a bookworm to figure out how to find everyone and get off the Fourth Stone. Mattie realized it was up to her to straighten it all out. She was the one who held the Spyglass, and she was the one who kept listening to Spyglass, let the Spyglass take control. Eddie wouldn't have done that. Even Geeta wouldn't have: she had pegged the Spyglass as a creep right from the start. But that was the old Mattie. No more time for fun and games. The Spyglass would be taking orders from her, not the other way around. She jerked the Spyglass through the hole to emphasize her point.

Above Mattie, the Spyglass awakened to hear the last of Mattie's thoughts. She took umbrage at the idea that *she* would be under orders from a *girl*. Oh, how she needed to be rid of this stupid child and her willful ways. It would come; soon the girl's soul would be hers. The Spyglass's body suddenly bristled with frustration—it wouldn't be so easy to trap this girl and grab her soul, for a pure soul was a slippery fish. *Trapped for eternity in this metal prison, bad enough, yes,* the Spyglass thought. *But now, thrown about, flung into Kurnigi, thrown into the grasp of the Snake Gneezy, almost in the clasp of the Beast Ashurnasirpal. Look at what this reckless girl has done! Oh, to find the Hidden Sister!* The Spyglass's thoughts ran on and on, the endless looping of the same wish. *Capture the pure soul and be freed from the metal prison. Find the Hidden Sister! Grab the Tablet of Destiny of Light from her! Power infinite!* For though the Spyglass knew she was thought to possess the knowledge of where the Hidden Sister lay, it was in fact buried within the murky depths of her consciousness. If only, if only she could remember who she had been, why she was trapped in this metal prison, and most important, where the Hidden Sister lay! The Spyglass lamented her amnesia. If her memory was recovered, what would she need a soul for? Then she could spin right there and grab the Hidden Sister herself. Take the Tablet of Destiny of Light… but how? No, it came back to her again that she must possess a soul to be released from her captivity. Still, if she knew where the Hidden Sister was, she could move Mattie there. *Think,* she commanded herself. *You've seen her. You know her. Who is the Hidden Sister?* But maddeningly, as in the eons before, nothing came.

Geeta's eyes were also shut tightly against the swirl of sand. Her black pigtails flew about, whipping her face, her thin body hitting the sides of the Hourglass. Her hands were alternately groping to find some way to steady herself through the sand and to keep her glasses firmly upon her face. In her mind's eye, she saw fleeting images: Eddie jumping away from her and Mattie on the Third Stone, Mr. Biddle and Dr. Wigglesworth blurred images as she and Mattie disappeared in the swirl of the bitter waters of the Fourth Stone, still trapped in the Hourglass. Oh, what would happen to them now? How would they ever escape its confines? ThaTha's words came into her mind: *Remember that what you see as real is bound by the steel bands of illusion. Find what is real, and you shall be freed.* His words were lost as a whooshing sound filled her ears. A force surrounded and spun around the Hourglass. Soon it was spiraling downward into a black sky toward a mortal city.

𒀭𒁺 𒂍 𒀭 𒁹

On the Harlem brownstone's rooftop, the wind gained in momentum, threatening to put out the flame of the candle. The four men dared not break the circle of their hands to cup the flame. One of them, bald-headed and with a pale thin face, uneasily cleared his throat. The wind's moan sounded eerily like the lamentations of the dead. Another shifted his body, his eyes narrow and close; fear shuddered across his wide, bearded face. *Trysts with the dead,* he thought. Another closed his eyes in pain, his bushy eyebrows knitted in worry over thin-rimmed glasses. So many tries to regain what was lost—would this be folly as well? And, too, they were trespassing up here, had broken into the brownstone: another felonious activity. But what was to be lost? The freedom to live worse than the rats with whom they shared the alleyways? The last man felt the tension of their desperation run like a current around the splayed hands upon the table, jumping from finger to finger. His eyes shifted about, the dark brown of his hair shot with white. A bell rang somewhere in the night. Slashes of light lit the sky. The roar of the thunder shook the brownstone. It was midnight.

The lightning stabbed the dark moonless sky like a dagger, tearing it with a jagged-edged light. For a moment it illuminated the scene: the spinning Hourglass that held Mattie and Geeta, a coffin with strong thick chains wound around it; the churning fog that was the Muhra released from Kurnigi but remaining trapped in the ether; the ugly form of the Crone held within it, like the queen bee in a bristling, vibrating honeycomb of evil. *Muhra! Muhra!* The sandstorm in the Hourglass grew as it tumbled downward in the velvety black sky. The tremors of evil formed an eddy around the Hourglass and shot through into the Spyglass.

Thunder shook the land, and lightning again brutally ripped the sky, lifting the darkness of the city in bright zigzags.

"Master Magician! Show yourself!" cried the four desperate men on the rooftop of the Master Magician's brownstone home.

The wind rose in response and filled the air with an eerie rushing sound: *Muhra! Muhra! Muhra!*

The men on the roof kept their hands splayed upon the greasy black cloth, the wind slapping their faces into a blur, lightning and thunder terrorizing the night. *Muhra*. It must be the secret chant, they thought. Amid the storm, the four men's eyes nonetheless reflected their determination.

"Muhra! Muhra! Muhra!" they shouted, not knowing whom they were calling…not knowing their voices were heard.

Darkness fell like a thick blanket, swiftly extinguishing the lights of New York City. The candle flickered, weak but steady. The vibrations of evil trembled through the men's splayed hands upon the black cloth. Terror seized their hearts. But it was nothing compared to their desire for gold. Fortune would be theirs. *Theirs!* Their eyes shut as they imagined the wealth that, like a sharp knife, would peel away all remnants of desperation that was the skin of poverty that they now wore.

"Muhra! Muhra! Muhra!" they called eagerly, their eyes lit with greed.

A great gale dashed the four men from their chairs to the ground. Their souls, rattling in fear, registered now that they had awakened dark spirits. The stubby candle now floated in the air, the light from it glowing with evil. The round table was thrown off the rooftop lifted, by the fierce wind.

A vibrating bolt of lightning struck the candle's flame, from which gray smoke billowed then grew larger. Out of this smoke faces ballooned out. Faces of the Muhra that once had held glamour and glitter strained against the atmosphere to be released. And the Muhra took in the situation—they were among the living! Not through the dreams of the greedy but actually in the land of the living. And here were four individuals with forms. Forms that they needed.

"We are *Muhra*!" they cried, a thousand eyes now upon the four men. They stood unsteadily from where they were kneeling on the rooftop, fear choking their hearts as the Muhra fog closed in upon them.

The four men didn't see the glint of their demise. They felt the presence of the Muhra and saw how the faces strained against the fog. This they misunderstood to be the presence of the Great Master Magician, showing his many faces like a magic trick from the beyond.

The bald one with the pale thin face, his teeth loosened by starvation now rattled in his mouth with greed as he demanded of the Muhra, "Give the key, Magician!" And the others immediately echoed the demand, "Give us the key, Magician!".

The Muhra's eyes bulged out of the smoke, straining to be whole. The mortals' demand meant nothing. Their mouths, outlined grotesquely in red, formed and then disappeared. Ears and arms came and went. Their eyes greedily took in the mortals. Living souls. Indeed, it was true: they were in the land of the living! They screeched in delight as they reached out to the men's outstretched hands. And the men, thinking the Great Master Magician was giving them key of fortune, opened their palms. Then it was that the Muhra fell upon the mortals. Their arms, hundreds upon hundreds, stretched out of the fog, their fingers plunging into the chests of the four men like sabers. The men's screams shuddered through their bodies. They were lifted into the air and mercilessly shaken, their eyes bulging in pain. The Muhra jammed against one another and greedily dug into the bodies of the four men. They must be seen! Old opera stars sang their arias now as they wrestled into position so their song could be heard again. Clowns with gruesome white faces and bald heads poured out from the men's bodies, along with long-dead actors and actresses of the stage, their lavish costumes glinting out of the ragged clothes of the four men then fading. Those who had found greatness through adulation over the eons appeared in droves, their bombastic sounds rising and falling from the mortal men's lips. Again and again these forms took shape in the men's bodies then disappeared as they were pushed out by Muhra behind them, greedy for their chance to be seen, to once again have form.

"Form!" the Muhra screamed. "We have form!"

But there were too many Muhra for only four mortal bodies. The hands of these relentless spirits grasped the men, and then they felt the Muhra's clasps in their hearts—so cold, icy, and sharp that they quelled the beats. As the grisly fingers squeezed, the desperate mortal bodies fell slack. Soon their eyes froze in lifelessness until all that was left were small gray wisps of dead souls. Their dead bodies then turned with bitter eyes at the Muhra, whom they now saw in the ether about them.

In the sky above, the spinning Hourglass suddenly struck a coffin bound with metal chains, causing the coffin and the Hourglass to fall onto the rooftop. The Hourglass shattered as it hit the roof. The coffin, however, bounced, first onto the rooftop, then out and over it. The newly dead souls of the four men took on the ghostly shapes of their former mortal forms. The Muhra reached to take them, to add them to their formless foggy hell. But the ghost spirits of the men were too quick to be captured. The four men, dead as they now were, cared not as they saw the Great Magician's coffin flying off the roof onto the street.

"We shall have our gold!" the four dead souls cried as they jumped from the rooftop into the dark night below.

"Geeta!" Mattie cried. "Get up!"

Geeta felt the tug of her friend upon her arm. Her eyes opened, and she automatically fixed her lopsided glasses before scrambling up. They were on a rooftop, the Hourglass lying in shards of glass nearby. Though it was dark, the fog that surrounded them cast an eerie gray light. Mattie's red hair frizzed like a ghostly halo around her head. She wielded the Spyglass at the encroaching fog.

Mattie whispered to Geeta, "There's something in that fog."

The Spyglass in her hand quivered in response. Geeta felt the vibrations of evil emanating from the haze that surrounded them.

"Evil," Geeta said, and shivered. She tilted her head in thought. What had her ThaTha said about vibrations? *Intonations can destroy or salvage the soul.*

Mattie gasped. "Eyes!"

From the gray fog, eyes bulged and surrounded the girls. Thousands of eyes were staring right at them. Horrible bloodshot eyes. Then arms and faces swelled out of the fog. Dozens of arms stretched toward Mattie and Geeta, each greedily intent on grabbing two forms.

Then the Muhra saw it, and a collective gasp rang through the fog. Spyglass. The Spyglass was in the hands of the red-haired one. They laughed in glee. Two forms, yes. But nothing to grasping the Spyglass. Soon the Spyglass would be within their clasp, and they who had once held in thrall tens of thousands with their songs, their dances, and their brilliance would rise again. They would assume their beautiful, talented, adored forms. Each Muhra thought of how once again mortal adulation, applause, and adoring eyes would be theirs. These thoughts tantalized them with glorious possibilities. The fingers of the Muhra poked out of the fog. Slews of arms impulsively reached to grab the red-haired girl and were pulled back by other Muhra. The Muhra moved to form a circle of wind, gusts that swirled with intense energy around the red-haired one and the brown-skinned owlet, each frustrated at the closeness of the prize and being thwarted by other Muhra from grabbing it.

Formless, with too many egos to succumb to one leader, a quarrel of voices broke out within the Muhra. Who? Who would take the form of the red-haired one to grasp the Spyglass? Who could be trusted? How could one among them be greater than another? Impossible. Each thought of his or her own greatness and how the others were but insignificant footnotes by comparison. Then other voices rose in a chorus. Formless they had been in this hellish eternity together, and form and power would be theirs *together.* If they attempted anything else, it would be sheer folly; they certainly would be doomed to failure. They needed to grasp the Spyglass with hands, real hands. For in their ether forms, they would just be air puffing around the amulet. If they all rushed to possess the mortals, they would destroy them—had they not already done this with the four mortal men? This time they decided that one Muhra would take the red-haired girl. Another Muhra would take the brown-skinned owlet, who would remain clasped to the red-haired one, a sort of check against the one who held the red-haired one from flying away with the treasure. Then the Spyglass would be used to benefit them all. All the Muhra. For its power when tapped was said to be great. Closer and closer they came until their breaths, coming from greedy mouths that strained out of the ether, fell like a foul wind upon the two girls, throwing them off balance.

Mattie crouched low upon the rooftop, slashing the Spyglass against the quickly encroaching fog.

Inside her metal prison, the Spyglass shuddered at the closeness of the fingers of death and the thousands of bloodshot eyes staring out of the gray ether. She knew these beings were formless creatures of the underworld. From the dark recesses of her memory, the word *Muhra* took shape. *The ether creatures that lay at the gates of Kurnigi!* The Spyglass was jolted into full consciousness. *Oh, is there no end to the peril this red-haired child will expose me to? We must escape this Muhra fog.* The Spyglass vibrated in Mattie's hands, its two gold bands glowing. Mattie placed herself protectively ahead of Geeta.

"Back!" Mattie screamed at the eyes within the fog.

Mattie struck the Spyglass at the hands that jutted out of the ether. Sparks flew and repelled the encroaching hands of the Muhra.

The Muhra drew back just ever so slightly. *The red-haired child can't be grasped while the Spyglass protects her,* the voices whispered, overlapping in the fog. *What to do? What to do?* Murmurs rose within the Muhra. The red-haired one's spirit had to be broken, for the holder had to be strong to channel the powers of the Spyglass. Then the Muhra could possess her and therefore the Spyglass. *How?* they wondered. *How to break the red-haired one's spirit?* Then the shrewd eyes of the Muhra saw—saw how the red-haired child protected the brown-skinned owlet. This was the red-haired one's weakness! They would take the owlet, kill her in front of the red-haired one, and weaken her will with fear and sorrow. Then, while despair brimmed in the red-haired one's heart, when the owlet lay gray and dead at her feet, the red-haired one would be overcome.

Then they would pounce to possess the red-haired one's body and then assume control of the Spyglass. The Muhra laughed with delight at this clever plan. So easy. They turned toward the owlet girl. Thousands of fearsome, bloodshot Muhra eyes cast their gaze upon Geeta. The energy ebbed away from Mattie and spun around Geeta, whipping her black pigtails about her face. Her knees scraped the rooftop as she pulled away from Mattie.

Geeta's eyes watered against the force of the wind; she tried to crawl back toward Mattie. Dimly she heard Mattie in her mind: *Move toward me!* And then there was ThaTha's voice: *Beware of deception that clouds the eyes.* Fear stung Geeta as the force of the Muhra's gusts pushed her away from Mattie as if she were no more than a twig. Then other faint words came to Geeta beneath the sound of the foul Muhra wind.

They're after Geeta! the Spyglass thought with relief as she saw how the Muhra were no longer intent upon Mattie, how the winds died down around Mattie and rose up around Geeta. The Muhra were after Geeta! The Spyglass was filled with relief. Incredibly the Spyglass thought it seemed that the Muhra didn't know what she was. They wanted a body. That was all they wanted. To show her full power to the Muhra would tempt them to take her. *Let them think that Mattie is holding a weak amulet,* she mused, for, the Spyglass thought, she had shown only some small sparks. *Stay still. I must stay still.* Once the Muhra had Geeta, then she and Mattie would escape somehow. *The brown child is dispensable,* the Spyglass thought, as she went inert in Mattie's hands.

Sharp musical notes rose from the fog: *Death awaits you. Death is upon you.* The notes rang morbidly, filling the air. Somewhere far off within the maelstrom of the Muhra, a chant, familiar but not discernible sounded, but Geeta's fear of the Muhra's terrible prophecy was so great that the death notes easily overwhelmed the chant. The terrible death sounds richoted in her mind, her thin body shaking as she fell to her knees on rooftop. *Death holds you now.* With their jagged edges, the fractured notes plunged toward her. Geeta's eyes were wide with fear and anguish, such as one who know death's fingers are at her throat.

"Oh no!" Mattie cried, moving toward where her friend now lay prone on the rooftop, her jerking legs the only signs that she hadn't yet perished.

The Muhra winds swirled like bars around Geeta and repelled Mattie back. Then the black slashes of the death notes leapt toward Geeta. With brutal precision, the musical notes of death struck Geeta, their small black ends jabbing into her bent body with a hypnotic, sedative-like effect. *Life whispers no more in your ears, for the sound of death and demise circle your soul.* These words filled Geeta's mind.

Geeta! Mattie's voice cut into her consciousness from afar. *Keep your eyes open!*

Geeta's eyelids fluttered, but the Muhra had prevailed. Her eyes went blank then rolled back. From somewhere faraway she heard ThaTha's voice, but the words were muffled. Then a far-off chant rose. First it was just the sound of ThaTha; then it was the low voices of many, blending in a hypnotic rhythm as her eyes shut. *Om Namaha Shivaya, Om Namaha Shivaya, Om Namaha Shivaya, Om Namaha Shivaya* the ancient Sanskirt words calling to Shiva formed. The sounds of the chant faded as Geeta's body gave way to the Muhra's poisonous spell. She lay crumpled on the ground, her legs splayed out. Cold tendrils of poison coiled around her heart to hold her so the Muhra could grab her body then her soul. She was unable to resist the death notes that vibrated throughout her body. As Geeta shuddered on the ground, her vibrant colors—the purple of her dress, the mustard of her tights and turtleneck, the brown of her face, her black pigtails—all turned gray.

The Muhra moved back. The owlet's spirit was somewhere far off—no matter to them. They wouldn't take her body, for to break the red-haired child, she must touch the owlet's cold dead body.

Mattie sprang toward Geeta, who lay flat upon the rooftop, and jerked her friend's motionless hand.

"Get up! Oh, Geeta get up!" she screamed. But Geeta lay still, like a lump of clay. The ether energy of the Muhra hovered above them, a sharp and deadly waiting current.

"Geeta! Please. Please, God, don't let Geeta die!" Mattie pleaded, her voice filled with desperation.

Mattie yanked the unconscious Geeta's arm again and again. Geeta's skin was cold, and its pallor gray; black notes embedded within her neck protruded out. Tears welled in Mattie's eyes. *Is Geeta dead? Oh, she can't be!* The Muhra eddied gleefully around the red-haired girl and the brown owlet, moving around, upward, and downward.

"Geeta!" Mattie sobbed. Tears splashed down her face as she knelt by her motionless friend.

The Muhra hovered around them in a giant storm cloud over the rooftop of the brownstone, forming a doughnut around the two girls and moving closer and closer to envelop them. Tens of thousands of eyes stared out at them now. Sobbing, her face splotched red with grief, Mattie held Geeta's cold hand. Her mother's voice was soft with her reprimand: *Yea, though I walk through the valley of the shadow of death, I will fear no evil.* "That's what people say at funerals!" Mattie whispered. "This must be Geeta's funeral." Her body shook with sobs.

The red-haired one's spirit is broken by grief! the Muhra thought, rejoicing. The Muhra's collective glee rose as they saw the Spyglass weaken under the red-haired one's despair, for they knew its strength ebbed and flowed with the thoughts of the mortal hand that held it. Their delight rose in force against the Spyglass; they saw that its mistress—the red-haired child—was deadened by anguish for the brown-skinned owlet who had fallen still upon the rooftop. Now they would seize the Spyglass. Every Muhra was awakened now. All wished to see the taking of the Spyglass. Once it was under their control, they would direct the power of the Spyglass to take over the bodies of mortals here in the land of the living. Once again they would rise in glory, fame, and adulation. There would be plenty of bodies for all.

On the street below the brownstone, the coffin crashed hard onto the pavement. The chains around it snapped, and the top sprung open. The four men, now dead souls, followed it downward, plunging to surround it. As soon as they landed, their ghostly hands reached into the coffin but were repelled by sparks.

The body within the coffin sat up. The man was young, clean-shaven, and had curly brown hair. Muscular, bare chested, bare legs, bound in large chains over bulging arms, clad only in small, striped swim trunks, this man, this Master Magician, wiggled his shoulders against the chains that bound him. His eyes blinked to see.

"Bess?" he said.

Then as the images around him sharpened he stared with incomprehension at the dead souls of the four men reaching toward him.

"Give us the key to fortune!" the four snarled in one voice.

On the rooftop of the brownstone, the ghastly Opera of Death began. For the Muhra, whose mortal veins had been filled with drama and the grandeur of the stage, the taking of the Spyglass would be marked as befitting a momentous event. The Muhra rose as an ominous choir, casting the first notes of the song of capture and possession. The sounds vibrated throughout the air.

AaaaAaaaAaaaa! Once again the deformed musical notes flew out of the cloud of Muhras. This time the tone was strong as thunder. It actually shook the brownstone. The morbid notes formed a circle of malevolence that swarmed ever closer around and around the prone Geeta and sobbing Mattie. The song of the coming of the deceased increased in volume as it prophesized the Muhra's possession of the red-haired one and their capture of the Spyglass.

Soon it will be the Muhra the Spyglass will hail.
To fame we once again soar.
Gasping and quivering will our spirits be,
When our formless prisons fall to set us free.
AaaaAaaaAaaaAaaa!

With utter horror, the Spyglass realized she had been wrong. They knew! They knew who she was. They had killed Geeta to weaken Mattie and grasp the Spyglass! Within her metal prison, she heard the Muhra's sing their song of her capture. The Spyglass summoned her energy to lift Mattie against the Muhra's oppressive force. But the Spyglass's strength ebbed under Mattie's will, which was nearly broken by her sorrow. Though the Spyglass was still encircled within Mattie's fingers, her hold was loosening. Mattie was losing her will to live. Spyglass felt waves of grief rise like steam from the girl, felt her spirit wane under despair.

The Spyglass panicked. *Mattie, stupid girl! Move! Move! Geeta is nothing! Move!*

Mattie did not—could not—hear the Spyglass, for her sobs filled her as she grieved over her friend. Mattie heard her mother's voice again in bits and pieces: *Be sober minded…The Devil prowls around like a roaring lion, seeking someone to devour.* She looked through her tear-filled eyes to see thousands of eyes peering greedily at her from the fog. Her fingers tightened protectively around Geeta's still arm; when she felt its deadweight, her mouth emitted a sob. Mattie thought of how good a friend Geeta was, how she had saved her in **Madame Lina's** auditorium when that horrible bat creature had her roped. She felt her heart beat heavily with anguish. Now the tears flowed without control, a great rushing river of regret that streaked her cheeks. Mattie bent over Geeta protectively with her body as the Muhra fog edged in closer and closer around them. She hurt with sadness. Why couldn't she have been stronger? Smarter? Oh, where was Eddie? He would have beat off this evil fog. He should have been the one to hold the Spyglass, not her. She wasn't a warrior. She was a weakling. She had let those creatures get Geeta. Then Mattie's thoughts ran with bitterness toward the Spyglass, who never showed her magic when she needed her. She felt the metal body against her fingers, cold and still; although she didn't know it, the Spyglass was trying to summon strength against overwhelming forces. She was calling to Mattie to help her, to channel her will into her. But Mattie's thoughts were obscured by bitterness toward the Spyglass, then despair for **Geeta.** She lamented if only she had been a stronger Mistress of the Spyglass! Then she could have gotten Geeta help. Against the sounds of the death song, Mattie sobbed. Her body bent over **Geeta's,** she threw her arms over her friend's prone body.

AaaAaaAaaa! The great Muhra pageant of the Opera of Death continued unabated. The Great Diva appeared; her face and upper torso emerged from within the fog as thousands of Muhra eyes surrounded her like lights upon a stage. Illumination for the Great Star. She had been a great—no, *the greatest*—opera singer ever to grace the stage. Unlimited mortal fame and fortune had been hers once. No wish of hers had gone wanting in the land of mortals. The powdered white face, the golden curls of her wig twisting down over her green satin dress, her bulging eyes—they all painted a ghastly caricature of beauty, reflecting her last mortal form before her body had been interred. A large beaked nose sprung out above wide red lips covering enormous donkey teeth. The Muhra Great Diva dramatically spread out her sagging fat white arms, with veins that ended in long bony hands. The long black nails of her white hands scratched the air above Mattie and Geeta.

The Great Diva then sang death's aria:

AaaaAaaaAaaaAaaa!
Drooooowning in the daaaaarkness,
Gaaaaasping in the bloody waaater,
As life beats its last notes,
You shall succumb to the Muhra's slaaaughter.

The Great Diva flung her head back as she raised
her voice high.

AaaaAaaaAaaaAaaa!
The winter sun of life has set,
Its pallid rays upon their mortal bodies frail.
The deaths of the red-haired one and the brown owlet are surely met.
AaaaAaaaAaaaAaaa!

Applause emanated from the Muhra fog. The Great Diva bowed her head in reponse and disappeared into the spinning ether. The gray doughnut-shaped fog descended closer and closer to envelop Mattie and Geeta. The Muhra would possess the red-haired one's body and manipulate it as their own. They pushed forward an old Muhra, ancient enough that he would have just enough strength to take over the red-haired one's body and small enough that he would lay fully under the control of the others. The small, ancient form of the old Muhra sprang out toward Mattie.

𒀭𒅗𒁹𒄑𒅗𒀭

Below the brownstone and the horror of the rooftop opera, the four dead souls lunged toward the Great Magician, who sat up in his coffin looking confused.

"The key! Give us the key to fortune, Master Magician!" the four dead souls cried.

Their four pairs of hands greedily jerked up the young shackled man in the coffin, their fingers wrapped around his neck. The man's throat made a warbled sound. He threw his curly head back then coughed to regurgitate something. Then he spat a small brass key into the air. It flew in a great arc, throwing a stream of bronze light in its wake. It flew over the four men, who quickly let the Master Magician go. They scrambled toward the key as it made its descent in the air. The young man in the coffin heard the yelps of glee of the four dead souls.

"Mine!" each one said, as they in turn grabbed to hold the key, which was flying just in front of them.

They ran after it, their hands outstretched to grasp the key as it zigzagged into an alleyway.

The Master Magician's eyes were lit with mischief. He laughed a small laugh at how easily even the dead could be fooled by the trickery of illusion. Then he quickly regurgitated another key, one of fine diaphanous glimmering gold. This key flew like a hummingbird around his chains. The metal melted away, unbinding him in an instant. The Master Magician stood up in the coffin, stretched and flexed his muscular body, and shook his dark curly head. He had been waiting these ten years for his beloved Bess to call him from the dead. How surprised she would be to find him back in again in his youth as he sauntered in through the front door of their brownstone. And not dead at all! At least he didn't think so—look how he had regained his strength. It was more like a long refreshing nap than death.

The Great Diva's head, a bobbing white blob with its yellow-haired wig, suddenly burst out of the fog. She headed straight toward Mattie, flinging the ancient small Muhra who would possess the red-haired child. The Diva's greed for the Spyglass couldn't be contained. Though she could only escape the hold of the Muhra's fog in parts, she was determined to do so. Her hands, with their bony white fingers, shot out of the fog and flew about her head. The Great Diva's treachery caused a break in the pulse of the energy of the Muhra force as voices of shock at her actions rippled through the doughnut-shaped fog. *The Diva sprang out of the ether!* Still they were in awe of the Great Diva, who had, even within the Muhra's collection of extreme and unrelenting entitlement, always gotten exactly what she wanted, no matter how unreasonable.

No, Diva. We must be one, the Muhra cried as they moved to pull her back.

In doing so, they grabbed the golden wig, which, like all that was Muhra ether, came apart in wisps. The Great Diva's wigless head revealed a ghastly scalp covered with short gray bristles. Still she struggled to escape the Muhra, her powdered white face elongated, the beaked nose stretching as it was pulled like taffy by the Muhra back into their ether.

The Diva's red lips, with their donkey teeth, shot out of the melting face like a missile from the Muhra fog. Her disembodied hands flew toward Mattie, their wispy fingers wrapping around the girl's arm. A great whisper of disapproval emanated from the fog, but the Diva ignored it. Her hands and mouth were all she needed to capture the Spyglass for herself. The Great Diva, even though she was just in parts now, must be the one to own the Spyglass, and all the other Muhra would bow to her as queen, naturally. The Muhra, who heard these thoughts, protested; a great riot of dismay rose within the ether at this betrayal. Though, truth be told, each lamented that they hadn't thought first to act exactly as the Diva had—to somehow try to grab the amulet first.

The Great Diva's garish red lips parted to reveal her snapping donkey teeth, which clicked and sprang like a rabid dog toward Mattie, intent on biting the hand that held the Spyglass. The Muhra could capture souls, could grasp the hearts of the living, but only collectively. This was yet another of the hell that they, a collection of inflated egos, were condemned to: never to be glorified as one but always as a group. The Great Diva was allowed only the smallest of departures from this, as she was able to keep the honorific of Diva and to sing the solo Opera of Death. Even with these allowances, she was still just ether, with no power of her own and reliant upon the rest of the Muhra.

Still, the Great Diva wasn't deterred. She had slipped out of the ether that was the Muhra—true, it was only her teeth and hands, but still she was out. And too, the Diva knew that the power of the Muhra always had risen from the strength of the fear of the assailed one—in this case, the red-haired girl. This fear allowed the Muhra to enter the world of nightmares, to secure promises from the dreamer, and then to exact their payment in the form of the dreamer's soul.

So it was that the Great Diva's teeth were just phantoms, although Mattie didn't know this. Her eyes went round with terror as the Diva snapped them at her. Mattie screamed, but her scream was like one has in a nightmare, where no sound emerges. With her intense fear, Mattie opened the door of her being to the Diva. The Great Diva's teeth snapped at her, penetrating her wrist.

The Spyglass felt Mattie's hand loosen its grip. *Oh, stupid girl! The teeth aren't real!* she cried, and tried again and again to lift Mattie up but to no avail.

Mattie was paralyzed by fear. All that she was aware of was a sharp electric bolt of pain. The Muhra's bite had invaded her with the acuteness of a nightmare. Against this, Mattie's thoughts came in spurts: *Mr. Biddle! Mom!* A soundless cry for help sprung from her mind. *Someone help us!* The disembodied hands of the Great Diva plunged their nails into Mattie's wrist. Overwhelmed by the excruciating pain, Mattie's fingers loosened their grasp around the Spyglass, and her eyes closed shut. The Spyglass clattered to the rooftop.

Even before the last note of the Spyglass falling from Mattie's hands to the rooftop was heard, the dam of the Muhra fog already had broken loose. Every Muhra who could plunge out of the ether in whatever parts were available to do so did: hundreds of horrific eyes, hands, feet, arms, legs, toes, mouths, faces, torsos, glimmering blood-red lips salivating with desire for the Spyglass. Parts were all they were. The Muhra had been torn apart by the force of their ravenousness greed for individual adulation and power.

The Great Diva's donkey teeth and red lips were overwhelmed. Hundreds of outstretched hands were blown away from Mattie by the Muhra fog. The Muhra rolled over and around her, but only one of them could take her form or her body would be torn asunder. The Muhra, in their ghostly parts, rolled over the Spyglass, desperate to pick it up, forgoing the laborious step of just one of them taking over a mortal body and then controlling it, for to do so meant delay and, more important, trust—trust that one of their duplicitous brethren would follow a plan that benefitted all and not just one. The improbability of the Muhra putting aside selfish need for collective glory already had been proven, for—as the Diva had tried—any one of them would only take the precious amulet for themselves alone. Emotion rather than logic ruled the Muhra's consciousness, in death as it had in life. *Muhra! Muhra! Muhra!* Their voices sprang upward, greedy with need. One of them would be the victor, and each held the grandiose thought that it would be them.

Muhra! The Crone's ear caught the sound in a blanket of blackness, her mind reeling with all the horrific possibilities of who and what were the Muhra. The Crone was a forgotten creature in the confusion of the battle between the Snake and the Four Terrors. Her greasy robes were covered with dirt when she landed by the gates of Kurnigi. These gates, once guarded by fierce monsters that allowed no escape, had been pulled from the ground. They had flown up into the sky, hurled up by a radiating force from the eruption beyond. Chaos reigned hard in Kurnigi. The noise of the battle between the demon gods and the Snake's creatures raged in the Crone's ears. She gasped for breath as her mind rapidly turned over the events. She could escape. But how? Where? Suddenly she felt a hold upon her, invisible but tight.

"Who clasps me?" the Crone cried from where the great gates of Kurnigi once stood. "I am just a helpless old hag!"

We are Muhra, the voices echoed in the Crone's ears.

Muhra. Muhra. Muhra. The Crone saw that the ether was a force of creatures—and they were trying to escape the fog that imprisoned them. Then she felt the Muhra upon her. They spun around the Crone, wrapping her ever more in their invisible iron grasp. She was pulled upward as the sounds of the battle in Kurnigi receded. The last sensation the Crone felt was the heat of the flames that engulfed her as she lay helpless where the Gates of Kurnigi once stood. Then she saw and felt blackness as the Muhra whirled about her. She felt the blackness take hold and pull her through the vibrations. Now the blackness was lifting, but the terrible presence of the Muhra fog pressed all around her.

𒀭𒄑𒂍𒄑𒀭

In the darkness of street below, as it flew back into his palm, the Master Magician's golden key was just a brief flash of light. He popped the key into his mouth, swallowing it whole. Then he jumped nimbly out of the coffin. The cold air hit his almost-bare body. It felt good after the hot confines of the coffin. A decade was a long time to be cooped up. He stretched his muscular arms. He snapped his fingers, and his body instantly was clothed in an elegant dark wool suit. His feet remained bare, and he wiggled his toes. Oh, well. Some rustiness was expected after a ten-year hiatus. He was about to wave his hands for shoes when his eyes caught a strange gray light hovering above the roof of his brownstone. The Master Magician's forehead furrowed in puzzlement. His ears heard the buzzing of evil energy, but beneath it he heard another sound: "Help!" It was a plea for help. Bess was in trouble! The Master Magician snapped his fingers again.

"Up!" he commanded.

Immediately one of the chains that had bound him appeared and rose straight up from the coffin toward the rooftop. He jumped onto the chain and adroitly began the climb to the roof, his toes wrapped around the chain, pulling him up with the nimbleness of a gymnast.

The Master Magician landed lightly upon the rooftop's edge. The chain rope he had climbed was clasped like a whip in one hand. He squatted low then tilted his head to hear, for all that he beheld with his eyes was an ominous whirling gray fog. A fog that was thick with sounds. He heard a moaning low beneath the fog again. "Help...help!"

Bess! the Master Magician thought. It must be his beloved wife, trapped within the evil fog. The Master Magician quickly threw the golden chain like a rope toward the sound.

Bess! Grab the chain! his thoughts shouted toward the voice.

The golden chain hovered in the fog over Mattie's head. *Grab the chain!* The words of the Master Magician burst through the mist.

Mattie reached out. *Grab the chain!* She felt a surge of hope—someone was trying to help them! Maybe Mr. Biddle! In a quick motion, she grabbed the chain, holding fast to Geeta's limp hand with her other hand. Immediately the chain swung up into the air, lifting Mattie and Geeta, and then flung them around. The movement served to repel the Muhra fog. Eyes, teeth, and grasping hands moved past Mattie and Geeta. She felt the wind against her face as the chain went round and round, beating the Muhra fog away.

The Spyglass cried out for help as she rolled on the rooftop. *Mattie! Don't leave me!*

The Muhra then veered downward toward the Spyglass. Mattie heard the Spyglass's plaintive cry: *Mattie! Don't leave me!* The chain swung around and around the fog, pushing away the Muhra with a wide swath. Below her the evil fog rolled around, their ethereal hands reaching out but unable to clasp the Spyglass.

Mattie! Please! The Spyglass tried another tactic. *I'm so scared.*

The Spyglass's beseeching tones filled her ears. She looked down and swore the Spyglass was looking straight at her with big accusing eyes. Even so, her heart was hardened against the Spyglass. *No!* Mattie bit her lip hard. Geeta swung below Mattie in a deadweight, pulling her downward. No matter what, she wasn't going to let go of Geeta—somehow she would figure out a way to get her to wake up. Somehow.

The Spyglass, upon the rooftop, locked her gaze upon Mattie. An intense ray of light glinted angrily from the eyes within her metal body, straight through the fog and into Mattie's eyes. *You cannot leave me. You will not leave me. You cannot leave me. You will not leave me.*

Mattie willed herself to shut her eyes against the Spyglass's will, but they remained open. Her face felt hot. *You cannot leave me. You will not leave me. You cannot leave me. You will not leave me.*

Mattie's head was woozy, cotton headed, as the spell of the Spyglass penetrated her. *Drop Geeta and pick me up!* the Spyglass ordered from below.

No! came Mattie's response.

The Spyglass's penetrating will grew in proportion to her fear of being left to be captured by the Muhra. It formed around Mattie's fingers, which clasped Geeta, and began to pry them open, one finger after another.

𒁹𒄷 𒁹 𒁹𒄷 𒁹

The Crone was tossed out of the Muhra ether and fell onto her back on the roof of the brownstone. Her snaggly yellow tooth shook in her ugly face. *Where am I?* she wondered. She righted herself but remained low to the ground on her knees, moving her grizzled head about, her narrow eyes scanning for clues. The greed of the Muhra had thickened the fog upon the rooftop, and all the Crone could see above her was a gray light. She heard the evil buzzing of the Muhra but couldn't make sense of the sounds. She felt the cold night air. The Crone lifted her beaked nose and sniffed. The long hairs that sprung out of her nostrils vibrated in response to the smell of mortal blood. She lifted her hands, palms up against the fog, and felt the pulse of life around her. Yes! She was in the land of the living! The Crone grunted in pleasure. She had escaped Kurnigi—and the Snake.

Her yellow eyes caught a movement, a glint beneath the fog. She scurried upon her knees toward it. The Crone's palms then vibrated again as her long fingers moved toward and encircled the Spyglass. Somewhere a blood-curdling scream rang out. Evil held the Spyglass. The Crone was stunned at first: the Spyglass! In a flash she recalled all the eons upon eons she had scurried through: she had lost her great beauty, held the Black Book of Magic and lost it to the Snake, and lost control of her spirit. Now at last the Spyglass was hers! *Hers*! She clutched the Spyglass tightly. She threw back her grizzly head; the gray hairs were now lit by the fog swirling around her. Still on her knees, she held the Spyglass tightly in one hand as the Muhra fog descended lower, their fingers reaching to grab her. The Crone stood up, her back hunched, the small lump rising to her shoulders a testimony of her ugliness soon to be shed, she thought. She would rise again in astonishing, mesmerizing beauty and rule supreme! She was fierce in this determination.

She shook the Spyglass at the Muhra fog and, with one hand beckoning, snarled with glee, *Come closer, formless ones, that I may capture you inside my evil amulet!*

The Muhra fog receded immediately, and a small hiss rose from their lips—the hiss of defeat. They had lost the chance to hold the Spyglass as their own for now, but they were in the land of the living, and there were many forms to be had. Then would this withered, wizened Crone feel their might.

AaaaaAaaaaa! The Muhra's voice raised as they lifted off the brownstone roof and moved toward the city streets to capture their prey.

The Muhra fog sped past Mattie, over and up and away from her, then disappeared. She heard a scream that felt like a knife cutting through her. The force trying to pry open her fingers had suddenly stopped moments before, and she had grabbed Geeta's limp hand before she fell. It was difficult to keep hold of the swinging golden rope with her other hand; it was slippery and moved as it fell from the fog somewhere above. The Muhra fog was also creating the wind as it moved past her. The wind violently swung the golden rope in Mattie's hand. Then suddenly the rope went slack. Mattie and Geeta were thrown downward and hit the brownstone's cement rooftop. Mattie tumbled awkwardly before righting herself to a kneeling position. Her knees hurt—they felt scraped—as she looked up into the yellow eyes of an old woman with frizzy gray hair and grimy clothing. The old one had a single yellow tooth, and in her hand she held the Spyglass and shook it at Mattie; she cackled happily then disappeared.

Good riddance. Mattie felt relief wash over her at finally being rid of the Spyglass. *It was evil, just like Mr. Biddle said.* Then a sudden jab went through her conscience.

A vision of the small man from Nineveh, the one with the large ears and crisscrossing veins, appeared in her mind. He softly chastised her, *Oh, child, what have you done? See how you have given over that which holds power to one who has a heart that devises wicked plans? Oh, child, I grieve at your thoughtlessness.* As quickly as he had arrived, the small elfin man from Nineveh disappeared from Mattie's vision.

Mattie was stricken with guilt. The old woman *did* look like a witch, and she, Mattie, had allowed evil to take the Spyglass. *But the Spyglass is evil anyway, so what does it matter?* Mattie groaned. *What was I supposed to do? Where was Mr. Biddle?* Mattie knelt by Geeta. Her owl eyes were closed behind her black-rimmed glasses. Her thin legs, encased in her mustard-yellow tights, were splayed. *Geeta is still here.* Mattie felt another wash of relief. Geeta was so smart. She would know what to do. They'd get that two-faced Spyglass back from the old witch, somehow, and then she'd let Geeta take it. Then the realization hit her, as Geeta lay still upon the ground: *Geeta might be dead.*

Mattie pulled at Geeta's arm and shook her. "Geeta!"

But Geeta didn't budge. What would happen now? Mattie moaned as she fell back on her haunches. *Think,* she commanded herself. *Think!* It was silent on the rooftop. Far off, the noises of the city ebbed and flowed in an eerie song that sent a shiver down Mattie's spine. She looked down at Geeta, who lay quiet and still. *Be strong!* Mattie told herself, and set her mind to believe that Geeta was alive. She'd have to get some magic dust or something to wake her up. Or maybe that nice little man with the big ears would come back and tell her what to do. Mattie had on her green-checkered pants, which were good against the cold. She looked around warily—who knew if those ghosts in the fog would come back or not? But no spirits formed against her. The darkness on the rooftop was relieved by a small flickering candle on a round table. Somewhere beyond it in the black night air, Mattie heard ghostly wails and screeches. Her heart shivered in fearful beats.

What could she do now to help Geeta? To help herself? Her mind felt like it was filled with gray fog. No answer came. Oh, why was she chosen to be the Mistress of the Spyglass? She wasn't qualified—after all, she had only just begun as a milk-money monitor at Fairmount Grammar School. Her thoughts went round and round: Mr. Biddle should have taken the Spyglass from her given it to Geeta or Eddie. Mattie looked at her arms.

Yes, they still had the faint undertone of gold, and she remembered how in Nineveh she had been strong—how she had led the people to the beautiful Tree in the Garden, the one with the shiny blue glass globes. How she had been the one they held up on their shoulders, and she had called them her people. But that was then. In her mind, Mattie heard her mother's voice faint as a breeze: *Take the shield of faith, with which you will be able to quench the fiery darts of the wicked one.* Tears brimmed in her eyes. *Oh, Mom! I don't get it!* Why couldn't her mom just appear and help her? Why couldn't she just be back home in Hackensack and be a simple fifth grader?

Mattie's heart brimmed with sorrow, regret, and bitterness. Though she couldn't give it voice, she found herself in that place and time when the weight of one's destiny rises larger than one's shoulders can hold; when it bears down, daunting to the soul, testing every bit of strength of will and courage as it exerts the excruciating and raw pain of the metamorphosis from the ordinary to the extraordinary.

To fulfill this destiny, one must move away from the known comfort of the shell of who they are to the unknown of who they're supposed to be. As it takes courage to fulfill this destiny—courage not often innately present—this mantle often is flung off at the first pangs of change. But as a bell once rung cannot be unrung, the first steps upon this destiny's path forever alter one's fate.

So it would be that Mattie would find that her journey already had thrown her so far from her world of drinking hot chocolate with marshmallows, of watching old reruns on television on snow days, of being snuggled in the warm cocoon of her life as a fifth grader in Hackensack, New Jersey, that she was no longer that Mattie. Her reality was now this fantastical world, and she must grow to accept this or be destroyed.

Mattie's mind couldn't articulate these thoughts; instead she felt them as deep, sharp pangs in her soul. Tears spilled down her cheeks. She thought angrily of the Spyglass and all her lying ways. *Now I'm a failure just because I couldn't hold on to that double-crossing Spyglass. It's not fair.* Before she could give voice to the wail that rose in her throat, a barefoot man wearing a dark suit dropped to the rooftop holding the limp golden chain.

"Where's Bess?" the Master Magician demanded of Mattie. His voice was commanding and angry, his eyes flashing ominously.

He seemed surprised by the two figures: a frizzy red-haired, red-faced girl kneeling over an unconscious thin brown girl with black braids.

Mattie looked with confusion at the man looming angrily over her. She opened her mouth, but no words formed, only tears that now ran down her cheeks.

The Master Magician's heart remained unmoved. He knew that evil spirit creatures could take the form of innocent children to trick the unwary.

"What have you done with her?" he shouted, and then snapped his fingers. A long thin black wand formed with a sharp steel point springing out. He pointed it menacingly at Mattie. "Speak or be hurt!"

CHAPTER 5

the drowning of the king

Gilgamesh, the seventh king of ancient Uruk, understood the dark. He had lived in it for eons while trapped within the confines the Tablets of Creation and then again in its pieces, which had been held within the secret tunnels of the British Museum. But this blackness into which he had plunged was wholly different. It was the Abyss, so dense that it blinded his eyes. As Gilgamesh fell, he felt the coldness of this hell under hell wrap around him. The blackness wasn't empty, however, for Gilgamesh felt movement all around him. He recognized that he was in a funnel spinning downward. Its serpentine coils imprisoned his body and moved around the sacred spear, which he held firmly. He struggled to thrust the sacred spear to repel the force of the Abyss of Blackness away from his vulnerability: the one-quarter-mortal portion. The energy of the blackness moved in. Tendrils of death tried to penetrate his golden armored vest, the only thing that guarded his heart, which held the one-quarter portion of him that was his mortal soul. This was his weak point in this the realm of the mortal dead, and the forces of darkness sought it.

Gilgamesh moved against the shadowy force that pinned his arms and his spear to his side. He struggled to see the faintest outlines of the flame at its tip, but only the darkness greeted him. It was then that Gilgamesh feared that the blackness had forever swallowed the sacred green fire at his spear's tip. The relentless darkness marked the strength of the dark world to blanket all that was light—the ascendancy of evil over good. Gilgamesh's spear was a noble weapon from the ancient times when the gods had offered strength and power to deserving warriors. It originally had been crafted from the mighty metals forged by the six kings of Uruk before Gilgamesh, each adding his valor to its power. Then it was that Gilgamesh had beseeched to the Mother Tiamat to strengthen this weapon so he could battle the evil that had threatened to erase light and goodness from the memory of man. Silver flames had sprung, and from them eleven warriors mighty in strength rode forth on winged white horses: five goddesses and five gods, and the eleventh Kingu, the warrior mate of Tiamat. The ten god warriors clashed their mighty spears with Kingu's spear, and the eleven spears formed one spear. Such was the spear: eight golden feet in length, with the strength of eleven gods, which Gilgamesh wielded now as he fell downward into terror. At its tip the sacred emerald flame burned bright with hope.

Gilgamesh heard sudden frenetic cries and felt touches light as a feather but with the electric sharpness of a current. These too thrust their evil force toward his mortal heart. The king of Uruk felt their sharp pings, followed by something that was beyond fear, beyond terror: the coldness of emptiness. Then the memories came to remind him of his duty, which brooked no fear. In his mind he heard the voice of the ancient priestess Nana. "Go forth, Gilgamesh, king of Uruk," she had said, her voice wavering in pain and her black eyes shining with tears as he had set foot on a treacherous path and impossible journey. The brown walnut face of the wise priestess of Uruk, Nana, flickered in his mind; her eyes were black like wet pebbles and held in their depths both wisdom and kindness. She was ancient in age, and therefore her knowledge held the tale of Uruk, across the seven kings, some said, of which Gilgamesh was feared to be the last.

"Go, Gilgamesh," the priestess had ordered, "and find the secret to eternal life. Bring it to us so that we, the last of the peoples of Uruk, should not fall into the clutches of evil."

Now in the darkness, voices rang out, but his own thoughts were even louder: *Gilgamesh, king of Uruk, you have failed.* Shame coursed through his veins. Yes, he had failed his people, for had he not allowed himself to be trapped within the Tablets of Creation? To lie still and helpless for eons while his people perished and were plunged into the darkness of Kurnigi? And had he not also led his warrior brother, Enkidu, to his entrapment in the City of the Condemned? *Gilgamesh, king of Uruk, you have failed.* These were the thoughts of weakness, meant to poison him with doubt and guilt. It was the evil ones' poison seeping into his mind to weaken him through doubt. Gilgamesh struggled yet again against the invisible force that bound him. He was still blind, for blackness was all that he saw in his spinning downward journey. Gilgamesh's thoughts ran to Nana and her prophecy that he would be plunged into the Abyss.

Ti-a-met-e-li-ti Ti-a-mut-e-li-tu, echoed the soft chant, the song that faintly rose; it was the voice of Nana,. He felt the ancient priestess's presence, for somewhere deep in the Land of Darkness, Nana and the people of Uruk lay trapped, awaiting their king to bring them back to the light. *Ti-a-met-e-li-ti Ti-a-mut-e-li-tu.* Her soft voice grew in Gilgamesh's mind to counter the evil force. He knew she was whispering to him the ancient chant of the Mother to unleash the light of the spear. *Ti-a-met-e-li-ti Ti-a-mut-e-li-tu Ti-a-mat-e-li-ta.* Her words came to his lips. He murmured them to bring forward the flame. He felt the current of the evil that surrounded him register the sounds. These words were dangerous, for the name of the Mother was an enemy to evil. He felt the dark energy tighten a rope around his neck.

Still Gilgamesh chanted, the words growing louder:

> *O Three Mothers, O sounds before the Nothingness!*
> *Ti-a-met-e-li-ti Ti-a-mut-e-li-tu Ti-a-mat-e-li-ta!*
> *O Mother, whose waters are within, below, and above!*
> *O Mother, bring to this sacred weapon I hold*
> *The light of the stars and moons of old.*

A deafening quake broke and shook the blackness; Gilgamesh felt its painful vibrations. The tip of the spear flickered against the blackness riding up to drown it. But the spear's light prevailed. It was the color of the green of new shoots, glimmering just enough to show Gilgamesh the contrast and how unrelenting the blackness of the Abyss was. Gilgamesh felt the hold of the evil force lessen as the flame grew into a glittering emerald light. He used the spear to right himself. Then Gilgamesh saw who was falling with him, around him, above and below him, and who reached their hands, sought to plunge their teeth and claws into him: it was a torrent of monsters, evil spirits, and ghouls of old falling as the skin of Kurnigi was torn. These creatures had been imprisoned in the Kurnigi but had been set free by Chaos, only to be plunged downward into the Abyss of Blackness. Their eyes were bloody, their fangs sharp and jagged. Some were serpents, some dragons, other rodents. Some were shaped like fish with claws and wings or had fins and shark teeth. Others had misshapen human heads, eyes bulging with fear, faces scratched and torn asunder. Some rode horses, chariots, carriages made of skeletons; others were only fragments: heads with chomping teeth, bony hands with long curved nails, eyes that blinked in rage. Some had bodies preyed upon by maggots; still others had crazed faces and voices that fell in nonsensical tones. All possessed their private fury, their special punishment for their mortal sins. This torrent of monsters fell—a rain of all the released spirits that had been held in darkness plunging, plunging downward into the Abyss.

"Aaagh!" Gilgamesh cried when these evil spirits crashed against him.

He tumbled upside down and sideways. He thrust his spear repeatedly against the evil souls falling in and around him. The hold of the malevolent force lessened against it. Into the Abyss of Blackness he plummeted, a depth from which no one returned, even with blood that was three-quarters god. *Asuru-alim-nuna*, he thought. *The forgotten mighty ones, the gods of old.* Gilgamesh knew that indeed chaos reigned, and the revenge the forgotten mighty ones had threatened against the rule of Marduk was coming to fruition. Chaos for darkness also meant Chaos for light and no return surely for those who fell into the Abyss. Gilgamesh forced this thought aside. He must not let doubt enter his mind. He had deliberately plunged into the Abyss to find the *muktablu* and would not fail the young warrior.

Gilgamesh felt a whoosh of wind and was thrown sideways. Abruptly the blackness lifted to reveal a steel-gray sky. He was still falling, as were the evil creatures around him. Then beneath him a great expanse of gray-green liquid rose, churning with choppy waves. He heard the frantic murmurs of the evil spirits as they fell around him toward the liquid. *Sea of Abyss. Sea of Abyss.* It was a sea beneath mortal oceans, filled with creatures of death that lured mortal men and took their last breaths with glee and held their souls ever after in their watery coffins. This was all Gilgamesh knew of the Sea of Abyss, which was said to lie within the Abyss of Blackness. So fearsome was it that even the monsters who had escaped Kurnigi feared it, for Gilgamesh saw how they frantically moved their wings, their fins, their arms to avoid plunging into its waters. Their screeches filled his ears. Some, with their death fingers, reached to grab Gilgamesh's spear. He swung its emerald flame, and the spirits moved back.

Brother. Gilgamesh heard the voice of the *muktablu*'s warrior father as he fell with the rain of the ghouls and spirits toward the strange liquid rising beneath them. Gilgamesh's brow furrowed.

Deep within the green flame, he saw a vision. Lush leaves of a mortal jungle and the anguished face of the warrior father of the *muktablu* appeared. *My son drowns in the Sea of Abyss*, he heard him say.

As the image disappeared, the words reverberated in Gilgamesh's mind. Suddenly he was thrown back in the sky as a deafening sound erupted from below and stupendous winds whipped the sea. His black braids, which hung like ropes about his head, moved with the wind, wrapping around his face and obscuring his vision. Gilgamesh felt the monsters collide against him, smack against the golden armored vest that covered his torso; his giant feet struck others below. He shook his head to move the braids away from his face. His eyes grew large as they took in what was had caused the sound.

An earthquake rocked the Sea of Abyss, from which a gigantic island rose. It was ringed in fiery molten lava that quickly became solid; it was turning into obsidian, the smooth black glass formed by the hardening of lava. Upon the island, mountains shot up, the trees upon them rising into giant forms in an instant. On the highest peak, spires pierced the mountain's skin, and then a jagged form emerged then took shape. It was an enormous dark castle of old forming, and Gilgamesh was falling toward it. Turrets now formed a rectangular perimeter of the castle. These giant towers sprouted one after another. Great conical metal roofs stabbed the air. It was a fortress among fortresses, so gigantic that it was a city unto itself.

The City of Fiends. The monsters, the ghouls, the dragons, the spirits dropped onto the island, some at its perimeter. Others fell onto a road that cut into the mountain like a bloody slash up toward the castle. The creatures fell and fell onto the island, forming an unrelenting torrential rain of evil. Where the obsidian edges dropped into the Sea of Abyss, other creatures crawled forth: amphibians with wings, fish with legs, crabs that were hundreds of feet in diameter with claws that snapped the air. In an instant they had traversed the heights of the mountains and were crawling toward the castle to join their brethren who rained down from the sky.

Gilgamesh was upside down, falling headfirst toward the island. He fiercely lashed his spear against the funnel of the wind that pulled him toward the island. He slashed at the creatures that fell above, below, and around him. The sacred spear cleaved a path. Gilgamesh pointed the spear downward as he veered away from the island and into the Sea of Abyss. As he fell close to the sea's surface, thousands of gigantic sharks the cold color of death sprang from the roiling dark sea then fell back into the water. Into this sea, teeming with death, he knew he must drop. Gilgamesh shuddered then steeled himself for the plunge into the deadly waters. Just then the sharks sprang up and out, baring their jagged double rows of teeth as they broke the sea's hold. Hundreds of them flew up into the air and pressed against Gilgamesh. So close were they that his feet touched their bodies, and his head hit their underbellies. The sacred warrior spear was so tight against his body that he couldn't wield it, pressed as he was by the throngs of rising sharks.

The king of Uruk's blue face beaded with droplets of fear. The stink of the sharks filled his nostrils. Their teeth, jagged blades that filled their cavernous mouths, were close upon his face. But then they abruptly flew up past him then toward the island, ignoring him entirely. Gilgamesh swung his spear toward the sea as he dropped toward it.

Then before the Sea of Abyss swallowed him, a dim chorus of voices, sharp with anticipation, floated up from the island: *The Prince of Demons rises!*

Eddie lay unconscious, curled upon the floor of the Sea of Abyss, which was littered with broken skeletons of other mortals. His yellow hair waved like sea anemones about his handsome face, the firm lines of his jaw still set in warrior resolve. Eddie was so much like his father—a *muktablu* even as death's cold fingers clasped him. In the recesses of his consciousness, he realized he had fallen prey to the Roanes, those hideous sea demons with long fangs embedded in their seal faces.

Eddie's body jerked, his heart faintly beating the last notes of the song of his life after he had unclasped Death's scythe. *Trina, Trina, Trina.* The deep notes of his broken heart filled his ears as his eyes fluttered inward against the pain that rose in his chest. Trina was lost to him again. Then, like the dim mists of fog rising over a dawning horizon, the memories of how in endless lifetimes he had found and lost Trina beat in his heart. The pain within his chest rose to claim his mortal body. He was drowning.

The beautiful sea-maiden he had thought was Trina had persuaded him to drop his weapon, Death's scythe.

Eddie heard her words again as consciousness ebbed: *O my lost love, I cannot come into your arms when you hold the scythe, for it will shred me to pieces. Drop you must the scythe.* As soon as his fingers had unclasped the handle of the scythe, the deadly waters of the Sea of Abyss had begun to fill his lungs. Eddie knew that a warrior who dropped his weapon only faced peril, but that paled in comparison to losing his beloved Trina. Somewhere far away, from deep within the Vietnamese jungles of his war, Sergeant Petersen had cried to his son in alarm, *Eddie! Never drop your weapon!* But Eddie knew he couldn't live without Trina and had unclasped the scythe only to learn his folly. For it wasn't Trina at all, but a Roane who had taken her form in order to trick him.

Now the liquid of the Sea of Abyss filled him, squeezing his life out, for no mortal could live within these death waters. Eddie realized this too late. It had been Death's scythe that had kept him alive. His last memory was that of the false Trina, whose face had disappeared to reveal long sharp walrus fangs moving toward him in anticipation of the taste of the warm blood of a newly dead mortal. Now the sea-demon creatures ringed Eddie. Their faces turned from beauty in order to show their true selves: long-toothed snarling seal heads, perched on human shoulders and torsos that blended into marine-mammal trunks and tails. Their luxuriant hair, the color of ripe persimmons, still waved garishly about their faces. They had captured this living *muktablu* who held Death's scythe, and now they would possess it. Their greedy fingers reached out then drew back: Death's scythe, which vibrated near its dying master, sent warning sparks that kept them back. The Roanes shook their long orange tresses impatiently in anticipation of the death of the yellow-haired *muktablu*. Their lips moved over their fangs as they let out high-pitched staccato yelps. Eddie's body jerked slightly then lay still.

The Roanes pounced as one toward the scythe, their faces alit with triumph, when a stupendous quake erupted from the sea's bottom. They flung themselves against the roar of the quake toward Eddie, whose limp body tumbled away from them. They scratched their fingers against the trembling waters, desperate to grab Death's scythe. Eddie's body rolled along the bottom with the rippling of the quake, and the scythe followed. More quakes shook the Sea of Abyss with a relentless vengeance to empty it of its denizens. Then the sea's bottom quivered as a body; the thunderous sounds were the sea's moans of pain as the Abyss gave birth to the island. The island's mountainous peaks ripped through the bottom of the sea as it erupted upward to gash the sea's surface.

At the bottom the tremors juddered the underwater world with their fury. The quakes freed creatures long held captive in the sea: the skeleton sailors, the half-eaten human forms, those who had thrown themselves into the sea when desperation had flown through their mortal veins, together with sea dragons, serpents, and sharks, all of whom swam up to the call of the island. It had been said in tales whispered by the creatures of the dark underworld that one day a lord of the Abyss of Darkness would rise and defeat the Dark Master Marduk and take possession of Kurnigi for himself.

The Prince of Demons rises! The Roanes heard and understood that the Sea of Abyss was to be emptied to greet the prince.

But the Roanes ignored this call, for here was Death's scythe to be theirs, and with it they could swim the waters of the land of the living freely, harvesting souls from mortals and culling the power that the souls would give them. Then it would be they, the Roanes, who would demand their fair share of Kurnigi from Marduk. For was not the Dark Master's power only as strong as the souls he held?

These thoughts rang within the greedy minds of the Roanes as they were caught in the cataclysmic force of their rising brethren, the sea spirits who had been called by the formation of the island. Everywhere the sea rang with the cry, *The Prince of Demons rises!* Chaos had broken Marduk's hold of Kurnigi, and Chaos now reigned as the released *Asuru-alim-nuna* rose mightily in the Abyss. Their Chosen One, the Prince of Demons, would rise up as well, and Marduk would be destroyed, the creatures of the Sea of Abyss had prophesized.

As the underwater world of the Sea of Abyss was set loose, the words from above the water's skin rang in echoes throughout the sea: *Prince Prince Prince Demons Demons Demons Rises Rises Rises!* The Roanes heard and felt the command, for all the creatures of the Sea of Abyss had been set loose. Every creature within churned upward, for every evil spirit heard the call—heard it and rose to greet the prince. Every sea spirit but one: the Roanes. They alone ignored the call. They swam against the storm of rising sea creatures toward the bottom, for the scythe was there still, their eyes saw. Now it lay near its master, the *muktablu,* who was sprawled on his stomach, his arms above his head, the blade vibrating just a hair's breadth away from his fingertips.

The dense, suffocating liquid of the Sea of Abyss enveloped Gilgamesh. He opened his eyes to dark murky water, instinctively tightening his grasp on the sacred warrior spear. The flickering light from the green flame of the spear revealed a horrific sight: he was surrounded by terrible creatures of the Sea of Abyss. They swam, intent upon rising to the surface. There were monster sea serpents with scales that shimmered a silvery green, fish with spikes that shot up like arrows upon their humped backs, sailors misshapen into the gruesome forms of their last moments of battle with the sea, mortals of every age. Some had jewels grasped in their hands, others weapons; others had the crazed bulging eyes of those whose last gasps had been consumed by fear, anger, disease, or despair. Their bodies slammed into Gilgamesh, who struggled against the creatures to swim downward. Even with his ten feet of height and muscular form, he was but a leaf in the wind against the force of their energy as they all propelled themselves toward the surface.

With his feet pointed toward the surface, his head facing the seafloor, Gilgamesh brandished his spear, but suddenly a force reeled him up. The long braided ropes of his hair and beard moved with the sea's thunderous rolls as he was flung up to the surface. He shook his head as he bobbed upon the surface of the roiling Sea of Abyss. His eyes looked beyond him to the rising giant island on the horizon. All around him creatures of the Sea of Abyss sprang up. They broke out of the choppy waves and flew toward the soaring island, ominous in its presence with the jagged edges of mountains that ruthlessly scraped the sky. These creatures joined the others who were falling from the skin of Kurnigi through the Black Abyss and onto the island.

The Prince of Demons rises! Their cries filled the air as they buzzed with anticipation.

Brother, hurry, for my son's heart beats its last notes. Gilgamesh heard these thoughts of the warrior father of the *muktablu* cry out to him.

Gilgamesh was pinned to the surface of the sea, moving up and down like a cork. He struggled against the force that held him as he repeatedly tried to plunge down. In the spear's light, a vision flashed: Eddie lying deadly still at the bottom of the Sea of Abyss.

Gilgamesh's blue face deepened in desperation for the *muktablu*. His muscular blue arms tensed. He brandished the spear high in the sky and called to the consort of Tiamat. He called to the ten god warriors who had clashed their mighty spears with the sword of Kingu's in order to form his weapon.

O Kingu! O warrior gods of old!
I beseech you to help me fall to the bottom of this death water,
Where the deadly liquid takes the muktablu's last breath to hold.

Nothing happened. Gilgamesh continued to bounce up and down on the surface of the waves. His call had gone unheeded. Then he saw the spear glow from within, shining and golden.

Within the flame appeared the dark walnut face of Nana, her black pebble eyes glinting with sadness in the flash of the emerald spark.

O Gilgamesh, to save the muktablu,
Stab you must the sacred spear into your heart.
Plunge you must the tip to where it holds your mortal soul.
Surrender you must this one-quarter-mortal soul,
Before the Sea of Abyss can sink you.
Beware, Gilgamesh for should you do this,

Like all mortals who fall into these deadly waters,
Lost to the sea's bottom for eternity will be
The last king of Uruk.

The face of Nana wavered and disappeared into the tip of the spear's flame.

Gilgamesh instantly grabbed the sacred warrior spear with both hands, his legs pedaling against the dense water to steady his body. He thought not of himself but of his brother warrior. In one swoop he thrust the point of the spear into his chest, which was covered with the golden armor of Uruk. The emerald flame of the spear's point penetrated the armor in an instant. Gilgamesh threw back his head and howled in agony as the spear plunged deep into his heart. His back arched in the water in pain. Then he pulled it out, his blue face trembling. His one-quarter-mortal soul was a small blue wisp that became the center of the emerald green flame. The golden body of the spear then elongated and wrapped around his body. All ten feet of the great warrior, the seventh king of Uruk, melted until all that was left of Gilgamesh was only the faintest blue thread of a line running through the spear. Then the spear sped downward to the bottom of the Sea of Abyss.

𒀭𒌋𒁹𒀭𒁹

Upon the floor of the Sea of Abyss, Death's scythe vibrated. The smallest of spaces separated the scythe's handle from the fingers of its master, whose heart was sounding the tones of its last beats. The sea's bottom was empty of all but Eddie and the twelve Roanes above him, who left unheeded the call to rise to greet the Prince of Demons. They would wait for the mortal *muk-tablu* to die so they might grasp Death's scythe.

Eddie's comatose form rose and fell with each quake of the Abyss.

The sea's bottom convulsed in fits and created fierce winds. The force of the undersea winds flung Eddie up from the bottom. The Roanes, with their seal flippers, swam fast against this storm, their orange hair waving like flags of triumph around their greedy eyes. Their walrus fangs protruded from their open mouths, gleaming with danger. The creatures circled the *mukta-blu*, beating their tails against the tornado of energy created by the quakes.

Eddie's body was flung up, suspended at the center of the eye of this storm. His body was a crescent—his back arched, his arms tossed back over his head—while his eyes were shut against awareness. The scythe stayed close to its master. Its serrated blade remained within millimeters of his fingertips, willing him grasp it, for the scythe was lost without a master. The Roanes moved within the conical shape of the fury under the sea, coming closer and closer to the scythe. Small sparks emitted from the scythe, warding off the Roanes, for its master's mortal soul hadn't been surrendered, and his claim as the living master of Death's weapon thus remained. The sea winds too kept the Roanes back.

The Roanes' slit eyes then saw it. They let out a long blood-curdling cry of triumph: Eddie's body, floating within the calm of the storm, showed his face pallid with the gleam of death, signaling that the last beat of his mortal life had struck. They saw his mortal soul rise from the space between his brows, a tendril that was purple in color where flickers of crimson and violet flashed. The blade of Death's scythe turned up toward the tendril of Eddie's soul that was suspended above this forehead.

A current ran fast between the tip of the scythe and its master's soul, moving it like a magnet to cull it. The Roanes beat hard against the winds of the sea toward the scythe. Their movement propelled the scythe away from Eddie, who floated upward, as the dead do in the sea, the wisp of his soul fluttering above him.

The scythe vibrated in protest, for as Death's weapon, it held first rights to take the *muktablu's* soul into the ranks of the dead. But the Roanes cared not for these rituals of the scythe and Eddie's meager soul. They wanted the powerful weapon of Death. They pushed toward the scythe, slapping Eddie's body, now a useless piece of human waste, away. They swam hard, placing themselves between the floating *muktablu* and the scythe. They threw their hands open with splayed fingers; all were to touch the scythe so that no one Roane would be its master. They grabbed the scythe—some grasping the twisted wood of the handle, others the deadly serrated half-moon-shaped blade itself. Their long howls rang out in a song; they sang the tale of how they now held Death's scythe. How they would now cull mortal souls and grow fat with power as they swam the skin of the sea as the Master of Death!

Into this maelstrom the sacred warrior spear sped, the flame with Gilgamesh's soul glittering within. It moved directly toward Eddie, whose limp body was carried in the circles of the energy of the sea's storm. The tip cast a bright light, green with a center that was a wisp of blue. The spear's tip then pierced through the tendril hovering over Eddie's forehead, which was his soul. It glimmered with the hues of his warrior lineage, shining purple then crimson.

The green flame glowed brighter as Eddie's soul became a filament within. Then the blue wisp that was Gilgamesh's one-quarter-mortal soul entwined with Eddie's soul. Into Eddie's forehead the spear's sharp tip plunged into that sacred region of the third eye, between the brows. Then it was that the soul of Gilgamesh, born from the royal warrior mortal lineage of Lugalbanda, the second king of Uruk, ruler for 1,200 years, whom, it had been said, the gods had given the gift of the speed of a thousand cheetahs, entered Eddie's empty third eye. It racked Eddie's unconscious body with jolts. The spear moved away, its tip now only a green flame.

Eddie's eyes snapped open, and within them was the small blue wisp of Gilgamesh's one-quarter-mortal soul, entwined with the purple and crimson threads of his own soul. He saw the warrior spear floating by him then quickly scanned for the giant blue form of Gilgamesh. *Where is the king?* The Sea of Abyss answered him with silence. Eddie quickly grabbed the Gilgamesh's spear and felt its strength rumbling under his fingers. Then he threw his head back and shouted the shout of war that came from the strength of the seven kings of Uruk coursing through him from the sacred spear. He was energized by having one and one-quarter-mortal souls within. The golden body of the spear glimmered under the fingers of the young *muktablu*, while the blue thread within it glowed. Eddie spotted the greedy Roanes below, who clutched at Death's scythe.

They must have captured Gilgamesh! Eddie thought. Then the memory of how he had been tricked by the Roanes exploded in his mind. *They must have conned and captured Gilgamesh too.* Eddie's anger rose. He swam downward and swiftly plunged the spear into the Roanes. Those he hit recoiled in pain, twisting their heads toward Eddie their walrus fangs bared, but their greedy hands clasped the scythe tightly, their ugly faces twisted in snarls.

Still, to defend themselves against the *muktablu*, some among them had to unclasp the scythe. And this was not something that any of the dozen Roanes, piled one on top of another, clutching even just the smallest portion of the scythe, was willing to do. Death's scythe hadn't vibrated, hadn't sent its signal that they were its new master. Therefore the Roane who unclasped the scythe before this happened would not be Death's master but relegated to a lowly creature with no power.

As the spear struck the Roanes, Death's scythe registered the *muktablu*'s presence as it coursed through its handle. The scythe lay still under the greedy grip of the sea demons, for its master remained. Although the Roanes glowered and turned their fanged heads at Eddie at each strike, they held fast to the scythe. *Under these monsters must be the king of Uruk. I have to get to him.* Eddie cried out a call that came from deep within, from the warrior memories of the ancient kings. This shout rang loudly and vibrated against the whirls of the sea storm. With a vengeance, he plunged the spear again and again into the Roanes. Then he spun the warrior spear as a shield against them. It struck their fangs, which shattered in an instant. Still they held tight to the scythe.

Right then left. Eddie heard his father call the commands. The Roanes moved to ward off the blows of the spear. Eddie heard his father call again: *Up then twist under!* Eddie's moves confused the creatures for a millisecond. He used that millisecond, quickly swimming under them, and spotted a small space between the tails of the Roanes. He pierced the spear through this space, hitting the scythe above. It vibrated in answer to its master's call.

The Roanes howled in pain as the spear's force went through the scythe and into their hands, arms, and bodies. In the one-thousandth of a second that it took their greedy fingers to unclasp the scythe, it twisted. Eddie reached out with one hand and grasped the scythe's handle; with the other, he wielded the warrior spear. His eyes scanned the sea's bottom: there was no king. Eddie swam up. *The king must be here somewhere.* The spear's blue thread, which was Gilgamesh, glowed in response, but the message was unheard.

The Roanes turned downward as one, looking at their empty fingers in dismay. The scythe was gone. They growled, revealing broken fangs in their seal heads. The *muktablu*, they saw, was swimming with the scythe. The Roanes moved toward him; as they were tricksters, they intended to prey upon this mortal's weakness. One of the Roanes turned into the form of Trina. She looked up, her face pale and oval and entrancing. Her hazel eyes were shot with pain, her chestnut hair flowing outward. This Roane Trina flung her arms toward Eddie. She sang beseechingly into his heart, *Muktablu, my love, come into my arms.* Eddie heard and turned to look downward. His heart stopped in a beat of pain. Even though he now knew the Roanes were tricksters, his eyes and heart were taken by the sight of the pleading Trina.

The Roanes made a mistake, for so greedy were they for control that they thought that if one Trina held power over the *muktablu*, then a dozen would be that much stronger. Each Roane turned into the shape of Trina. A dozen Trinas swam toward him, arms out imploringly. They encircled him. The scythe and spear were in each of Eddie's hands, each filling him with their strength. The dozen Trinas faced him, and though he saw the face of his beloved, the sheer number of them, rather than weaken him toward the Roanes, made him shut his heart. For a dozen Trinas spoke only of falsehood; there was only one true Trina for Eddie. He swung the scythe and hit an approaching Roane Trina, who plaintively sang, *Muktablu, my love, come into my arms!* Eddie moved the sharp blade and swiftly cut off her head. As the Roane Trina's head tumbled down with a trail of blood,

Eddie cried out instinctively in anguish, despite knowing it was a Roane and not his love.

The Roanes sensed Eddie's pain. Weakness was what they targeted. They swam toward him, crying sorrowfully, *Muktablu, my love. What have you done? Muktablu, my love.*

But Eddie's pause had been momentary; he was now deaf to their false pleas. *Destroy them and rescue the king*, he commanded himself. He swung the sharp curve of the scythe's blade to meet the Trina head of each approaching Roane, shutting his eyes as the scythe moved, silently slicing their heads off their necks. Then the Sea of Abyss, still roiling with the storm, churned with decapitated Trina heads. They swirled deliberately around Eddie. He opened his eyes and saw the bloody heads of Trina that surrounded him then began to sink. They stung him with horror as his heart pounded with fear and dread. The Sea of Abyss churned, and muffled chants echoed from far above.

The weight of the sea was dense with emptiness, for all its creatures, save the Roanes, who had been slaughtered, had left. It sought to claim Eddie as it pushed him down, down. The sea pressed hard with all its strength upon Eddie's head. His weapons, the sacred spear in one hand and the scythe in the other, also were pushed by the weight of the sea to become anchors that dragged him toward the decapitated heads. He struggled against falling into the bloody horror beneath him. *Swim! Swim up before the sea swallows you!* Eddie heard his father. As he struggled against the ever-deadening weight of the sea, his arms rang thick with pain. But Eddie wouldn't yield the scythe again, and he never would allow the king's spear to fall into the hands of the enemy. He sank toward the swirling bloody heads below, which now skimmed the bottom of the sea. Eddie moved his legs to pedal up against the sea's pull, but each move only pushed him down farther.

The Sea of Abyss would claim all three: Eddie, the scythe, and the sacred warrior spear. The blue wisp within the spear glowed, and Gilgamesh within spoke to the *muktablu: Two weapons are too heavy to hold. My brother, drop the sacred spear, for it cannot keep you alive to swim to the surface as Death's scythe can.* Eddie heard these thoughts of the king of Uruk only as buzzing sounds, for his mind was upon one thing: to break the sea's hold upon him. He gritted his teeth against the pain in his arms and the pressure of the sea upon his head. He knew he needed the scythe to breathe, and the spear was now a liability. No. He would never surrender his brother's sacred warrior weapon to the enemy. He would break the Sea of Abyss's hold. Wherever the king was in the Abyss, Eddie resolved, he would somehow find him. As long as the scythe kept him alive, he could roam the bottom of the sea and search for the king. Yes. He would find them both, the king and Trina.

The spear's blue filament, which was Gilgamesh, glowed in frustration as he heard the *muktablu*'s hopeless resolve. Gilgamesh mustered his strength, for although what he was about to do would bring to reality Nana's grim prophecy of his disappearing within the Sea of Abyss for eternity, it must not be that both he and the *muktablu* should be so lost. Gilgamesh's energy rose and surged through the spear. It stung Eddie's hand with shocks, rapid and brutal in their strength. Eddie cried out in pain; still he wouldn't let go of the spear. This spear, Eddie knew from Gilgamesh, had been forged from mighty metals by the six kings of Uruk before him, each strengthened by the valor of the warriors before them. It would dishonor every warrior virtue, Eddie thought, for such a weapon to be given up to the enemy.

The shocks increased, and the blue within the spear turned as hot as a burning flame. It burned off a thin layer of skin on

Eddie's hand until the spear broke away. As soon as it did, Eddie's body, now freed of the weight of the spear, shot up toward the surface of the Sea of Abyss.

Eddie was pulled by the great current of energy that had pushed the underwater sea spirits upward. He fought back, swinging the scythe, and tried to turn downward to swim toward the falling spear. But it had disappeared, sinking deep into the sands of agony that formed the bottom layer of the Sea of Abyss. The blue filament of Gilgamesh's one-quarter-mortal soul glittered within Eddie's eyes as it sensed its three-quarters-immortal form sink with the spear. Eddie felt these notes of sorrow pound within his heart. Gilgamesh's mortal soul remained tightly wound around the crimson and violet of Eddie's soul to strengthen him against the force of the deadly waters.

A deep sadness rose in Eddie's soul, its forlorn notes ancient in form. A warrior leaving to the enemy his brother's weapon was a terrible thing. He felt profound shame that he hadn't been a capable guardian of the spear. For as the weapon was precious to the king, so too was it cherished by Eddie. It had saved him in the forest of Humawa, and he also knew it held the story of Uruk. What he didn't know was that it held the immortal part of his comrade.

As Eddie was lifted toward the sea's surface, the spear sank deeper toward the bottom. It twirled a final blue glint as it disappeared into the murky depths of the sands of the Sea of Abyss.

So it was that beneath the waters of the Abyss, the sacred spear, which unknown to Eddie held his brother warrior, Gilgamesh, the seventh king of Uruk, was now enveloped by the death sands and lost to the Sea of Abyss.

CHAPTER 6

menðicant of yasnaya polyana

L. Rufus Wigglesworth was caught in the blinding Fourth Stone's windstorm. Its unrelenting grasp whipped even his obese body as if he was of no more substance than a twig. The great roar of the storm's gusts filled his ears as he was rushed into its maelstrom. Still it was not the wind that bore into his soul but the Seven Widows' lamentations, sung upon the receding Fourth Stone of Bitterness. The widows' song had just moments before cruelly risen with the wind. It had torn from Herman Biddle his cape, which held the White Book of Magic. The cape's dark purple folds were pitted with the yellow acrid tears of the Seven Bitter Widows' curse:

Our loves' last garments, tattered and bloodied,
In our arms weak with sorrow, have we carried.
Come you now to this stone, hardened with our tears.
Now these shrouds shall fall upon you.
Lose shall you, as did we, that which is precious,
So your heart, as does ours, may beat with agony and despair.

Wigglesworth moaned in distress, his three chins shaking at the memory of how Biddle's hands had sought and grasped the cape, only to have it fall into shreds. *Oh, if only Biddle had heeded his call to hold fast, to not yield to the bitter wind!* For Wigglesworth as holder of the Cape of Ša Nagba Īmuru would have been impervious to the widows' curse and so could have captured and saved Biddle's cape. But Biddle fell to the curse, and at his desperate touch, the cape had disintegrated into pieces. Such was the malicious capriciousness of the Bitter Fourth Stone: to allure you with the promise of what is taken, and then as you touch it, destroy it in front of your eyes. Now it was too late. Biddle's cape lay in shreds, and the White Book of Magic held within it also was in tatters, its holder torn by bitterness. What would happen now that the White Book of Magic had been ripped to pieces? Would the power of the Black Book of Magic rise in proportion so that its holder, that reptilian Uri Gneezy, could capture Mattie and therefore the Spyglass? Now Wigglesworth and Biddle were swirling within the vortex of the Fourth Stone's biting wind.

The bitter wind played him well, Wigglesworth thought of Biddle. *Dragon of chaos.* The warning entered his mind. Chaos had set the dark underworld demons loose—all started by Mattie, who in guilelessness had grasped the Spyglass, opened the treacherous Path of the Virtuous, then cheated the darkness of those ancient souls trapped in Nineveh by freeing them into the Tree in the Midst of the Garden. Wigglesworth felt deep regret, for despite all of his and Biddle's schemes to keep the Spyglass buried, fate had risen strongly and placed it in the hands of a gullible child, Mattie.

When the moon no longer rises, when the stars sparkle no more. The refrain of the beautiful moon goddess Anunitu rang through Wigglesworth's mind. What would become of the Tablet of

Destiny of Light? His heart pounded against how the prophecy of the evil demon gods of old, the Asaru-alim-nuna, was taking shape: that the spirit of light would be drowned as the demons rose strong; that man's soul would fall into the pit of blackness, without free will, for destiny would now only be darkness.

Wigglesworth heard the faint beats of Biddle's broken heart sound in his ears from somewhere within the storm's clasp. The bitter winds of the Fourth Stone spun like a tornado. Soon the White Book of Magic would be lost completely as the winds tore Biddle into a state of helplessness. He thought now of the goddess of the moon, Anunitu, with her beautiful silvery translucence against the deepening opaque sky when he and Biddle were on the Third Stone. Her almond eyes, shot with bolts of silver light, had turned toward Wigglesworth, and she had spoken of how the night sky would soon swallow her and how a promise made eons ago must now be kept. *Then they will soon be upon the land of mortals, called by the Prince of Demons. Evil demon gods of old, Asaru-alim-nuna, will rise again. Asaru-alim-nuna. The forgotten mighty ones.* Then the soft silver gray Cape of Ša Nagba Īmuru had formed. Wigglesworth had been appointed as the protector of the Cape of Ša Nagba Īmuru so many lifetimes ago, should the Asaru-alim-nuna escape from the depths of the underworld, should the light of the moon goddess darken.

Wigglesworth felt the Cape of Ša Nagba Īmuru move about his shoulders with the spinning wind. Deceptively light, the cape in fact was dense as fate, heavier than the earth upon Atlas's shoulders. The wearer bore the burden of the knowledge of the fates of others but did not possess the ability to speak it. The Ša Nagba Īmuru was also a shroud, one the moon goddess had lain upon the Wayfinder, He Who Sees and Understands the Deep. This cape was woven from the moonbeams that the goddess had lain upon the Wayfinder in order to catch the last beats of heart-ache for mortals as they heeded the false prophets that divided one against the other. As mortal man had rejected this Wayfinder again and again, the cape had grown heavy with the sadness for man's folly. Too it was said that only one more Wayfinder would come to mortal man.

Wigglesworth's thoughts ran to the story of the fate of the seventh king of Uruk. Gilgamesh, breaking with grief at the loss of his brother warrior, had beseeched the moon goddess to help him find and rescue Enkidu from the underworld. The moon goddess's heart was touched so profoundly that she placed the Cape of Ša Nagba Īmuru upon Gilgamesh. The goddess had said, "Gilgamesh, this cape you may wear that you may see your mortal brother Enkidu's fate." Then the she warned, "Do not look directly into the cape itself, for it holds the sorrows that form the Mysteries, that which can only be borne by he who is the Wayfinder." When he donned the cape, the vision showed him only that Enkidu lay tortured deep in the whorls of the underworld, but it did not tell him where. Gilgamesh did not heed the goddess's warning, for he removed the cape so he could look at it and see where his brother warrior was being held. The Cape of Ša Nagba Īmuru swiftly transformed into a small translucent gray globe within which the fullness of the Deep shimmered. Upon this Gilgamesh had gazed, and so it was that the Mysteries filled and broke his vision. He was not the Wayfinder and therefore could not understand the Deep. The Mysteries were woven of knowledge as deep and wide as all the oceans, infinite as the universe, rushing into Gilgamesh, whose heart and mind were but a thimble-sized vessel. It thundered through him as jolts hard and fast as the earth does when it is torn; then it receded, Now his spirit was damaged. All Gilgamesh could do was stumble in fits and starts, prodded by courage and penned in by fear in his search for Enkidu. The moon goddess had told this story as a warning to Wigglesworth: even Gilgamesh, who was three-quarters god and only one-quarter mortal, could not withstand the knowledge of the Mysteries woven into the cape.

The moon goddess had taken back into her hands from Gilgamesh the silvery ball of beams that formed the Cape of Ša Nagba Īmuru, to hold until again she had the sorrowful task of placing it as a shroud upon the Last Wayfinder. Though it would be many eons before this Last Wayfinder would journey to the earth, the goddess whispered that she had always been present, that the knowledge of the Deep was not lost—for if mortal man and woman glanced into the night sky when the fogs formed, they would see the moon goddess surrounded by the misty blanket that was the Cape of of Ša Nagba Īmuru. Now all that had changed, for the curse of the forgotten mighty ones, the Asaru-alim-nuna, was realized: the moon goddess's light was dimming, and the Cape of Ša Nagba Īmuru also would fall into darkness. So it was that Wigglesworth had to be the holder of the cape, so that the Mysteries would not be lost to the blackness.

Wigglesworth was jolted from these thoughts as sharp pieces of the Cards of Time, torn from Biddle's cape, began to fly loose. Splintered images rose and struck him: long-dead dictators and brutal warlords, with their bloody victories; mushroom-shaped clouds rising like thunder and destroying cities; the dark times of disease, the light times of peace; men upon horses and ships; jewels upon queens; and pompous men and women living in splendor as those around them perished in squalor. And then the terrible vision of his old friend Biddle's fate appeared—his thin body writhing in lunacy, his kind blue eyes streaked with agony as he fell into a dark alley.

Was there nothing Wigglesworth could do to alter the fate of the bitter wind, the one he saw that showed only blackness? The one that showed the end of Biddle and the White Book of Magic? Was there no way to save his friend by again making Biddle's cape whole?

Wigglesworth then heard his old professor's grumbly voice—from the days when he himself was just a young academic—the gruff pronouncement: *It is easier for a camel to go through the eye of a needle than for a rich man to enter into the kingdom of God.*

Then the small piece of the Card of Time that was hurtling toward him formed its image: the peaceful green grove of a Russian estate by the name of Yasnaya Polyana. He saw the bearded old man as he sat upon a simple chair formed from branches, his contemplative eyes always somber. Bits of yellow dust within the wind gathered and viciously stung Wigglesworth's eyes. He tried to grab the piece of the Card of Time, but it moved away within the wind.

He who saw the light, Wigglesworth thought. *Yes, if I can get to him, Biddle might be saved.* He and Biddle would have to pull away from the wind's grasp so they could move into that snippet of the card that held the green canopy. But how? For the bitter wind grew stronger, and as it whipped about him, Wigglesworth grimly realized that he had to alter the fate that the bitter wind of the Fourth Stone had set for Biddle. The impossibility of it hit him stronger than the wind. *What is man that you are mindful of him?* Wigglesworth heard the words of his old friend in the Russian grove. *Man was made lower than angels but still crowned with glory.* Wigglesworth steeled himself, his old portly body shaking, as he knew what he was about to sacrifice: the free will that his mortal soul held. It must be done quickly, he realized, as the yellow dust began to clog his vision.

Wigglesworth began a chant against the growing gusts of the bitter wind:

Goddesses, you who walk with spindles!
Weavers of the Threads, with which the mortal story is told.
O three daughters of light, dusk, and night, I beseech thee!
O you Spinners of Fates, weave this, the soul I hold!

He willed his soul out and prayed: *Weave it into the cape that it may hold my soul, my free will; weave it that I might swing the cape away from the story of destruction that the bitter wind of the Fourth Stone has spun.* He then resumed his chant:

Spinners of Fates, your help I beseech for this flight.
Sharp in point! O Moirai, your needles bright,
Take this, my will, with its shining silver light.
Spin the soul, amorphous in shape.
Thread it fast upon this cape!

A thousand needles with points like daggers entered Wigglesworth's rotund body as he arched back in pain and fell into unconsciousness. The needles traveled through his body and moved as one into his third eye. Then his soul was pulled out as a silver thread upon a needle. An invisible weaver darted the threaded needle in and out of the swirling Cape of Ša Nagba Īmuru. Soon Wigglesworth's soul formed upon the gray cape as tiny bolts of silver glimmers.

A light behind his lids shimmered the soft golden color of the autumn sun. Wigglesworth opened his eyes in relief to see small snippets of an indigo sky framed by a great canopy of leafy green branches. His heart was elated to see that verdant aisle: the great column of trees whose branches reached to the sky and to clasp one another and sway in brotherly love like a great, green wand. *Yasnaya Polyana. I'm at the Russian estate.* Wigglesworth smiled as he felt the hardness of the mound under his back, and the soft breeze, fragrant with the smell of cut grass and spring flowers. He had miraculously reached the forest of the old order. He saw the outline of his great belly and laughed in delight. The old body had survived intact. He had feared that the vessel—the fat, old form that held him—would have shattered as his soul was woven into the cape. If it had, the sacrifice of his soul would have been for naught, for without a wearer, the cape would have been reduced to a small gray glow dimming in the ever-darkening universe. But that hadn't happened, and for this he praised the spinner goddesses in happiness.

"So you've managed to step upon the Path after all." Wigglesworth heard the man's voice over him.

"Help me up, Lev Nikolayevich," Wigglesworth said. "I am old and fat."

Two gnarled, old hands quivered as the voice grumbled, "And I am old and dead."

Yet the hands reached toward Wigglesworth's raised arms and pulled him up. The Cape of Ša Nagba Īmuru upon his shoulders, gray with darts of silver threads gleaming here and there like a small school of minnows, swayed. Wigglesworth grunted, his bald head bearing drops of sweat and his three chins wobbling as he sat up on the grassy knoll upon which flowers of many colors and shapes had been placed.

Then the man who had helped him up moved back to crouch low upon his haunches, facing Wigglesworth. He took in the color of the Cape of Ša Nagba Īmuru, with its gleaming bits of silver shining as small slashes upon the soft once-pure-gray cloth, but said nothing of this. In one hand he held a staff made of a crooked tree branch, which he pointed to the mound, and said, "My grave wears spring flowers, Wigglesworth, you see, though soon the breath of the winter wind will blow."

"Were you buried in peasant clothes, Lev Nikolayevich? I didn't remember that." Wigglesworth said, as he grunted again to stand up.

The old man, Lev Nikolayevich, born in this Russian estate of nobility and great wealth, wore the garments of the poor. Lev Nikolayevich looked the part of a Russian peasant with his long, loose white shirt and a worn brown leather belt around his thickened middle, over baggy black pants. His feet were bare and dirty; the bulb of his nose rose above a raggedy salt-and-pepper-beard, which he touched absently with long fingers that spoke of the aristocratic life he had sought to shed. His white face was crisscrossed with wrinkles, and great bushy eyebrows loomed over meditative eyes. These dark eyes were close set, with sadness painted on them, for they had seen the fate of Mother Russia. His hairline receded to reveal the mound of his fore-head, from which long strands of gray hair fell back. Although he played the role of the mendicant, this role fit him poorly, for Lev Nikolayevich was no beggar. Rather he was a man whose pen had been heavy with wisdom and warning that ran freely in inky scratches so that his fellow mortals would be guided to walk in the light.

"You did not remember," Lev Nikolayevich said with mild dis-approval, "because you, my friend, were not in attendance."

"True." Wigglesworth smiled at his old friend with fondness. "So in the end, you made what you would call 'the most beautiful choice.'"

They had argued about this in the past, the beautiful choice of austerity: of whether poverty was indeed the route to godliness as Lev Nikolayevich believed. Wigglesworth had countered: was not austerity merely deprivation, as ostentatious in its absence of the material as wealth was in its presence? Why would God offer the wonders of the earth, Wigglesworth had asked, if not for man's enjoyment? And what of those who argued that God was but a drug for the poor to distract them from their meager lives by keeping their eyes upon of what lay in the kingdom of Heaven? Would not this then lead to godlessness? And if mortal man did not care about his soul but only his body, what then?

Lev Nikolayevich had shaken his head firmly against such ideas, for he was convinced that wealth corrupted, that no one man should have more than another; everything was God's blessings to be shared. He had asked Wigglesworth, "Do you not believe it as it is written in Acts 34:2? Although we are of one heart and one soul: but aught of the things he possessed his own; but they had all things in common."

Wiggleworth shook his head sadly in response, "Lev Nikolayevich, I cannot say that it is true that all believers are united in heart and in mind, for my mortal eyes have not seen it as such; that they would feel that God's bounty is for all to share, that no man owns a thing more than another."

Lev Nikolayevich closed his eyes, and behind them flickered sorrow. Though he had left his mortal form, his spirit saw in anguish that though the wealth in Russia was said to be shared by those who were once peasants, greed rose in the hearts of all men, and those once poor readily killed those once rich and took as their own this bloodstained wealth. For godlessness ruled his beloved country, and there were no apostles in that land upon whose feet gold could be laid to give to those in need.

Lev Nikolayevich patted the dirt off his white shirt and said gravely, "What is the end, Wigglesworth? Has not now the fate of light churned to Chaos? The Asaru-alim-nuna have been released, the doors flung open to darkness for the rise of the Antichrist." He irritably struck the ground with his crooked staff. "By a heedless child, no less," he continued, his bushy gray brows bristling with anger, "from whom you could not keep that evil amulet. And you... you have sullied the sacred shroud of the savior with your soul."

"For a purpose, Lev. Not for nothing have I done this," Wigglesworth said firmly.

Lev Nikolayevich's expression remained unconvinced. A bright light flashed through the canopy behind Wigglesworth. Lev Nikolayevich wordlessly pointed with his staff to the figure of Herman Biddle tumbling down. Wigglesworth turned to see his old friend fall upon his back on the grassy mound. His body was writhing as he babbled nonsensical words, while his thin translucent fingers tightly gripped the purple shreds of his cape. Wigglesworth grew solemn at the sight of Biddle riddled with lunacy. In his happiness at having found Lev Nikolayevich, he momentarily had forgotten about Biddle. Even though they had escaped from the storm, the bitter curse of the Seven Widows had taken effect anyway. The heartbreak of losing his cape and the White Book of Magic had left Biddle senseless.

Lev Nikolayevich said sharply, "So now it is that the boy Dmitri, who avoided his destiny only to have it bite him in the neck, falls from the sky as an old man uttering madness."

Wigglesworth replied, "Biddle has fallen to the curse of the Seven Bitter Widows. See the shreds of bright purple cloth in his hands? Those are his cape, and within them the White Book of Magic lies in tatters." Here Wigglesworth paused and said, rather than asked, his request. "The White Book of Magic must not be lost. You, Lev Nikolayevich, who walks in the light, must restore Biddle before he is fully given up to insanity."

"Cold...cold," Biddle cried. His eyes suddenly fluttered open then shut; his lips were turning blue.

Lev Nikolayevich moved and stood over the prone figure. His shaggy brows were knitted together in concern. "He lies in two worlds."

Biddle sat up suddenly, his hands opened to release the purple shreds of the cape. As they fluttered up from his open fingers, he desperately clawed the air as if to hold on to an invisible ledge.

The shreds of the cape spun, and out flew more Cards of Time. The images were blurred and then became frenzied, stirring wind as they flew and hit Lev Nikolayevich. They slapped his face and body and tore at his long beard. They flew in a torrent of splintered images: here now was Tsar Nicholas riding the night train; then his head rolling as the sharp blade of a guillotine cut it; now the cold frozen Siberian ground littered with the bodies of Russian soldiers; now a mushroom-shaped cloud forming over a land as the bodies below it melted; now a pockmarked one who rose to the cheers of millions. Lev Nikolayevich pushed the horror away; he deftly stabbed his gnarled wooden staff in the air against the torrent of the Cards of Time and speared shreds of the purple cape.

The wind ceased as soon as the cape was captured. The Cards of Time disappeared. Wigglesworth blanched at the sight of Biddle's face and figure, which were fast becoming ghostly outlines. He was beginning to disappear.

"Quickly! Quickly!" Wigglesworth cried, his three chins shaking desperately. "Lev Nikolayevich! Bring him back with your mendicant's wand!"

Biddle was now a ghostly figure, his back arched as he let out a bloodcurdling scream at some unseen enemy, for his eyes were filled with an awful vision: the Crone's filthy, black-nailed, clawed hands holding the Spyglass tightly; her grizzled head thrown back; her ugly mouth open with shouts of glee and triumph.

Lev Nikolayevich said softly, "My friend, it is too late."

Wigglesworth jumped to grab Biddle. It was indeed too late, for Herman Biddle disappeared like a mist within his hands.

𒀯𒌋𒁹𒀯𒁹

It was Halloween at the midnight hour. Certainly the screams of anguish unleashed within the Dorothea Dix Insane Asylum were fitting.

"Hold him tight!" the doctor who was directing the procedure shouted. He wore the requiste white coat, that emblem of medical authority, and held clipboard in one hand and in the other a small pen, readying to record the agonies to come. His face was masked by a beard, though his excitement glittered in his eyes behind his thick glasses.

Two muscular male attendants, splattered with water, plunged the babbling old man again into the ice-cold water of the deep tub. The old man screamed again—a scream that tore against the walls of the bleak rectangular room, lit by one large hanging bulb. The floors were once white tile, but the horrors that the room had borne witness to had stained it yellow. In this room of the institution, the hydrotherapy center, as it was called, were four deep tubs lined horizontally, one next to the other. A large window framed the black sky. The tree branches outside scratched the window as if screaming in empathy with the writhing old man within.

The doctor's pen momentarily froze over his clipboard while he was timing the patient's submersion. He felt a sudden chill knife through him when the old man screamed in a voice that seemed from the beyond. The doctor looked at the attendants to see their reaction. But the other men seemed not to have noticed; their heads were bent as they pushed the old man down. Or perhaps if they did hear it, they were hiding it well, he thought.

A cold wind carrying a premonition of an amorphous evil whispered in his ear. The doctor shook his head to clear it. After all, this was the modern time of 1936, and he was an experienced doctor overseeing the administration of a treatment. *October 31, 1936.* The date echoed in his mind. *When the bell rings at midnight…*The old childhood tales of those who had died rising at the midnight hour on Halloween flew into his head. *Stuff and nonsense!* the doctor sternly told himself. He again pushed down the uneasy feeling that rose within him. It was most certainly a time beyond superstitions, a time in which insanity was a medical disorder, not a sign of possession by demons. And this, after all, was the Dorothea Dix Insane Asylum, New York City's oldest and most prestigious institution for the treatment of the insane. Cold-water therapy was thought to be an effective way to shock the lunacy out of the insane through sudden hypothermia and heart attack. The hypothesis was that there was a narrow window of time for the treatment to be effective—just enough to cause vasoconstriction to make the heart pump faster and faster until cardiac arrest. Then brain would be shocked by the lack of oxygenated blood to reset itself. It worked rarely; most times the heart gave way and the person died.

Timing was everything. If the hypothermia could be titrated into precision, its efficacy would be improved, and there would be fewer negative outcomes, such as death. The doctor had a hunch that a new sequence might work: plunge and cause a heart attack, revive, plunge again for another cardiac arrest, revive and then plunge again, with each time of "death" slightly increased for a specific ratio of arrest to revival. It had worked reasonably well on the cats in which he had first surgically induced seizures to mimic mental illness. Now, after many months of trial and error, he was approaching a nearly zero feline mortality rate. But his colleagues had opposed his trying out the sequence on humans; too many deaths at the hospital already had occurred and were bringing negative attention to the asylum. These mortalities were from insulin shock treatment, he protested, and not the cold-water therapy sequence he was proposing. To no avail had he had argued this to colleagues. They were cowards, he thought. In these times, money was scarce, with much of it coming from the do-gooders of the Dorothea Dix Foundation, those matriarchs of old money who urged for humane treatment of the insane. His colleagues feared that the doctor's sequence was unproven and therefore too risky, too likely to bring about the wrath of their patrons, and it was thereby rejected.

The old man they were now treating had been found prone just outside the hospital doors minutes before, writhing and babbling incoherently. He was yet another casualty of the Depression, the doctor thought, one of the many who wandered about, too old to ride the rails, too young to die quickly. This one wore tattered trousers tucked into worn boots spattered with yellow dirt, the same stains that were also upon his torn brown woolen jacket. His white whiskers, which ran into his sideburns, and long thinning hair bore the same yellow substance—who knew what it was? The poor slept in alleys and carried the stains and stench of their death and decay. Perhaps he had money once, the doctor thought. His clothing looked old but as if it had once been of quality. No matter now, for now he was nobody, with no wallet, no name. "Perfect!" the doctor had declared.

Strangely the attendants couldn't remove the old man's clothing. It stuck to him as if it were a skin. They had plunged him into the tub anyway; the doctor said the water was so cold that it didn't matter that the man was clothed. This was even better, the doctor thought, for if the experiment failed, the body could be more quickly disposed of without all the bother of reclothing it. He would have the attendants take the corpse down to the morgue in the basement for appearances' sake, but later he would personally remove it and throw it into one of the numerous alleyways where death was a common occurrence. Perhaps he wouldn't even have to go through the sham of transferring the body to the morgue. His attendants were unlikely to raise protests about the disposal of this beggar anyway, the doctor knew. They were glad for a job. Yes, this was his lucky day indeed! No one would be the wiser: the old man was just another nameless, faceless, forgotten bum—just another cold-weather casualty. But were he to succeed! Ah, glory days! Then the doctor could tell his colleagues that he had performed, out of compassion, the sequence upon the poor old man teetering on death's edge from madness just as a last-gap measure, and—behold—look at him now: recovered from lunacy! Then he would be allowed to perfect the sequence upon on others, hailed a genius, and move out of the hellhole of the Dorothea Dix Insane Asylum and into a respectable hospital with well-heeled patients.

And the dead rise as the clock strikes midnight to wreak their revenge.

The doctor was jolted out of his thoughts as the clock began to strike midnight. His face twisted in fear at the sight that rose behind the dark glass of the window. Ghostly palms and outlines of faces straining out from a fog were upon it. The window facing the black night shattered. The doctor heard the bloodcurdling scream first then realized it was his own voice. Through the broken window, a fog poured in first. Then from the fog moved several pairs of searching hands, which grasped his neck and flung him up and around. The doctor's body was swung high up to the ceiling, and he felt his legs hit the hanging light bulb. Below him the attendants were scrambling to run to the door, but they too were lost causes, like him. The Muhra, with their quick reflexes, some of whom once had been dancers, spun out and took the hefty bodies of the attendants as their own, throwing the attendants' spirits into the fog, which now served as a receptacle for newly collected souls. But there were plenty of bodies to be had, and those who could move with lightning speed secured the strongest vessels.

The Muhra moved through the hospital like a tornado. The cries of those whose bodies were being taken ricocheted within the walls of the Dorothea Dix Insane Asylum. No hydrotherapy sequence would cure these screams, for they were now the screams of the dead. The doctor heard the voices of his captors as he struggled to hold on to his spirit. *Muhra! Muhra!* they cried. *We are Muhra!* Then the hands that grabbed him seemed to be fighting one another as they possessed his body. He felt his spirit being pushed out, and then a force grabbed it until he was within and part of the faceless, shapeless Muhra fog. He was hit with the realization—shocked at first, stunned next—that he had no body, no form, just an amorphous presence and a bitter longing to be back in his body. He screamed again, but this time there was no sound, for now his spirit was thrown into the miasma of the fog, and he had now become one of the newly formless. The new Muhra.

The Muhra's cries filled the wards of the Dorothea Dix Insane Asylum as the formless spirits savagely moved through the hospital, grabbing bodies, pulling the souls out of the bodies and throwing them into the ever-growing fog of new Muhra, and lastly, taking the bodies as their own. Those who lived within the Dorothea Dix Insane Asylum were easy prey: the evil ones, those who had tortured the vulnerable, were picked as effortlessly as low-hanging fruit. And the will of the insane was weak and therefore readily overpowered by the Muhra. Now the fog bulged with the spirits of the newly formless, as those who had long been held by the Muhra fog found form in the bodies they had taken over. The spirits of the recently dead within the Muhra fog moved in restless confusion, hitting one another in swarms. The old Muhra moved out and grabbed bodies, and new Muhra—the spirits that were pulled and thrown into the receptacle of the fog—grew in number. The new Muhra saw with astonishment how the old Muhra filled their bodies like clothes that were too small or too large, but it didn't matter. These Muhra cared not that their bodies were ill fitting; they finally were in a form. The Muhra with forms ran out of the hospital ward to wreak havoc upon the city. The fog of the new Muhra then moved swiftly to follow the old Muhra to reclaim their bodies.

In the cold tub, the old man lay still, for Herman Biddle had been bypassed by the Muhra, as his body lay stiff and he was presumed dead. The light bulb that hung above swung in the now-silent Dorothea Dix Insane Asylum, casting its melancholy shadows upon Biddle's face, which was swiftly turning the blue of his kind eyes.

𒀸𒌋𒁹𒀸𒐊

Wigglesworth trembled at the terrible vision of Biddle that appeared before his eyes: his old friend lying stiff and dead as evil rose all around him. L. Rufus Wigglesworth had altered the Cape of the Mysteries for nothing, for Biddle's fate hadn't been averted. Wigglesworth held up his pudgy hands in front of his eyes. Regardless, more images sprung to his consciousness. He moaned. There rose now Uri Gneezy, a giant serpent with great black wings, whose poisonous tongue mercilessly lashed Herman Biddle.

He turned toward Lev Nikolayevich, his voice hoarse with pain, "All is lost, after all, to the cruel Fourth Stone of Bitterness."

Lev Nikolayevich shook his head. "Wigglesworth, my friend, how quickly you surrender. Where is your faith?"

Wigglesworth did not respond, for he was blind and deaf to everything but Herman Biddle's awful fate: his body broken, his eyes hollow as he was torn and twisted and thrown into the Corkscrew of Terror.

Lev Nikolayevich nonetheless raised the gnarled mendicant's staff into the air. Upon it hung the purple shreds of Herman Biddle's cape like moss upon the branches of old oaks. He thrust the staff toward the canopy of leaves.

Then Lev Nikolayevich closed his eyes tightly until all that Wigglesworth could see were his bushy brows and the ferocious expression of determination with which he spoke:

O Lord of my salvation!
Mortal will draws near to the grave,
As this wretched soul, adrift in fright,

Is buried in the enemy's pit without sight.
For when he falls into shadows deep and dark,
Upon all men's souls will the Devil make his mark.
Allow mortal man this hope's last spark.
I beseech you, O Lord! You who hold all might,
Restore these shreds into the Cape of Light.

The sky turned a steely gray. The cold winter wind rose in mighty gusts. It snapped the vision of Biddle's demise away from Wigglesworth's eyes. He looked up as the canopy of leaves above them changed color from green to oranges, reds, and yellow. Then there was a great rustling sound, and a storm of brown leaves rained upon the two old men. Between the branches large clouds formed in the winter sky, which was quickly darkening into dusk. Beams of light shone from the clouds through the bare brown branches of the columns of trees. The colors were those of winter dreams: lavender and vermillion pink of the setting sun; these beams of light danced like small fairies around Lev Nikolayevich's gnarled mendicant staff. Then winter's icy breath blew again so that wisps of purple and dark pink were lifted and swirled into the shreds upon the staff. The wind lifted the yellow pits from the purple cloth, weaving, weaving, weaving. Then Biddle's cape fluttered above the old men. It appeared as a web of light—a patchwork of purple and the golden-hued pink, purple, and red of the setting winter sun. The cape slowly fell. Lev Nikolayevich thrust his mendicant's staff up to catch Biddle's cape. The enormous canopy, the green wands of the branches of the old trees, appeared again.

Lev Nikolayevich gingerly lifted Biddle's cape off the mendicant's staff with his old fingers. It was no longer the thick cloth it had once been, made as it was from a patchwork of light and gossamer thin in substance. One had to be careful with this cape; it was that delicate.

Wigglesworth felt a light lift of hope in his heart when the winds blew and the cape was rewoven, but then the flimsiness made him pause. "This cape...is changed. I wonder how the White Book of Magic can lie within its folds. And if it doesn't, what good is it now?"

Lev Nikolayevich knitted his bushy eyebrows. He knew that doubt filled Wigglesworth because his mortal soul was an open wound, with every vision like salt falling upon it. This was what came when one had the arrogance to attempt to alter fate by sullying the sacred shroud of the Cape of Ša Nagba Īmuru with mortal will.

Lev Nikolayevich spoke, though his voice took on the tone of a reprimand. "By grace you have been saved through faith. Discipline your heart away from despair, for that is the doorway for bitterness to take hold. Come, Wigglesworth, let us journey to this place of the Bitter Fourth Wind where Biddle lies."

Wigglesworth shook his head, for though he saw Biddle's fate, he could not speak it.

Lev Nikolayevich said, "Yes, yes. I know: you cannot speak of his destiny, but his cape will take us where he now lies if you will say the chant."

Wigglesworth shut his eyes tightly and raised both arms through a blanket of despair, born of the visions he had seen of his friend Herman Biddle.

Elish nab la shaman u enuma
Ammantum shaplish la suma zakrat

Wigglesworth shuddered, for the ancient words were scrambled. Then in desperation he called the three sacred names of the Mother:

O Tiamet, O Tiamut, O Great Mother Tiamat!

No silvery fire appeared; no wind shook the mound upon which they stood; nor did the face of Tiamat, with seven moons shining about her head, appear. Instead there was only the quiet silence of the forest grove and the gray winter sky above the again bare branches of the winter trees.

Wigglesworth knew that the Great Mother's powers had ebbed, but why this silence?

O Great Mother Tiamat! He felt a small rustle of hope as he heard the softest of whispers.

Then he heard her voice, faint but discernible: *Blessed is he who walks in the light, whose prophets say the Last Wayfinder will rise again. His words have power.*

Wigglesworth opened his eyes. Lev Nikolayevich's bushy eyebrows were raised in question.

Wigglesworth said softly. "You must help me," as he began the ancient chant:

When Heaven was not yet named,
And the earth beneath did not yet bear a name.

Lev Nikolayevich replied:

The earth was without form, and void,
And darkness was upon the face of the deep.

The wind rose and rustled the brown leaves at their feet, growing stronger until all the leaves were lifted into the air and moving like dervishes, forming a tornado around the two figures on the mound.

Wigglesworth then called out the ancient words that formed on his lips:

Enuma elish la nab u shaman
Shaplish ammantum suma la zakrat

Lev Nikolayevich stamped the gnarled mendicant's stick upon which the rewoven cape hung. He struck the staff again seven times upon the mound that had held his body.

And the spirit of God moved upon the face of the waters
And God said, "Let there be light," and there was light.

The green grove of the forest became a mist as it gave way to a ghastly, blinding green light.

When the light lifted, the two old men found themselves standing on the shattered glass of the window that framed the hydrotherapy room of the Dorothea Dix Insane Asylum. The last wisps of the Muhra fog had moved out of the shattered window, and the asylum was now as silent as a morgue. Herman Biddle remained submerged in the tub. The lone bulb over the deep tub that held him swung over his deathly blue face as if restless to light the ghastly deeds that it once had illuminated.

Quickly Lev Nikolayevich lifted Biddle's cape. It moved in light, spreading its gossamer form like the clouds of the soft pink-and-purple sunset from which it had been formed. The cape hovered protectively over Biddle's body as it drew him up out of the cold water. At the touch of the edges of the cape upon his body, the water instantly evaporated. Biddle now floated horizontally above the tub, the cape blanketing his body. As the cape nourished his soul to life, the blue in his face dimmed. Biddle opened his eyes and stared wordlessly at the lone light bulb that swung above his face.

Lev Nikolayevich moved toward Biddle's head. He raised the mendicant's staff and hit the bulb. The light from the bulb above began to grow. It shone first a yellow then gave way to the blinding brightness of a full moon.

Wigglesworth shouted, "Spell of light! Spell bright! Move us from this cursed plight!"

𒀭𒂍𒀭𒉿

A persistent rap brought Wigglesworth into consciousness. It was Lev Nikolayevich striking his mendicant's staff on the wooden floor. Wigglesworth opened his eyes. He was seated in his chair behind the mound of clutter on his desk in his office at Columbia University, lit by his small desk lamps and a floor lamp in the corner. The silence of the empty university building was as dark as the night and only served to render an echoing eeriness to the sound of the mendicant's staff. Lev Nikolayevich stood over Herman Biddle, who lay on his back on the floor, the cape under him, his eyes open, his mouth moving soundlessly.

"He's still wordless," Lev Nikolayevich said. "The cape has revived him, yet it has not fully restored him."

Wigglesworth heaved his body away from the desk and joined Lev Nikolayevich. "Catatonia from the shock," he said. "He will come to his senses as he recognizes these familiar surroundings."

In a quick movement, Biddle lurched up to his feet to face Lev Nikolayevich and Wigglesworth. Rather than in recognition, his blue eyes flashed in confusion and paranoia. His hands were in front of him, as if to thwart off assailants. He stood in his old expedition clothing, spattered with yellow dust, his feet set apart, and arms ups in a fighting stance.

"Herman..." Wigglesworth said softly. "You are safe."

The sound of Wigglesworth's voice seemed to fall as a threat rather than assurance upon Biddle's ears. Biddle moved as if he had been hit, his head thrown back, the white of his hair moving in an unseen wind, his mouth open in a soundless scream. He lunged toward Wigglesworth, his face filled with anger and suspicion. He then swung his cape—that gossamer cloth that glimmered pink, purple, and golden—forward, as if to ward off Lev Nikolayevich and Wigglesworth. Then he vanished.

L. Rufus Wigglesworth was now the one in shock. Quickly he touched the Cape of Ša Nagba Īmuru to locate Biddle. Darkness rose in front of him. The sharp teeth of fear bit him. But he did not know where his friend was—only that he had been swallowed by the night.

"He moves in madness," Lev Nikolayevich said. "A madman who holds the Cape of Light and the White Book of Magic."

Wigglesworth moved toward one wall of bookshelves laden with dusty tomes, the Cape of Ša Nagba Īmuru fluttering behind him. His hands moved rapidly over the volumes.

"The goddess Ninazu," he said, "gave me the Small Book of Spells, which disappeared in the chaos ensuing from the Fourth Wind of Doom. But fearing that a foe might one day grasp it, I took the precaution of hiding within this book the Last Spell, the most potent spell of all. With it we will find him." He removed a large volume with a hollowed-out middle where he had secreted the Last Spell of the Small Book of Spells.

"It is gone!" he exclaimed, panicked.

CHAPTER 7

aB-Gal-lu: captain of the ship of outlaws

Eddie's head broke the turbulent surface of the Sea of Abyss. Beneath, the energy of the waters was unleashed as the seafloor erupted. On the surface, it created a titanic wave upon which he was catapulted. He held tightly to the scythe as he rode its crest then tumbled within the curl of the wave. The force of the wave then thrust Eddie out like a cork into the sky. *Intel. Get the intel,* he instructed himself as he moved into an airborne position. Eddie quickly scanned his environs, catching a glimpse of a dark castle upon the giant island that was jutting from the sea. Terrible creatures fell upon this island and rose from the sea to scramble upon its shores.

He heard their cries: *The Prince of Demons rises!* The evil vibrations of the chant reverberated through Eddie's body. In his eyes the blue wisp that was the one-quarter-mortal soul of Gilgamesh, entwined around the purple and crimson threads of Eddie's soul, quivered with warning.

Eddie felt it as sharp stabs of anxiety; he pushed it down. *Fear leads to doubt. Doubt leads to indecision. Indecision leads to failure.* His mind quickly turned over the possibilities. The wave he rode would soon mercilessly fling him against the shores of the island. Then, in short order, he would be captured by the demons upon the shore, which numbered in the tens of thousands, from what he could see. These thoughts flashed through his mind in milliseconds. He swung the scythe into the air to keep him from falling back into the wave. He reconned the fury of the sea beneath him; the scythe would keep him aloft with its repelling death energy, but not for long, he knew.

𒐚𒌋𒌐𒐚𒀀

As they fell toward the seafloor, the Roanes' bloody Trina heads transformed into their original seal forms, with broken walrus fangs protruding out of their gaping mouths and their long orange locks waving over their hideous faces. When they hit the sea's bottom, the sandy kernels stung their bulging eyes. They shrieked curses against the *muktablu*, upon whom they swore to exact a torturous revenge. Their bodies, with disembodied torsos that were half human and half seal, fell with their long arms reaching to grasp their decapitated heads. Then the sea's bottom exploded. A long wooden pole stabbed through the sand, the force lifting the separated heads and bodies of the Roanes upward. The bloody heads slammed against furling, torn black sails. The shape of the thing that rose from the sands into the water became clear: it was an ancient vessel, that of the *Condemned Ship of the Outlaws of Hell*, which was an assembly of pieces of wrecked ancient warships now set free as the Sea of Abyss emptied itself of its creatures.

On each side and beneath the ship was the bottom deck, which held the empty spots for rowers; on the top deck were catapults to fend off invaders. The vessel rose from the sands where it had been buried eons ago. With it were flung its ancient seafarers, with blackened souls in life, who had roamed the waters of the living to pillage and cheat. These were the sea raiders of the ancient times of Sumer, of Babylon, of Mesopotamia, of where the Tigris and Euphrates ran rivers of life, and of those peoples who had fiercely guarded their treasures of precious metals, myrrh, and exotic woods as they traveled the Red Sea. All were those whose evil deeds upon the waters against their fellow mortal man gave them a place in Kurnigi, only to be later sunk into the Abyss and deeper still into its seabed. Then the sands of the sea gave another heave, and great chests of treasures were flung up, spilling their contents: diamonds, rubies, pearls, large urns, chains of gold, coins engraved with the heads of long-ago kings, all rising like glittering bubbles. The *Condemned Ship of the Outlaws of Hell* rapidly rose from the depths of the water to the surface. Its sails broke the angry waves that were the skin of the Sea of Abyss.

Gigantic waves slashed the sea. In the brooding, gray sky of the Abyss, crimson clouds hung low. The Roanes' decapitated heads and dismembered bodies rode the crests of the colossal waves. The waves surged in a fury toward the island, upon which a great castle for the Prince of Demons had formed. They crashed against the black obsidian shores of the island, flinging the Roanes splintered bodies against it. The Roanes felt their fellow sea demons as they were trampled by the creatures' feet and hands, and they too heard the call: *The Prince of Demons rises!*

Eddie saw it. A behemoth ship had risen from the waters beneath him; it tossed and tilted against the winds that howled about it, its black sails of doom battered by the wind. It looked like it was empty, but appearances could be deceiving. Eddie's mind turned over the situation. Should he jump on to the ship, which seemed empty, or risk being captured by the enemy on the island? Holding the scythe below him, Eddie tightened his airborne position and jumped, breaking away from the wave.

He uncurled himself from the airborne position to land feet-first in a crouching stance on the wide wooden planks that made up the ship's deck. He stood up and swung the scythe in a swift circle as a warning to any enemies that might be aboard. Eddie quickly scanned around him for a hidden enemy. The deck of the ship appeared to be empty, with no one manning it. The wind lashed his face. The waves of the Sea of Abyss rocked the ship back and forth, threatening to swallow it. Eddie steadied himself with the scythe; the planks were slippery and wet. The ship swung violently to the side, blurring his vision as the sea's poisonous spray hit him, stinging his eyes. The force flung him to the hull's bow. He had to find a way to stabilize the ship before it capsized. Then the ship tilted again and threw Eddie back upon the wooden planks of the deck. As he righted himself, he saw through his blurred vision why the ship had tilted: demon sailors, one upon another, were scrambling up from the sea onto the ship.

These creatures were varied in aspect and looked to be of an ancient world. Some bodies bore the slashes of whips and were clad only in rags, upon which were emblazoned the insignias of those they had captured. Still others had grizzled beards that hung below their chests. Their faces were angular, and they wore turbans and bandannas that were slashed and bloodied, marking them as defiant to the rulers of land. Their eyes were hollow and streaked with wrath, for they had ridden the ancient rivers as thieves. They were of kingdoms long gone: of those whose veins held the waters of the Nile and had traveled the Red Seas. They hailed from from the kingdoms of the Assyrians, the Babylonians, the Akkadians, and the most ancient of all, the Sumerians. They rose from the dynasties of old—riders into the Lower Waters and the land of the dead. Some were male, while others came from the reign of the long-forgotten female rulers of the sea. Some faces were velvet in blackness, others the color of walnuts, still others the pale brown of milky coffee; still others were as white as the rising moon. Then rose those more ancient still, whose faces were brown and smooth, who wore small, pointed, braided beards. These dark souls had traversed the waters before they were known as the Euphrates and Tigris, thousands of years earlier, and had made a pact for bounty with the forgotten mighty demon gods of old, the *Asuru-alim-nuna*. Now these demon sea raiders of old, creatures who for eons had not felt the brush of air against their skin, who had lain buried under the sands of the Abyss for eons, stood up. Miraculously they were no longer encased in their sandy coffins, but free. They howled in delight at their newfound liberty as they scrambled for the tilting, rocking the ship. Their *Condemned Ship of the Outlaws of Hell.*

Eddie crouched low, now hidden beneath the curving demon ship's bow, clasping the scythe close. It vibrated in response to the energy of the evil spirits of old. The sea's poisonous spray still smarted in his eyes, but his vision had cleared. With alarm, he focused on the demon seafarers. Though Eddie didn't know their exact numbers, it was one hundred fifty-two. It was a number that would come to sear itself in his mind, a number that would seem impossibly large and impossibly small at once. Still more, fate would seal their journeys together in a way that for Eddie, who was now crouching low and scanning the scrambling demon sailors with suspicion, would seem impossible. But now Eddie was only aware of how the ship was straining under their weight. If they were spirits, how could they have weight? But everything in this sea moved in a manner that contrasted what Eddie thought defined reality.

He peered out, careful to keep himself hidden from view. He needed good reconnaissance before he made any moves. One of the demons looked like he could be the commander. That one's head was covered in a large red turban that ballooned upward in a pear shape. He was shouting what sounded like orders. *This guy doesn't have much authority*, he thought, as sailors who looked low in rank—who wore only loincloths and whose upper torsos revealed slash marks—were snarling their resentment, their faces defiant. But then several others jumped up when the ship tilted downward. They moved into position, grabbing the handles of a dozen paddles that poked through the sides of the vessel. Then two of them scrambled to steady the ship against the outraged waters, moving a T-shaped wooden bar that twisted the tattered black sails against the winds. *Black sails*, Eddie thought. *Is this a ship of death?* Then suddenly some of the demon sailors grabbed a large net from the side of the vessel and threw it into the choppy sea. The rowers called out a chant, their rhythm moving them in unison as they rowed.

Their songs vibrated through Eddie, although he couldn't make out the words, for the sea outlaws sang their story in their old tongues as they rowed against the rising winds that tore the sails of the ship.

Creatures once of the living mesh,
Seafaring thieves, born of woman, wearers of flesh,

Ferried into the Boat of the West,
Our last breaths taken, dead but not at rest.
Our souls with evil stank;
Dropped into the dark underworld, we sank,
Landlocked in the underground of the dead,
Beneath the watchful night eyes of the Master of Dread.

Longed did we for a ship of glory to sail against the ocean's tide.
Longed did we for such a chariot to ride,
To grab treasures of rubies, pearls, and gold.
But for our greed, punishment was foretold.
To the Counselor's cunning lure, our seafaring minds were bent.
To his plan to overthrow the Dark Master, we gave our assent.
For treachery against Marduk, so said the Counselor, our reward would
be a ship to sail,
And the plan, this treacherous one claimed, would not fail
And too our hands would bounty hold,
For betrayal in exchange for mounds of gold.

Instead the Dark Master plunged us within this Sea of Abyss's fold
Nowhere were the promised treasures we were sold.
Instead, imprisoned upon the sea,
Demon sailors were we.

This ship of outlaws was tossed against the gale,
Till the sea rose to swallow us, leaving no trail.
Condemned, drowned, and coffined in the sand.
Thus for our betrayal, were we banned.
Remained did we, buried with our vessel,
Until chaos shook the sand with thunder
To mark the Sea of Abyss's surrender.

From his vantage point, Eddie saw that the surface of the sea was now littered with bobbing treasures: gold pieces swimming like fish between glittering rubies, ropes of pearls, golden goblets studded with diamonds, swords, sabers, and dirks of old. The demon sailors shouted in glee as they moved in unison toward the bounty. They heaved their net up onto the ship. It was heavy with the treasures that clanked onto the wooden planks of the deck. The snarling seafarers, those pirates of the ancient world—and even their slaves, who had pitched the net aboard—all threw themselves forward to grab the treasure. Even those who were rowing left their posts to catch what their arms could hold. Slaves and the nobility of old—all were petty thieves of the sea. Moreover, it didn't matter, for all were equally condemned, and all had a right to these treasures, which they had sought for so long. They snatched as much as they could carry, these treasures fallen to the sea over the eons. Their shouts of greed mixed with the howling wind that billowed the ship's dirty sails against the crimson sky, where heavy dark clouds hung low and ominous.

Then one among the demon sailors—the one who had issued the order, he whose face wore command, his eyes black and hair like a lion's mane, falling in waves upon his back—rose up, piercing the air with his roar. The others growled at him in protest, their mouths open to reveal rotting, blackened teeth. They raised their fists toward him, away from something that was in the net. He brandished a gleaming silver sword mounted with coral and slashed the air about him. His face was smooth and the color and shape of a peeled almond. He wore robes of red with ballooning black sleeves, and upon his head, he wore a peaked red headdress with a black band. Everything about him, from his manner to his garb, signified his superior status. The object that had caught the sailors' attention lay on top of the other treasures, which paled by comparison. Loud, angry, threatening shouts rose in waves against the one with the headdress.

Eddie twisted his head up to see what was causing the ruckus. Then he saw it. His eyes widened. It was Gilgamesh's warrior spear. Its long body, wrought with its story of ancient Uruk in lines and ridges, glimmered golden with a thin translucent blue line wrapping around it; the flame of green at its point was shining. His heart beat rapidly. *The king's spear. Stay still. Listen. See. Process*, Eddie commanded himself as he crouched low.

A drumbeat rose among those who surrounded the pile of booty, on top of which lay the spear. From his hidden spot, Eddie heard the chants, fearsome and staccato in sound, but the meaning of the words remained lost to him. The rowers who had abandoned their posts to grab the booty now circled the mountain of treasure, holding their oars vertically and pounding them to the beat of the drums. The ship pitched violently against the waves. Even those who had commanded the T-bar that controlled the tattered sails had left their posts to grab the treasure. The arms of all the thieves of the ancient seas were heavy with gold and jewels, which they clutched to their chests. They gazed as one upon the spear. Then they raised their voices high and told the tale, their song blending into the wailing winds.

> *This mighty weapon of the gods of old*
> *has appeared as foretold.*
> *Its splendor shines brighter than gold.*

The Once-Noble One in the red headdress, in whose veins the blood of nobility once had run, shouted. His eyes glinted with greed and evil. He slashed his coral-handled sword at the others to move away as he arrogantly climbed the pile of treasures to reach the spear. The demon sailors, bristling with resentment, jumped back to allow the Once-Noble One through.

The ancient demon seafarers cried out to the Once-Noble One:

Beware, demon brother,
Though you once sailed with Hannu in the Red Seas,
Then ruled high and mighty in your plundering and pillaging sprees,
Now in the Death Waters of the Abyss, you will fail,
For here you are no more than the lion's tail.
See how it is that the sea rises and splits its skin.
See how it is that Chaos rules from within.

The Once-Noble One shook his red headdress, his robes of red and black flowing as he ignored their admonitions. He bent to lift the spear, his dark eyes flashing in triumph. His fingers, fat with greed, encircled the warrior spear and moved to raise it in victory. Suddenly the spear elongated then twisted and squeezed the Once-Noble One's body like a python would its prey. His red headdress flew off to reveal a balding peaked head, upon which his wisps of hair had been lit afire by the green flame of the spear. The spear then quickly twisted off and flung the Once-Noble One onto the deck. He rose, his face stinging with shame and anger, as the others around him laughed derisively.

Eddie craned his neck. The intel was this: the enemy combatant with the red-and-black get-up had been roped and thrown down by the king's spear. He heard the enemy's laughter at the demon's failure. The spear straightened and fell back onto the pile of booty.

So this one with all his noble veneer was not the One. The demon thieves of the ancient seas ridiculed the Once-Noble One:

Now in the Death Waters of the Abyss, you fail!
For here you are no more than the lion's tail!

But if this one could try, the other outlaw seafarers thought, why not them? The ancient laws of the living did not matter: slave, master, rich, and poor were all one. The outlaw seafarers circled close upon the warrior spear, their fingers voracious with the need to conquer, to rule over the others. One after another tried to grasp the spear: slaves and masters. But as each came close, the spear struck them back again and again. The ship rocked against the sea's turbulent waters and tilted in the rising, violent wind. The demon sailors were hurled down the mountain of treasures, their fingers scratching at the glittering, wet jewels as they fell to its bottom.

The scythe vibrated in Eddie's hands. He felt the filament in his eyes, the one-quarter mortal soul of Gilgamesh's keeping him still. *Stay where you are. Do not move against these demons.* These whispers of caution sounded in his mind. Eddie, however, was deaf to these words. He shot up. He was going to act. This was the sacred spear of the seventh king of Uruk. It could not fall into enemy hands. One to at least a hundred—those were the odds, he guessed. But he wasn't going to hide like a rat while the enemy took his warrior brother's weapon. *Move and conquer or be destroyed*, he thought.

Eddie struck the scythe against the wind. His body was lithe and muscled, that of a young warrior in his prime. He shot up from the hull with quickness and ease. So it was that Eddie would find his warrior destiny, though he didn't know this as he jumped with the vigor of a young man's youth and recklessness high into the air, the scythe lifting him. He dropped straight into the center of the pile of booty, standing strong in his combat boots. He brandished the scythe in broad swaths around him.

He shouted the primeval cry of warning: "Aaaee! Aaaeee!"

The warrior spear now lay at Eddie's boots. The outlaw seafarers below him jumped back, startled. They snarled in surprise. The smell of the blood of a living mortal filled their nostrils. A living *muktablu* brandishing Death's scythe! Tall, with yellow hair, his clothes not of the ancient world, and eyes that glittered with a filament of blue then purple. The demons' greedy eyes saw the scythe. A weapon to hold, if not the spear, it would also give them power. This *muktablu* was just one, and they were many. They scrambled up the mountain of booty, their gnarled fingers bent to reach him, moving in unison toward Eddie, who stood at the top.

"Stand back!" he shouted, swinging Death's scythe in broad swaths at the ancient sea thieves.

The sea demons' fingers clawed at the treasures to reach and surround him, but the spear at the *muktablu*'s feet kept them back.

Eddie kept his eyes fixed on the enemy combatants as he swung the scythe forward. In a swift move, he dropped down and grabbed Gilgamesh's spear with his free hand. As his fingers wrapped around the spear, the energy of the ancient kings of Uruk, noble and brave warriors of old, rose. Generation after generation, in ancient Sumer, the spirits of the kings of Uruk had weaved the material of their mortal souls into the spear. Eddie felt their spirits run strong in his veins. The blue filament of Gilgamesh's one-quarter-moral soul glowed deeper within Eddie's eyes when the spear's energy flowed through him. Then in turn the blue that was Gilgamesh within the spear's golden body also shone. The divine warrior energy of the spear flowed through Eddie's body and met its fourth part, the filament of the soul of Gilgamesh.

Eddie didn't know that he had found Gilgamesh. He only felt the great surging energy of the ancient lineage of warriors. He flung his head back as he jumped up and stabbed the warrior spear into the crimson sky with its steel-gray clouds. The old ship, with its tattered black sails of death, tossed Eddie and the demon sailors back and forth upon the roiling waters. A primal cry formed in Eddie's throat and sprang out, low and growly at first and then a roar. It was the sound of the warrior kings, who had formed the spear for one of their brothers. The force that flowed through him held the speed of a thousand cheetahs and the strength of the six kings of Uruk and the hidden one within the spear. It coursed through Eddie's veins. His eyes, which held the mortal soul of Gilgamesh, flashed. Then sparks of light shot from the spear's tip, the burning green flame. The light grew to bathe Eddie's body until he was alit in a phosphorescent green glow. Though he wore the camouflage battledress of a foot soldier, he looked like a warrior god with his yellow hair shining like the sun and the two mighty weapons he held aloft, one in each hand.

The demon mariners moved back, fearful and filled with wonder. They turned toward Eddie. A living soul was holding in one hand Death's scythe and in the other the ancient warrior spear. Had the One come? Their cunning souls sought to find a lie in the tale of their rescue. Was this yellow-haired one true or a fraud? For frauds were plentiful, but those of sincerity and truth did not exist in the Abyss. Still the prophecy that they would redeem their souls from the Dark Master was something they yearned for, though they hadn't the heart to believe it, for why should there have been a path out for scoundrels such as themselves?

Liars, thieves, and outlaws were all they had been in their mortal lives. But blackness only covers light, and what is covered could be uncovered, although, with their spirits so twisted by deceit, the outlaw mariners couldn't fully comprehend this. At least not then, not at the moment when Eddie stood before them, in his battle garb of a modern soldier, shouting the guttural and ancient cries of the six kings of Uruk and the last one, that of Gilgamesh. They all knew the tale that had been spoken, but they had turned it away from their minds long ago, so outlandish was it: that the One would come and lead them out of the Abyss. Then something deeply buried in the spirits of these thieves of the ancient sea awakened. At first the ancient sea thieves only sensed the faintest of feelings of it. It was a small pinprick of hope in a blanket of black that covered the light. Even so, it broke their despair, for it was hope. With hope came belief, and with knowledge came the surrender of their disbelief. Then it was that they bowed to the One, to Eddie, whose face was lit with the green glow of the spear.

The demon sailors bowed their heads as they bent down on their knees around the perimeter of the mountain of treasures, their arms outstretched in supplication. Although the glow of the spear now dimmed, the weapon's energy filled Eddie's heart with strength. The demon sailors rose to their feet, their song blending with the rising vicious storm around them—the displeasure of the Sea of Abyss at the increase of hope in the hopeless. The vessel was a cork bobbing in vast waters, so small and insignificant was it against the Great Sea of Abyss. The demon mariners raised their heads and continued to sing as their spirits rose.

Shining, shimmering, glimmering
To only One, it holds no fear.
A weapon that crushes its foe,
Stronger than a god's arrow and bow.
Invincible is this spear.
Who is He Who Commands the Chariot of the Dark Waters?
Ab-gal-lu! Ab-gal-lu!
He Who Commands the Chariot of the Great Waters of the Underworld,
To you we yield!
To him we bestow the title
Ab-gal-lu! Ab-gal-lu!

The demon sailors bowed toward this mortal, strangely here in the land of the dead but their Ab-gal-lu nonetheless. True, their demon souls were blackened with their acts of cruelty, their pillaging and plunder of those who had ridden the seas. Truer still was the fact that they had defied Marduk. No one ruled over them. No one but the prophesized rescuer, Ab-gal-lu, the great water man. He would be the commander of the outlaws, for only the One could lead them out of the Abyss, through Kurnigi and out of the dark underworld to regain their spirits. To this One they knew they must submit their will fully. They knew well how readily good could turn to evil. But could evil indeed transform to good? For only the good were freed from the dark underworld. But as Eddie would learn soon enough, robust of all remained the sea outlaws' true nature, where loyalty was a thing of expedience that fluttered with the winds of the moment. The One who ruled them would do so only as much as a vessel ruled the wild waves of an uncontrollable sea.

Eddie warily steadied himself on top the pile of treasures, his body surging with the energy of the spear as the ship beneath him tilted against the Sea of Abyss. His camouflage vest was wet; his pants and boots were sodden. Eddie felt their wet coldness against his skin. Two weapons he held, and these formed his defense. The enemy had surrendered. Eddie took in the intel about the enemy combatants: some were ragged, with bloody eyes and torn ears, and wore shreds of clothing; others were more grandly dressed, like the one with the red-and-black outfit. Some were male; some looked like they were female. All but one had bowed to him.

Could be a trick, Eddie thought. Somewhere deep within him, he also felt the spirit of their hope in him. But their surrender was too quick, he thought, to be trusted. The spear was powerful, true. But that didn't explain the why of it fully. The enemy had made him their leader; he figured this out by all the bowing and the singing. Still, he was cautious and kept the spear with one hand pointed at the demon sailors, who now stood at the perimeter of the mountain of treasures, their heads bowed. *Wait. Watch. Listen,* Eddie commanded himself. His jaw set itself in resolve. The scythe he held in the other hand, its deadly point facing those who surrounded him. Eddie again flourished the spear, his arm straining against its weight. It wasn't easy holding both weapons, for the king's spear was cumbersome and long. He wished the king were here. Still, he wasn't going to lose either weapon, no matter what. Suddenly the throng of outlaw seafarers parted. Eddie jumped back. Were they going to ambush him?

The Once-Noble One, who wore the peaked red headdress and whose face was that of the peoples who had ridden the waters of the Tigris and the Euphrates, was fast approaching Eddie, who stood at the top of the mountain of treasures. He stomped through the treasures and laid down his coral-embedded sword at Eddie's feet. His voice was deep and throaty, for in the depth of the sands where he had been buried for eons there had been little need for it. When he spoke, the sounds were garbled at first then cleared, and Eddie understood what he said.

"To you, Ab-gal-lu, He Who Commands the Chariot of the Dark Waters. He who now commands us, we who were thrown from Kurnigi and buried in the sands of these terrible waters. You, who shall lead us out of our terrible fates. To you, I give your crown and robes."

"Ab-gal-lu, He Who Commands the Chariot of the Dark Waters!" the others cried in return.

Eddie heard the word: *Ab-gal-lu,* He Who Commands the Chariot of the Dark Waters. Or, he thought, captain of this ship. He glanced warily again at those who surrounded him. The crew looked to be in worse shape than the ship.

Suddenly the peaked red headdress with its black band flew onto Eddie's head.

"Hey!" Eddie said, startled.

Then the ancient noble demon's red-and-black flowing robes lifted from his body like the wings of a bird. It left him clad in the white undergarments of the subservient. The robes appeared over Eddie, covering his khaki camouflage pants and his T-shirt and flak jacket. The nobleman's garments changed colors: from red and black to purple and crimson, the colors of Eddie's soul. A long, thick, braided rope of crimson fell across his shoulder, symbolizing his noble stature. Threads of blue shot through the robes and the headdress.

A great cry rose from the throats of all the ancient seafaring outlaws, for surely now they would be freed under the leadership of the One, who was strong with two weapons: one of Death, one of the Divine Warrior.

Their voices rang out:

> *To him we shall bestow the title*
> *He Who Commands the Chariot of the Great Waters of the Underworld!*
> *Ab-gal-lu! Ab-gal-lu!*
> *Who is master of our fates?*
> *One who can hold this weapon of old?*
> *Out of the Abyss he will lead us,*
> *He who is strong and bold,*
> *For he who can this weapon wield,*
> *The secret of the journey through Kurnigi will be revealed.*
> *He who shall sail us out of the Abyss,*
> *He who shall break our fates that were once sealed,*
> *To you we yield!*

Eddie was surprised by his feelings: he liked the strength of the weapons and, more still, liked the feeling of being promoted to leader. The spear glowed in warning, and a whisper fluttered in his ears: *Beware.* But Eddie was deaf to this. He felt the headiness that comes when one is suddenly elevated to power. A primal cry formed in his throat as he shouted, "I am Ab-gal-lu!"

The ancient thieves roared back in delight, "Ab-gal-lu! Ab-gal-lu! Greatness to He Who Commands the Chariot! He who shall free us from the Abyss!"

In response, a ferocious wind, holding the tempest of a hurricane, struck the ship in swift and strong strikes. The waters beneath seemed to have heard the outlaw seafarers' chants and had risen in opposition. The Sea of Abyss rocked the ship with its angry waves. It tipped toward the waters, threatening to capsize. The mountain of treasures was overtaken by a great wave of water that licked its top.

Eddie slid down and fell onto the slippery wooden planks, where he stabbed the spear into the deck to steady himself. The sting of the sea's acid spray hit his face. All around him the demon sailors scurried to stay aboard. The black sails of this doomed sea chariot fluttered and tore against the sevenfold winds of the Sea of Abyss. There was no way to steer this ship, as the T frame that controlled the sails had broken against the wind, and the sails were just tatters. The ship rocked back and forth with a ferocity that spoke of the great rage and vengeance of the sea. The demon sailors took up positions, as rowers on each side of the ship were powerless against the waves, their oars breaking against the churning sea.

"Ab-gal-lu!" they cried, and the tossed-about seafarers turned their desperate eyes toward Eddie.

If you're the captain, you'd better take command, Eddie told himself. The spear held the magic of warriors. But since he wasn't the king, he didn't know the right words.

Fierce waves struck the ship again. Stabbing the spear into the sky, Eddie shouted, "Warrior kings! Help us steer this ship!"

The spear's tip glowed in response to the call, for though Eddie was not of Uruk, though his lineage was not of the ancient kings of old, he held the one-quarter-mortal soul of Gilgamesh. And to the old kings whose spirits were held in the spear, Gilgamesh beseeched. He called to his ancestors to help his warrior brother. The purple-and-crimson robes flew back behind Eddie as the flame in the spear grew. From his throat sprung the voice of Gilgamesh:

Mesh-ki-ang-gasher,
drowned son of Utu!
Break these winds that howl!
Tame this sea that roars!

The words were a chant of old, a song that was said in the land of light, not darkness. They cut the sea's force in two halves, creating a window of calm between them. The black sails grew and took shape again, and the broken T mended. The demon sailors cried their hurrahs.

"Grab the T to wield the sails!" Eddie commanded the outlaw sailors nearby.

The sea thieves scrambled to grab the T to use the sails. But the smooth waters had lulled them. The Abyss was stronger than the power of the warrior spear. The ship suddenly lurched forward on its own course. Eddie tied the scythe to the back of his shoulders with the crimson braided rope. A force was pulling the ship toward the island. He assessed the situation: he had plunged into the Abyss of Blackness to find Trina but had ended up in its sea. Now they were headed toward this dangerous island. The ship moved still faster, with lightning speed, toward the island, which rose large and ominously on the horizon. The Once-Noble One, in his white undergarments, faced the island with a grim look. With dread, all the mariner outlaws spied the fast-approaching island.

Eddie asked the Once-Noble One, who stood by his side, "What's this island?"

The Once-Noble One's long, smooth face furrowed as he spoke. "Ab-gal-lu, it is the island that has risen for the Prince of Demons, he whose power comes from the demon gods of old Asaru-alim-nuna. All creatures of the Abyss must surrender themselves to the prince when he rises."

Eddie's eyes narrowed. The Prince of Demons. That pock-marked one who had kidnapped Trina had called himself that. He was right where he needed to be, to crush him and rescue Trina. Surely too, the king must have been thrown to its shores if his spear had been in the sea's waters.

"Good. Let the ship crash right into the island.," Eddie said. "We're not surrendering. We're going to take it by force."

The Once-Noble One grimly shook his head. "We are meager in numbers, Ab-gal-lu. They are in the tens of thousands. Too, we are branded outlaws of the land of the Abyss. We must not land upon this island, for we shall swiftly be captured and become slaves of the Prince of Demons."

The demon sailors felt bleakness course through them, and the sliver of hope in the One began to fade, for how could they overthrow all the powerful creatures of the Abyss when they were but a drop of water to the sea of the enemy?

Eddie paused as doubt etched its way into his mind. The odds were bad. The enemy greatly outnumbered them. And he didn't even know the island's terrain so he could form an attack plan. He felt the doubt of the ancient sea outlaws of hell rising around him. Then he heard his father's voice: *No one follows a leader who doesn't believe in himself.*

The ship was tearing toward the black obsidian island, closer and closer. All that appeared upon it was a large jagged mountain, on top of which sprouted a massive, dark, looming castle. Eddie now saw that thousands of hellish, fiendish creatures were climbing the mountain. He took in the intelligence. He had to infiltrate the castle and find the king, and together they would find Trina and rescue her. But how? *Bounding overwatch maneuver when the enemy is certain,* Eddie heard his father's command. *Yeah, Dad.* Eddie thought. *When you have a real platoon that works—a platoon that watches each other's backs—you leave no brother warrior behind.* But these were sea criminals, ancient pirates. They'd likely just as soon stab him in the back as protect it. Still they had called him Ab-gal-lu. Eddie made a decision: he had to trust that they'd meant it when they said he was their leader; there was no other choice.

"Move together!" Eddie ordered.

The demon outlaws formed a close circle within which Eddie stood, all of them swaying to the ship's rapid movement across the waters. The scythe, tied with the crimson rope and flung behind his back, vibrated ominously as the outlaw seafarers came close and surrounded Eddie. He held the spear as a shaft, gripping the middle to steady himself.

Eddie spoke quickly. "Grab what you can for weapons. When the ship hits the shore, listen for my commands. We'll move in three groups of fifty. You!" He pointed to the Once-Noble One, who wore only the white underclothes of the subservient but who already had picked up his sword with the coral inlay. Eddie shrugged off the robes that he had been given. They flew up, fluttered, and fell over the Once-Noble One, turning red and black again.

"Take these men." Eddie pointed to a group of what seemed to be roughly fifty seafarers. "All of you behind this guy are Platoon One, First Bound. He's your leader."

Then Eddie shook his head, and off came the peaked red headdress. It fell upon a female seafarer of the Nile, whose black-velvet skin glowed. Her eyes were hazel, like those of a tiger, and her hair rose in black spikes, within which were bright sapphire beads.

"You," he told her. "Take command of Platoon Two. All of you behind her are Second Bound."

Eddie turned to the remaining sailors. "We're the rest of the moving force. When we hit the island, move off the ship, listen to my commands, and obey them. No matter what."

A little more than one hundred fifty demons and one living, yellow-haired *muktablu* intended to confront the thousands upon thousands of creatures of the Abyss. The Once-Noble One, now clad in his red-and-black robes, thought ruefully of their fates. He was of an ancient land with two rivers that crossed it and was born to royal parents. He had killed his own brother to ascend to the throne. He had betrayed Hannu, the noble ancient seafarer, and then fallen when he was thrown out of his land to live his mortal life as nothing but a scavenger of the seas. He and his brethren were thieves who had sometimes used cunning and charm to steal, other times brute force. They knew the twists of the mind that thought only of itself—how good could be interpreted as bad, and evil as good, as long it served a purpose for oneself. Once, his heart had beat the song of loyalty and goodness. But that was eons ago; since then, his heart had been covered with layers upon layers of deceit, of promises made to be broken; "leader" they would call you one day and make you slave the next. The young Ab-gal-lu, who held his head with the proud spirit of an unsullied and true warrior, did not know about about such things.

"Move! Grab your weapons!" Eddie commanded, hoping the demon sailors indeed had weapons.

As the ship moved with a thundering vengeance toward the island, the demon outlaws were thrown back and forth within it. Still they obeyed Eddie, scrambling to pick up the remaining treasures that hadn't been washed into the Sea of Abyss to use as weapons: gilded daggers, jewel-encrusted dirks, swords whose handles were inlaid with lapus lazuli, ropes of pearls, golden globes.

A deafening sound cracked the air. It was that of a rising titanic wave. It shot up and formed a great claw in the sky. Then this weapon of the Sea of Abyss grabbed and pitched the *Condemned Ship of the Outlaws of Hell* like a ball against the ruthless shores of the island, where it shattered into pieces.

CHAPTER 8

the Broken wand

The midnight hour of October 31, 1936, was not ordinary. Though the basement of the Great Master Magician's Harlem brownstone was dank and drafty—with every corner, it seemed, filled with cobwebs—the seriousness of purpose of those stalwart few who had gathered there gave the room dignity. To enter, they had broken the low window that rimmed the sidewalk, for the old back room of the magic store where they used to meet had fallen victim to the Depression and had been found dark, locked, and shuttered tight against unlawful entry. But meet they must, and indeed what better place than this, the basement of the Master Magician's home? It was the tenth meeting of the Society of Phantom Magicians since their president, the Master Magician himself, had passed on to the spirit world. Yes, the spirit world. For though the Master in his human form had sneered at spiritualists, he was a secret believer.

The Society of Phantom Magicians understood that magic was fueled by an undercurrent of power, the source of which was the dark world. *Real* magic, not the tricks perpetrated by frauds. Those Phantom Magicians who had died and were now in spirit form were the key to the group's living members harnessing that ability; to have genuine powers, one had to communicate with these magicians who had moved on to the otherworld. Then these magicians' wizardry would dazzle, as had the Master Magician's. Though he had shunned séances when he was alive, many believed the Master Magician had tapped the energy of the dead Phantoms. How else could he perform his incredible escapes when naked, shackled, and submerged in icy waters? The magicians who had gathered in the brownstone basement this night longed to tap that energy of the Phantom Magicians, to become what the Master had been: a wizard.

Once their roster had boasted thousands: magicians who had (or claimed they had) glimpsed the electric power of *real* sorcery. Now only six remained. Spending time and money to seek pure wizardry seemed a childish thing when the demands of daily living weighed upon their shoulders as the Depression wore on and on. Magicians, as all entertainers, were the first to feel the chill of reduced circumstances. Who was going to pay for a magic show when bellies rumbled with gnawing hunger? Who was going to use the last coins in his or her purse to see disappearing acts when life was a series of disappearances: jobs, homes, people? Now, ironically, it was the Society of Phantom Magicians that had all but disappeared, reduced to its gathered half dozen loyalists.

The Master Magician had sworn an oath to return in the midnight hour of his death. "Ten years," he had said to them. "Give me ten tries upon the midnight hour of my death. If I do not appear, then you shall know there is no spirit world. Know, Phantom Magicians, that you have been tricked by fakery."

These six in their middle years—three men and three women—looked ragged; they held none of the glitter and glamour of their old stage days, when they paraded their skills to appreciative audiences. They deliberately had left the light on, a bright glaring bulb that hung from the ceiling and would not soften, as would candlelight, the price of poverty upon their gaunt faces. Also, for this last try, they would not mask with doubt whether the Master Magician's spirit rose under the cover of a dusky light. They had to know! Know with certainty that if the Master Magician rose, it was not due to the trickery of one of them, conducted as a sleight of hand under the cover of a dim candlelight. They had had made a bet with the Debunkers Association, a group of dry academics from Columbia University, who were to hold a séance in their office, presided over by a medium. The séance there would be filmed and would prove decisively whether the afterworld of phantom spirits indeed existed. It would decide whether the Great Magician was one of the phantom spirits or whether, as the Debunkers said, it was all bunk, and the spirit world was a great fraud, now exposed.

But the six of the Society of Phantom Magicians ultimately could not allow this last opportunity to communicate with the Great Magician to be wasted in the environs of an academic office. Therefore, the Debunkers would be left to their own dry devices without the Phantom Magicians presence.

"Ten tries," he had said. And too, the widow Bess had declared it to be the last séance, and without her coming here, they knew the Great Magician never would appear. No. They must know without a doubt that there was a spirit world, and they would not, could not, let this chance pass. For the Depression had taken their profession, their homes, and most terribly, their sense of self. Now all that was left was this: to know with certainty that the spirit world existed. And if it did not, then it would be dust to dust for their weary bodies. Their eyes were filled with the question as they gazed upon a bright gleaming crystal ball on a round wooden table. How the Master Magician had despised such accoutrements of the frauds, those gypsies whose black eyes and mysterious gasps and utterances over just such a crystal ball led the gullible to give over their earnings for the promise of hearing the voice of a long-lost loved one. But this was all they had. Candles, incense, magic boards, dolls, cards, the breaking of a wand, incantations, strands of the Master's hair, pieces of the ropes that once had bound him—all these had been tried as lures to lift the Master from the spirit world in the nine séances preceding this last one. None had worked. So the crystal ball it would be—that despised symbol of fakery. It was all they had.

The six of the Society of Phantom Magicians clasped hands as they sat around the wooden table that held the gleaming crystal ball. Three circles: of hands around a round table upon which was a round ball. Three men. Three women. It was propitious, their hearts said. It was all bunk, their minds replied. Still they gazed into the ball. As one, they placed their clasped fingers on the crystal ball. Then they said her name—Bess—for they knew that the Master Magician's widow had fled to the lure of sunshine and was rumored to have finally abandoned the ritual of the death-anniversary séances. For her—certainly, for her—the Master Magician would come.

"It is Bess who calls for you! Your beloved calls for you!" the six murmured over and over.

Through her tears, Mattie squinted up at the man who held a black stick with a sharp blade at its tip. It was pointed straight at her!

A mix of emotions rose within her: fear, sadness, frustration. These feelings fell like a hailstorm and collided with one another and scattered her thoughts. It was all too much. Geeta hadn't moved at all. *Oh please don't be dead, Geeta!* Mattie wailed to herself. She had to figure out some way to get Geeta help, some way to bring her back to life—maybe that tree in Nineveh? Maybe they could go there again, and the nice small man with the large ears could help her? But how? *How?* There was no Mr. Biddle to help her out, and Eddie had gone off somewhere with the king of Uruk. Her mom—who knew where she was?

In the milliseconds that these thoughts ran through her mind, she returned again to this: it was all because of that rotten, double-crossing Spyglass and her rat-fink ways. Now this man wanted to hurt her, and she didn't even know him!

Mattie felt the injustice keenly. She had done nothing to this man. Grown-ups were supposed to be…well, grown-ups! Maybe she wasn't book smart like Geeta; maybe she wasn't a warrior like Eddie, but she was the one the people in Nineveh called their leader. She was the one the Spyglass—two-faced rat fink though she was—had chosen.

Now another emotion, red-hot, rose. It flushed her face. It surged through her, heating her head and frizzing her red hair until it was a halo of fury. She'd had enough! No one was going to boss her around anymore. Okay, maybe she had made some mistakes—mainly letting that fink Spyglass control her—but now it was all going to be different. That creepy Spyglass was gone into the hands of an old witch—just what that rat fink deserved. Now that the double-crosser wasn't around, Mattie could really take charge. Why they needed to keep that creep around she couldn't figure out; the Spyglass was nothing but trouble and more trouble. She would show that nice little man with the big ears from Nineveh that she was still their leader; she could be trusted.

She, Mattie O'Reilly, would get Geeta help. She would find everyone, and they would all go together on the rest of the stones of the Path. Then everything would work out, and everyone would be happy. Her eyes narrowed as she turned toward the nasty man with the sharp pointy stick. First she had to take care of this guy. Mattie jumped up, head low, and barreled toward the man like a linebacker.

The Master Magician started at the girl's ferociousness and deftly moved away before she could strike him. This girl wasn't a spirit but alive. It must have been this one whom he had heard calling for help, probably for the skinny brown child lying dead upon the ground. But where was Bess? This girl might know. The girl turned to run at him again. The Master Magician hadn't had much experience winning over children. His tricks in his mortal form had no rabbits, no puffs of smoke that were the cornerstone of those who peddled their wares to youngsters. No, his illusions had required the wits of an adult to be fully appreciated. The Great Magician adjusted his face to form a smile and kept his wand down. Yes, better to smile and not scare the girl if he wanted to get the information, he thought. The smile hadn't reached his lips when he felt the girl's hand bat the wand. Immediately his face twisted in pain. The force of her living strength ricocheted through the wand, into his arm, and through the fingers that held it with the potency of a thousand bee stings. He uttered a gasp as his fingers loosened their grip upon the wand. As it dropped in one deft move, Mattie jumped and grabbed the fallen rod.

She triumphantly waved it and shouted at the man, "Look!"

The man's eyes registered shock as he beheld the red-haired child recklessly waving the black wand. "Give it back, child," he said in a soft, placating voice. His hand was outstretched, though his eyes were wide with fear that the wand would be destroyed by this clumsy girl who was flinging it about mindlessly. "Please," he said. "I won't harm you. I promise."

Mattie backed up with the wand held firmly in her grasp. She stood protectively over Geeta's still body. The man in the suit seemed shocked and upset. But Mattie knew he was a trickster—she could just see it in his shifty eyes. *He won't harm me. Ha!* What would Eddie do? He would show his man—the enemy combatant—who was boss. And that was exactly what Mattie was going to do.

Again she slashed the wand in the air toward the man. "Get back!" she yelled.

The man moved toward Mattie. "You don't understand what you're holding. I won't harm you. Please just give it back."

"Back, I said!" Mattie proclaimed, and to emphasize her seriousness, she hit the wand against the stone floor of the rooftop patio.

The Great Magician's wand was a delicate thing of the phantoms, formed by incantations, and did not possess the strength of the solid things of this world. The force of the impact of the wand upon the stone floor made a terrible sound, like glass shattering. Then the wand broke in two.

At once, the Master Magician's body arched back. The magic wand was broken! In the living world, the breaking of a wand signified its retirement when a magician left his or her earthly form. But it meant much more in the spirit world, for the wand was taken to the other world as an amulet that contained all the powerful incantations of the one who held it; it formed one's being. The Master Magician began to writhe. The elegant suit disappeared. Now he was clad only in swimsuit trunks, his body wrapped in chains with several locks. His eyes jumped in surprise at the transformation.

Mattie's mouth was a big *O*, the kind her mother said made her look like one of those goldfish inside the fishbowls at Kashmir's Pet Store in Hackensack. She hadn't meant to break the stick! Now it looked like she had done something really bad to the man.

Mattie didn't have much time to consider the repercussions of her actions, for the rooftop began to shake and split. The piece of the wand she held flew from her hands. Now the wand was in two pieces on the roof. Instantly it melted, forming a black tar-like substance. It seeped across the roof to rise around and swallow the Master Magician and then engulfed Mattie and Geeta. It whipped a great black slash up into the air then turned into itself to form a small black spinning ball that shot downward, through the rooftop below.

𒀭𒁉𒊬 𒂍 𒀭𒁉𒊬 𒉺

In the basement of the Harlem brownstone, the light bulb flung about wildly from the ceiling. Six pairs of eyes lifted to confirm again and again that indeed the bulb was moving. Six pairs of eyes looked to one another. Yes, everyone had seen it. Around the round wooden table, hands clasped tighter in the small circle around the gleaming crystal ball; the magicians' hearts now beat giddily in anticipation. Their voices longed to call out his name, but they stilled their thoughts lest they disturb the spirit's journey into the living world. Still, the faces of the six members of the Society of Phantom Magicians revealed their words: they called his mortal name with their eyes, with the small and sound-less movement of their lips. Then the energy of the spirit world coursed through their clasped hands. A small black ball shot out of the ceiling, penetrating but not shattering the crystal ball it entered. Instantly the crystal ball began to balloon. It grew larger and larger until it filled the circumference of the wooden table. The gleaming glass pushed against the faces of the six around it until each one saw the small spinning black ball at the bottom of the crystal ball and just the barest of ghostly outlines of the person across from them.

Fear filled them, for phantoms were of the dark underworld, but not a single one unclasped their hands to break the spell. Not a single one uttered a word, paralyzed as they were by their first encounter with the phantoms from beyond. Within the crystal ball, the small black ball exploded. It sent three tendrils of gray smoke up, each shaped like a clenched hand. One hand unclenched, and from it formed a chubby red-haired girl wearing checkered pants, her eyes wide with surprise. Then from the second unclenched fist followed a listless skinny brown child in a purple dress and yellow tights, whose eyes were shut. Finally, from the last unclenched hand, the Master Magician emerged. Yes, the Master Magician!

All three of these figures floated within the crystal ball as if they were suspended in liquid.

Each of the six around the table uttered a grunt of surprise. Not at the youthfulness of the Master Magician or even the fact that he was naked, except for his swim trunks, and bound with chains, as in the escape tricks of old when he was shackled and submerged in tanks of water. He had been a showman in life; why not in death? No, it was the look in his eyes that startled them: a look of terror.

The Master Magician fruitlessly struggled against the chains as an unseen energy swirled within the giant crystal ball. It churned and churned, flinging the three figures against one another and the glass wall of the ball. The Master Magician seemed to be saying something as he was tossed about. The ball then turned black and abruptly was filled with a bright light. So blinding was this light that the six around the table instinctively shut their eyes against it.

When they opened their eyes, all that remained was a giant crystal ball, empty of the three figures. The crystal ball rapidly began to shrink to its original size. One word from the Master Magician echoed in their ears: *Hippodrome.*

The deep blanket of blackness that surrounded Geeta's consciousness was broken by sounds: first of Mattie crying, then of a far-off chant. The words vibrated in her ears in a hypnotic rhythm: *Om Namaha Shivaya Om Namaha Shivaya Om Namaha Shivaya Om Namaha.*

Consciousness rose slowly within her until she was aware of the sounds of a city. She recognized it at once as the cacophony of Bombay, for the language was a mix of Hindi, Maharati, and English. Intermixed were the sounds of the fishwives hawking their wares, as well as snake charmers, boiled-peanut vendors, beggars, cows, the honks of taxi drivers, the double-decker buses rattling their way down the buckling streets, and the sounds of a myriad of others who made up the vibrant, paradoxical weave of an Indian city: of the modern and ancient, of poverty and enterprise.

Geeta's eyes flicked open. She was seated, cross-legged, at one end of the daybed in her grandparents' living room, in their apartment in the Sion section of Bombay. This daybed, with its metal frame and sagging mattress, acted as a sofa of sorts. It was pushed against a window, beyond which was a small balcony that fronted a busy street—the street whose noises had filled her ears. She saw her ThaTha sitting across from her on the daybed. His old familiar brown face—with its shaven head and long tuft of hair—and his shirt over a dhoti—made her heart soar in happiness. "ThaTha!" she struggled to say; her lips moved but made no sounds. ThaTha too seemed unaware of her. Though his eyes were shut, surely he would have felt Geeta's weight fall upon the daybed. His spectacles were at his side, as was a crisp, unopened *Times of India*—highly unusual, for ThaTha read the *Times* with fervor, and Geeta never had seen it lying in a pristine state at his side. No, ThaTha always scoured the *Times*; with his prodigious memory, he retained everything. Then he would recall to Geeta the events of the day when she came home from school. "One must never become ignorant of what transpires in the world, for it is precisely such ignorance that invites evildoing," he would tell her. For in those days, before they had moved to Hackensack, New Jersey, Geeta and her parents had lived with ThaTha and Pa-tee (as she called her grandmother) in this very apartment in Bombay.

Geeta tilted her head in puzzlement: ThaTha's eyes were closed in meditation; she saw how his eyeballs flickered under the lids, crossed toward the third eye. But ThaTha never did his prayers in the daybed; that would be disrespectful. Instead he always did them in the small puja—or worship—room inside the kitchen, where fruits were offered to the golden statue of the Lord Vishnu, as the avatar form known as Srinivasa, which was laden with garlands of yellow and orange flowers.

ThaTha's lips were moving in a faint chant, not to Lord Vishnu but to Lord Shiva, who held both creation and destruction.

Om Namaha Shivaya Om Namaha Shivaya Om Namaha Shivaya Om Namaha Shivaya.

The hypnotic rhythm of the chant lulled Geeta, and her eyes fell shut. When she opened them, she was looking into a bright flame in an oil-soaked cotton wick within a silver lamp whose top was shaped like a lotus flower. Again she was cross-legged, her knobby knees covered in her mustard-colored tights. The flame in the lamp flickered as it lit a large black oval stone, the Shiva lingam. Around this stone lay the puja—offerings—of elongated delicate bel leaves, bright flowers of many colors, and bananas. The air was smoky with the smell of incense. It was a puja for Lord Shiva.

Geeta lifted her eyes from the offerings. Her eyes widened even more in surprise; she was in a small cave carved into the side of a cold, windy mountain. The low ceiling and sides, lit by the flame in the small lamp, were made of yellow stone. ThaTha materialized across from her in the smoky haze, sitting cross-legged and dressed in his dhoti, white cotton that was wrapped around his waist. Upon his bare chest hung a mala, or necklace, of seeds and a sacred thread that fell across his left shoulder and down to his right side, signifying his status as a Brahmin. ThaTha placed some fruit by the Shiva lingam.

Geeta saw they were not alone, for now a priest appeared, his forehead marked with a white-and-yellow trident, his lips moving in the chants of old. The priest's face was shrunken into itself, and he was bent over in concentration as he poured pure milk over the oval stone, the lingam, as an offering. The white of the dhoti around his waist shone brightly against his skin, which was so deep a brown that it was almost black. His head was shaven, as was the custom for a Brahmin priest, and on top of it was a small lock of white hair, the kudimi. This priest was even more ancient than ThaTha, Geeta noticed, for his fingers, gnarled with age, shook in a sort of rhythmic palsy as he rang a bell over and over, and his face was mapped in wrinkles.

Geeta instinctively felt that the puja had been offered on her behalf to Lord Shiva, who was a destroyer but the Creator too, she knew. Why was she here? Then she felt a prick of discomfort. Were her shoes off? But when and how would she have taken them off? Geeta knew this was a silly thought in the larger context of how she had even come here. Still, it was forbidden to wear shoes in worship, as it defiled the sacred and showed disrespect to God. She tried to wiggle her toes but felt nothing. But then, neither ThaTha nor the priest seemed to be aware of her. Why couldn't ThaTha see her? The chant rose, interrupting her thoughts.

"*Om Namaha Shivaya Om Namaha Shivaya Om Namaha Shivaya Om Namaha Shivaya,*" the priest and ThaTha chanted over and over. "*Om Namaha Shivaya Om Namaha Shivaya Om Namaha Shivaya Om Namaha Shivaya.*"

The flame within the lotus-shaped lamp rose, and the smokiness of the room increased. Then a yogi appeared, moving out of the very sides of the cave. This mystic seemed to be of the cave, for his robes were the yellow of the stone. The ceiling of the cave lifted higher. The yogi sat cross-legged and was suspended in the air over the priest and ThaTha, and across from Geeta. His tangled white hair was tied up in a knot over his head; a long white beard fell over his bare brown chest, while the sacred cord and mala of seeds fell over a skeletal body. His chest, with its protruding rib cage, revealed the vigor of his fasting. The yogi's eyes were shut; nonetheless Geeta felt his gaze sear through her.

The yogi spoke, his eyes remaining closed. "In this child, the steel bands of the questioning self—her ego—have bound themselves to Maya, to the illusion."

Geeta felt the sting of the accusation. Was her questioning mind an ego? But hadn't ThaTha told her to question that which was? Could she not defend herself? Then she felt another prick of realization: this might be what the yogi meant, for here was her questioning intellect once again.

ThaTha kept his eyes closed as he replied, "Sanyasi, it is true. Her imperfections were many, yet—"

The yogi interrupted him. "The greatest of which is the eye upon her heel, the ego of intellect that blinds true knowledge."

ThaTha fell silent, though Geeta could see his anguish rise behind his flickering eyelids when he spoke. "Sri Yogi, we beseech you still…Help us call Lord Shiva to restore her."

To restore me! Geeta thought in recognition. She *had* died on the rooftop. That was why Mattie was crying. And here was ThaTha praying, *beseeching*, for the yogi to revive her.

The priest with the gnarled palsied hands and the face whose features almost disappeared in its blackness, whose eyes were filled with kindness, looked straight at Geeta as he kept pouring the milk over the black oval stone.

"Sri Yogi," he said, "allow Geeta to continue her dharma upon the Path of the Virtuous. Allow it so that the Third Age of the Maha Yuga, the Dvapara Yuga, where the eternal dharma totters between good and evil, will flourish into good."

It seemed that the yogi remained silent for an eon as the smell of incense filled the air.

Then he said with sadness, "It is not the Third Age that rises but the Fourth Age, that of Kali Yuga: of misfortune and war; of moral degradation, where the grasp for the material pours like an acid upon virtue and darkness envelops the world."

Then, though the yogi's eyes remained shut, his searing glance nonetheless again filled Geeta. She felt as if she were transparent, her very soul open to his assessment. The yogi spoke again: "Still, though she is bound to Maya, in this child I see self-less goodness. For within the whorls of evil, she sacrificed herself for her friend."

The yogi then began to recite the one thousand names of Lord Shiva. The old priest and ThaTha joined him. "*Om Maheshwar, Om mahadev, Om shankar, Om pashupatinath, Om Kailash pati, Om uma maheshwar, Om Gaurishankar.*"

The chant rose and filled the cave with sounds, soft and rhythmic like a gentle wind. It filled Geeta's mind and soul with its sacred vibrations. At the thousandth name of Lord Shiva, the yogi disappeared back into the yellow stone, and a blue-black smoke filled the cave.

Geeta was flung to the ground, falling upon her back. A foot, heavy as lead, was upon her chest. She gasped at the vision that formed over her.

It was not Lord Shiva who appeared but Kali, the goddess of death, materializing above her. Geeta's eyes were filled the goddess's awful form. She was blue-black in color, with long hair that fell loose, fluttering like raven's wings upon her shoulders and across her back. Her eyes were fierce and bloodshot, and a long red tongue protruded from her mouth. Kali wore a garland of bloody heads around her neck, and across her waist was a terrible girdle of severed arms reaching out in desperation. She herself had four arms; the back two held a bloody bent sword and a decapitated head. Her breath filled the cave with the stench of death. With rage seething to her fingertips, Kali's front two arms reached down to grab Geeta to devour her. Her anger was thunderous as she howled against the prayers around her to take from her Geeta's soul, which already had been given to her.

Geeta heard ThaTha and the old priest again chanting, "*Om Namaha Shivaya Om Namaha Shivaya Om Namaha Shivaya Om Namaha Shivaya*" against the angry roar of Kali. She felt it rise in her, and then the chant "*Om Namaha Shivaya Om Namaha Shivaya Om Namaha Shivaya Om Namaha Shivaya*" struggled out of her mind to her lips, where she formed the words against the pressure of Kali's foot upon her chest, until the very cave itself seem to fill itself with the sound of *Om*. The heaviness lifted from Geeta's chest. Then she heard the snarling of the goddess Kali recede as she disappeared into vibrant colors of rage and destruction: red, black, blue.

The smoke cleared to reveal the yogi forming again from the yellow stone, suspended above the puja. His yellow robes faded to reveal Lord Shiva, luminous in aspect, sitting cross-legged, with two arms behind him holding a sacred spear and bell, and two arms in front, one with the palm raised. Lord Shiva's skin was sky blue, and his long matted mustard-colored hair fell like small ropes about his shoulders. The third eye upon his forehead glinted. On top of his head, little silver snakes were coiled atop a peaked mound of hair. The garland around his neck was the snake Vasuki, a gently undulating cobra.

Geeta was now sitting upright again, cross-legged across from the puja for Lord Shiva. She was beyond fear and now in awe at the luminous vision before her. She heard ThaTha in her mind: *Raise your right palm toward Lord Shiva so that your lifeline may be restored. Raise your left palm so that it may hold your dharma.*

Geeta raised her palms. A blinding blue light filled her eyes, and a searing pain burned her hands as the lines made their way back to her palms.

She heard ThaTha's voice again as she disappeared from the cave: *Now you know your dharma. You must not allow yourself to fall into the grasp of illusion, as does she who fights her dharma. You must be a guide and a lamp. To do so, you must grow and change.*

CHAPTER 9

marchio del consigliere

The Saber of Shadows glinted in Stal's left hand as he plummeted through the crimson sky of the Abyss onto the island. With arrogance, he rode upon the giant, dark, winged dragon horse that spewed pallid green flames. As the beast hit the black shining stones that paved the winding pathway to the castle, it grew two more heads: dinosaur-like, with large rows of teeth, narrow eyes, and twisted black horns on each side.

A sharp pain intruded into Stal's consciousness. Here before him was that yellow-eyed, rodent-faced creature Abaddon, who had sunk his teeth into Stal's right hand on the frozen land of the Russian Square. Abaddon flapped his bat-like wings in unyielding determination to reclaim his black and blue thumbs. Stal flung his hand back to throw off the creature, but Abaddon wasn't so easily dislodged, for he was determined to take back his thumbs and all the power within them. Then abruptly the center head of Stal's fearsome horse transformed into large serpent head with a long tongue that lashed around Abaddon's body and pried him off his master. Abaddon was flung onto the cobbled road, narrowly avoiding being crushed under the dragon horse's pounding hooves. The head turned back into the fearsome aspect of a dragon, flames shooting from its mouth. The two heads on each side opened their mouths to reveal their rows of sharp teeth and let out loathsome snarls.

The path that led to the castle was treacherous, for the island's landscape was severe: it jutted up from its shores into a harsh, steep mountain. At the peak loomed a formidable castle that breathed despair and desolation; its sounds echoed throughout the island in a moaning wind. For though the castle appeared to be made of stone, it was in fact the fossilized bones of spirits who were condemned for eternity to be walls and floors. As all things in the land of light were said to hold a spirit, so too was it in the land of the dead. So it would be that this castle of the dead, whose very floors and walls were miserable evil spirits, would hold the Prince of Demons. Upon the mountain rose trees and shrubs, all demon spirits themselves. The trees were gnarled, with bleeding bark, and their dried leaves cried tears of gloom. Their long branches scraped the ground with their pointed ends. They scratched the creatures that came their way and slapped others with their thorns.

The trail curved and twisted toward the top. Quickly it filled with even more creatures of the dark underworld: some with faces streaked with bloody tears, some with fangs set in green faces, others with misshapen heads, others with chains that they dragged forward. Some were birds of prey; others were man and bird, man and rodent, fish with claws, birds with serpent tails. Some were old, others young, some with maggots feasting upon their bodies, others with faces that wore insanity and whose cries were discordant notes of agony. Their horses, the skeleton carriages, the moving winds of insects that buzzed revenge—all were denizens of the Abyss or those freed from imprisonment in Kurnigi's Corkscrew of Terror.

> *Prince of Demons! Ruler of Creatures of Dread,*
> *Slice the sky with your saber,*
> *The Sword of Darkness. The Saber of the Dead!*

Stal brandished both sides of his weapon in response. Its shimmering blue-gray steel cast silver shadows upon the crowd. The demon creatures of the Abyss shouted:

> *Eyes of red that glow!*
> *Upon the dark lands of the Abyss you sow*
> *The seeds of the overthrow,*
> *For the skin of hell, its outer crust,*
> *Marduk's Kurnigi, is now ashes and dust!*
> *Prince of Demons!*

Stal's pleasure roared through his ears at the call of the creatures that lined the path. He waved the saber again and again, as befitting royalty. Yes, he was mighty. Yes, they were bowing to him. He felt all-powerful; the muscular form of the creature with the three heads that he rode was the physical manifestation of his sovereignty. But it was the euphoria of this welcome by the teeming tens of thousands of creatures from the Black Abyss that surged through him even more powerfully. He held all power, might, and prestige. He possessed everything, including Trina. Her thin body was now pressed against the dragon's neck, held fast between the beast and him.

Too, the sweet sound of his victory in the Russian Winter Palace Square echoed in exultant notes. He reveled in the fact that he, once just the son of a drunken Georgian cobbler and a washer-woman, an object of ridicule due to the pockmarks upon his face, had struck and felled the mighty Cossacks. Power had surged from his black and blue thumbs, given to him by the withered old Crone, and he suddenly had become a man, no longer a pockmarked beggar boy wearing tattered clothing. The admonitions of his mother, Keke, were pathetic and false: "He who is slow to anger is better than the mighty, so say the Proverbs, Iosif. Keep still in anger. Turn the other cheek, and the Lord will bless you." *No, old woman,* he thought now, *it is anger that rules. Turn the other cheek only to be struck again.* And that was exactly what those stupid Russian peasants, shivering with cold and hunger and turning the other cheek under Tsar Nicolas, had found out. He recalled how easily they, on the tsar's square, had fallen in response to his cry of revolution—"The sickle and the hammer for all comrades!"—as his banner, red with fury, and the sign of the sickle and the hammer had shone forth. But the peasants' adulation of him had been nothing.

For upon its heels came a greater triumph: the cry of the demon gods when they had called him Prince of Demons! The Snake Gneezy had tried to bend him to submission, shouting, "You are nothing but a pockmarked cockroach who serves me!" But now Stal relished the memory: the Snake was sadly mistaken. For it was to the Prince of Demons that the reptile had spoken, not a powerless pockmarked boy, and it was the demon gods who had surrounded him and sprung to grasp the Snake. And the Snake could only retreat in defeat.

Stal was no longer a cowering boy but a strong, powerful man—no, not a man but a demon, for he had long since lost his mortal body. Trina—once far removed from him, as she was the daughter of a wealthy tradesman, and he was just the son of her family's washerwoman and maid—also was his. Stal took in her beautiful, pale, oval face; the light-hazel eyes with dashes of green; and her hair, which brushed against his chin, shining like polished dark wood…so smooth, thick, and luxuriant. He relished it all. Everything was his now: power, glory, and even the wealthy Trina, whom he could only dream about when he was a poor boy. He was strong as steel, Stal, Prince of Demons, and Trina was his Princess of Demons.

Far above the waters of the Sea of Abyss, upon the rising island forming for the Prince of Demons, a stairway made of stones twisted up from deep within the mountain, straight into the castle, which sat atop the mountain's peak. It was the only way into the castle from its dungeon below. It was a treacherous, serpentine path and spiked with slippery, jagged, moss-covered stairs. The path curved upward in unpredictable slashes and hairpin turns, with darkness that fell upon one's eyes and gave no warning. If just one step was missed, one would be plunged downward, back into the mountain's bowels. The one who now took the path knew this. No word of derision could describe a soul so drenched in maliciousness and for whom no redemption was possible. For what is crooked, it has been said, cannot be made straight. The creatures descending upon this island were evil beings whose weight of wickedness was such that even the vilest circles of hell, the Corkscrew of Terror, could not contain them. It was then that they were plunged beneath Kurnigi and into the Abyss of Blackness. Though many blackened souls had been imprisoned in the Abyss, among them was one who rose far above the others in his twisted machinations for power.

It was this one who now trod the path, headed into the castle, one whose evil came not with blows but in the soft whispers of persuasion. He called himself Del Consigliere: the Counselor. Moments before, he had been held prisoner within the bowels of a mountain, chained to a stone wall in a dark, damp chamber. How he had come to be imprisoned there was yet another refrain in the eternal song of treachery that was the way of life for those who lived in the Abyss. A song that played itself over and over, with captors and captives changing roles. There was no reality to it; it was a story that ran in an endless loop. So too had the Counselor been trapped in the never-ending boredom and nothingness of the Abyss.

When the quake had hit, the stone wall crumbled, and miraculously his bony hands slipped free from the shackles. The Counselor's eyes were long used to the darkness, where he had gazed upon nothingness for an eternity. The story had changed—and change did not occur in the Abyss. So it was with surprise and pleasure that he saw it: a path forming in quick strokes into a winding staircase. This was the path that his dirty bare feet trod, leaving bloody footprints in their wake. But to the Counselor, blood was nothing, for he had no mortal body, just the shell he once had held. The mountain had reverberated with the cries of creatures falling upon it. Within the Abyss of Blackness, the Counselor's chance had come, as Chaos had exploded Kurnigi open, from which the demons of old now rose, and this island had formed from the shattered bones of the seafloor. The Counselor wore the black robes of a medieval priest; a red collar ringed the neck, and his feet were shoeless— all contrivances to give the appearance of humility.

The Counselor was anything but humble. The head above his collar was the shape of an upside-down pear, with a thin down of hair covering his protruding chin. His eyes were dark, his nose aquiline. His was face pale and framed with flyaway wisps of hair. All of this gave him the appearance of a commonplace, even timid man. But underneath this benign monk-like aspect lay another form: a ferret face greedy for power. Behind the obsequious brown orbs was a haughty glare, sharp with condemnation. In his mortal form, the Counselor, considered himself an esteemed adviser to those great families who owned all the land, held all the wealth, and controlled the papacy—idiots one and all, he realized. Even now, at the memory of those who had held themselves superior to him in mortal form—even now, so many hundreds of years in Kurnigi and the Abyss later—a bile of bitterness rose in his throat. He was the one who was brilliant, insightful, prophetic, yet he was the one who had been tortured and then condemned to poverty by idiots. Despite this, in his mortal form, long after he was thrown into abysmal poverty and, even worse, obscurity, the Counselor couldn't contain his ideas. He was the Counselor, though there was no one to counsel. Nevertheless he wrote down his admonitions for those in power regarding how to keep it, from one who had lost it. The Counselor advised that they set their hearts cold and cruel, if dominion over others was ever to be fully theirs. In his mortal form, he had failed, for no one read his thoughts. And even now the clumsy hands of idiots incompetently continued to hold the reins of power.

As it was on earth, so it was in hell. In the depths of Kurnigi, the Counselor also had failed, tried as he had to become the Dark Master's trusted adviser. Then he had been hurled into the Abyss with twin awareness: of yawning eternal nothingness and the sharp longings of his mortal desires. Eventually the gloom of the Abyss gave way, as it always did, like a cruel dawn that presaged no morning. But it gave way to a gray light, and the

Counselor, like all those condemned there, found that it was land, sea, and space at times and, maddeningly, nothing at others. The Abyss was not under Marduk's dominion—it was under no one's dominion.

It was, in fact, an existential damnation, and those who had believed in their mortal lives that only nothingness existed after death—and had lived their lives in deceit and cruelty—were given this reality. It offered at times presence, as well as the lure of giving, to those marked souls, and they grasped at it. So it was that wars were spawned among the denizens of the Abyss, and fickle allegiances were formed there, where all were aware of their nothingness, their pointlessness.

The Counselor had been endlessly engaged in these meaningless conflicts. The conflicts continued on and on, unrelenting in their predictability; hands that clasped power one day were rendered to servitude the next. The awfulness of Kurnigi, where Marduk reigned supreme, paled by comparison. For though Kurnigi had its petty disciplines and harshness, there was an order to it; there was a substance that at least gave weight to some level of existence and offered the promise of more clout as one rose among the ranks of Marduk's henchmen. In the Abyss, however, there was only eternal emptiness and meaninglessness. There the Counselor had resided— sometimes winning but many times losing the pointless wars— always stabbed by the sharp need for power that never would be requited.

The Counselor's hopes now beat fast as he jumped up the stone steps with surprising alacrity: Marduk, the Dark Master, who had hurled him into the Abyss, could be overthrown! The cries of the creatures falling upon the island raised his sense of urgency. He, who was so brilliant, would be indispensable to the

prince. He must be the first one to greet the prince in the castle and immediately ingratiate himself into his inner circle. His
mark must be made upon this prince. The calls of those upon
the island echoed within the winding stone staircase: *The Prince
of Demons rises!* So, too, thought this one, as cunning and shrewdness flashed in his eyes, does his counselor.

𒀭𒈾𒊩𒀭𒉌

A roiling blackness emerged within the darkening crimson
sky of the Abyss. It spread like an omen over the creatures of the
Abyss, most of whom were now at the perimeter of the castle,
although some stragglers were scrambling up mountain path.
Then, from the dark cloud, a sharp black streak shot out. It took
the shape of two large deadly talons of a predatory bird. Then it
moved straight toward Stal, who still sat upon his three-headed
dragon horse. In moments the giant talons dug into Stal's shoulders and lifted him off his steed. Stal cried out in surprise and
struggled against the hold, brandishing the Saber of Shadows
against the force that carried him up. But it was to no avail;
Stal was as powerless as a rodent in the clutch of a bird of prey.
Quickly receding below him was the landscape of the island and
the throngs of horrible creatures upon it.

Suddenly the Sky of the Abyss exploded, and from it emerged
the Four Terrors, those demons gods and goddesses of destruction, tribulation, confusion, and conflict: Nergal, Namatar,
Lamashtu, and Zaltu. They were one part of the triad of the forgotten mighty ones. They formed around Stal, whom the talons
held in the sky. A hushed silence filled the land of the Abyss,
broken only by the shouts of the Prince of Demons, his red eyes

glowing in confusion and anger at this humiliation. Below him the creatures of the Abyss surrounded the castle.

The castle doors flung open. The three-headed dragon horse no longer bore the Prince of Demons. The beast reared up on its back legs, its great black wings flapping, green flames spewing from its three mouths, and bearing only a frail female spirit, whose eyes were wide with fear.

𒀯𒀭 𒉽 𒀭 𒁹

The Counselor's bare feet hurriedly slapped the mottled gray castle floor. His black robes, with their red collar that ringed the neck, mimicking the collar of a medieval priest, fluttered around his thin body. His wisps of mouse-colored hair gave him the appearance of weakness, of an underling whose only desire was to serve. But as those the Counselor betrayed would ruefully come to know, his benign, monk-like aspect only thinly veiled his rodent face. It was his eyes that revealed his greed for power. The Counselor's sharp eyes now calculated the scene. He was in the castle's hall, a large rectangular room with enormous vaulted ceilings, beams blackened by fire, tattered tapestries hanging on its walls and telling tales of horror, and candles that flickered upon the stone walls in long shadows of gloom. In the dim, candle-lit hall, the Counselor's narrow face held a greenish sheen as his mind plotted his ascension. His mind took in the voluminous size of the castle. All of this meant one thing for the Counselor: the castle had risen to house the Prince of Demons not by chance. No, thought the Counselor, it rose in response to this prince's longing to be not just in power but one of the elite.

In short, the Counselor concluded, the castle told of the prince's deep yearning to be obeyed and admired, as befitting supreme nobility. It spoke to the Counselor as well of the prince's mortal background: this one had not held power in the land of the living; no, this one must have been trod upon—an ego that the Counselor would be only too able to stroke, to mold and manipulate to his needs. So it must be that the Prince of Demons was merely a puppet, controlled by he who held the strings: the Counselor. The Counselor's thin lips held a small smile. But just as quickly, his features adjusted themselves to their proper respect. He must become the prince's confidant at once.

Marchio del consigliere, he whispered to himself. *The prince must bear the mark of the Counselor.*

The Counselor's thoughts were broken by the sounds of hurrahs rising outside the castle. The prince had come! The vibrations pounded through the floors of the castle hall and shook the Counselor's body; it was the hooves of the prince's beast, striking the cobblestoned road. They were fast moving toward the castle. The castle seemed empty, but a sound, small and rustling, moved through it, soft as a slight wind. The Counselor suddenly knew he wasn't alone; evil spirits were held everywhere in this castle. Indeed bitterness was everywhere in the Abyss, for everything in it held a story of dreams lost when evil took hold. The floor stung his soles. The Counselor recognized immediately that it was the jealous barbs of the spirits that were trapped in the floors. Soon too it would be filled with creatures of the Abyss, who would rush in to curry favor with the Prince of Demons. The Counselor scurried across the floor toward a giant, heavy, wooden-planked door. It flung open at his touch. Then the cloying stench of death filled his nostrils.

The Counselor quickly moved away from the open door to a corner of the great hall. He peered through a narrow slit between the walls of the castle and confirmed that it was indeed as he had feared: the Four Terrors had arrived. He had studied the story of the Asaru-alim-nuna: how they had first tempted man to relinquish free will and clasp the hand of evil; how they had been used by Marduk to overcome his mother, Tiamet; and how they were betrayed by Marduk, who had imprisoned them in Kurnigi's dark tunnels. So it was true, the Counselor saw, that the Asaru-alim-nuna had been plunged into the Abyss by Marduk, but with the chaos in the cosmos, it would seem they were rising in strength. The Counselor's eyes narrowed in thought as he took in the scene from within the castle. How would the Prince of Demons fall under his control with the Asaru-alim-nuna present?

𒀸𒊒𒀉𒁹𒀸𒊒𒀱

Outside the castle, in the darkening crimson sky of the Abyss, the Four Terrors flew around the Prince of Demons; it was they who had formed the giant talons in which he was now clasped.

The Four Terrors roared for their brethren cave gods to appear:

> *Rise, my brother fiends! Rise, my sister devils!*
> *Winds of hell blow; rains of terror fall!*
> *Cave gods, demons of old, it is to you we call!*

The old demon gods erupted in the sky and swarmed like locusts around the Four Terrors. So many were they—thousands upon thousands—that their shapes were obscured. They formed and merged, thick and black. Their stench was heavy, and their chants, sung in ancient tongues, told of grisly sacrifices. Then too came the cave gods; stick figures they were, but power they held, for they too had been given mortal souls as sacrifices, when man was more beast than man.

Within the castle, the crafty Counselor took note: only two of the triad of the forgotten mighty ones were present: the Four Terrors, as well as their demon brethren and the more-ancient demon cave gods of primitive man. Where were the serpent-shark gods? The Counselor turned over the information in his calculating mind: the serpent-sharks, the oldest of the demon gods—they from whom the Counselor, in his mortal form, had taken his power; they who held man's deep, primeval fear, one he had used to manipulate other mortals—did not appear. Why? It spoke of a point of weakness of the Asaru-alim-nuna, the Counselor understood at once, and stored this nugget of knowledge in his mind. Too, the Asaru-alim-nuna drew power from the worship of mortals and had fallen to dust when no mortal offered sacrifices to them. Though the Asaru-alim-nuna had been freed from Marduk's imprisonment in the caves of Kurnigi, then thrown into the Abyss, the dark underworld still shook in chaos.

Who would ultimately rule Kurnigi? Marduk still did, but for how long? Would it be the Asaru-alim-nuna? The Counselor's eyes narrowed. No mortals had uttered their names for eons; no mortals had made sacrifices to the Asaru-alim-nuna. No mortal feared them as man still feared Marduk.

The Four Terrors, as befitting their status as demon gods of destruction and tribulation, shouted their tale in fearsome beats so that all of the Abyss would bow to them in utter obedience. The Four Terrors were indeed to be feared by the creatures of the Abyss as demons of confusion and conflict. Were they not once so feared that the sound of their names—Nergal, Namatar, Lamashtu, and Zaltu—shook mortal man in fear? The Four Terrors flew about the fading crimson sky, surrounded by the swarm of their demon brothers and sisters. Their faces shook the sky with fog, fire, and pestilence to show the creatures of the Abyss their might.

Their sounds thundered through the gruesome landscape below:

Hear this, dead souls of the Black Abyss!
Chaos in the cosmos has freed us.
Rulers of the Abyss are we, and you will heed us!
No longer are we held within Marduk's hold,
For Kurnigi lies in dust, its fiery embers cold.
Struck and beaten was Marduk. Sway and tumble did he,
As we struck his serpent servant, as we slashed the Sebitti!
Marduk reigns dimly as the lord of the waning Kurnigi!

Murmurs of anger rose among the creatures of the Abyss at the arrogance of the Asaru-alim-nuna. And those who had newly escaped from Marduk's imprisonment in the tunnels of Kurnigi, only to be plunged into the Abyss, bristled. How were these Asaru-alim-nuna different than them? All had once been prisoners of Kurnigi. To the longtime denizens of the Abyss, the Asaru-alim-nuna's words echoed of empty threats and hubris. For they were nothing but new spirits to the Abyss, these forgotten devils, whose names were unknown to many of the demon spirits in the Abyss—unknown to them even when they had been in mortal skins and had walked in the land of the living. The murmurs grew louder against the outrage of the Asaru-alim-nuna's arrogance. Who were they, these Asaru-alim-nuna? Nothing but long-forgotten demons.

Now these demon spirits dared to hold their prince, he who had been prophesized to rise and free them; their prince was held like a rat within the clutches of the talons formed by these Asaru-alim-nuna. "We bow only to our master, the Prince of Demons!" the creatures of the Abyss shouted in defiance.

The Asaru-alim-nuna thundered against the anger of the creatures of the Abyss:

Listen, dark and banished souls!
Hear the ringing winds and the roiling seas.
Hear the drumbeat! Hear the rolls,
As they tell for whom the bell tolls.
It is for Marduk; listen, as the story will soon be told
You will fight the battle; you will win the war.
So that Kurnigi will fall under the Asaru-alim-nuna's hold,
Risen have we again, the demon gods of old.
Asaru-alim-nuna! Asaru-alim-nuna! Not forgotten but mighty and bold.
Bend you shall to our will.
Into the land of the living, you will travel to kill.
Take then, shall you, mortal souls into our hold!
Bow to Asaru-alim-nuna!
Asaru-alim-nuna! Asaru-alim-nuna! Not forgotten but mighty and bold.

The creatures of the Abyss raised a primeval sound, a howl that was jagged with fury, a sound that carried the sharp marks of their opposition. The old demons' fight with Marduk was not theirs. Too, they knew Marduk was still mighty, despite the bragging of the old demon gods of their triumph, for who else but Marduk would have plunged the Asaru-alim-nuna into the Black Abyss? No one came to the Abyss freely.

The creatures shouted back, "We come for the Prince of Demons, not you old forgotten devils! Release the Prince of Demons!"

One among them, who wore a tarnished, blood-spattered gold mask of an ancient king, strode forward and struck his long staff at the sky. "It is for the Prince of Demons who rises that we bow. You are forgotten demons of old, Asaru-alim-nuna. You were never mortals but foes of Marduk. You waged a battle to control the dead and lost. And then you were lost and forgotten in the eons. You are *not* our rulers. Your fight is *not* ours."

The creatures of the Abyss echoed their assent. Some jumped up to try to reach the prince and free him from the talons. Others slapped long poisonous tongues into the sky. Still others hurled their ancient spears at the Asaru-alim-nuna.

"Old forgotten devils! Release the Prince of Demons! Release the Prince of Demons!" their cries shot up.

The Four Terrors laughed derisively as they flung off the spears of the creatures of the Abyss and bore no marks from their poison.

The Prince of Demons is our puppet!
He moves as we say.
See how he sways.

As they said this, the talons swung Stal like captured rat. His red eyes glowed in anger at this humiliation by the Asaru-alim-nuna.

They had given him power, but now they wanted to show everyone they could take it right back. But these creatures of the Abyss had once been mortal souls, like Stal. And these devil gods, the Asaru-alim-nuna, Stal recognized, were like the old priests in the church, with their drooling, mumbling pronouncements, relegated to the periphery by the young, who controlled the pulpit.

The Four Terrors shouted over the hisses and boos of the creatures of the Abyss:

Strike and slay shall you the Dark Master Marduk dead!
Aim shall you your blows at his demon faces.
Cut shall you his long tresses; blind shall you his red orbs,
Until of the Dark Master and his fold there are no traces.

The cries of protest of the creatures of the Abyss grew. They countered in raised and angry voices, "Why should we fight a battle for the Asaru-alim-nuna against Marduk? Marduk will destroy us, and you will be nothing, as you still are. You are no one to us!"

Still the Four Terrors, surrounded by the old demon gods and cave gods, shouted over the protests:

Creatures of the Black Abyss!
Question not our power. Slain shall be Marduk of Kurnigi,
And his name no longer will be sworn.
Into obscurity we shall send him, tattered and torn.
As he once betrayed us, so shall be his fate.
Soon shall it be that the newly dead,
As they bow in surrender at Kurnigi's gate,
Will call out our name: Asaru-alim-nuna!
Call for us they will, as they whimper in the Land of Misery and Dread!

The dissent against the Asaru-alim-nuna grew strong on the serpentine path through the mountain, and the energy of opposition gained in force. "We come for the Prince of Demons!"

High above Stal, the energy of the creatures of the Abyss rose as a vibrating beam toward him and through him. In the clasp of the talons, he felt the old sting of humiliation at his position, clutched and flung about. He was the Prince of Demons! Anger simmered then brewed strongly in him—born of the years of his youth, of the endless taunts of the rich boys at the Georgian church school. His anger rose and rode through his torso, lit the pockmarks of his face, and pulsed through his arms to the black and blue thumbs. The black and blue thumbs, which held the power of dead souls, pulsed purple then blue then black in response. Stal held still, for anger had betrayed him with impulsive action in the past. He felt the strength of the force of the creatures below him join in the energy that pulsed through his anger into the thumbs.

The ancient king with the blood-spattered gold mask shouted, "The Prince of Demons is our Master! Only he who is one of us, once a mortal spirit, it is prophesized, will be the one to come upon a dragon horse and free us from the Abyss. For him and *only* him shall we rise in battle."

In response the Four Terrors—Nergal, Namatar, Lamashtu, and Zaltu—shook the sky in anger. These trifling creatures would soon see and respect their might. Nergal, whose locks of flames burned all hope, shot out great licks of flame that enveloped the creatures of the Abyss.

Creatures of the Black Abyss!
Bow to us as rulers of the Abyss and heed us!

The creatures of the Abyss were long used to pain. Although Nergal's flames rose high, the creatures could not be consumed by the waves of fire, for the fire was an illusion that quickly turned to smoke. Then Namatar, with the stink of death and disease, raised boils and blisters upon the bodies of the creatures of the Abyss, which rose upon their bodies but quickly disappeared. Then Zaltu, with her long gray locks flowing like a fog of confusion, swirled as the old demon gods swarmed like stinging locusts upon the creatures of the Abyss, but this fog also disappeared into wisps. Then Lamashtu bared her bloody teeth and formed the face of a wolf. She hurled sharp talons of fear that spun like small snakes and stung those below but melted as soon as they hit the land.

Up and down the mountain, the creatures of the Abyss laughed mightily at the stupidity of these old devils. The Asaru-alim-nuna didn't know this: the punishment of the Abyss was that no battle was real; no win existed; no one triumphed. It was all meaningless. Nothingness.

The creatures of the Abyss cried out, "We feel not your punishments, old devils. We bow not to you but the Prince of Demons!"

And those who had fallen from Kurnigi shared in the laughter, for they too had been mortal spirits and had sold their souls and sworn their allegiance to their new brethren, the creatures of the Abyss. They joined the creatures of the Abyss against the Asaru-alim-nuna, their shouts rising in strength.

The one with blood-spattered gold mask spoke. "Hear this, Asaru-alim-nuna! You hold no power here, plunged into the land of the long forgotten. Corpses of souls are we. And know too that mortal man has forgotten you. Marduk, who has many names, still strikes fear in the blood of mortals. He still wins their souls as they tremble in his shadow of death."

The land below erupted with sounds as the Asaru-alim-nuna swirled about the sky, weakened and enraged. These old demons held power only as long as mortals feared them, gave sacrifices to them, and gave their souls to them. But these Asaru-alim-nuna were long forgotten by mortal man—unlike Marduk, whose many names invoked fear in nearly all mortals. The Asaru-alim-nuna could not wage battle against Marduk in the land of the living, for they were never mortal, and they needed spirits that were once mortal to invade the minds of the living with fear. They needed those who bowed to evil in the land of the living; those who feared Marduk, he who was known by a thousand names over the eons in the land of the living. They needed those, who, like the creatures of the Abyss, when they had worn their mortal skins, had done Marduk's deeds for earthly wealth, fame, and power in exchange for their souls—mortal souls captured in thought, in dreams, then in deed by the evil spirits of the once living.

Stal's black and blue thumbs surged with power as the creatures of the Abyss rose against the Asaru-alim-nuna. The old demons had forgotten that Stal's soul had been sold not to them but to Marduk. His subjects, the creatures of the Abyss, their souls sold to the Devil, were just like him: mortals once. Their cries to him rang loudly in his ears. He, Stal, was more powerful than these old demon gods! They held him in their talons only because he thought they did. When Stal's red eyes blazed with this realization, the talons upon his back disappeared. Freed from their clutches, he jumped from the sky directly onto the dragon horse beneath him, the quaking Trina still upon it.

He shouted, "Behold, I rise. Stal, the Prince of Demons!" and slashed the Sword of Deception to the triumphant cries of the creatures of the Abyss.

All the old devils and cave gods faded into the sky until only the Four Terrors remained. They vowed revenge for the defiance of the creatures of the Abyss.

Creatures of the Abyss! Prince of Demons! Hear ye!
Holders of both Tablets of Twin Destiny
Asaru-alim-nuna will be!
These curses we place upon you,
Creatures of the Abyss.
Defiant to the Mighty Ones, you go amiss.
Fogs of confusion, fires of fury, boils, and stings
Will be what your future brings.
Pockmarked prince, riding upon the dragon horse with raven wings,
No more prince but pauper will you be.
Like a cockroach will you scurry
Upon the dust of Kurnigi.

The Asaru-alim-nuna faded into the red sky, their curses drowned in the shouts of glee and triumph of the creatures of the Abyss as the Prince of Demons rode toward the castle.

𒂥𒅋𒌋 � 𒂥𒅋 𒀀

Trina felt the pressure of Iosif's body against her. She was pinned between him and the three-headed dragon as they rode toward a looming castle in this hell beneath hell. No, he was no longer Iosif, the small, pockmarked, beaten-down son of their washerwoman, Keke. No, this Iosif, who had shouted that he was Stal, was truly one of hell's creatures, the leader of these others, whose faces reflected the many shades of evil of the Abyss.

There was no escape, even when Stal had been lifted up from the dragon beast and flung around in the air. For then the creatures of the Abyss had risen strong against those forgotten gods of old. She heard them call to him, "Prince of Demons!" Then this Stal, this Prince of Demons, was upon the beast again.

Trina's body flung against the leathery neck of the three-headed dragon-beast—better this evil beast than to have Stal's form against her—as it strode toward the enormous doors of the castle. How to escape this Abyss? Now she feared for the spirit children. Had they also been thrown here, into the blackness below hell? Trina's heart ached for them—poor children, whose night terrors had opened the door to the robbing of their souls by the spirits of the Land of Darkness. Spirit children, little ones with faces filled with wonder, skin the color of caramel, eyes as black as pebbles; others with hair the color of ravens, skin black and like a velvet night; some with hair the color of cornfields, eyes blue like the sky; some with faces ruddy, faces white, faces of yellow, eyes the shape of almonds. These children had succumbed to the Reaper in sleep, in illness, in greed. How could Trina now escape the Abyss? For through the darkness of Kurnigi and then the journey of the Seven Tears—that was their only way to light. She stilled her thoughts to hear the spirit children, but she did not feel their presence, did not hear their voices call to her. They were not in the Abyss; of that she was certain. Relief filled her. But she must escape this Abyss and find them. She must lead her spirit children in the Journey of the Seven Tears.

The song played in her mind, its notes long and mournful.

Seven days is our
Journey from body to spirit
Until the cold breath leaves us.

Seven times our souls
Should be kindled.
Seven tears shall we shed
Until we weep no more.
Seven steps must we take
Until we are freed
from this sad land of the benighted,
Until we see the starlight
Dancing upon our mother's brow.

Then and only then could Trina allow herself to think about for whom her heart beat the strongest: her *muktablu*. How he had stubbornly run toward her when the Abyss had splintered the ground, when she had cried to him to stay back. How her heart's stirrings awakened the aching memory of their endless love, played in lifetimes over and over—love found and always love lost. She wondered at the lifetimes they must have had together, knowing them as one recalls a dream: misty, fleeting images that confused the soul. She wondered at how she had grown to womanhood in that moment. The yellow-haired *muktablu* also had grown into manhood, his form tall, his face achingly handsome. *Her beloved.*

Then Trina heard it, the far-off sound of her *muktablu* calling to her: "Trina!"

"No!" she gasped.

O pray do I, my loving warrior, that it is not true!
O pray do I that you step upon the land of the living,
For no mortal can pass through this Abyss!
I beseech you, O Great Spirit of Light, high above!
Though I have been cast to the Abyss, my spirit swallowed in darkness,
Let not my fate fall upon my dear love!

She felt the brush of Stal's face against her neck. He was whispering something: "My Princess of Demons." Revulsion vibrated through her. Then fear.

𒀭𒌋 𒂍 𒀭𒌋 𒀸

Behind the castle's stone walls, peering through a long narrow window, the wily Counselor readily perceived which way the wind blew: Asaru-alim-nuna had no power in the Abyss. He watched with glee as they faded, filling the air with their empty curses. The cheers of the creatures of the Abyss calling forth the prince were deafening. The pockmarked Prince of Demons, his face slashed with conceit, the Counselor noted, was riding in circles of triumph. The wings of his three-headed dragon beast slapped the air in glory as the creatures of the Abyss pressed around him. The Counselor's keen eyes saw too that the saber, that weapon of darkness and deceit, though forged by the Asaru-alim-nuna, remained in the possession of the Prince of Demons. It would have to be taken from him, for it was a weapon that held power, unlike the illusory ones forged in the endless battles of the Abyss. Oddly present, the Counselor thought, was the pale fragile beauty the pockmarked demon prince held tightly. Who this was or what she meant to the prince, and if she should be destroyed, the Counselor concluded, would be known soon enough. Now the prince was turning his beast toward the castle's entrance. The Counselor decided it was time.

Quickly he lifted his thin, translucent hands and fluttered them hypnotically in front of his face. His lips emitted guttural sounds—sounds of the agony of tortured spirits, whose souls the Counselor had stolen in the moments before death. It was the symphony of death rattles of the many souls who fell to this evil one, gurgling from the Counselor's throat. It rocked his body back and forth, and his eyes rolled back. His body writhed in pain. Then his drab brown monk robe disappeared, leaving the bare body of a man but covered with thin black fur. His angular face turned into that of a snarling creature with sharp teeth. From his backside grew a long rodent tail.

His body bent, he shook with tremors, threw back his head, and in a guttural voice whispered, "*Magna coronat!*" The Counselor was calling forth the crown, the *magna coronat,* for the coronation of the Prince of Demons. This *magna coronat* would be a circle of the purest gold upon which glittered diamonds and rubies. *Il Principe* were would be the words that these diamonds and rubies would form. Then, he the Counselor would meekly place upon the Prince of Demons, this crown. For he whose crown was upon the Prince controlled him And it must be the Counselor's. The Counselor's face wore the dismay that his yelp sounded at the shape of his *magna coronat.* It was not the Counselor's *magna coronat,* that formed. Instead, upon his hands appeared a mockery of a papal crown: peaked and golden, embroidered with glittering diamonds, with the inscription "*Il Principe.*" He uttered a sound, a deep growl of displeasure. He knew at once that his spell had been overcome.

Now the castle's architects were revealed. It was the Unholy Trio, the Tarnished Knights. They had been condemned deep into the Abyss for their hypocrisy. These knights had once worn the white tunics of the holy and had claimed to crusade for God, but instead they had clutched to their hearts man's base desires for wealth, glory, and worse still, indulged in acts of depravity. They had been fearsome in their mortal forms; now in the Abyss, the Unholy Trio of Tarnished Knights were the high priests of the unrighteous and rarely showed themselves. But their presence was felt, and even the Counselor knew they weren't to be trifled with. The Counselor saw their intent: the Prince of Demons was to be crowned the Unholy One and controlled by the Unholy Trio.

His rodent face bared his long teeth in anger. But the power that formed the *magna coronat* was his, culled and given strength from his own evil machinations. It was not for the Tarnished Knights to control. He flicked his tail. The Counselor's body transformed instantly back into the form of the humble, servile monk. Turning toward the open doors of the castle, he positioned himself, preparing for the entrance of the prince. It was imperative that the Counselor crowned the pockmarked one and brought him under his control. Then it would be that the *marchio del consigliere*, the mark of the Counselor, would be worn by he who bore this crown; the Tarnished Knights might have controlled the form of the *magna coronat*, but its substance held the power of his incantation. And whoever wore the crown answered to the Counselor. He bent down on one knee, his head bowed in servitude, though the wily one also felt the anticipation of power behind the scenes rising in his evil spirit. He would be the puppeteer controlling the prince.

The Counselor's face bore a thin sardonic smile. He bowed his head low and stretched out his arms, with the *magna coronat* held out.

O most-high prince. The Counselor's lips began to form the words as he heard only the pounding of the hooves of the three-headed dragon beast with black wings bearing the prince as he crossed the threshold of the castle.

CHAPTER 10

the hidden sister

The *Condemned Ship of the Outlaws of Hell* splintered against the unrelenting black rocks on the island's shore. The explosion reverberated in Eddie's ears as an endless ringing of bells, the force of it catapulting him through the air. Eddie held the warrior spear tightly with both hands, while the scythe remained firmly tied to his back. Instinctively he assumed an airborne position in order to land upon his haunches. He pulled the spear horizontally to his chest. Though he kept his eyes open, night surrounded him, blinding him in its blackness as he dropped. Eddie braced himself for the anticipated pain of falling against jagged rocks. But when his combat boots hit the ground, the impact was soft. The land was flat, and the air around him was humid. Eddie widened his eyes against the darkness, which was relieved only by the green flame of the warrior spear. He jumped up from his crouched position and jabbed the spear in the air, rotating it in anticipation of the enemy combatants coming forward. Death's scythe vibrated in warning to its master: *Beware.*

Silence greeted Eddie in response. He was alone. And in what appeared to be a cave. Where were his three platoons of demon sailors?

The spear's tip of light showed him the contours of the cave: its roof was low. He held the spear vertically to measure the height of the cave, knowing that the spear was eight feet in length. It just touched the roof of the cave, the flame flickering against the rocks that formed the ceiling. Beneath Eddie's boots, a liquid was bubbling up from the ground. He felt the gooey fluid rising, reaching his ankles, moving past the tops of his combat boots. The stench of it reached his nostrils, and it drove through his soul. This place was a cesspool of depravity and terror. The closeness of the space and its smell tightened around him. *Stay focused. Get intel.* Eddie felt the roof of the cave as a presence pressing down on him, its outlines flickering under the spear's light. It was just a little less than two feet above his head. *I guess I'm just a little over six feet tall,* he thought. *Just like Dad.* That realization sharpened his awareness. His father would be gathering information about his surroundings, would have already implemented plan B. Eddie kept the spear up. *Don't let fear hold you,* he reminded himself. Then he heard Trina's voice, loud and clear, as it sliced through his mind: *O my noble warrior! O my beloved muktablu!* He called to her through the vibrations in his mind. *Trina! Tell me where you are!* But no voice responded. She was here. That was all that mattered. Her presence surrounded him. He *would* find her.

The pounding of thousands of footsteps reverberated through the cave. *It must be the creatures I saw falling on the island, where Trina was.* The cave began to shake. Small stones then large ones rained like mortars upon Eddie. He held his arms up to move the spear above him, against the onslaught, but it was of little help. The stones hit him hard and pushed him down to the wet ground of the cave. The stench pressed in upon him. The walls of the cave seemed to be moving toward him, sandwiching him in. Soon he would be buried. Was there a way out? Eddie crouched further, lowering into the very earth of the cave, as the stones rained upon him; there was no way out that he could see. He moved the warrior spear up vertically. The scythe vibrated against his back under the rain of the falling stones. Eddie flickered his eyes open and shut to ward against the dust and small sharp stones. *Tunnels hold hidden secrets, turns and places that can kill.* Eddie knew this from his father. Vietnam was full of tunnels that held dark places of death. The closeness of the cave was filling Eddie with claustrophobia. Its spell was powerful: anxiety rose in his veins, mixing with despair and hopelessness. He was on his haunches. His back, upon which the scythe was tied, took the brunt of the falling rocks.

Eddie lowered his head even more, keeping his body in a bent position, as he continued to hold the warrior spear upright. The cave shook, unleashing a torrential rain of sharp-edged rocks that struck his head and body. They piled around and over him. Eddie crouched farther and farther into the muddy ground of the cave. He felt the rocks pressing against him like a coffin; they rained upon him relentlessly and were soon up to his neck. He was immobile. Dankness surrounded him. The evil spell of the cave entered his heart and filled it with tendrils of despair. *There's no way out! I'm going to be buried alive!* His heart pounded. *A warrior's will is only broken by the warrior himself,* he heard his father say. *You're only defeated when you surrender.* The words moved against the black spell of the cave. Eddie shouted against defeat, "My will is not broken! My will is strong! I am not surrendering!" He felt the pinpricks of an energy, a force, move through his hand and into the warrior spear. It surged against the weight of the rocks that were packed around it. Then the spear moved out of Eddie's hand. It moved with weightlessness, like a feather, and formed over him in the darkness of the cave. Eddie was still crouched, with only his head visible.

The dust of falling rocks filled the cave. Still his eyes, those that held the filament of Gilgamesh's mortal soul, saw it. A light. The green light of the tip of the spear flickered over him. *Move into the light* were the last words he heard as blackness blanketed his consciousness.

𒈗 𒂊 𒈗 𒁹

It was not darkness but a sparkling, gleaming, green glow that filled Eddie's consciousness as he woke up on the forest-ringed shore. His eyes cleared, but his head was woozy. Where was he? For though he could perceive his surroundings, he couldn't perceive himself. Was he still alive? He felt his heart beating and had an awareness that he was in a physical body. It was like a dream awareness, though, a distant memory dawning brightly. A glistening emerald lake appeared and glittered in front of him. In the middle of the lake, he saw her. She rose from the water like a song, her body tall and slender, her long tresses the color of sunbeams, her face the light green of a new leaf, her eyes the purple of amethyst. Though her hair wasn't chestnut brown, nor her eyes hazel, Eddie knew her at once. *Trina. Trina. Trina.* His heart jumped in elation. The notes of his love for her rang again and again as the beats of the heart. The memory of who he was faded from his consciousness as Trina in her true form filled his vision, and he too began to change. Eddie's body changed as the memory of Eddie

Petersen faded, and the person he was now at the shore of the lake rose strongly. As he ran toward the lake, his muscular brown arms were outstretched as she disappeared into the green waters. He shook his long braided black hair and, through his dark eyes, saw in surprise that the beauty in the waters had gone.

She moved through the water like a fish. As she rose to its surface, she saw that upon the shores of the emerald lake was a mortal man with his arms outstretched toward her. This man was tall and strong; his chest was bare; and he wore the skin of a spotted deer as his garment. His long hair was the deep black of the darkest night and braided with the feathers of the owl, the eagle, and the hawk. His skin glistened the color of the brown earth after rain. His dark eyes beheld her with enchantment as she walked out of the water onto the shore. The man held out his hand to her—a hand that told a tale of hardship. When she touched it, she felt the roughness of his fingers, calloused with the tribulation borne by all mortals. She saw his strength in his body, which spoke of battles won. She saw how his face carried courage and honor as she held his gaze. She was enchanted.

His voice was low and strong as he called her name, "Sister of Light." For she was clad in a flowing gown of golden light, its very threads made of rays of sunshine. He spoke in a tongue in which the words rose like the wind, but when they fell from his lips, it was like a gentle rain that showered her.

The Sister of Light listened, but it was with amethyst eyes that she took him in. Her heart, a thing of which she hadn't known before, fluttered. She raised her hand and touched his face. She felt its contours and its texture: the high cheekbones, the leathery roughness of his skin. She took in his scent, the muskiness of the earth, the freshness of the pines, the sweetness of spring flowers waving in the meadows.

"Mortal man," the Sister of Light said.

"Sister of Light," he replied, his face alit with love.

The man showed the Sister of Light the land he held sacred. She saw for the first time the things of the earth: the black mountains that reached in splendor toward the sky; the tall and wondrous trees of the forest, their leaves rustling the song of love. In the golden morning light, she saw the great eagles soar above them against a dark blue sky. In the afternoon, she watched as her mortal man fished the emerald lake. As the day darkened to dusk, they sat by a fire, which her mortal man had built upon the shore. Then they stood, and he held her tightly in his arms. She placed her palms on his chest and felt the rhythm of his beating heart, which sang his love for her. And so the Sister of Light returned the mortal's love with her own trembling heart. But then the rhythms of the heart of her cherished one began to slow. Her eyes, those eyes of glimmering amethyst, saw her beloved's fate unfold before her: that he would grow old and wither and die before the night was done.

The Sister of Light cried in anguish, "Oh, why do you die, my love, my mortal man?"

And her mortal man said, as his hair turned the white of the first snow, and his eyes grew the rheumy blue of the old…her mortal man said with sadness, "All things of this earth live and die, and so it is as well for me, my beloved."

But the Sister knew not of death, other than as the land where her Dark Brother ruled, for she was divine and lived eternally. She shed tears of despair, which her mortal man wiped gently with his fingers. "Cry not, my love," he said. "Let us be happy in that which we can have and not despair for that which is impossible."

The Sister of Light felt her heart breaking as the darkness of the night deepened upon the shores of the emerald lake. The time her mortal love had been allotted upon earth would soon be over. She held his body, now wracked with age, his eyes shutting out life. She felt the heart that beat within him, its rhythms broken; in starts and fits it came.

"Oh, why does mortal man die?" she cried out again, holding her beloved as his heart beat slower and slower. This time her cry was heard—heard by a creature, a lower-spirit creature who had been both revered and reviled then forgotten by mortal man; she was trapped in the form of a bird.

"Eeeawa," this spirit bird cried out from the forest.

The mortal man, lying on the shore upon his love's breaking heart, caught sight of the bird: Anza of the Land of the Dusk, fluttering about in the canopy of leaves above them. Anza was a small bird with feathers of gray and gold, and her song only brought bitterness to those who listened. *Beware the Anza bird as you take your steps toward the journey of the night,* the mortal man had heard as a boy from the old wise ones as they readied for their journey into the spirit world. The feathers of Anza of the Land of Dusk wore the stains of deceit while she waited for her prey in the limbo world between the gods and demons. Anza was a thing of trickery.

"Eeeawa," the bird sang, and her voice filled the mortal man with terror. He struggled to warn his beloved of this bird.

For the bird, Anza, was of the Land of Dusk, yet here she fluttered above them in the land of the living. The mortal man saw how the bird's eyes looked at the Sister of Light with cunning and knew at once that she sought to trick his beloved. The mortal man tried to form the words, "Beware, my love."

"*Eeeawa,*" the bird sang again.

"Who is it who speaks now?" the Sister of Light said, catching the warble of the bird but not her words.

Anza's thoughts were indeed upon the Sister of Light. Her sharp eyes were ever watchful for her opportunity, for all knew how weak willed the Sister was and how she, so naïve, held in her hands the Tablet of Destiny of Light. Anza knew that the Sister, away from the Mother Tiamat, could be persuaded through trickery to relinquish the Tablet of Destiny of Light. But until now the Sister always had remained protected by the Mother in the Milky Trail of Stars. Then, in the battle between good and evil, when light had dimmed, Anza saw that the Sister of Light had tumbled out of the Milky Trail of Stars and wandered into the Garden of Dusk, before falling into the emerald lake in the land of the living. This bird spirit, Anza, had followed her, flying behind the Sister of Light, down from the land between darkness and light, on the Dusky Path into the land of the living. So it was that Anza, hidden within leaves of the forest, had watched and waited. She saw how upon the shores of the emerald lake the Sister of Light had fallen in love with the mortal man.

In the tree where she was perched, the tricky Anza saw the Sister's amethyst eyes brim with tears as her palms lay flat upon the chest of her beloved in despair of his impending death. Purple tears ran down her face, which was the color of new spring grass. They flowed in rivulets until her face was stained in sorrow.

As the darkness descended blacker, Anza flew near the ear of the weeping Sister and whispered, "Why is it you cry so, Sister?"

The mortal man willed his heart to beat again. But he had no strength to form the words to warn his beloved, for the pulse of life was almost gone. He could not leave his beloved to this creature. Then the mortal man cried from within to give the only thing he had. "Spirit of Darkness! My soul I trade to you, that I may remain here to protect my beloved."

The mortal man felt his spirit rise from within toward darkness, but it was stopped because his heart was too pure to be held by evil and stayed within him. The mortal man's distress was great. His eyes were dimming, as the evening shores of the emerald lake were now just shadows. His lips formed a warning: "This one you must not heed. Please beware, my love." But no longer did the sound rise sharply as the wind, for his heart was beating its last beats, and only puffs of air moved out of his withered lips.

The Daughter turned her head to the small bird and said, "Oh, see, little bird, how my love withers and dies? Oh, why does mortal man die?"

The little bird's eyes turned to the mortal man, whose hair was now wisps of white, his body bent and his face ashen. His eyes were sallow as death's shroud descended upon him.

The bird murmured feigned concern. "Mortal man lives not long upon the earth. This is true. But as to why, I do not know."

The Daughter now held the gaze of her love lying in her arms, his eyes nearing death, his body old and broken. Her heart was breaking fast, and she cried as her mortal love's life was falling rapidly away. "Oh, little bird, I cannot live in eternity without my love!"

The tricky bird again murmured, "Oh, Sister, but that I could help you."

The Sister of Light beseeched, "Oh, little bird, if you could, what I would not give you as a reward!"

Then the devious bird paused. "It is told that there is a Tree of Everlasting Life, that one leaf of this Tree placed upon the tongue of a mortal will make him eternal."

The Sister cried out, "Take me to this Tree!"

Her love, the mortal man who lay helpless and dying in her arms, stirred, for he knew and feared the evil of the little bird.

"My love," he whispered, the words again just small breaths of air with no sound, "listen not."

But the Sister only had ears for knowledge of the Tree of Everlasting Life. "Oh, my love, please live but a little longer. This little bird will take me to the Tree of Everlasting life, and I shall return with its leaf. Then you shall be immortal, and we will forever live in happiness."

The little bird fluttered its wings and spoke craftily. "But Sister, the price is mighty. For the owner of the Tree of Everlasting Life parts not cheaply with the leaves of immortality."

The Sister shook her hair of sunshine and said determinedly, "I am the Daughter of Tiamat. I can pay whatever the price is. Let us go now!"

The mortal man, old and dying, felt all the malevolence of the bird and pleaded, "My love, trust not this bird." But the again the Sister of Light did not hear the dying man's voice.

She gently placed him down upon a bed of soft grasses and whispered, "I will come back soon, my love, and upon your lips place the leaf from this Tree of Everlasting Life. Then we shall be together for eternity."

The mortal man struggled to protect his love, but his dying breath was feeble. His heart saw all that was to happen, but he could not warn his love.

He saw his love lift her arms up to fly and say to the little bird, "Which way is it we go?"

When Anza saw upon the Sister's palm the mark of the Tablet of Destiny of Light and knew it was hidden upon her breast, greed beat fast in the bird's heart. "This way," she said.

Anza flew up toward the Dusky Path. The Sister followed, flying fast behind her. Quickly they were in the Land of Dusk. Unbeknownst to the Sister, this bird had evil intentions, for the

Tree of Everlasting Life was not in the Garden of Dusk at all, and the Tree, which held the fruits of eternal life, was blocked from man's reach, with only one branch held by Utnapishtim, who was lost in a vast sea. All this the Sister knew not. Anza whispered an incantation, and before them appeared an enchanting Tree, glistening with lush green leaves and filled with fruit shimmering like blue gemstones: turquoise, the bright blue of lapis lazuli, and sapphires. The Sister ran to the Tree to pull a leaf from it, but the Tree became like mist. The little bird flew by the Sister, her wings beating deceit.

"Where did the Tree go?" the Sister cried. "I must return to my love quickly, else he shall be gone. Oh, help me little bird!"

Anza said cunningly, "You must take the Tablet of Destiny that lies close upon your breast and place it under the Tree. Then a leaf will fall into your fingers, and you can take it to your mortal love."

The Sister paused. *The Tablet of Destiny!* Her face was anguished, for many a time the Mother Tiamat had cautioned her against the trickery of her brother, Marduk, who wished to take the Tablet of Destiny of Light from her, and she had been warned never to remove it. The Sister hesitated, for although she didn't own the Tablet of Destiny, it was hers to guard.

Anza, seeing the Sister's hesitation, spoke rapidly and cunningly. "Oh, Sister, the owner of the Tree asks not to keep the Tablet of Destiny of Light but to have it at the base of the Tree to strengthen it. For when you take one leaf, only through the power of the Tablet of Destiny can he replace it with another. He asks for the tablet to stay there only for the time that you take the leaf to your mortal man. Then, when he too is immortal, you can return and retrieve it. I shall stay here to guard it for you."

The Tree suddenly reappeared.

The Sister felt relieved. "Oh, thank you, little bird! That I can do."

The Sister reached to her chest and pulled out the Tablet of Destiny. It was a thing of dazzling light, bright and golden. Carefully, the Sister laid it down at the base of the Tree.

She reached up, and a leaf fell onto her palm. The Sister then said to the little bird, who flitted by the tablet, "Please guard the tablet carefully while I go to my love."

The Sister held the leaf tightly in her hand and turned to the Dusky Path to return to her mortal love in the land of the living. She speedily flew through the waters and onto the shores of the emerald lake and found her mortal love, whereupon his last breath was upon his lips.

"Here, my love!" the Sister cried, as she placed the leaf in his mouth. But the leaf did nothing, for it had no power of eternal life.

This her mortal love knew. "Oh, my love, the evil bird has tricked you!" he whispered. He closed his eyes as the Sister cried in anguish.

Then the mortal man died. Now the Sister of Light held but the vessel of her love and wept. She placed him gently back upon the bed of grass, her eyes blurred with tears.

Though the mortal man's spirit was light and pure and would have soared to heaven, it was bound to his heart, which lay in heavy anguish for his love. He called to her again and stayed in his withered body, willing his soul to remain bound to the dead vessel, though he was to make the journey of the spirit into the stars. But this he could not do; he could not leave his beloved to be destroyed by the tricky Anza.

Despite his attempts, however, his spirit could not be stayed. It rose out of his body and moved around his beloved, crying, "Oh, my love! What have you done?"

The Sister of Light was deaf to her beloved's spirit. Nor did she see her love's presence, for it was no more than the slenderest threads of light. She knew she had to get the Tablet of Destiny back, and then somehow she would revive her love back to life.

The mortal man's spirit followed the Sister of Light as she ran swiftly to the Dusky Path and flew up to the Land of Dusk. He cried to her, "Oh, my love, that you had but known. Man's soul is like an eternal flame that never extinguishes. Oh, my love, you should have feared not!"

In the Land of Dusk, the Sister of Light saw the tricky bird flitting about the Tablet of Destiny, trying to take possession of it. But the tablet's size and force were such that the bird could not touch it.

The Sister now was upon the creature. "You evil bird!" she cried, and reached to snatch back the tablet from under the tree.

"Stay back, you stupid girl. The tablet is mine!" Anza then flew at the Sister.

Her feathers slapped the Sister of Light's face, leaving their marks upon each cheek and dusting them with sleep.

"Oh, my love!" the mortal man's spirit cried in despair as the Sister's slender body collapsed.

He quickly flew around his beloved, weaving a blanket of love to protect her, for he feared that if she were to fall upon the cursed Land of the Dusk, she might never rise. He wove his love around and around her until it held her aloft in a nest. Inside, she lay curled, her eyes shut in a deep, drugged slumber. His soul then hovered around his sleeping love.

Desperate to take the Tablet of Destiny, Anza, that evil bird, cried another incantation. For to be the owner of it, she had to have it upon her.

"I call you mine!" Anza cried, her feathers flapping hard, but the tablet didn't shrink.

It was too large to overcome, and she was too small to lift it and place it on her chest. Anza flew again and again, speaking incantations to make herself more substantial, but failed on every try.

Then the Land of Dusk shook, and the mortal man's spirit shook too; he feared that his weaving of love upon his beloved was too weak against the evil that shuddered the sky. For above them, the giant red orbs of the Dark Master Marduk filled the dusky sky.

Marduk now knew that the Tablet of Destiny lay unguarded and away from his sister, the Hidden Daughter of Tiamet. He shot his red-hot gaze upon the bird.

But Anza would not move away. "It is mine!" she cried.

Marduk laughed at the bird, his face ever changing into the thousand faces of the Devil. From his mouths shot flames that seared Anza's feathers, and she fell, still screaming, "It is mine!" The ram's horns that protruded from Marduk's fearsome head scratched the sky. Then he moved those horns, sharp and ragged, pointed at the ends, to pierce the Tablet of Destiny of Light.

Triumph, however, was not yet to be Marduk's. A great divine storm born of Mother Tiamat's breath rose against him with fierce, gusty winds that drove Marduk out of the Land of Dusk. The windstorm then lifted the unconscious Sister, cocooned in the mortal man's weaving of love, and into which moved the Tablet of Destiny of Light.

As Anza struggled on the ground, flapping her wings, she saw the tablet within the cocoon in the windstorm. She flew toward it, determined to claim it, screaming again and again, "It is mine! It is mine!"

Though the evil bird's feathers were torn asunder by the strength of the gale-force whirlwind, she penetrated the cocoon of the mortal man's weaving of love. Then Anza head and body, with its outstretched wings, hit the tablet. She fell unconscious. The bird's body fell into the robes of the Sister of Light, who was curled up in a drugged sleep as she reached up to hug tight the Tablet of Destiny of Light.

Then the spirit of the mortal man spun and was torn away from his beloved; he cried out but to no avail, for his soul was destined to move on.

The mortal man's soul, however, was stubborn. "O Great Spirit, part me not from the Lady of my Soul, whom I must protect," his spirit cried.

His soul hungered not to join the infinite but to be with his love. So it was that the mortal man's soul, that thing of shimmering light, spun up then moved not to the heavens but to a place where he would wait to be born and reborn again and again: a warrior in search of his maiden.

Mother Tiamat appeared from the milky stars, wearing her robes of gold, a crown of stars upon her head, to where her child lay sleeping in a tattered weaving of mortal love.

"O Daughter, heedless one, what have you done?" she cried, and turned with a fierce expression toward her demon son. "Marduk, I will battle you fiercely."

Tiamat put her hand up and swept away the storm. Her flowing robes of gold cast a mist, a transparent golden globe that enveloped the Tablet of Destiny, the Daughter, and Anza too. Marduk took on a monstrous form: ram's horns upon his head, a beard of black-and-orange vipers upon his face, his eyes flaming red with greed. He reached his devil hands toward the golden globe but couldn't penetrate its enchanted mist. He snarled at Mother Tiamat, whose hands held the globe as she flew upward to return to the milky stars.

Marduk cried out to the Great Spirit of the Universe, his head thrown back, the beard of snakes swinging mightily back and forth, his great arms thrust up toward the heavens:

O Great Spirit, stop you must Tiamat in her flight!
For you decreed two Tablets of Destiny: one of darkness
and one of light,
So that the souls of mortals belonged by their choice to heaven or hell.
Only when secured in the hands to which they were given
Did the Twin Tablets remain as two,
As you, Great Spirit, decreed. Is that not true?

I ask, O Great Spirit, has this Sister, this Daughter of Tiamat,
guarded it well?
She who put one mortal man above all and rang the Tablet of Light's
death knell?

A tempest blew upon the Land of Dusk and shook it. The Mother Tiamat was held back in the air. Marduk too was pushed back. Then the sky split into two halves: one filled with the golden goodness of the Mother Tiamat and the other with the evil darkness of Marduk.

Tiamat felt the displeasure of the Great Spirit as the answer shook the air.

Tiamat, your son, the Dark Master Marduk, speaks the truth,
For your Daughter holds the love of one mortal
Higher than the fates of all.

Marduk's face glimmered in satisfaction. Tiamat bowed her head then spoke.

O Great Spirit, I have chosen poorly for man's fate.
In one hand placed did I the Destiny of Darkness
In he who now embodies evil and hate.
In the other hand placed did I the Destiny of Light
In she who is weak and naïve in trait.
But O Great Spirit, I beseech thee!
Punish not mortal man for my folly: let his will still be free!

Marduk then protested:

O Great Spirit, I ask your blessing divine
To take the Tablet of Light that is now rightly mine!

The Great Spirit spoke again, the voice ringing like thunder.

Tiamat, your Daughter shall remain the holder.
Should Marduk find again unguarded the Tablet of Light,
It shall be Marduk's as his right.
Go now, Tiamat, in your flight!

The Land of Dusk shook again, and the presence of the Great Spirit was gone. Tiamat quickly rose, her golden robes lifting her up.

Marduk's evil face glowered as he spoke.

O Tiamat, beware my wrath,
For strong have I grown in mortal man's greed.
He has all but forgotten you,
As well as your Daughter, my Sister.
Soon it will be me whom she will obey.

Stronger still I will grow, and upon my breast
Both tablets will soon lie, as they are rightfully mine.

Then Marduk too disappeared.

As Tiamat flew away from the Land of the Dusk, her heart was greatly troubled. She took with her the golden mist that held the tablet; her Daughter, who lay in the mortal man's weaving of love; and the bird Anza caught within. Into the trail of milky stars, Tiamat flew, though her face reflected sadness not relief. Her Daughter was weak. Too, Tiamat's power was diminishing as mortal man forgot her, the feminine divine, and her ability to protect mortals longer shone not strongly but was faint. Within the milky trail of stars, Tiamat placed the golden globe of mist. There her sleeping Daughter's thoughts rose. They spoke of her longing, her love for her mortal man, and her yearning to find his soul—for her mortal man had said they would meet again. Tiamat saw that her Daughter's love for the mortal was binding, and the temptation to find him in the land of the living—where mortals, whose desires bound them to material forms, returned to lives again and again—would be ever present.

Tiamat's heart was anguished. *Oh, my errant child! O my Daughter, so meek and mild!*

The demon bird, Anza, of the Land of Dusk now knew the face of the Hidden Daughter and knew well her weakness, and would tempt her again with trickery to give up the Tablet of Light to be reunited with her mortal love. And so the greedy bird would lead the Daughter into Marduk's grasp. But Tiamat knew that she should not hold the evil spirit of Anza in the milky trail, as it was a spirit with powers of its own. It belonged to the Land of Dusk, which was not within her dominion. The Daughter, with the Tablet of Light, must be hidden again somewhere where the eyes of Marduk would be blind. But the spirit bird had to be imprisoned.

Tiamat held her arms up high, her fingers brushing the great trails of milky stars. Then the milky stars parted, and Tiamat spun a great breath that lifted the Tablet of Destiny and the sleeping Daughter out of the golden mist. They were held floating in the milky stars, with the arms of the Daughter upon the tablet. Then Tiamat held the golden globe of mist in her palm, where within the small, sleeping spirit bird Anza lay, still and silent.

Tiamat's heart was filled with anguish for her Daughter and with hate for this evil spirit that had tricked her child. She spoke a chant mixed with her fury, her hatred of this creature who sought to hurt her child.

Cunning bird of the Land of Dusk, evil spirit, demoness of old,
Lose shall you all memory of who you are and of the face of my
Daughter, the tablet, and what has been foretold.
Into this slumber will you fall, and lay shall you in this prison of gold.
Sleep shall you for eternity, forgotten, sealed in this tube of metal,
your birdcage.
Safe shall my Daughter then be from Marduk's rage.

A golden mist churned and churned until it became solid and formed into a small tube of metal, with one end larger than the other. The metal tube twirled. The small end, open and like a vortex, drew Anza into it, and then the tube sprung into Tiamat's hand. Tiamat held the metal tube aloft, but as she prepared to hurl it from the milky stars back into the Land of Dusk, a force rose and stopped her.

The tube flew out of Tiamat's hands. Then the thunderous sound came. It was the voice of the Great Spirit.

O Tiamat! See your folly! Look upon your Daughter's face.
There you will find the bird's trace.

The imprint upon your Daughter ties their fate,
Bound evermore with a chant that you cast with your hate.
See too the tablet, upon which
The imprint of the feathers of the bird Anza lay.
See how the Destiny of Light is to pay.

With pain, Tiamat saw how the fine lines of Anza's wings were upon the cheeks of the Daughter. And too, the Tablet of Destiny had upon it the traces of Anza's head and feathers, from when the bird had crashed into it and fallen into unconsciousness. Tiamat's revenge against the evil bird now bore the imprint in stronger grooves upon the Daughter. The evil being of the Land of Dusk and the Daughter were now bonded together; the fate of one reverberated into the fate of the other. Tiamat's golden face saddened, and the stars that shone like a crown around her head dimmed. The metal tube twirled in the milky sky.

The Great Spirit said:

O Tiamat, a great folly have you done to imprison this spirit, and for
this you shall weep.
The spirit bird Anza of the Land of Dusk you cannot keep.
The demon bird will soon awaken in the metal tube, her prison,
in a huddled heap.
To your Daughter, the bird Anza spoke with crafty zeal
To get the tablet she sought to steal.
Cunning in her tale of the Tree,
For her punishment, this spirit bird's memory will no longer be.
She will only know the longing to be free.
Fall shall she into the land of mortals.
From one end of this tube, springing from her greedy spirit, she shall see
Nothing but duplicity.

Tempt will she mortal man's hands to grasp her,
For her magic powers still will she hold.
Believe will she wrongly that her freedom comes from inhabiting
a mortal soul,
That then her memory will be whole,
And that the tube that binds will she shed like a husk.
But her fate will be wound upon the tube that imprisons this
spirit of dusk.
There lay three glittering bands of made of precious gold,
Three bands of gold that mightily will she hold.
But this demon spirit is deluded by what she thinks she sees.
Prized and protected by Anza will this treasure be,
But the greedy bird will not know that only when the three bands of gold
Are broken and shed will she be free.
Know then shall she where the Daughter flies
And where the Tablet of Light lies.
Bound are their fates by the trace
Left upon your Daughter's face
And the Anza bird's imprint upon the Tablet of Light,
Etched forever so that she, this trickster spirit, may hold its might.

Tiamat's face was filled with anguish and love for her
Daughter, who lay innocent in sleep upon a soft bed of the mist
of the milky stars, her arms around the Tablet of Destiny as she
dreamed of her beloved mortal man. Tiamat heard the prophecy of the Great Spirit and spoke with sadness.

So it shall be, Great Spirit, that I shall pay for my folly,
That Anza, if she awakens in the mortal lands,
Shedding the three golden bands,
This bird, this grasping deceitful creature,

Shall strive to take from my Daughter the Tablet of Destiny of Light.
But my Daughter I shall hide in these milky stars, away from this
bird's sight.
Then it will be that light shall live as a destiny still,
For mortal man's soul to fill.

The Great Spirit shook the milky stars with a thunderous voice.

No, Tiamat, your Daughter cannot stay in these milky stars.
Her desires are her bars,
For her heart beats too strongly for one mortal man,
He whose spirit is now bound upon her.
Into the land of the living will she be sent
Until she repents.
For her actions, which risked the souls of all for the love of one,
Into one thousand mortal lives will she be born
As a maiden in heartbreak forlorn.
Endless days will she seek her mortal man's face.
Endless times will she find and lose his embrace.
Endless notes will she hear of the sweet voice heard and lost,
Of her beloved mortal's call.
Into this cycle of life and death will she fall.
If she should live out all one thousand lives as a mortal,
Then she will once again be allowed to cross your portal.
But should the demon spirit bird Anza break the three bands of gold
Before the Daughter's one thousand lives unfold,
Know, Tiamat, that the bird spirit will clasp the Tablet of Light,
And have it to hold as its right.

Tiamat began to protest, *O Great Spirit,* but the Great Spirit
thundered,

Raise not your protests, Tiamat; I know the smallness of the Anza
bird's spirit.
Should the bird break the gold bands,
Marduk will crush Anza quickly and possess both Tablets of Destiny
in his hands.
Then mortal man shall lose free will.
O Tiamat, this is the prophecy of your errant Daughter's fate that
I have spoken:
Live one thousand mortal lives before the three bands of the bird's
prison are broken.

The Tablet of Destiny melted into the right wrist of the
Daughter, moved under her veins, and shone as a ringlet of silvery gold. The Great Spirit's wind then shook the stars that cradled
the Daughter and blew her away. The Daughter disappeared into a
wisp of golden smoke.

Tiamat' tears splashed into the dark sky and onto the milky
stars. Then her thoughts were sharpened by her pain: the Great
Spirit's prophecy would be fulfilled; she could not thwart it. Nor
to mortal man could she tell the prophecy's terrible spell. But
mortals, those who worshiped her still, she would she seek. She
would not tell them of the Great Spirit's prophecy, only that they
must find the golden tube with the evil spirit and bury it deep
within the earth's fold. To do so would ensure that the Anza bird
would not rise and that the Daughter's one thousand mortal lives
would be lived, after which she would once more returned to the
milky stars. Then the Tablet of Destiny of Light would be saved.

Tiamat reached to the milky stars and took seven in her hands
and blew upon them. The stars sparkled brightly and moved
toward one another to form a Cape of Light. Then, upon this
wondrous cape, Tiamat with her fingers wrote the White Book

of Magic. She then wove it into the Cape of Light with magic chants. To one thousand mortals, Chosen Ones, she would give this cape. One thousand mortals for each life that the Daughter was cursed to live. One thousand mortals to guard the Daughter and keep buried the golden amulet that held the Anza bird. One thousand mortals who would in one thousand lives see that the Daughter lived and died. One thousand mortal lives guarding against the Dark Master Marduk's eyes. One thousand lives during which the evil one in the golden tube would remain coffined in the earth.

But it is said that a mother's love is blind, for she cannot see how weak her child is. And when she moves fiercely to shield her child from harm's way, wisdom fails. And so it was even for the goddess Tiamat. In her zeal she had forgotten to protect her child that it was darkness that was first was upon the face of the Deep before the Great Spirit had divided light from darkness; light was always linked to the dark, and where there was one, there must be the other.

So the blackness that held the milky-white stars now moved to form the Cape of Darkness and the Black Book of Magic. This book fell upon the mortal land and would open to those mortal souls heavy with evil. Its journey would be similar to that of the White Book of Magic; it would travel from mortal soul to mortal soul that gave itself to the Dark Master Marduk. Throughout the eons its grimy leathery cover would hold the fingerprints of deceit and wickedness. It would grow with strength as mortal man's eyes were lit with greed, with desire for power over the other. It would strike out the chords of agape, of loving-kindness, and become fat with strength as more and more souls turned to darkness over light.

This Tiamat did not know when she formed the White Book of Magic, for her eyes were upon the mortal land, seeking the first Chosen One upon whom to place the Cape of Light. But Tiamat would soon discover the existence of the Black Book of Magic as Marduk grew strong and as the Tablets of Creation, which told the story of Tiamat as a force for good, were buried. The story of Marduk as the false prophet of light would rise as Tiamat became a myth in mortal minds, a story, something that held no power but was thought of as born from the spirit of primitive man from the ages. The tale of her milky stars and golden light would be blanketed by the darkness of mortal man's slender and flawed mind. Mortals would look upon the heavens and no longer see the Mother Tiamat clothed in the sun, the moon at her feet, the milky stars a crown upon her brow, but instead only see pricks of light in the night sky, which in their arrogance, they would name and which these mortal minds would claim to be no more than rocks flying in the universe, reflecting the light of a great ball of fire.

𒀭𒌓 𒁹 𒀭𒌓 𒁹

Blazing green light flooded Eddie's eyes as he staggered awake against its brightness. Where was he? Then he remembered the last words he had heard before he had fallen unconscious: *Move into the light.* A beam of light had illuminated the cave. What had happened? He felt the weariness that one does from a long day's travel. He was sure he had been somewhere and was now back. Back here. But where was here?

There were no coordinates here upon which he could form grid points. Light surrounded him.

Am I in the spear's flame? Eddie wondered. But there was no heat. He sensed he was somehow suspended in whatever substance this was, for it felt both like light and mist.

That was the extent of the intel he could gather from his senses. Then fragments of memory punctured his consciousness: the emerald lake ringed by a forest, his body bent and old as he gasped for breath. Where had he been? It wasn't his mind but his heart that answered: *Oh, my love.* And beneath his vision, he saw her slender body crumpling, his heart breaking as he wove a light of love around and around her. The sense of who he was in all of his lives sped through his being, vague, amorphous, leaving a trail of loss. Then the thousand faces of evil flooded Eddie and shook him.

CHAPTER 11

il principe del abyss

The sharp desire of the Prince of Demons for pomp and circumstance rose like a cold winter wind bringing a deadly storm. It blew through the great hall of the Castle of the Abyss, gaining strength from the thunderous cries of the creatures of the Abyss as they proclaimed the prince their prophet, the conqueror of the Dark Master Marduk. It shook the stone walls of the great hall and transformed them. It ripped across the Counselor as he knelt by the threshold of the castle's entrance; it tore through his obsequiousness and lay bare his cunning. It lifted him, his brown monk robes billowing to reveal his thin white legs and the dirty bare feet of his false humility. It threw him against the bottom of three steps that had materialized and led up to a dais. From his hands, the *magna coronat* flew to land upon the foot of an enormous throne made of gold. This unholy dais was a thing made of blasphemy and deceit; the raised platform was constructed of smooth black stone culled from the innermost region of the Black Abyss, the Altar of Despair.

From it the whispers of the prophecy rose as small tendrils that swirled into the Counselor's ears: *On this night he comes, strengthened by the steed of darkness, riding upon the three-headed dragon, carrying the mighty weapon, cutting the cords of the bondage of those exiled to the Abyss.*

The Counselor's bloodless hands reached desperately toward the *magna coronat* as the tendrils of the dark altar's prophecy lifted it into the air. He felt the presence of the Tarnished Knights and knew it was they who had lifted it from his hands. The Counselor snarled against this theft. He moved over the steps and placed his palms flat upon the stone platform of the dais. His body writhed in sharp jolts from the dark altar stone as a warning to leave. The Counselor, however, would not be deterred. He scratched the stone with his nails, clawing his way against the sharp currents of the opposition of the dark altar stone. He must place his *marchio del consigliere,* his mark, upon the prince in order to hold power over him! The *magna coronat,* with its peaked and golden form, this mockery of a papal crown, glittered brighter with deceit as it fluttered above the throne. The Counselor's face was bitter with despair as the dais's force flung him back to the bottom step. Above him he saw his *magna coronat* fall to the control of the Tarnished Knights, the Unholy Trio. The tendrils of the dark altar stone turned into a black feather, its tip writing over the Counselor's inlaid inscription, "*Il Principe,*" to change it to "*Il Principe del Abyss*"—the Prince of the Abyss.

The floor and ceiling of the great hall began to move and grow. The dome elongated higher and higher until it was like a cathedral in scope. Large carved stone columns broke from the floor, one on each side of the great hall, and sprung toward the vaulted ceiling. Illuminated by the flickering light of stout candles that were ensconced in the wall, giant tapestries depicting scenes of Hades unfurled from the ceiling: terrible images of fires, of bloody battles, of horror that came from the cruel treachery of mortal man against one another.

These tapestries were hardly decorative; nor were they random. They told the story of more prisoners of the Abyss being thrown out of Kurnigi by Marduk. Although they once lay trapped within the stones of the earth of the Abyss, they now moved in their painted circles of hell, impatiently waiting to be released. Some of their hands were gnarled with deceit and hatred; others held gruesome bloodied instruments of torture. Still others were just pieces of bodies. But they all snarled with pleasure. These were creatures who had, in their mortal forms, wrenched from their brethren confessions of false sins. Their blasphemous words and deeds had led them into the Corkscrew of Terror when they had left their mortal forms. Threads of rust-colored blood dripped from their long nails. These droplets rained from the ceiling of the great hall, turning into red threads that swiftly entwined with one another, weaving a carpet of deep burgundy that fell between the giant stone columns that divided the great hall. This carpet then rolled toward the large golden throne that sat upon the black stone platform at the end of the hall.

The castle's stone walls expanded as tens of thousands of the creatures of the Abyss instantly appeared inside the hall on each side of the rich burgundy carpet. These spirits of evil, these painted devils, heard the chant of the creatures of the Abyss as they filled the great hall. But the painted devils remained silent, moving in the dome softly, like sea serpents under dark murky waters.

The creatures of the Abyss chanted:

In this night rises the prince.
Spirit of injustice,

Breath of ruthlessness,
Song of our vengeance,
Mightier than the wind!
Stronger than the driving storm!

More and more creatures of the Abyss lined the great hall on either side of the dark-wine-colored carpet that led to the throne. Their chants rose and reverberated in deep lugubrious notes through the castle.

The Prince of Demons burst mightily upon the great hall, riding his dragon steed and holding close the frail spirit female. His red eyes glinted wickedly as the candlelight cast dark shadows upon his pockmarked face. He pierced his Saber of Shadows toward the dome then turned it downward to show it as the Sword of Deception. The three-headed dragon beast spewed red flames and flapped its great black wings against the otherwise-still air of the great hall. The black and blue thumbs glowed upon Stal's hands. These thumbs, which held the anger and anguish of death culled into them by Abaddon, vibrated amid the evil notes of the chants of the creatures of the Abyss and drew more strength ever from the sword wielded by Stal.

Trina's eyes widened in horror at the scene unfolding in front of her. The power of evil pressed against her, its stench overwhelming her.

As Stal swung the steed toward the throne and maneuvered it through the crowd, the cries of the creatures of the Abyss were deafening as they rose in unison. Those in the great hall pounded their feet against its hardened heart of stone.

The bonds of the Abyss that holds us,
With his sword our prince slashes.

In a hailstorm of revenge, our hatred flashes,
Trampling upon the Dark Master's land of trouble
Until it is nothing but a city of rubble.

In this soil of adulation, Stal's arrogance grew, mounting in proportion to the tens of thousands in the castle shouting for him. Him! Prince! Stal took in the castle, its enormity, and the throne at the end of the hall, above which glittered a crown. *His crown*, though it was shaped like a crown worn by a pope. With pleasure, Stal's mind moved rapidly over this thought: *Master of the Abyss, Prince of Demons.*

Then his thoughts went to Marduk and Kurnigi, how the Snake had shuddered under his stare. How mortal man had feared him: "Satan," his mother would warn. "Beware of Satan." The Abyss was not enough. He wanted to be Prince of All Hell. Satan. Master of Darkness. If Marduk were to be overthrown, then it would be he, Stal, Prince of Demons, who would be the rightful ruler of hell. But these creatures of the Abyss would serve for now. Master of mortal souls, worshiped and feared by all—that was Stal's goal.

Stal waved that weapon forged from the shadows, the Sword of Deception, again to the shouts of "Prince of Demons!"

From the domed ceiling, the trapped devil spirits broke forth from their painted prison, their gnarled hands reaching toward their prince. Perhaps it was he who would free them, for his form was sinister, and the weapon he held was powerful. But then they stopped.

They did not like this prince's thoughts, he whose ears rang with the praise sung by creatures of the Abyss, who themselves were deaf to the aspirations of this pockmarked one. The prince's thoughts of treachery wafted up to them—they who were finely tuned to the stink of deceit, being masters of it themselves. This pockmarked one wanted to be the ruler of hell, the Master of Darkness.

These evil spirits, however, wanted no master, only the freedom unleashed by Chaos. They only wanted this prince to lead them in the exodus, lead them out of the dark whorls of the Abyss and Kurnigi until they were released in the land of the living to prey upon mortal souls. This was the promised journey spoken by the Unholy Trio. Not to be subjugated to another master. This one would be taught to do his duty only. Soon this prince would be shown his place and learn who was master and who was slave.

Long hands reached down from the ceiling and yanked Trina off the dragon steed. Stal was jerked out of his thoughts of glory.

"Drop her!" he commanded. He thrust his sword at the creatures as the dragon steed's great black wings lifted him into the air.

The painted devil spirits moved toward the prince in unison, like waves of locusts readying to descend upon a field. Their force pushed the prince and his steed back onto the hard stone floor. Their faces wore their sins. Some, snarling with maliciousnessness, had small sharp horns that protruded from their foreheads. Others had faces burned to a blur by their lust for gold or for dominion over others or for the desires of the flesh. Some bore their sins as ribbed bodies racked with insatiable hunger. Others had small heads with large mouths whose teeth clicked in gluttony. All of them moved out of the dome and swarmed in and out of their painted prisons.

"I command you to drop her!" Stal roared as his dragon steed skidded on the stone floor of the castle.

Trina's scream lay trapped in her throat, but her eyes revealed her terror as the evil spirits held her tightly against the dome. The painted devils snarled their response:

O Prince of Demons,
Know this well:
None of us is master over the other in this hell.

Great jolts from the stone floor stung the hooves of the three-headed dragon steed. The beast snorted in pain and shook in convulsions, the flames from its three mouths now just wisps of smoke. It reared up on two legs, whinnying and flapping its great wings against the stinging jolts. Stal was flung off the beast. The front legs of the steed came down, one of them slamming into his head.

He felt the old shame burn through his pockmarks; the taunts and laughter of the rich boys at the church school rang in his ears. He tried to scramble up, but the stone floor pinned him, stinging him with sharp jolts. What was this? Was he being tested again? Had he not already overcome the Asaru-alim-nuna? His red eyes narrowed in realization. He was the prince, as they called him, yet these painted demons were controlling the events to let him know that he was the master in name only. They were all Criminals of Hell after all, and none of them was to be greater than the other. He was to free them from the Abyss and be called "Prince," but he would also know his place. The thought enraged him as he lay writhing on the stone floor; it evoked the memories of how he once had been beaten, mocked, derided. Around him, the cries heralding him "Prince" dimmed as another voice rose.

My eyes waste away in grief, he heard the voice of his mother, Keke, *for my son perishes as the unrighteous.*

His mother's meek piousness raised his anger to a higher pitch. *No, you stupid beaten old woman,* he thought. *I am not your son. I am the Prince of Demons.*

The creatures of the Abyss murmured their fear of the painted devils, who had been held deep in the black heart of the Abyss and bore its mark. Look at how they held the prince with their jolts upon the floor, as he struggled like a dying rat! Still they needed this prince with his sword to cut the cords that bound them to the Abyss, to lead them out. The painted devils could not be thwarted easily; rather, they had to be persuaded to let the prince rise and lead. Then one of the creatures of the Abyss stepped forward with his mask of gold spattered with blood, for he understood the painted devils and their power, but he knew too that the prince was needed, that he must be raised up and crowned to lead them out of the Abyss. He spoke as he had as a mortal, with the smooth tongue of a diplomat and the shrewdness of a politician. He raised his arms to the dome then bowed in appeasement to the Prince of Demons, who lay writhing on the stone floor. His voice carried a tone of respect but underneath it too a warning.

> *Painted devils, listen here: Chaos will free us, as it is told,*
> *But first this prince must be the leader of our fold.*
> *O Prince of Demons, harken to this:*
> *Ruler are you only until we are no longer in Marduk's hold.*

Stal's red eyes glowed angrily as he raised his head from the stone floor against the jolts. These creatures of the Abyss would see who the master was. They didn't know Stal. He was steel. He was stronger, smarter, mightier than them, for he held with him powers they did not: the black and blue thumbs of trapped souls, the sword given to him by the Asaru-alim-nuna—not weapons of illusion, as were the things of the Abyss, but real powers.

Stal fought the power that held him to the floor. In a quick motion, he was up and then brutally stabbed the point of the Saber of Shadows into the stone. A cry of terror and agony rose as the spirits which formed the floor broke, and a bloody gash appeared. He lifted the sword out and raised it to the dome. He then jumped high, flying onto the back of three-headed dragon steed. It felt its master's strength move through its flanks, flowing from the evil energy of his sword. As the dragon steed flapped its great black wings, Stal jabbed the beast's sides with his heels.

"Up!" he shouted.

Around him, sharp curses fell from the dome. The creatures of the Abyss were hushed. Stal's pockmarked face bore determination as he flew toward the throne. His ears were still ringing with the calls and jeers of the painted devils, who had wanted to humiliate Stal so he would know from whom his power came. Soon they would see who ruled whom. The *magna coronat* floated, suspended over the golden throne, its red-velvet cushions and its arms of wood from the black forests of the Abyss showing it to be the Great Seat of power. Stal thrust his saber forward, its tip showing itself as the Saber of Shadows, and pierced the *magna coronat* through its peaked, golden center. He then turned it so that the other side the, Sword of Deception, glinted. The *magna coronat* vibrated as the power of the sword surged through it; the gold tarnished and turned black, then turned a deeper gold. The papal peaked face of the crown became pitted and pockmarked as he who would soon wear it. Stal withdrew the sword. With its pointed tip, he slashed the inscription "*Il Principe del Abyss.*" Those words disappeared, and in their place appeared Stal's inscription, "Prince of Demons."

Stal shouted, "Do you see how I mark the crown as my own?"

There was now silence. For those of the Abyss, this was a drama unfolding, a story that had not been told and retold, as everything had been in their condemnation to nonbeing. The *magna coronat* fluttered above the throne.

Flames erupted and engulfed the throne, and from the fire, three tall headless figures—those of the Tarnished Knights, the Unholy Trio of the Abyss—emerged. They were clad in long hooded cloaks the gray of the sea under the dark clouds of a storm. Each knight carried his mummified head, each face bearing his sins of the spirit: greed, arrogance, and hypocrisy.

The Tarnished Knights placed their mummified heads upon their necks, deep within their hooded cloaks. The creatures of the Abyss who lined the great hall were in awe: the Unholy Trio had held the place of the high priests of the Abyss. The hollow eyes of the Tarnished Knights glowered in displeasure like lamplights within their hooded cloaks. Underneath each cloak was a black tunic upon which was embroidered in large red letters, "*Radix malorum cupiditas*," or "The root of evil is desire." Just as it had been in the mortal world, where these knights had crafted lives of unbridled indulgence fueled by cruelty, so too was the cloak of hypocrisy worn in the underworld.

For eons this Unholy Trio had resided in the Abyss as the High Priests of the Unrighteous. The root of evil was desire, they preached. And for evil to flourish, so must desire in mortal man's heart—desires not of the flesh or heart, but wishes to overcome, overpower, control and step on the necks of their fellow man to rise higher. This, the Unholy Trio prophesized, would occur with the arrival of the prince who would lead them out of the Abyss. The Fallen One, not from the heavens, but from the skin of the land of the living. He, this prince, would come when

Chaos splintered the Lands of Light and Darkness, where anarchy in mortal time took hold. All those souls in the mortal world were ripe to be picked for evil, for all knew that mortal man was weak, that he didn't know the value of his soul, and could easily be overcome. They, the Unholy Trio, now out of the Abyss, would then defeat Marduk. The Dark Master himself would fall, and the Land of Darkness would be theirs.

It would be theirs not to serve the Unholy Trio's own desire for evil but for the evil of all to flourish. They would grow and protect a Land of Darkness for the Great Spirit of Darkness himself. That was the will of evil through the principle *Radix malorum cupiditas*. But in truth, within the spirits of the Unholy Trio, personal desires still ran rampant, and the need to be all-powerful sprung strongly. Each one of them suspected of the other that there was hypocrisy in their pious verbalizations but not in themselves. Flames surrounded the trio, a cape of fire, a warning to the prince of their anger. For it was they who had lifted the castle from deep within the black heart of the Abyss, so that this *prince*, this *savior of the unrighteous*, might be crowned at the Altar of misery, be the anointed Unholy One to lead them out of darkness onto the soil of the living—so that they, the knights, might once again rule. But this pockmarked one had slashed the crown with *his* desire.

The Unholy Trio cried to the creatures of the Abyss, and the painted devils above, "Behold the false prophet! He is not a prince but a pockmarked pauper who comes to trick us!"

The Unholy Trio extended their arms, their long hands seeking to recapture the *magna coronat*. This prince had defiled the crown with his will; he had not submitted to them, as he should have.

But the story of the rise of evil is twisted, much as the hearts of those who possess it. So it was that the *magna coronat*, bearing

Stal's appellation of Prince of Demons, spun past the grasping hands of the Tarnished Knights. It fell upon Stal's head and crowned him Prince of Demons, ruler of the Abyss and its denizens. The flames around the throne were extinguished. Upon his head, this mockery of a papal crown sat, bearing his inscription, "Prince of Demons." It drilled into his head the force of the dark incantations held within the *magna coronat* from the Counselor and from the altar stone of the Trio of Tarnished Knights. It blended with the power of the Saber of Shadows and its underbelly, the Sword of Deception.

Stal turned his dragon steed around, and its giant black wings flapped. His red eyes showed the mark of his ascendancy with glints of cruelty that were yet to be realized. He slashed the sword to show its two sides as darkness and deception. Then the memories of the ancient souls within his thumbs, trapped by Abaddon, their last moments painted by pain, rose. He flung back his head and threw open his mouth. From it spewed wave upon wave of fire. He brandished the sword and kicked the flanks of the three-headed dragon steed, whose enormous black wings flapped, and the dragon horse rose with its rider over the creatures of the Abyss.

Stal's black hair grew long upon his shoulders. Upon his pockmarked face appeared a sharp and pointed beard. His arms and body grew until he sat upon the dragon beast ten feet tall, his body covered with a tunic of shimmering silver scales, each glinting with evil. A black cloak, a weaving of silk made by the spider of death, formed and fell about his shoulders. No more puny pockmarked beggar was he. No one would *ever* humiliate him. And for those who did, only the direst of punishments awaited before utter destruction descended upon them—as it did for the painted devils and this Unholy Trio.

The creatures of the Abyss in the great hall stomped their feet on the stone floor to mark the triumph of the prince over those who would try to rule him. For here, in the Abyss, was a spirit who ruled rather than be ruled. Stal hit the flanks of his three-headed dragon steed to reach the dome. He swung his sword toward the painted devils' arms. They too knew that this prince was not to be taunted. They released Trina to fall upon the steed. Stal then rode the dragon steed in fury, flying over and over the creatures of the Abyss, who erupted again in adulation for this new prince. He had broken the painted devils' hold. He had taken control of the *magna coronat* from the Unholy Trio and crowned himself the Prince of Demons.

As cries of celebration of their impending freedom from Kurnigi rose from the lips of the creatures of the Abyss, discontent and rebellion were still stirring in the painted devils and the Unholy Trio. Those creatures of the Abyss, the devils in the painted dome whispered now, what did they know of imprisonment? Had they been trapped in the stones of the black earth of the Abyss for the eons? Resentment grew among the painted devil spirits. No, those creatures ran about the skin of the Abyss to play their games, while they had been trapped, stagnant and silent, within the strokes of a paintbrush. Prince, he may call himself. Master too. But once the skin of Kurnigi was broken, once these painted devils rode upon the land of the living, this pockmarked one would see who ruled supreme.

Stal then jumped from his three-headed dragon steed, leaving Trina upon it. He strode with the confidence of the powerful before the throne upon the Altar of the Unholy, the scales of his silver tunic gleaming with arrogance, the black cloak of the weaving of the deadly spider giving off the scent of death. The Tarnished Knights stood by the throne, emanating their displeasure.

Stal shouted to them, as one would to the lowest of slaves, "Bring my princess robes of silk and necklaces of gold and rubies."

The Unholy Trio stood still. Silence now filled the great hall, for though the Abyss was a thing of illusion, these unholy ones were still the high priests of the unrighteous, to be respected.

"Move!" Stal shouted as he seated himself on the throne.

The Unholy Trio, with their cloaks of gray, rose toward the ceiling. "Beware, Prince of Demons: the eyes of the unrighteous are upon you. And the face of evil will soon destroy you." They uttered an incantation before disappearing into a black mist that covered the painted dome and its devils.

Now the creatures of the Abyss unleashed their chants once more, for they held no doubts. The prince had risen. The prince would free them.

O Prince of Demons,
Friend to the wicked, foe to the righteous,
Lead us with your Sword of Darkness!
Pierce it into the land of the living
Until we are departed spirits no more but conquerors of the earth!

The creatures of the Abyss moved forward in their broken forms: some man, some beast, some with bloody eyes, some with rusted swords clashing in triumph. All bowed low to pay their respect to the prince on his throne. Stal knew he held the might and power of the dark underworld now, for the evil that surrounded him entered and vibrated through him. His red eyes glowered with anger and arrogance.

Through it all, crouching low and unobserved and hidden behind the throne, had been the scheming Counselor. He smiled to himself at the turn of events. Distrust, deception, twists in the plots of the ruled and the ruler—these were his milieu. His forte. For he was the supreme weaver of webs of deceit. The prince would need him indeed. The Counselor moved from his place of hiding. He lowered his head in humble service and assumed the face of the most obedient servant; even his brown monk robes radiated obsequiousness.

He bowed low and said, "O Mighty Highness, Prince of Demons, please let me be of service to your princess."

CHAPTER 12

the unlooking glass

The six members of the Society of Phantom Magicians stood in the bitter-cold night air on Sixth Avenue shivering, for their coats were threadbare and no match for the icy wind that mercilessly stung their faces. Too, the night was bewitched, as they heard the dreadful long moans carried within the wind. *Dead souls rising upon the midnight hour,* they thought with a shudder. They were risking being possessed themselves. But *Hippodrome,* the Great Master Magician had said, and they had come, for they were certain that soon they would hold the great currency of powerful magic that would flow like electricity from their fingers to entice crowds and fill their pockets with gold.

The six stared up in awe at New York's Hippodrome Theatre. To perform here once signified the pinnacle of one's career. It was a monumental edifice indeed: a vast redbrick-faced building that proclaimed grandeur and spanned an entire corner of the city street. Also, its design, with its terra-cotta coloring, was meant to recall the Moors, those great architects that had crafted the Alhambra in Spain, that colossal fortress upon a hill, that "pearl set in emeralds." Though the city streets didn't allow for the forests to encase the Hippodrome, nonetheless, just like a fortress, it had two towers, each of which had a globe that once shone with electric lights. That was not now, however—not on October 31, 1936, when the grinding poverty of the Depression made the once-legendary Hippodrome a shabby diva deteriorating in neglect.

The massive Hippodrome was a silent, dark mass. This grand forum, with its 5,300 seats, once dazzled audiences with circuses with elephants, tigers, baboons, and clowns and even had reenacted the Union cavalry riding on horses, with gunfire and explosions to boot. This was the same theater where the Great Magician himself had made an elephant disappear under the bright glare of the Hippodrome's spotlight.

The six members of the Society of Phantom Magicians had come to the Hippodrome expecting…what? Something. Lights flashing, the Great Magician flinging the Hippodrome doors open. But not this: the building shut tightly. No, not after the supernatural doings they had just experienced. One member of the group had brought with him the crystal ball that had ballooned then shrunk again in the Great Master Magician's basement. The crystal ball had showed the Master Magician within it. Perhaps that would happen again. The man lifted the crystal ball to the dark doors just as a great gust began to blow. It was the wind created by the Muhra possessing bodies.

The wind grabbed the crystal ball from the man's hands as if it were light as a leaf. Suddenly the Hippodrome's doors flung open, and the crystal ball dropped to the pavement. The six felt the sudden thrust of Muhra reach into their bodies, possess them, and fling their spirits behind them toward the ever-growing fog forming at the theater's threshold. Their Muhra-possessed bodies rushed into the Hippodrome.

Now the six members of the Phantom Society of Magicians knew with clarity what it was that made up the dark spirit world: it was them. But into the Muhra fog they would not go. They swiftly flew as six tendrils of fog toward their crystal ball, which was still rolling on the sidewalk in front of the Hippodrome's doors. They moved in one quick movement into the ball, escaping imprisonment within the growing receptacle of the fog of dead souls.

The crystal ball then rolled into the Hippodrome.

𒀭𒈾𒁀𒀭𒁹

The bleak New York streets were alive with the sounds of the dead. The cold fog of the Muhra, those formless spirits that had risen from Kurnigi's gates to take possession of whatever hapless humans fell across their path, deftly grabbed souls and moved themselves into their bodies. Windows flung open, with souls thrown out like refuse into the growing Muhra fog, now a receptacle for newly dead souls. Everywhere in the city, bodies were assumed by the long-trapped Muhra. These Muhra were the old opera divas, the long-dead theatrical performers, the clowns, the silent-movie stars, the vaudevillians, the performers of shows of long ago. These Muhra, who once had sipped greedily from the enticing elixir of fame, were now grabbing any mortal body, any form that came their way with reckless abandon: ill-fitting bodies of those snatched in their sleep from dark alleys, hobos mostly; some lunatics from the insane asylum; still others who had been asleep in their homes and in the dead of sleep had become the dead.

The streets were littered with the dead crashing to the ground and rising again as the Muhra possessed them. The bulging fog, made up of the newly dead souls, moved tentatively into the dark theater. These spirits were still in that dazed, paralyzed state that comes when life leaves with no vessel to hold it, for now the fog moved slowly and settled at the perimeter of the theater. Soon these newly dead souls would awaken to begin the long, endless awareness that they were formless and would come to long for the bodies the Muhra had robbed from them. The bodies of those possessed by the Muhra moved into the dark theater much like an autumn wind rises and lifts dead leaves in a flurry of sudden motion. New to form, the Muhra tentatively moved their arms and legs.

The Great Diva, who had been ripped to pieces as she had pierced out of the Muhra fog to grab the Spyglass, had roamed the streets as a veritable hurricane force of self-centeredness in the form of growing tendrils of gray fog. Her disembodied hands scratched the path in front of her for a body. Her head, with its moon-shaped forehead, bulging eyes, and great snapping donkey teeth, flew behind her hands. *A suitable body*, she thought. The Great Diva was in the market for a very particular type—not a hobo or lunatic for her. She was too egotistical for that; to play the starring role, she needed a lithe body with flowing dark hair. Then a hapless young woman who had the misfortune to be leaving her shift as a waitress at a nearby diner emerged, her feet aching and a few meager coins clanging in her pockets. The chill of the wind stung the woman's eyes and froze the horror in her face as the Great Diva pounced upon this one, extracting her soul to dump into the Muhra fog.

The Great Diva strode imperiously into the Hippodrome in the body of the waitress. She brushed past the other newly occupied bodies stumbling in, shouting orders in her domineering manner.

"Turn on the lights!" she commanded. "Prepare my dressing room. You! Stagehands! Ready the set for *Aida*!"

Muhra everywhere jumped up to obey. Several scrambled up immediately and moved to become the stagehands—for what the Great Diva wanted, the Great Diva would get. They manipulated their fingers to deftly pull at knobs. Lights came on. The buzzing noise of excitement of a performance in motion moved through the Hippodrome. The theater, so lately dead to the world, had been awakened by the dead. For the freed Muhra, long trapped in formlessness, who wanted to perform again—hear the applause and adulation, feel the heat of the stage lights upon their faces, smell the grease of makeup, and feel their sweat roll down their faces as their feet tapped out routines—the Hippodrome was too much to resist. Their thoughts ran to one thing. *A performance tonight by the Great Diva. A performance like no other!*

𒁹𒄸𒌋 𒂍 𒁹𒄸 𒀹

The alleys near the Hippodrome had been swept clean of any reckless soul who had thought that refuge from the cold wind could be had there, for they hadn't reckoned that the midnight hour would bring the Muhra's great, greedy grasp for form.

There was yet another being who was greedy and giddy with power: the Crone. She had flown from the rooftop of the Harlem brownstone clutching her stolen treasure, the Spyglass, in her gnarled hands. The Crone had landed with a thud onto the street and scurried with rodent-like movements to hide in a nearby alley already emptied of bodies. Thus it was a safe refuge—though what could the Muhra do to her? She heard her own cackle in her ears. *Oh, no more. No more.* Soon she would be beautiful, and her voice, her tinkling laugh, would fall melodically upon the ears of her admirers—of which there would be many.

The Crone lifted the Spyglass to her eyes and peered into it. It was dark.

Inside her metal prison, the Spyglass shivered with rage at the yellow eye looking in. Mattie—that reckless, disobedient, mortal child—had left her to be captured! Spyglass paused in surprise as she took in the yellow eye and felt the clasp upon her. It was not a living entity but dead hands that held her. Still, even the dead held on to their spirits, but this one had none. It meant that the one who held her was under someone else's control. Serpentine undulations swirled within the eye.

Then the Spyglass saw the image of an ugly old woman and recoiled at once in the knowledge of who owned this hag: the Snake. The Spyglass's thoughts whirled rapidly. Oh, the terror! If the Snake took hold of her, then soon Marduk would possess her, and never would she be free. Then the Spyglass stopped. This hag's needs were small and stupid, for her longing for beauty rose like steam does from freshly dropped cow dung. This old withered one gave off the stink of bitterness at her ugliness. She must be quickly tricked to give up the Spyglass before the Snake came to take possession of this hideous creature. Mattie, that impudent girl, was somewhere nearby, for she felt her presence. Spyglass would take possession of the girl at first sight. She would take over Mattie's soul at once; it was possible now that the power of White Magic was dimming and that meddlesome Biddle wasn't around to interfere. The old endless loop played again: somewhere in the deep recesses of her memory lay the knowledge of who she was and therefore where the Hidden Sister lay. She would access it and find the…oh!

The Spyglass shuddered. The Crone's fingernails were prying at her two precious gold bands of protection.

In the dark alleyway, the veined hands of the Crone, with their long, dirty nails, were indeed digging around the Spyglass's gold bands. The Crone had an unerring instinct for the weakness of those she wished to dominate. When she had first clasped the Spyglass, she had felt the heat from the gold bands radiate into her and at once recognized that they had been formed from White Magic. Then the old one surmised, *Bands of protection.* This metal amulet was a prison to the spirit entity within. She would peel away the gold bands to keep the spirit entirely under her control. In the days when she had possessed the Black Book of Magic, she had learned much. This creature within was linked to the Hidden Sister and therefore knew the location of the Tablet of Destiny of Light. The Chosen One was who the Dark Master had directed the Crone to find (and control) in the frozen Siberian land. Then this Chosen One would grasp the amulet and bring the entity under his control. In turn the Crone would turn him over to the Dark Master, and her beauty and power would be returned for eternity. But it hadn't worked that way, for she had erred, mistaking the cockroach Uri Gneezy for his twin brother Dmitri as the Chosen One. Chaos had ensued, and she had lost both the Black Book of Magic and her spirit to the control of Uri Gneezy, now in a serpentine form.

None of that mattered now. It was she who held the metal amulet—the Spyglass—and not the Snake! A thin spittle, a drool of greed, rolled down from the edge of the Crone's cracked lips as she cackled in glee. Soon the Crone would wield the power of the Book of Destiny of Light, be in equal with the Dark Master, seize her spirit back from the Snake, and cut that vile reptile into pieces. That pockmarked cockroach who called himself the Prince of Demons also would be brought under her control. The demise of Marduk loomed real. Greater even than the Dark Master would she be, for Chaos had been unleashed now, and the Asaru-alim-nuna were rising mightily. But all that could wait, for now the Crone was hungry to be restored to her beautiful self. She felt the cold deadness of the metal amulet in her hand.

"Creature, trick me not with your pretended sleep," the Crone hissed menacingly. "Think not that you can control me as you have the mortal child."

The Crone dug out a small bit of a foul greasy substance from her fingernail. Under her nails, in the form of slime, were the spirits of mortals who had sought spells and incantations so that all they touched would turn to gold, pledging in return their souls to the Crone. This was when she had held the Black Book of Magic. When the time came for them to surrender their souls, so dirtied by their abuse of their fellow man were they that they did not go to Kurnigi but instead were held as oily encrustations lodged under the Crone's long gnarled fingernails.

"Give me dazzling beauty!" the Crone commanded, raising the Spyglass to her yellow eye.

The entity did not respond to the old one's command. The Crone then spread her slime of evil spirits just underneath the two gold bands. Black pits formed upon the gold bands, for this foul oily substance of evil had the power to corrode anything it touched.

The Crone felt the entity within the metal tube stirring. "Beauty will be mine, and you will be under my control!"

The Crone snarled as she pulled at the gold bands as more and more black pits formed like cancer upon them.

Then the old one felt one of the bands loosen from the body of the metal tube. The Crone yanked off the loosened gold band in one motion. A sound of pain, guttural and primitive, rose as if the amulet were being skinned alive. The band fell into the Crone's gnarled hand limply and softly, like a rotten peel, then dropped to the ground.

"Creature! Make me beautiful! Do it now!" the Crone ordered as she began to dig at the second band of gold upon the Spyglass.

Spyglass panicked. She couldn't lose her last gold band of protection. She would have to fulfill the Crone's demands. Quickly she shot off small sparks.

The Crone's fingers paused in their digging. The sparks formed into a gold swirl that melted over the Crone.

Intense heat overcame the Crone as the gold swirl, like molten lava, covered her face and body. Her fingers no longer sought to ply away the gold band, for she swayed as the golden liquid dripped over her face. It melted away the gnarled features, smoothed the ridges and bumps of the Crone's nose. Soon the hideous countenance disappeared, and in its place was an exquisite one. The Crone's body was changing as well: the hump upon her back disappeared, and her arms and legs elongated. Soon she stood tall and statuesque. The old rags formed into a silky gown that draped over her curvaceous body. Now the Crone felt the cold night air once again against her skin. She moved to touch her face and felt its softness. A swoon rose from her perfectly shaped red lips. Her face was soft and smooth, not bumpy and rough.

Then the pitted gold band that had been thrown to the ground flew up. It swirled and transformed into a mirror. The Crone grabbed it with her left hand, as the right one still held the Spyglass.

She was greedy to admire herself. It was a small oval glass framed by gold edging. The Crone peered into the mirror and gasped. It was *her* face, her long-lost self. Not just a beautiful face, but *her* long-lost face. Tears of happiness rolled down her cheeks as she greeted her face in the mirror: high cheekbones; deep-set emerald eyes speckled with gold and fringed by thick, long lashes; long, shiny, silky dark locks of the deepest blue-black framing her face. Her skin was a pale golden hue, as if gold nuggets had been melted into cream, and upon her cheekbones was a dusting of rose, a faint maiden blush. Her neck was long and swanlike. As the Crone moved the small mirror to glimpse at the rest of herself, she saw that she wore a silvery satin gown that showed bared shoulders and a shapely figure. Ah, she was beautiful! Enchantingly, bewitchingly so. Just as she had been. She lifted her arms to admire them. Her bare arms, with their golden tinge, ended in long beautiful hands, one that elegantly held the Spyglass, the other the small oval mirror. She was restored. This was indeed her face—the visage of a goddess, just as she had been when she was worshiped by mortal man, who had fought wars because of her. The memory of that time stirred within the Crone, when her face had moved mortal man to do her bidding. *Before…before…*The Crone quickly repressed the thought, for secrets that spilled into the night air surely would be caught by the malevolent Muhra spirits that churned in this night of the dead in the land of the living.

𒐋𒀭𒌋 𒐘 𒀭𒌋 𒁉

Within the bowels of the Hippodrome, the gigantic glass water tank shuddered like a great sleeping mammal awakening from a deep winter's sleep. It rose like a specter, commanded not by a séance but by the sudden switching on of power. The tank had been another casualty of the Depression: long forgotten to the draconian fiscal measures taken by the Hippodrome's management to stay alive. The giant tank was designed to hold up to 4,000 gallons of water; in its glory days it was the venue for amazing, glittering aquatic productions—all much too costly for the paltry sum that theater tickets could command in these desperate economic times. In fact, the Hippodrome had been largely dark, given that few could risk the cost of a producing a show anyway, much less one with the costs associated with water spectacles.

The bare bulb that lit the stairway leading into the Hippodrome's basement cast angles of dim light. It threw shadows onto the tank, which was rapidly filling to the top with a liquid, not the clear water of the old aquatic shows but a dark, murky, blue substance. Something was held prisoner within as the liquid moved. Then the bottom lights of the water tank snapped on, and its captive was revealed: the Great Magician, shackled in chains and naked except for his swim trunks, was struggling without effect.

Mattie was inside the tank as well, her red hair moving like seaweed around her face. Her eyes were wide open in surprise. She looked around for Geeta but didn't see her. Then Mattie quickly moved her legs in the jackknife technique she had learned at the Hackensack YWCA last summer. She moved past the Great Magician—a murky silhouette, struggling against the chains that bound him, pushing his body toward the top of the tank. Mattie's head hit the lid of the water tank and pushed her back down. Her chest was hurting. She was running out of oxygen. Her heart fluttered in fear. She remembered how she almost quit her swim classes at the Hackensack YMCA because it took forever to learn how to swim. The water over her head made her panic and choke; she was always so afraid she would sink and drown. She had told Mr. Biddle this in the basement of Sears in the furniture department, where he had sat at his desk, listening to her and looking at her thoughtfully with his kind blue eyes. "Mattie," he had said, "panic is what drowns the swimmer, not the water. If you stay calm, you'll float." Remembering this, she forced herself to calm down. *What would Mr. Biddle tell me now?*

In response to her call, it seemed, Mr. Biddle's gentle face rose before her: his blue eyes; those old-fashioned white whiskers around his chin, rippling in the water. But there was something different: his face was drawn in worry, and his eyes had a haunted, lost look. Mattie felt a ping in her heart, as you do when you know that someone you love is in deep pain. She moved her arms instinctively to comfort him, creating a ripple in the tank. Mr. Biddle's lips moved in the watery vision. He mouthed a word then disappeared. Then something floated up out of Mattie's pocket, glinting in the watery light. It was one of the Cards of Time that Mr. Biddle had given Geeta and Mattie so long ago on the Third Stone. She grabbed it, and it moved her toward the glass wall of the tank and through it. Mattie landed on the hard cement floor of the basement of the Hippodrome. Her face was flushed, her heart beating rapidly. She stood up. She was dry. The Card of Time was in her hand, slick and black.

Mattie moved toward the water tank. "Geeta!" she yelled.

The tank's light shone from the bottom. It lit the murky waters so that Mattie could see that its only occupant was the Great Magician.

Where is Geeta? Is she still alive? This last thought she dismissed at once; it would only jinx things. *Geeta is alive. Geeta is alive. Geeta is alive!*

Mattie was jerked from these thoughts by a tapping on the side of the water tank. The Great Magician was knocking his chains against the side to get her attention. Suddenly, creatures were forming in the murky water. Mattie's face contorted in fear. She couldn't give these creatures a name, as the fear evoked by these beasts was primitive, instinctual. For these were the ancient creatures of the forgotten mighty ones, the most primeval of the three groups of demons that made up the Asaru-alim-nuna. Though they were only seven of in number; their shark mouths held a thousand sharp teeth; they emanated a primal evil that struck fear in both mortal man and demon spirits. One by one, these demon gods with the bodies of pythons and the heads of sharks began to take form. One sprang to wrap itself around the Great Magician.

The Great Magician's body was quickly being wrapped by one of python tails of the ancient demon gods. This shark-snake creature's head twisted down upon the Great Magician. It opened its mouth to show a fearsome double layer of sharp teeth preparing to swallow the man.

"Help me! Please!" The Great Magician mouthed these words, his face flat upon the glass.

This man had threatened her on the rooftop—why should she help him? His eyes were bulging, and he looked really, really scared. *Oh, boy.* Mattie felt mixed emotions; he had threatened her—that was true—but she had also broken that wand of his, and that was why he was all bound up in chains now.

"Help me!" the Great Magician mouthed again as the primitive sea serpents flung him against the glass.

Show mercy, Mattie, she heard her mother say. *Show mercy that you may receive it in your time of need.*

Mattie had a split second to act before the sharky-snakey creature swallowed the man whole. She slapped the Card of

Time on the side of the water tank. In an instant it sucked the Great Magician out. He fell, still in his shackles, upon the cold basement floor, not a drop of the strange liquid upon him. The demon python-shark creatures were growing and spinning inside the tank. The water tank began to shake and shudder. Its sides started to expand. It was going to explode.

Mattie lifted the Card of Time and waved it. "Card of Time, take us away from here!"

The Card of Time flew from her hand, slashing the shadowy light and enveloping Mattie and the Great Magician into its blackness.

𒀭𒈾𒈲𒀭𒁁

The Hippodrome's gigantic water tank burst open. The seven demon gods, with their shark-python forms, now fully formed swam out of the liquid, which now rapidly rose toward the ceiling of the basement. But they weren't the only creatures within, for to the surface of the now-roiling liquid ascended the Brotherhood of Evil: first the Beast with his bull face and hairy, humped body, condemned from a king to the body of a beast. The other three were nearby: Khan of the Huns, round faced, sallow colored, with a forehead large and protruding. His almond-shaped eyes were askew, with one higher than the other, and he wore a cap of bloody leaves. Beyond Khan bobbed a pale man with a balding head fringed by coarse hair and a long face that seemed to melt into his beard. His bulging eyes and sloping nose showed him to be an aristocrat: the Grand Duke of Muscovy, the first Tsar of Russia. Lastly, shooting out of the water, came the Prince of Wallachia, with his narrow ferret-like face, a long nose that haughtily presided over a mustache that served as a roof of sorts over red pouty lips and a sharp jutting chin. His skin had a greenish hue and an oily sheen. The prince, with his foppish dark-red velvet hat, bobbed in the liquid, his black hair floating about his head in long coils. Although his name was Vlad, no one dared whisper it—for all his foppishness, the prince was a deadly foe, as his unsaid moniker, "Impaler," implied.

The Prince of Wallachia sniffed the air as one might a fine wine. The hairs within his sensitive nostrils vibrated with pleasure. Yes, it was indeed that fabulous aroma: the sea-salt smell of the blood of living humans. He and his cohorts had escaped the red orbs of Marduk and were indeed in the land of the living.

He gleefully pronounced, "Bravo, Beast! We are in the land of the living!" Then he added commandingly, "I have a horror of liquid. Beast, have your demon gods take it away at once."

His high-handed tone was not lost upon the others. The Beast bristled. But truth be told, the liquid was irksome. His heavy bull body was not meant for swimming.

He called the desecrated names of Marduk to the demon-serpent gods. "*Ankia-en-lugal Ugug Umum Tudu Udud Gar-gash Bilulu-en!*" Instantly they swam around the Beast.

The Beast grunted:

Ankia-en-lugal Ugug Umum Tudu Udud Gar-gash Bilulu-en!
Remove these liquid bars
That lie like chains upon myself and my brothers: the prince,
khan, and tsar.

The serpent gods' shark heads thrust up through the liquid. They spoke through their teeth with a whistling yet guttural voice, "We are *Ankia-en-lugal Ugug Umum Tudu Udud Gar-gash*

Bilulu-en. And to you, Beast, who first called us after our long sleep, we belong. To you we bow and obey all commands."

The liquid instantly disappeared.

The Brotherhood of Evil dropped to the cement floor. The basement ceiling was high, as it had to accommodate the storage of all sorts of props, and therefore the seven demon-serpent gods could still remain aloft. They moved about in the space above the Beast. Now it could be seen that four of the serpent gods clasped within each of their tails the prey that the Beast had ordered captured. These four—the fat man with the orange hair and mustache, the yellow-haired woman, the lunatic spirit with the frog legs, and the muscular one—struggled to little avail against the tight clasp of the python demon gods.

The Beast stood upon his two hooves; his beefy arms, covered in dark fur, were flung out. His head was tilted up as if to keep the liquid out.

Unconsciously the Beast moved the tip of his tongue to the side of his mouth to feel the Droplet that held Marduk's demise. The Droplet had fallen from the eye of Marduk in the ancient battle when he and the other gods had fought for control of the underworld. This Droplet was formed from the waters of Apsu and Tiamet, who were said to have conceived Marduk. The Beast, as the ancient King Ashurnasirpal, knew that the Droplet marked the beginning of the true Seven Sacred Tablets of Creation. These tablets lay buried so that the other tale—that of Marduk as invincible and all knowing—lived, while the true tale lay dead to the ears of all.

It was the dead gods—the forgotten mighty ones, the Asaru-alim-nuna—who had whispered into the Beast's ears that the kingdom he held in his mortal hands was nothing compared to the one he could possess if he helped them overthrow Marduk.

These forgotten mighty ones yearned for Marduk's defeat, but for that they needed one of his legion of the underworld to overthrow him. They told the Beast of the Hidden Sister of Marduk, she who had been born of Apsu and Tiamet, to whom the Tablet of Destiny of Light had been given. They told him that this Hidden Sister's whereabouts were known to an entity trapped in a metal amulet and that, once Marduk was defeated, they would share with the Beast the power of both Tablets of Destiny.

The Beast, who was in the mighty, handsome form of a mortal king, had recoiled at so great and dangerous a treason against Marduk. He knew that even the thought of it rendered him at great peril. Then the forgotten gods told him of the Droplet of weakness that had fallen from Marduk's eye in the Great Battle of the Gods. They tempted him with tales of how the possessor of the Droplet, together with a secret incantation, could be rendered invisible to the eyes and ears of Marduk. After that, they said, it would be just a matter of gathering others in the underworld of like mind to overthrow Marduk. Then the gods would be set free, and imagine what power he, the Beast, would hold.

The gods gave the Beast the incantation; now all he needed was the Droplet. "Seek it, for it is here, under your palace, that the Droplet fell," the forgotten ones told him. And so he, though he was already a mighty king, had succumbed to their luring him into possessing an even greater kingdom than his mortal hands held. But he didn't find the Droplet. It was Marduk who had discovered his treachery and turned him into a foul-breathing beast and held him as an underling through eons.

Then incredibly the Droplet was in his possession, through that ugly hag, the Crone. How this smallest drop lay glittering upon the dirty nail of the Crone, the Beast had no idea. But he knew the Crone, remarkably, did not know she held the Droplet and in fact did not even feel it. The Beast knew she was greedy for her beauty, which had been lost in the eons due to her greed for more beauty and the power it held. The Crone also was greedy for something that she did not speak of, something that drove her through the eons, imprisoned in the cast of ugliness.

The Beast had taken the Droplet from her dirty nail as he was giving her the thumbs of Abaddon, purportedly in exchange for spells the Crone had to allow him to stand on two legs. The Beast had opened his mouth to the Crone, and his tongue shot forward, holding the two thumbs that were upon it. The Crone reached to grab them; as she did, the very tip of the Beast's tongue snatched the Droplet, which sat upon her long black nail. Quickly the Beast retreated his tongue into his mouth, feeling the Droplet's sharp blades cut his mouth. Mesmerized by the black and blue thumbs of Abaddon, the Crone wasn't aware that the Droplet was gone. She cackled with delight as she held the thumbs in her bony hands.

The incantation of the desecrated names of Marduk given to the Beast by the Asaru-alim-nuna had indeed rendered him invisible to the Dark Master. and from it the Brotherhood of Evil had formed. But it hadn't been a force enough to destroy Marduk, for by then the Asaru-alim-nuna had been imprisoned by the Dark Master deep with the walls that formed the bowels of Kurnigi.

The Beast knew that the forgotten gods were tricksters of mortal man and condemned spirits alike. He also knew that the knowledge of how to unleash the Droplet to destroy Marduk was held tightly by the Asaru-alim-nuna—and the incantation given to the Beast was only enough to gather forces for them. But he held the Droplet, not the Asaru-alim-nuna, and the Beast wasn't going to give up possession of it for the promise of the trinket of controlling Kurnigi.

Now, in the basement of the Hippodrome, the Droplet glinted within the darkness of the Beast's mouth.

The three others of the Brotherhood saw the motion of the Beast's tongue but not the glint. It was obvious that the Beast was hiding something from them that the serpent demon gods knew was powerful. The Sign of the Four that lay on their foreheads was invisible to all, but each pulsated a blood red, as if to remind the Beast of his sworn allegiance to the others. It was a bond, born of their resentment of Marduk, that the Brotherhood of Evil had formed when they were in Kurnigi. A dance of loyalty by the treacherous, much like the dance of honesty of the pathological liar. Still, as it was expedient to pledge allegiance to one another, the Brotherhood of Evil had remained intact. Walking upright on two hooves, the Beast, with his hulky bull shape, though he was once the ancient King Ashurnasirpal, was viewed by the other three with disdain. The Beast was more animal than man—certainly not like them, in whose veins ran aristocracy, their being and manner clearly demarcating them from lowly peasants. Khan, the duke, and the prince each were waiting for the moment to overthrow the Beast and take over the reins of command, which was their due.

The serpent demon gods spun downward toward the Beast. The Droplet's glint had flickered for a millisecond in the Beast's mouth, and they had seen it while swimming in the air above him. That was time enough for the serpent gods to be mesmerized. They were the most ancient of the Asaru-alim-nuna, older than the cave gods even, but held in low regard by the gods about whom mortal man had crafted myths; these revered gods considered the serpent gods to be just above maggots in their place in the song of death. These old demons of death and destruction had once moved silently and unseen in the seas, evoking fear but not mortal worship. The serpent demons moved downward, their tails pointed toward the ceiling. They elongated their bodies so that their shark faces were close upon the Beast. The Beast grunted in surprise.

The smell and sight of the Droplet bewitched them. Their scaled python bodies glimmered as they wove around the Beast. Their shark teeth glinted in hunger. Then suddenly they moved into the air, as silently as they had in the days when they had lived in the sea. It was they who smelled the Droplet upon the Beast. Their pledge to serve him had broken under the Droplet's enthralling gleam. Here it was, the thing that held the demise of Marduk, who had imprisoned them for eons! They had called the Beast their master, for he had uttered their names, but the Beast was not a demon god as they were. The whistling, guttural voices of the serpent demon gods rose: this Beast they would break; this Beast they could destroy, as they swam not in the bowels of Kurnigi under Marduk's control but where mortals' blood froze in fear of them— in the land of the living. As they moved toward one another to form a deadly circle, their scaly bodies shed a sickly yellow light, the color of decay. The scales of light then formed a net that fell upon the Beast and lifted him up toward the serpent demon gods.

As the prince, Khan, and the duke watched the Beast being lifted him away from them, this thought instantly sprang into their minds: *He escapes so that he alone may rule mighty!* They weren't about to let the Beast have such triumph. Then Khan, the duke, and the prince flung themselves into the net of light. Once they were inside it, they grabbed the Beast tightly—one each upon his arm, the other grabbing his head.

The tails of the serpent demon gods unclasped the Beast's four prey, which they had held under his orders. What did they care for the Beast's commands? The fat man with the orange hair and mustache, the yellow-haired woman, the lunatic spirit with the frog legs, and the muscular one all tumbled to the ground.

The serpent demons swung their tails around the net of scaly light. Each tail end wove over the other, forming a tight circle of control around the Beast and Brotherhood of Evil, who clung to him. The suffocating yellow net of scales had formed a cage around the Beast and his brethren, who now understood thoroughly that they were prisoners of these demons. The serpent demons then moved their circle of bodies toward the cage, intent on crushing the Beast and the Brotherhood of Evil with their python strength. Closer and closer they moved. The Beast's hairy body stunk with frustration as he struggled against the pressure. Then, as the circle grew tighter around the four it held, it became a bright yellow flash just before it vanished, taking the Brotherhood of Evil with it.

𒀹𒀹𒀹 𒀹 𒀹𒀹𒀹 𒀹

The floor of the Hippodrome's basement met Paddy O'Reilly's back with unrelenting hardness as he dropped upon it. He yelped. Lying on his back, he glimpsed, through his foggy glasses, the terrible creatures that had held him disappear in a yellow flash. This was a dim awareness, for most prominent were the sharp pains that shot through him. He moaned at this additional assault to his portly body, which had been punctured by the stings of the serpent demons' sharp tails and the bites of disembodied heads deep within the bowels of Kurnigi.

Paddy's expedition clothing was in ruins: tattered, torn, and stained by all the unseemly exertions, the jig-jags in time; bitten, beaten in a dark underworld. Oh, all he had endured since

Biddle and those children had come upon him in Nineveh while he was attempting to discover the Eighth Tablet of Creation! His round face was flushed and framed by frizzy red hair; his orangey-red mustache lay like a limp rag under his nose. He had started his expedition in Nineveh in 1938, but he had no idea where they were now or even what year it was.

Paddy groaned under the weight of these thoughts. *Oh, my. Oh, my.*

In contrast to Paddy, Sir Henry Layard, tall and dashing in his crisp expedition clothing, landed on his haunches and stood up with the ease of a natural athlete. He took in the disappearance of the primordial creatures but wasn't foolish enough to believe he and his companions were out of danger. Beneath his white shirt, the outlines of his muscular form could be seen. Layard wore his brown hair parted on the side, dark locks of which fell over his forehead. He had a small mustache and two dimples that permanently lined each check. His nose was a long aristocratic one; his cheekbones were prominent; and his jawline was well defined and square. His sleeves were rolled up to reveal arms kissed brown by the desert sun.

The old man that he once was—the haggard Sir Henry with the coarse white beard, the one who was lacking in courage, the one with the careful demeanor, the avoidant one, the one Biddle and Wigglesworth had found in his reading room at the British Museum—that self had been shed fully. Biddle and Wigglesworth had come traveling through time, visits that he dreaded and that made him question his sanity. They had come this last time brandishing his research paper "Discoveries in the Ruins beneath the Tunnels of Ashurnasirpal."

In seeking the tunnels to find their lost companions, Biddle and Wigglesworth, with their chants, had landed all three first upon a mound in Nineveh. There Layard had been given a choice by fate: beams of light that showed a safe path and an unknown path. True, Layard had first flung his trembling, palsied hands toward the beam of the known path: the path of safety and old age. But a vision had stopped him: that of himself as an old man lying upon his death bed, gray in face and soul—he who had taken the path of cowardice. Layard had swung toward the beam of the unknown and the dangerous path of courage.

It was her eyes within the glimmering beam that had drawn Layard. *Oh, Lady of My Soul!* Her dark shining eyes; her long hair falling in ringlets about her shoulders; the graceful arch of her long neck; the face carved into the slabs excavated by him on the mound in Mosul, which he had sought again and again in the desert, but never found. *The Queen of the Desert! Oh, Lady of My Soul!* Her face had enchanted his dreams and whispered words of endless love. The blood of youth instantly had flown through him, and he was as he once had been: the dashing explorer of the 1840s who branded pistols, fought with valor the Turks and Persians, and had been imprisoned but escaped.

Layard, for Sir Henry was no longer how he thought of himself—that was an accolade for the old man who had hidden behind the safe walls of the politician, the diplomat. No, he was Layard now: strong, fearless but not foolhardy. His deep-set dark eyes were alert. He quickly scanned the environment, lit in the harshness of the bare bulbs that illuminated the basement. Layard saw that the round, hot-tempered academic had fallen on the other side of this cellar. But Smith…where was he? And the woman? As he thought this, the woman fell, almost at his feet. Layard was alarmed by her state of unconsciousness.

The web-footed, emaciated, ragged George Smith fell beyond the prone Dottie O'Reilly and quickly sprang up like a jackrabbit.

He immediately moved his arms in front of him, palms up, eyes zigzagging about. Smith felt little relief at being unleashed from the serpents' clasp—the Land of Darkness was an endless series of punishments. As well, Smith's long years in Kurnigi's bowels had taught him this: *Know at once the power of the enemy spirits that inhabit the realm in which you are plunged, for there are only two denizens of the Land of Darkness: predator and prey.* He was not going to become prey.

"Dottie!" Paddy cried in relief as he turned his head toward the opposite side of the basement.

Paddy remained flat on his back, pinned by the pain that shot through his body. He wasn't the dashing explorer that Layard was. Though he was only in his midthirties, his wiry red hair was already thinning, and his body reflected his dedication to scholarly pursuits: soft layers of fat served as testimony to his discipline of spending long hours poring over various assyriology tomes in the library. His 1938 expedition to Nineveh, self-funded, had been curiously interrupted by Herman Biddle—a mysterious ally of Dr. L. Rufus Wigglesworth, the chairman of his department at Columbia University—and three children, one of whom, Mattie, was his daughter from the future. But most miraculous of all, he had been reunited with his beloved wife—though how this could be, as she was from the future, his empirical mind did not quite grasp.

Dorothea, Dottie in the short form. Dottie! Paddy was jerked out of his thoughts. He turned his head to see that his beautiful Dottie was now crumpled in a heap, clearly unconscious; her blond hair was undone and lying in silky strands across her pale face. Her plain skirt and blouse showed the evidence of the wear and tear of their journey in Kurnigi. Paddy's heart ached at seeing his love so vulnerable. He grunted as he sat up, grimacing in agony as he did so.

Layard deftly lifted Dottie. She was so light that he barely felt her in his arms. As her head fell back, her pale complexion and closed eyes and stillness gave her the look of a porcelain doll. Layard again wondered whether a creature this delicate could survive the travails of their journey.

Paddy's face flushed to the tips of his frizzy red hair as jealousy pinched his heart. *The scoundrel! That cad Layard had Dottie cradled in his arms!* His bushy orange-red mustache bristled with indignation.

Paddy's myopic eyes were magnified behind his black-framed glasses, which sat askew upon his face. He flashed anger as he staggered up, sharp pain rolling through his chubby form. He had to save Dottie from that rogue! His thoughts ran upon one another, weaving in and out of the excruciating pain that moved through his body. The bites and beatings of Kurnigi had taken their toll on Paddy, who was made for a different type of battle, one that was fought in the annals of peer-reviewed journals—not in the corporeal world.

Layard tapped Dottie's face lightly to see if he could awaken her. "Madam!" he said.

Paddy was jolted up out of his pain. *Now look! That rascal is caressing my wife's face! Outrageous!* He had known from Layard's writings of his "discoveries" at Nineveh (a thoroughly worthless work, a piece of fluff by a rank amateur adventurer in the mid-1800s, if you asked Paddy, who was an assistant—almost associate—professor at Columbia University's department of assyriology) that Layard paid an inordinate amount of unseemly attention to the women he encountered in the desert.

Layard felt confident that the woman who lay limp in his arms had gone into shock; this he knew was highly dangerous from his many experiences in the desert. Shock led to the body shutting down; shock led to death.

Layard shook Dottie gently as he held her in his arms. "Madam!" he said. "Madam!"

"Unhand her!" Paddy shouted, his face distorted in pain as he stumbled toward the other side of the interminable basement, each step accompanied by shooting sensations.

Now, Paddy thought grimly, he fully understood the many allusions to the "pretty eyes" and "the remarkably beautiful women" of the tribes that littered Layard's account of his expedition in Nineveh as he arrogantly floated down the Tigris River. No true academic wrote such nonsense! Yes, it was time for Paddy's groundbreaking work, the rejected *JASA* paper "The Eighth Tablet of Creation: Moving Beyond the Hegemony of Layard and Smith," which directly exposed the scholarly arrogance of this...this *womanizer* Layard (and the madman Smith), to be given the full airing it deserved. Perhaps an addendum piece adding the personal knowledge acquired from the recent strange occurrences (how to explain these he would have to leave for now) would merit—yes, it *did* merit—an entire edition of *JASA*, *The Journal of the American Society of Assyriologists* devoted to it.

Layard's face was low to Dottie's as he held her in his arms. She hadn't stirred. *Is she still breathing?* he wondered.

Good God! Is this man now kissing Dottie? Paddy thought, alarmed.

"You rogue!" Paddy screamed, jumping up, his arms flailing, and then, leveled down by a shooting pain in his hip, he fell flat on his face.

Layard frowned as he saw the chubby man with the red mustache fall to the floor on his face, floundering and angrily blabbering some nonsense. The man was almost as much of a lunatic as George Smith. Layard's eyes caught hold of Smith, once hailed a genius, now touching the walls of the basement, his frog feet slapping the cement floor as he paced and muttered about, assessing the spirits he sensed were inside the building.

Clad in unkempt, torn expedition clothing, Smith was emaciated, his hair and beard filthy. His eyes screamed of madness—what horrors had he suffered in Kurnigi, that evil underworld? Layard shuddered in wonder. This was the same Smith who had deciphered the cursed tablets that Layard had unearthed in Nineveh, of the ancient Semitic peoples, the Chaldeans; no wonder it was called the "bitter and swift nation," for such appeared to be the destruction of those who touched the Tablets of Creation. The tablets were the Chaldeans' first documentation of the early account of the Great Flood, the story of Creation, and within that was the story of the lost Gilgamesh, all of which Smith had dangerously deciphered from the cuneiform.

Even with his formidable authority, Layard had failed to stop the task George Smith had proposed in 1876: to find the missing Twin Tablet, the counterpart to the one held by the Dark Master Marduk. Smith had said he felt certain that the secret lay within the elusive Eleventh Tablet, which finished the tale of the deluge and of Gilgamesh and would lead to the other half of the Dup Shimati.

Ah, Smith, why did you not stay away from the blighted tablets, as I warned you? But did not Layard himself not heed the warning in the visions that had come to him during his excavation near Nineveh in a dream in 1845? He had seen the labyrinth of caves, chambers upon chambers, where he heard the cries of tortured souls as well as a warning: these secrets should not be unearthed.

Smith's final letter to him came again into Layard's mind. Smith wrote that the story of the Twin Tablets of Destiny, the

Dup Shimati, was not as it was thought. Smith's last ominous lines now rang in Layard's head: *I fear I will soon be plunged and imprisoned beneath the black earth, for the forces of the Dark Master surround me. I feel the evil breath of the curse of the king of Ashurnasirpal upon me, his hooves treading on my neck as I awaken in sweat each night…and see the shadow of the Snake behind him.*

Layard forced these thoughts to stop. It was true that he himself had brought the cursed tablets to the British Museum, and years later the eccentric Smith, with no formal education whatsoever, was able to decipher them through some sort of black magic. And for that—for Layard bringing those tablets out of the earth—Smith had paid the price. So, Layard recognized, he was now responsible for Smith, whatever he was. A madman? Tortured spirit?

Layard frowned, for the stout academic shot up, red-faced, angrily waving his hands and babbling nonsense, only to collide against the lunatic George Smith. The portly one yelped as was caught under Smith's webbed feet.

Paddy struggled to untangle himself and sprang toward Layard. "Unhand her! You…you…rapscallion!"

Smith scowled, jumping over Paddy. "You boob!" he said irritably. "Now you've done it—you've disturbed my assessment of the spirits!"

Layard tapped the unconscious woman again. The color in her face seemed to be returning.

Smith, he saw, had again resumed his flapping movements about the room. Yes, Layard was responsible for George Smith, but to what end? How was he to traverse and overcome these treacherous depths of the underworld—to walk the Path of the Virtuous—with two companions such as these and this woman, who was so delicate? And where on earth were Wigglesworth and Biddle?

The door to the basement flung open. From above, the eyes of those who were dead, yet alive with the spirits of the Muhra, saw the four figures below. They moved downward in jagged movements on the stairs to stave off rigor mortis. They were the stagehands coming to retrieve more materials for the Great Diva's performance.

George Smith's dark hair was as wild as the storm that raged within him. The vibrations from the evil spirits pulsated into this palms and shot through his webbed feet. *Damnation!* In alarmed recognition, he cried, "Muhra!"

At once Smith recognized that these were bodies possessed by the evil spirits from Kurnigi's gates. He, who had been trapped in the depths of the underworld after his strange discoveries in Nineveh, knew and feared the Muhra. They were the first of the spirits encountered in the dark underworld, and because of their bitterness over their formlessness, they maliciously tricked newly condemned souls to give to them whatever trinket of magic or spells or knowledge that they held. Smith's eyes darted in confusion. His palms hadn't detected the underworld's usual vibrations of terror. Where were they? His eyes jumped from the Muhra to the bowels of the Hippodrome. *What hell is this?*

As Dottie lay within Layard's arms, her eyes fluttered, and her lips were moving. *Mattie...be sober minded. Be watchful.* Then from one of Dottie's pockets flew out Wigglesworth's lost Small Book of Spells. Dottie had placed the book there after Geeta had thrown it down upon the Second Stone when the Snake had clasped Paddy and herself. There it had remained through her travels deep within Kurnigi, forgotten. Truth be told, Dottie had little idea of what it was, for Dr. Wigglesworth hadn't disclosed that he held it. The Small Book of Spells was light as a sparrow. It opened and revealed itself to be empty of pages, for the Last Spell had been ripped out. The Small Book of Spells moved with the flaps of the cover serving as its wings, stretching out, at first a muddy brown as if it had just been unearthed from the ground but then glimmering and glittering, as the feathers of a wondrously colored bird might appear under sunbeams. It flew about the four—Dottie, Paddy, Smith, and Layard—and covered them with its luminescent glow and absorbed them into the cover. The Small Book of Spells then flew through one of the basement walls.

The Muhra saw something fly out of the basement walls. *Escaping spirits*, they thought. The small crystal ball holding the Phantom Magicians' spirits clattered down the stairs past the Muhra. Then the crystal ball hit the wall and shot through it. *Dead souls recently imprisoned escaping*, the Muhra stagehands thought. *Not our problem.* They were no longer guarding the gates of Kurnigi. This was the Hippodrome. They had a show to put on.

𒀭𒉿𒍝𒂖𒀭𒉿 𒅋

The fire's warmth fell like feathers brushing against Mattie's face. She opened her eyes to see flames about her and the man in chains—flames that slashed the air like giant red swords. She was surprised at where the Card of Time had taken them: right into a fire! Mattie had expected to be whisked somewhere safe and far away, not to be burned up! The flames sputtered up, sending some sparks. Mattie quickly patted her pants pockets for the Card of Time to get them out of the fire, but it wasn't there. Trapped. *Stay calm. Get the intel like Eddie would*, she told herself. The warmth remained the same, Mattie registered. She and the man in chains were sort of floating within the flames.

There didn't seem to be any ground underneath them—just the fire. And they weren't burning up; it was as if they were sitting around the fire and not in it. Mattie looked over at the shackled man next to her. His lips were moving. She couldn't understand what he was saying, for she became aware of music coming from beyond the fire, permeating it with notes—long, beautiful notes that filled her. A violin's melancholic strains were lifted by the rifts of a guitar, the haunting voice of a woman weaving in and out of the sounds of the instruments.

Mattie felt the strains of the song move into her heart. Like cool waters that soothed, the song poured itself over her. *When you walk through the fire, you will not be burned. The flames will not set you ablaze.* Mattie heard her mother's voice move in and out of the beautiful notes hypnotically. She felt her eyes become heavy as the lids closed. She lost sense of who she was until all she was aware of was the music.

The darkness of the New York City alleyway gave way to the flickers of light around a garbage can in which a fire had been lit. The flames shot in spurts, greedily devouring the combustibles within. Men with long beards and black hats, women wearing brightly colored scarves to fend off the cold—their swarthy faces surrounded the fire as it rose from whatever in the days of the Depression could be marshalled to be burned. Now the fire grew ever larger as the mystic chords of music that surrounded it rose to feed it. The colorful scarves around those who made the music glimmered in the light of flames. Some played guitars. Others played violins; the notes, wrung from the strings of their instruments, were taut with sorrow. Music moved across their souls like a wind across the face of a calm sea. Those who played these instruments did so as one might sing a hymn in worship, for that was what these gathered individuals—numbering less than a dozen men and women, derided as fortune-tellers, thieves, and gypsies—were doing.

The notes were vibrant and sorrowful at once; they were a chain of connection from those gathered around the fire in a New York City alley to those who secretly had kept alive the worship of the Mother Tiamat from ancient times to now. They whose hands were clasped in an invisible bond of spiritual links across time and place. They who had ventured out knowing that deadly spirits rose to capture their souls. Among them, they held up a tall, thin, frail old man with light-blue eyes and white whiskers that grew into a long beard that lay flat on his chest. They had found him in this very alley, a pathetic heap, in worn expedition clothing, boots spattered with yellow dust, his eyes twitching in madness. It was the cape that fluttered above the old man—a gossamer web of light, a patchwork of the golden-hued pink, purple, and red of the setting winter sun—that showed them who he was. They had lit the fire in the garbage can to warm him. But the old man could not be warmed, for he shivered not from the cold but from the weight of his loss. In their song the voices of the tribes of past and present blended into the moans of the terrible night wind. This old one's sorrow blew in tendrils into the air and into their music, as the night of rising dead souls fell with a vengeance.

Then the fire rose high until the tips turned blue and licked the cold night air.

From the blue flames, a small brown girl dropped into the alley. Her owl eyes sat behind large black-framed glasses, her long black braids framing either side of her thin face. She wore a purple paisley-print dress and mustard-yellow tights. The brown child's palms were up, and within them the blue lifelines were bright.

Immediately the gypsies murmured in reverence. They moved back, as they recognized her from the tale they had carried through the generations—the tale that had come as they had traveled out of the old land one thousand years before, when they had been cursed with wanderlust to travel aimlessly upon the globe, forever derided, strangers always, until she came to lift the spell of their restless spirits. *A princess of old; upon her palms, the dual blue lifelines of her royal veins will shine bold.*

Geeta heard the murmurs of the gypsies calling her, "*Princess, Princess.*" But the memory of ThaTha and the cave was still strong. *Om namaya Shivaya:* she had been pulled from death by Lord Shiva, and her dharma was to guide Mattie to fulfill her destiny. Her old ThaTha had sacrificed something to allow this, for the puja had been held in a cave far from his home in Bombay. His words filled her ears: *Now you know your dharma. You must not fall into the grasp of illusion, as does she who fights her dharma. You must be a guide and lamp. To do so, you must grow and change. Om namaya Shivaya.*

ThaTha's chants faded as the gypsies' song filled her ears. Where was she? Where was Mattie? She saw the men and women— gypsies, she thought, for they reminded her of the people in Siberia who had lifted her upon their shoulders when Rasputin, with his mesmerizing eyes, was among them. Geeta took in the darkness of the alley and surmised that she was in a city, not the barren fields of Siberia.

Then she saw Mr. Biddle, hunched over on the grimy pavement. His white whiskers and the wispy strands of hair upon his head were embedded with twigs and debris, as if he had been rolling in the dirt. Geeta never had seen Mr. Biddle in such a disarrayed state. The cape about his shoulders was different: a beautiful changing color of both the setting and rising sun, but it was fragile in appearance, and he was shivering uncontrollably. Mr. Biddle's light-blue eyes, streaked with fear and confusion, flicked over Geeta with no recognition. Something was terribly, terribly wrong.

She immediately moved toward Mr. Biddle. He looked down as she took his hand. "Mr. Biddle, you must warm yourself by the fire."

Her touch upon his hand momentarily took away his fear, though his confusion remained, his voice hoarse as he muttered incoherently. Geeta looked into his eyes and saw that Mr. Biddle still didn't recognize her. Maybe if he warmed up, maybe then he would come back to himself. Geeta thought of how wise Mr. Biddle was, though now he seemed so uncertain and confused. She would have to warm him up then pull out the White Book of Magic so they could find Mattie.

Geeta led Mr. Biddle toward the flames as the gypsies parted to make room for them. Mr. Biddle seemed mesmerized by the fire. He then let out a small gasp.

Geeta looked closely at the fire, where she saw Mattie's face and body form within the flames. Mattie's eyes were shut tightly. Immediately, and unthinkingly, Geeta thrust her hands into the flames to pull Mattie out.

𒀭𒌋𒁹𒀭𒁹

Mattie heard a voice rising with the flames, a voice telling her to open her eyes. She opened her eyes and saw two hands reaching into the flames. They were small. She saw that the palms had deep-blue glowing lines upon them. Mattie clasped both hands with her hands.

Behind her, she heard the man cry out. "Please…don't leave me."

Mattie let one hand go and reached down to grab the shackles upon the man.

Then she felt the pull, and suddenly she and the chained man were tumbling out of the fire onto the ground. Mattie sensed the men and women form around her to help her up. She stood up and looked around in surprise to see that she had been trapped in flames from a fire that rose not in a mystical or magical place but from a garbage can in a dark alley.

As the darkness was relieved by the orange glow of the flames, she saw her.

"Geeta!" Mattie cried, and tears of relief rolled down her face as she hugged her friend tightly. "Geeta! You're alive! I knew you would be."

Relief flooded Geeta as well. Then she moved away from Mattie's clasp and adjusted her glasses. No time for sentimental forays. She remembered ThaTha's instruction: she was Mattie's guru, her guide to fulfill her dharma. The responsibility was heavy upon her thin shoulders. For this, ThaTha had performed a puja, had pulled her from the clasp of Kali, the demoness. For his prayers, Geeta's lifelines had been returned. What ThaTha had pledged in return for her restoration she didn't know. Most assuredly, the time for childishness was over, she resolved. She must grow and change, as must Mattie. For Mattie must complete the Path of the Virtuous. She had no idea where they were right now or where Eddie was, for that matter. How they would achieve this Herculean task also remained elusive to her. Surely, Mr. Biddle could be of guidance in these arenas once clarity was restored to him and once they had consulted the White Book of Magic.

Geeta turned to tell Mr. Biddle her thoughts. Then, with alarm, she saw that he was not by her side but was running down the alleyway, the cape moving like wisps of the setting sun, away from them.

"Oh! Mr. Biddle! Stop!" Geeta shouted, racing toward him. "Stop!"

"Do not worry. We shall get him, Princess," one of the gypsy men said, as he and two others ran down the alleyway.

As Mattie ran behind Geeta, she saw a bit of the cape as the figure moved out of the alleyway. "What's wrong with Mr. Biddle? Why's he running away from us?"

"Oh, Mattie! He's not himself!" Geeta cried in anguish, giving way to the very emotions she had chastised herself to refrain from. "He's confused."

The gypsy men already had run toward the end of the alleyway and come back. "Princess, the old one has disappeared into the night air."

Geeta gasped. Oh, this was indeed not fortuitous. Mr. Biddle must be under some evil spell of amnesia. They had to restore him. But first they had to find him.

"Mattie, employ the Spyglass to find Mr. Biddle," Geeta ordered, as she and Mattie made their way back to the fire.

Mattie paused. She was happy to have Geeta back, but she seemed different. Plus, she definitely didn't like her bossy tone.

Mattie shook her head. "We don't need that rat fink to find Mr. Biddle."

The man in the shackles was stirring at her feet. The gypsies warily moved away him. He was of the spirit world, but the red-haired child and the brown owl were not.

"What does that mean, Mattie?" Geeta asked, alarmed. "Please don't tell me that you've lost possession of the Spyglass!"

Mattie shrugged noncommittedly but again felt a little annoyed at Geeta's tone. She pointed at the man. "He'll help us. He owes me," Mattie said.

"I don't understand, Mattie!" Geeta saw with incredulity that Mattie was pointing to the almost-naked man wrapped in shackles.

"Princess," one of the women by the fire warned, "beware of this one. He is of the spirit world."

The man, curled in a fetal position, was moaning in pain.

"You are the guardian of the Spyglass, Mattie." Geeta's words were stopped by the murmurs of surprise from the gypsies around her, for the man coughed, and from his mouth flew a small golden key right into Mattie's hands.

Move this key over my chains so that I can be free. I promise to help you, the man's voice echoed in Mattie's mind. Quickly she passed the key over the air above his prone body.

The chains instantly melted. The man was still clad only in swim trunks and remained in a fetal position, holding his abdomen and moaning in pain, for without the amulet of the Phantom Magicians' wand, he was destined to be imprisoned within his last mortal moments before death.

The gypsies moved back farther to give this groaning one a broad swath. They fixed their eyes upon him in hypervigilance and remained protectively gathered around Geeta.

Mattie considered the writhing man and his pain. She held the key up to her eyes. She saw that it had writing engraved on it, but it was so small that she couldn't read it.

"Geeta, what do you think this means?" Mattie asked. Maybe it was some kind of instructions to help the man feel better.

Geeta leaned over to squint at the key's words.

Then the writing grew larger and larger until the words were floating, like oil on water, above the key.

Mattie read them out loud, remembering what Mrs. Elmwood had said about long words: to read them in chunks and pronounce slowly. "Anti-do-tum-mith-ra-da-ti-cum!"

At the last of the words, the key flew out of Mattie's hands. It turned into a small honey-colored drop that fell onto the man's tongue. Immediately the man's pain stopped, and he jumped up. The drop turned back into a key. As it fluttered out of his mouth, he grabbed it deftly.

"Clothes!" he commanded, waving the golden key.

Instantly he was in his black tuxedo, with a white shirt that came to his chin. This time his feet were shod. His face remained clean-shaven, and without the chains about him and the pain now lifted, a friendly smile formed.

The gypsies smiled in recognition at the curly-haired man before them and clapped appreciatively. "It is the Great Magician!"

Of course, it was the tenth anniversary of his death, was it not? Though in life he had been their foe—he had derided them as phonies and frauds in their efforts at contact with the afterworld—they celebrated his appearance from the spirit world and clapped in admiration that he had realized his promised return from the dead.

The Great Magician flung the key up in the air, tilted his head back as he opened his mouth, and with a showman's flair, swallowed it whole.

Then he bowed his dark curly head toward Mattie. "Thank you. Now I can help you."

Mattie made a little face at Geeta that said, *I told you so.*

Geeta's head tilted in puzzlement, her black braids falling to one side, her black-framed glasses magnifying the brown eyes behind them. Her encyclopedic mind was at work. The Great Magician? Was it… the legendary magician Houd..? Geeta thoughts were interrupted by the Great Magician's shout.

The Great Magician said, "Stand back," and the gypsies moved back. The Master Magician reached into the fire and pulled out a black, burning lump. He held it within his palms and blew a puff of air upon it. The lump of coal turned a pearly white and grew and formed into a crystal ball.

The Great Magician handed the crystal ball to Mattie. "Take it, child, and in here you will find where your friend, the old man, has gone."

Mattie and Geeta gazed into the crystal ball. The gypsies peered over their shoulders to see the vision form. But the ball remained opaque. Mattie and Geeta looked puzzled.

Mattie shook the crystal ball, but it still remained dark. "Do we need any magic words?" she asked the Great Magician.

The Great Magician made a motion for Mattie to be quiet. Surely he heard her call—faint, true, but did he not just hear it, the secret song they had pledged to sing to each other? Yes, he was certain that he heard the song!

"Sweet Rosabelle!" he sang. "For me you hold a spell!"

𒀭𒈾𒂗𒈾𒀭

The office on the second floor of the department of assyriology at Columbia University was austere, even for Depression-era standards. It clearly had been rearranged. A desk with neat piles of paper and a half-filled pitcher of water was pushed to one side, against a heavily laden bookshelf.

The emaciated academic, Dr. Milo Peasely, wearing an ill-fitting suit, with a dark-black toupee perched precariously atop his egg-shaped head, under which a fringe of wispy gray hair poked out, scanned the room. A madame known for her "prowess" in contacting the beyond (or the ability to make money disappear from the pockets of the gullible, as the academics had sneered) had agreed to participate in a séance (for a fee—pooled resources that in reality amounted to a very paltry sum).

Even with the absence of the six members of the Society of Phantom Magicians, Peasely's office felt crowded. He knew that it was too small a venue to comfortably hold ten people (not to mention a *spirit*, he snorted). But it was the best he could do, for he had organized the séance in stealth, knowing full well that Dr. L. Rufus Wigglesworth, chair of the department of assyriology, would have nixed it. Wigglesworth and his new ally, Biddle (a man whose academic footprint was hazy indeed), seemed inordinately fearful of the otherworld. Wigglesworth had taken it upon himself to chastise Peasely, saying, "Tempt not the spirits of darkness! For they will swallow you whole." That Wigglesworth was a believer of such nonsense was astonishing. The Debunkers Association (a rather inflated name, given the present membership of three) were academics—two in archaeology and one (Peasely) in assyriology—and had made a bet with the Society of Phantom Magicians (another rather impressive name, contrasted by their larger but still meager membership of six), who remained steadfast in their belief that the Great Magician would appear from his lair in the spirit world. The bet had no monies associated with it, just the satisfaction of proving one or the other party wrong. Yes, on this Halloween night, surely momentous in that it was the tenth anniversary of the death of the Great Magician, it would be a feat indeed to expose psychics for the frauds they were.

"Tonight the Debunkers Association will decisively demonstrate that mediums are frauds—one and all!" pronounced Dr. Milo Peasely. "Gentlemen, the hour of midnight is upon us, though the members of the Society of Phantom Magicians have yet to show. Cowards."

Peasely continued, "Madame Luludja has graciously agreed be the *medium* for this event."

He snickered derisively, and the two other men, the remaining stalwart members of the Debunkers Association, superior in their scholarly acumen and wearing the requisite black-framed eyeglasses, joined him in his laughter, each man merrily shaking his balding head.

Madame Luludja was vaguely middle-aged, having one of those faces that appeared neither young nor old. She wore the usual costume of the psychic: a long-sleeve black-velvet dress—nubby with wear—that reached to her ankles, along with a pair of pointed black boots. Her eyes were a dark brown and her hair a similar shade, parted down the middle and worn back in a tight bun. She sat expressionless in the stark, brightly lit office, in the assyriology section of Columbia University, in an otherwise dark and empty building. Madame knew that the sour professor had deliberately sought a sterile atmosphere, one that was stripped of all the mystery that a psychic created: the scents of the whispering olfactory spirit oils, the soft darkness around the light of the candles, the hushed voices, and minds that were open to the otherworld—all to allure the spirit in. Money, meager though this séance's fee would be, was something in a time when not much was to be had.

A small, square, wooden table sat at the center of the room, around which were Madame Luludja's seat and two additional chairs at each side, provided for the Phantom Magicians to form the circle for the calling of the Great Magician. Madame had asked for a round table and noted here too that the peevish professor had defied her. On the table directly in front of her was a fishbowl that was filled with water—a proxy for a crystal ball. Madame Luludja's crystal ball had cracked in a particularly vicious séance just days earlier, in which the spirits called had been angry at being disturbed. She had no funds to replace it, a fact she had conveyed to Peasely, who had waved his hands dismissively and said with a sneer that a fishbowl would suffice.

Two stout candles were placed on either side of the bowl. Their wicks were dipped in Abramelin oil; the candles themselves were infused with aromatic oils, three parts Abramelin oil of old and one part the secret mixture of myrrh. Fire drew the spirits, and the mystical scents made the pathway clear for the travel from the otherworld. Thus Madame Luludja had insisted upon the expense of these candles. She struck a match. As she lit each candle, her lips moved silently as she called for the strength of the scent and fire to make the journey of the spirits an easy one. Instantly the candles seemed to come alive; their scent traveled through the office like a spell: now the whiff of bay laurel, then cinnamon, then the smell of burning birch, then the sudden aroma of pepper nigrum, and then the bracing smell of camphor melded with the oils of eucalyptus and ginger.

Peasely sneezed, creating a tremor that shook his toupee. He adjusted it automatically. The Great Magician had been their ally as a Debunker. Indeed, it was he who had set up fraud exposures in 1925: shows all over the country, offering $10,000 (what a sum! Ah, for those were the glittery days before the economic crash, when cash flowed like a gushing geyser!) to anyone who could demonstrate supernatural powers that he could not duplicate. He had shown over and over how these trickster gypsies spat out "ectoplasm" (in reality a mixture of egg whites, entrails, and other foods swallowed and regurgitated), levitated tables with invisible strings, and so forth. Those who preyed upon the bereaved, vulnerable in their grief and desperate to hear the voice of their dearly departed, were an outrage to decency! It was rumored that these efforts had angered the mediums, who in turn placed a curse upon the Great Magician. The academics had sneered at first, but in the fall of 1926, several strange events occurred: the Great Magician's wife was struck by ptomaine poisoning; he himself suffered an ankle fracture during the Chinese water torture trick; and then ultimately he died from punches to the abdomen in a ludicrous bet with college students. One of the academics was now struggling with a bulky camera, circa 1929, a remnant from the heady days before the crash, to memorialize the process.

"Begin your proceedings, Madame Luludja. The midnight hour has long struck and moves forward," Milo Peasely peremptorily said as he looked up from his watch, twitching his nose. The scent was overpowering, and he felt another sneeze brewing. "Our cameraman, the good Dr. Brewster, is ready,"

"A ring of hands is needed for the magic circle," Madame said. "I have told you this already."

Peasely snorted. "Well, as the members of the Society of *Phantom* Magicians were to form your *magic* circle, but have held good to their name and have not appeared, Dr. Leadbetter and I will substitute. Camera, Brewster!"

The two academics seated themselves at the small table and clasped hands with Madame, one on either side. Madame closed her eyes and said, "Behold, O spirit, O Great Magician!"

Both Debunkers snickered.

The Madame ignored this and continued, "Three parts Abramelin oil of old and one part the secret myrrh scent this air, that you may move from the spirit world to our lair."

She kept her eyes shut; she was not a fraud, for there had been times when the otherworld had appeared to her, though not necessarily giving the bereaved what they wanted to hear. Many times the deceased would air the same petty complaints and grudges they had held in life. Madame had been shrewd enough to take editorial liberties with such communications, sometimes causing her to become the subject of the wrath of these spirits. Tonight she did not expect the Great Magician to appear here. Yes, it was the tenth anniversary of the Great Magician's death, but these foolish professors thought that his spirit would appear to them and not his widow, Bess, an extremely unlikely occurrence. This was most likely why the Society of Phantom Magicians had not appeared. Still, a séance she would perform. Who knew? Perhaps on this night of All Hallows' Eve, when dead souls were said to wander the earth, spirits would come to her calling. Then perhaps she could have one of them rip the toupee off the egg-headed one. *Now that would be a trick!* Madame inwardly snickered. Then she disciplined her mind to be silent.

"O Great Magician, O Great Seer. Phantom from beyond, appear!" Madame called.

𒀭𒇉𒂊𒀭𒅕

The Great Magician threw his hands up as if reaching out to someone. "Bess! Oh, I will come, my love!" His face and arms began to fade.

Then he felt a tug at his tuxedo that yanked him back to the New York City alleyway. He frowned at Mattie, who clutched his coattails, binding him to this place. Desperation rose in the Great Magician's heart. The moment was short; the midnight hour—sixty minutes only—of October 31, 1936, was quickly fading. He felt Bess's doubt that he would rise from the spirit world to meet her. Ten tries to reach him in the spirit world he had asked her for. This was the last. She would never try again.

The Great Magician struggled against the hold of the red-haired child. "Please, child, I have helped you as promised. Now I must leave...my wife, Bess, calls."

Mattie shook her head as she held up the opaque crystal ball. "There's nothing in here. It's broken."

The Great Magician ignored Mattie, for he heard a female voice calling him. He flung his arms up and sang the song of their pact. "Sweet Rosabelle! You hold me in your spell! Oh, Bess, I sing the secret song! Sing it back, my love, that I may come to you!"

A gust came through the alleyway. It blew like a small spiraling wind as it formed over Great Magician. From the wind emerged two disembodied spectral hands that reached out with ghostly white fingers. They wrapped around the Master Magician's neck, yanking him up, but not before Mattie, tightly clutching the tuxedo tail, yelled as she too was sucked into the gathering wind, "You promised to help me find Mr. Biddle!"

Geeta instinctively grabbed Mattie's dangling foot. As she was her guru, it was imperative that she keep close to her side. As Geeta was pulled into the spinning wind, she called to the gypsies, "Please find Mr. Biddle!"

The gypsies below saw their princess disappear. Their eyes stung from the force of the wind. Find the old man they would.

𒁹𒌋 𒉺 𒁹𒌋 𒁹

The vibrations of spirits ran through Madame's fingers like small pricks of electricity. She opened her eyes to see the water within the fishbowl rippling. The lips of Peasely and the other academics were set in sarcastic smiles. They unclasped hands.

Madame Luludja's eyes suddenly turned inward, the whites of her eyes gleaming as her body shook.

"Really, Madame Luludja, such cheap theatrics?" Peasely said. "Shaking the table through tremors from your hands is such an old trick that I'm—"

His words were cut short as the fishbowl levitated from the table and sat suspended in the air. Then a wind rose from beneath it and flew into the bowl. The water was sloshed back and forth then suddenly erupted out like a geyser as the fishbowl shattered. The room shook. The candles fell.

The night of spirits was in full force, for a crystal ball shot out of the fishbowl. It gleamed like a new moon as it fell into Madame's hands. She cried out, for within the crystal ball, she saw six spirits with their eyes upon her. The crystal ball was clasped tightly within Madame's hands; such a thing, powered by phantom magicians, was not to be lost.

Two disembodied, ghostly hands flew out from the crystal ball, growing ever larger. The hands hovered over the academics and Madame and flung out three figures. These three were circling above them, just below the ceiling: the Great Magician, whose coattails were tightly held by a chubby, red-faced, red-haired child, whose foot was held by a thin, bespectacled brown child. Peasely's toupee had flown off his head, revealing a shiny bald head fringed by a ring of gray hair. With shocked eyes, he turned to Madame, and then, with a gaping mouth and uncharacteristically speechless, he pointed up.

Madame's body quivered as she saw the three figures fly above. Yes, it was the Great Magician. But that was not why her body shook. For she caught a glimpse of the bright-blue lines upon the palm of the outstretched hand of the brown child with the long black braids whipping about her face.

The Great Magician's arms were outstretched as he called, his eyes furtively searching for his beloved, "Oh, Bess, it is I…"

Then the three figures flew through the walls of the room and into the city streets.

The crystal ball turned from solid to light. It flew through Madame's fingers then through the wall, following the three figures.

Peasely ran to the window and yanked the curtains aside. The two academics followed him. They all peered down. The city lights revealed no sign of the three figures, just an empty street.

Madame stood up. She did not mourn the loss of the crystal ball. *A princess of old. Upon her palms, the dual blue lifelines of her royal veins will shine bold.* The beats of her heart rose in excitement; she had no time now for the nonsense of the Debunkers Association. She left the office and swiftly moved down the stairs, her pointy black boots marking in staccato sounds the commands that rang in her mind: *The Mother's name you shall call for protection, for into the night of dead souls you must go. Our princess seeks the old wizard, who holds the Cape of Light and whose mind unravels in madness.*

She flung open the heavy doors to the building. Three hobo bodies lay dead and discarded, their arms akimbo, upon the threshold. Madame gasped as wisps of cold gray fog rose from the dead bodies. They wove up, formless Muhra who had to abandon the rigor mortis–ridden old forms they had possessed. They moved toward Madame.

"Tiamat!" Madame cried, her hands flinging up to ward them off. Repelled by the word, the wisps moved away with a hissing sound. The fog entered the building as the doors shut.

Peasely and his fellow academics heard the heavy door to the building slam shut and saw Madame run out and disappear into an alleyway. They moved away from the window. Peasely stooped to retrieve his toupee and placed it upon his head. He straightened his glasses. The three academics looked at the shattered fishbowl upon the floor. The candles lay in the water, their flames fizzled out. Was it proof that something had happened? It was all so quick. Had the Great Magician indeed flown out of a *fishbowl* above their heads with those two children? None of them wished to give voice to what they had seen, lest they prompt snickers of disbelief from their colleagues. Doubt began to form in their minds.

"Brewster did you…" Peasely began, as the academic with the camera shook his head and pointed to the floor. The camera lay broken in pieces on the floor.

Brewster said, "It shattered within my hands when…when… the wind came."

As president of the Debunkers, Peasely felt it was his duty to clarify. If anything had been seen, it was only hallucinations formed from whatever potion was in those candles. "Wind. Most certainly a wind came in through the window."

"Hear, hear." An anemic assent rose from the lips of Peasely's colleagues, for they doubted that it was just wind.

"We have definitively debunked the myth of the return of the Great Magician. See how Madame Luludga has scurried away in shame! Fraudluent woman! We have exposed these thieves, decidedly." Peasely's face held a sneer of a smile as he turned back to point out the window where the gypsy had run away into the black night. "Hear! Hear!"

Peasely heard no assent from his colleagues. He turned away from the window, and his eyes widened in shock. A fast rising fog had seeped through from beneath the office door. From this fog fingers formed to take hold of Brewster and Leadbetter by their necks. Their eyes bulged, and they made their last mortal sounds as Muhra hands moved into their bodies and flung their souls into the wisps of fog that eddied about the floor.

Peasely's backed toward the window. Then he felt the cold Muhra fingers around his neck. His body jerked back. His toupee flew off as the Muhra possessed his body, his soul joining those of his colleagues in the fog. Now the three academics were debunked of their souls. In their fog receptacles, they rose up, confused, tearing apart into smaller wisps. The Muhra opened the office door. The wisps of the newly formless Muhra followed, each one winding around the legs of his old body but unable to penetrate it.

Peasely's form, now inhabited by a Muhra, reached in jerking movements for the toupee and placed it in a lopsided way upon his head. The Great Diva was in the midst of a production at the Hippodrome; the night air had vibrated with this knowledge. And everywhere that the Muhra had dispersed into the city, gray wisps of fog were in search of bodies. They could not miss being a part of the production or even in the audience, if need be. Their hobo bodies had been rotting even in life, and in death they had worn out quickly. Now, with fresh forms, they could proceed to the Hippodrome. As the three newly possessed forms moved toward the stairway, a thud in the next room shook the building.

The thud startled the Muhra. It came from the office, where the door was shut. Whatever it was, it was none of their business.

Likely more Muhra in search of bodies. They had their bodies. They hurried down the stairs of the assyriology building and into the street, running toward the Hippodrome. The Great Diva would be furious if the performance was delayed.

The wispy fog of the souls of Peasely and his fellow Debunkers moved about in stunned confusion in the hallway: Debunkers no more but the Debunked.

𒀭𒌅𒂖𒀭𒁹

Behind the office doors, it was Paddy who recovered his senses first. It had been his chubby form hitting the floor that had caused the thud. He grimaced in pain. The office was very familiar to him, of course, given the many unfruitful discussions he'd had here with its owner, Dr. L. Rufus Wigglesworth, chairperson of the department of assyriology. Paddy saw that Layard was standing confusedly with *his* beloved Dottie still cradled in his homewrecker arms. That madman Smith immediately lifted one of his frog feet to feel the vibrations of the room.

At last Paddy felt he was at an advantage. He moved as swiftly as his pained limbs would allow toward Layard. The cad would have to be brought into immediate obedience.

"Layard, unhand her at once," he said, pleased that he did not address the rake as *Sir* Layard.

Layard lowered Dottie to the floor of the office. "Fetch some water," he ordered. "She's moving dangerously close to shock." He grabbed a piece of paper and fanned it over Dottie. "Madam!" he said. "Stay awake!" Her eyes opened to reveal large, blue-rimmed, black pupils. Then her eyelids shut.

Paddy sputtered, but the sight of Dottie, her pale eyes flickering open and shut, scared him into action. Dr. Wigglesworth's desk was cluttered with papers, and the whole room looked as if a whirlwind had moved through it. Water? None here. He'd have to try Peasely's office next door or, failing that, the faculty room. Paddy opened the door, and as he moved into the hallway, he felt the cold wisp of the fog of the three spirits of the trapped academics move about his ankles; they recognized Paddy and hoped their old colleague would rescue them.

Paddy shook his foot; it was a disgustingly slimy feel. His nose wrinkled against the smell of the newly dead spirits that rose from the fog winding about his ankles. *What is that stench?* he wondered. *Rotting fish?*

Paddy knocked on the door. "Peasely!" he said.

The fog about his feet moved in rapidly jerking movements. Paddy shook his foot again. Most bothersome, this sticky, odiferous fog. He pushed open the door to Peasely's office and observed at once the odd arrangement—everything pushed to the side, a small wooden table, glass shattered on the floor. A large camera also lay in pieces on the floor. The window was open to the night, the curtains billowing out. Well, Peasely was an odd duck. A *debunker* he had called himself, with not much to show for his work in the way of publications, in contrast to Paddy, who pursued assyriology in its undiluted form rather than being distracted by magicians and legerdemain—once again demonstrating the folly of Wigglesworth, who tolerated such nonsense in an academic venue. The fog again rolled around Paddy's ankles, as if protesting his internal criticisms. Then Paddy spotted it: a half-filled pitcher of water on the desk. He grabbed it and swiftly headed to Wigglesworth's office, the fog following him like a needy dog.

𒐚𒌍𒈬𒐚𒈬 𒐏

The Crone's eyes were mesmerized by the face in the mirror.

Her face. Emotion overtook her. To be back again. To be herself again after so many eons trapped in the humped, odorous, ugly shape. She moved her arms down as her lips emitted a small sob of relief. Then the Crone raised the mirror again just to make certain: yes, she was there, still her beautiful, beautiful self.

The Crone looked admiringly at her emerald eyes with their sparkles of golden specks.

A sharp heat jerked her from these thoughts. The amulet in her right hand was burning. Her body suddenly felt hot and heavy as a flush of sweltering heat moved through her. The Crone was disoriented, her body swaying. Her vision blurred for a moment. Then the heat dissipated, and her vision cleared. She looked down at her left hand, which held the mirror, and let out a gasp: it was old and wrinkled, splotched with ugly brown spots. In the mirror, when she turned it to look at her hands, they were soft and smooth. The Crone moved the mirror about her body: she wore a beautiful silvery gown. Then she looked down without the mirror. Outside the mirror's reflection, her clothes were rough, stinking, black rags—not the smooth, perfumed silk of the gown that the mirror reflected. The Crone touched her face with the back of the hand that held the mirror: it was bumpy, and the nose was large. Her right hand brushed against her coarse, grizzled hair. She realized with a start that she was now only beautiful in the mirror.

"Aaagh! Aaagh! Turn me back! Turn me back!" she screamed, as she brought the metal amulet to her yellow eye.

The Spyglass now looked out, her eyes glinting with evil at the Crone. When the Crone had pried off the gold band, the Spyglass felt as if she were being flayed. From the pain something stirred; something formed: an idea, a glimpse of twilight. Then the Spyglass's bitterness at her imprisonment had been released. The bitterness moved into the gold band as it was yanked from her.

The Spyglass felt something change within her. With only one protective band of gold left, she was paradoxically lighter. Her thoughts were clearer; though still she didn't know who she was, the power of what she once had been was rising.

Into the pitted gold band flung upon the ground by the Crone, the Spyglass had cast a spell. A spell of real power, not the fantastical things she had done before for the mortal men and spirits who had held her. But one that held her old black magic. Black magic, strong with trickery and cunning, was returning to the Spyglass's consciousness. She didn't know who she was, but the spells she once held seemed to be bubbling to the surface, begging for release. Even so, she felt exposed, vulnerable, for she had only one gold band left—that must explain the strange lightness she felt. It didn't matter for now, as she understood how to control the Crone, how to get what she needed. As the Spyglass's bitterness had fallen upon the pitted gold band, it had mixed and churned, and then it had turned into the Unlooking Glass. Within this Unlooking Glass lay a trap, as she who looked into it would soon find out.

The Crone was shrieking, her yellow eye bulging in anger as she looked into the amulet to find the creature within. "What trickery is this? Where is my beauty! Return it at once, or I will rip you to shreds. Play not with me, creature!"

The Crone moved to bring the amulet down from her eye to make her threat a reality. She would rip the gold band that remained upon the amulet, tear it open, and gut it. She should have done so to start.

Crone, you hideous being, the Spyglass spoke into the Crone's mind, her voice sharp and cold. *Into the Unlooking Glass, I have now imprisoned your true beautiful self.*

The Crone moaned as she tried again and again to move the amulet from her eye. But it would not budge. Her bulging yellow eye was held glued to the opening.

The Spyglass continued, *Obey these commands, Crone, and your beauty will be returned to you. Disobey, and my spell will shatter the mirror into a thousand shards. Your beauty will be flung across the dark underworld so that you never recover yourself.*

Cold sweat formed under the Crone's arms and dripped down her body. Her beaked nose caught the stench that rose from her. What a contrast to the alluring scent, the smell of velvety red roses, she had exuded in her beautiful form. She stared deep into the amulet, with her yellow eye held against it, for clues as how to control the spirit, but only darkness confronted her. Once the amulet let her go, she could rip off the last gold band, but if she did so, she knew the Spyglass would make good on her threats to scatter her beautiful self in a thousand shards. Oh, to lose herself forever! The pain of it rattled her body.

The Crone knew she was defeated. "Creature, tell me what you want."

The red-haired child, the Spyglass snarled.

C H A P T E R   1 3

seven sista

Fat Man's body rippled to the smooth notes of the horn. Though his girth was indeed worthy of his name, his motions were like song notes themselves when he moved to music. Although he was in his middle years, his dark-brown face was smooth as a balloon. A raised circular platform functioning as a stage was built in the center of the room, which had a high, peaked ceiling. It was one of the many buildings of the late 1800s now languishing in disrepair; it had seen sparks of revival, the last of which had ended the year prior, 1935, after the race riots had made the clubs in Harlem too dangerous for the white folks to come and spend their money. Crammed upon the stage this night were a bony, deeply black-skinned, frenzied drummer; a trumpeter whose honey-colored cheeks puffed in and out; a pianist with long, elegant brown fingers that flitted across the black-and-white keys; and Fat Man. Around Fat Man and his band, smoke carrying a bitter and cloying smell rose like pillars.

The drumbeat picked up the pace of the piano. The small tables were pushed to the side. Those were for the flush times when the patrons sat and drank overpriced whiskeys and vodkas, when Prohibition ran strong and the riots of 1935 hadn't happened. Tonight the shoebox-shaped, smoke-filled tenement club in Harlem was packed, not with paying customers but root doctors and conjurers: a patchwork of men and women—brown, both dark and milky, and deep blue-black. These were the black spiritualists who practiced hoodoo, that weave of the mystic with the magical, with healing herbs and exilirs, secrets formed in the slave days and passed on from generation to generation. It was their pots of herbs—potions to unleash the spirits from beyond—from which the smoke rose.

Their faces were marked by the hope that gleamed in their eyes. Their dress was shabby, as the Depression had reduced their trade with a vengeance even greater than it had the white magicians. Murmurs rose within the music. *The treasures of darkness, the hidden riches of secret places.* Fat Man's songs had been rumored to draw Hoodoo spiritualists from the dead; when his voice rose in song, the sounds held all the otherworldly power of their hoodoo purveyors of old—of the chants that were said to have been first sung in the African night, of the rituals and sacrifices that formed that mystical bond.

This date, October 31, 1936, was propitious. Fat Man's notes held the vibrations, those powerful sounds that could call forth their departed brother conjurer, Black Lazarus, "the world's greatest conjurer," as he had billed himself, having left his mortal form exactly one year earlier on this All Hallows' Eve right here in Harlem, just as the white Great Magician had died ten years before. But Black Lazarus's magic was real; it had been dug and nurtured from a deeply spiritual place, while the white man's feats of magic, they believed, were just tricks, illusions that had no power. So it was no wonder that he never had risen from the dead. Black Lazarus was often possessed by the hoodoo spirits. Those who had witnessed it told of how he would collapse to the floor, where he'd thrash about like a fish in a net. The secret powers in the Book of Psalms had been whispered to him, and thus his power as a hoodoo practitioner had grown. Black Lazarus also had been a formidable root doctor, with potent potions that used the light roots to heal and the dark roots to repel the evil. He was a conjurer too, calling forth the beats of the ancient songs and sounds that were the backbone of the Psalms. The Holy Bible, it was known, was the greatest book for conjurers; just look at how Moses was honored as a miracle worker. Those who practiced the art of conjuring without the knowledge of the Books of Psalms were foolish, inviting devils who roamed like hungry lions to devour them. They who walked in darkness rather than light had caused the curse of the hoodoo evil spirits upon the land and had brought in the insidious poison that was poverty, which leeched people's wills from their bodies.

Black Lazarus had said he had practiced his art first in the Deep South, learned from those who had lived in the slave days; those who knew the roots, the stones, the rocks that could repel the evil ones. In the old days, they'd said, they had seen slave masters wither and die when a spell was cast; they had prevented whippings, had brought to life stillborn babies or made whole those with shriveled hands or legs. These old ones, who had lived with the ever-present force of the invisible serpent that was darkness, had held it by its tail and swung it to bite the oppressors of their souls. *Quench not the spirit, saith the Lord.* And those oppressors would learn how heavy the yoke of slavery was that they had inflicted, as they would wear it for eternity in the underworld.

Black Lazarus had traveled north, first to Chicago and then to Harlem. He drew crowds, black folk, brown folk, white folk: no one was immune to his lure. Some said it was because he brought the power of the spirits of the black conjurers of old; others said he was not mortal but spirit. Every show was sold out until he became a very rich man. Who he had been before he became a conjurer was unknown. He had no wife. He had no child. He rose as if from the mist and called himself Black Lazarus, for he would bury himself and rise from the grave four days later—until the last time when he did not rise. He came and went like a sparkling star.

Tonight, when the city streets were filled with dead souls, the gathered conjurers hoped Black Lazarus could be called and beseeched to give them his touch, to transform their acts, to draw crowds and turn the ashes of their poverty into gold. For what need did he have for those secrets in the afterworld?

Outside the club, just moments before, dark-brown and black hands had shot up, holding blue bottles aloft as talismans—bottles that could imprison malevolent souls. These were an effective repellant against the dead spirits that rose in wisps of gray fog, their fingers reaching to grab the conjurers as they made their way to the club. Those who had eluded the deadly grasp had run down the stairs into the club, and now the small space could hold no more. The doors were locked. The music had begun.

Fat Man snapped his fingers to the beat. His body moved with the rhythm. His stomach jutted out here, then there, his stout legs acting like anchors. He threw his head back.

The vibrations of the melody flowed through the packed room.

Lalalalalalalalalalalalalala
Babababababaabababababa

Men and women swayed to the beat. They held their blue shimmering bottles above their heads and tapped them against each other. "Son of Moses, son of Moses," they sang to the drumbeat, for that had been Black Lazarus's claim, and who could doubt it? "Brother Lazarus, rise, we say! Rise!"

The drumbeat sped up; the drummer blurred into the beat as it came faster and faster. The sweat dripped down Fat Man's face into the rolls of his neck as his body shook to the beat.

Raralalalararalaralarararalalarara
Raralalalararalaralarararalalarara

Fat Man was lifted out of the smoky environs of the shabby club into that hypnotic place where the music always took him. He never knew the song he would sing, for the words and music came through him and were not of him.

Bababarrarum babararararum!
I say it right now... the heartbeat goes crazy
Whenever I see you, darlin'.
My mind goes hazy
As I fall under your spell.
O R-R-R-R-Rosabelle... O R-R-R-R-Rosabelle.

The crowd murmured in surprise. Rosabelle? Who was Rosabelle? They were here to call Black Lazarus. But Fat Man was swept away by the music. His head was thrown back, his eyes shut as he sang the song that bewitched him.

Wanna be, wanna be, wanna be, wanna be, wanna be
With a you, with a you, my sweet baaaaybee.

With a you, with a you, with a you, my sweet baaaaybeee.
I walk in love...I walk in love...I walk...in laaaoove...can't you see?
Because you, my darlin'...you, my darlin',
You got me under your spell,
O dark-eyed, sweet R-R-R-R-Rosabelle!

The beat of the drums pounded and shuddered within the blue bottles held aloft. The bottles flew up from the fingers that held them; they shimmered and suddenly shattered. The very ceiling of the basement lifted into a dome. The shards of glass flew like a thousand bluebirds and melted together to form wings made of shimmering crystals. An elegant figure in a black tuxedo embedded with white circles materialized and somersaulted out, floating just beneath two giant wings made up of the blue shards that flapped above him. A pyramidal necklace, with the large open Eye of Providence at its point, worn upon a chain made of links of silver and copper, glittered upon the man's neck. In one hand he held a large brass key.

It was indeed Black Lazarus, sleek and handsome, his dark-brown face with its trim black mustache and little V of a goatee under his lower lip. *He has risen!* The conjurers' thoughts snaked through the smoky room like a spell until their words rose from their lips, moved their hands to clap, and sprang out of their throats with joy.

The club was now a field of swaying hands. "Alleluia! Black Lazarus! Black Lazarus!"

Fingers stretched to touch Black Lazarus as he floated right above them; they reached out to grasp the brass key that would open the doors to fortune. They didn't notice that Black Lazarus's characteristic showman smile was absent from his face. Indeed his lips were twisted in fear. An unseen wind pummeled him up and down; he flew hither and thither, caught in a ghostly current. Now he was turned downward, his necklace hanging low, the brass key clutched in one hand. The blue shard wings whirred just above him.

Then suddenly three flying figures materialized. As they collided into Black Lazarus, he was flung backward and turned over, his back arched. The crowd below immediately recognized the white man as the Great Magician, but clutching his coattails was a red-haired, red-faced girl, and holding on to her was a skinny brown child who looked like an owl.

Black Lazarus was pulled up close to the arch of the ceiling. The blue shard wings chasing him flew upward.

The three figures fell upon the small stage, almost right on top of Fat Man.

The band had stopped playing, in astonishment at those who now shared their stage: two spirit children, white and brown, and the famed Great Magician himself.

Fat Man was in that hypnotic zone, his eyes shut, sang on unaware.

O dark-eyed, sweet R-R-R-R-Rosabelle!
I will love you whether in heaven or hell.
Sweeeet baabeee doll, you got me under your spell.
O my deaarrrr R-R-R-R-Rosabelle!

Fat Man stopped singing; he suddenly felt woozy, as if he had risen too quickly from sleep. On the stage in front of him, he saw blurry figures that then sharpened into clarity. He shook his head. A chubby white child with kinky red hair, a skinny brown one with long black braids, and...? And a white man...the Great White Magician, dead ten years. What song had he sung? Then a small crystal ball suddenly materialized above him, spinning like a top.

Ghostly hands from the crystal ball sprang out, grabbing the tails of Black Lazarus's tuxedo. As he disappeared like a wisp of fog right into the crystal ball, the crowd shouted in dismay, "Black Lazarus!"

The blue crystal wings flapped in confusion at the dome of the ceiling, for Black Lazarus, to whom it had been formed to adhere, was gone. The black spiritualists stretched up, their bodies jumping to try to grab the crystal ball as it spun high above their grasping hands.

Rosabelle. The Great Magician was sure he had heard the song, though not as it had been when he and Bess had sung it. Nonetheless it was the secret sign known only to the two of them. Bess? Where was she? The Great Magician scanned the surprised brown and black faces of those reaching up to grab the crystal ball as it flew about the room. *Who is Black Lazarus?* The Great Magician now felt the sting of all of his mortal works: how he had derided the spirit world, how he had made a fortune being a debunker of frauds. Yes, there were fraudulent mediums, but as he knew too well, having spent the last ten years buried and never able to break the coffin that held him, there was a very real spirit world. He was not a magician in the spirit world but a phantom magician of the spirit world. Oh! His heart cried that Bess had believed his foolish mortal words that there was no spirit world. "Bess!" he cried out. "Call me, my love. Call my spirit again. Bess, believe!"

That plea remained unanswered, for the spinning crystal ball turned at a high speed and aimed itself right at the Great Magician.

Geeta ducked. With perfect timing, Mattie thrust her left arm up to intercept the crystal ball and catch it.

"Got it!" she proudly said, as she made the lefty catch. *And to think Eddie never wanted me on his softball team!*

The crystal ball glowed in Mattie's left hand; she held it aloft; it fit perfectly in her hand. It was a rheumy blue—that clouded color that one saw in the eyes of the blind. Within the crystal ball, there was a swirling movement; it was the Phantom Magicians' spirits swimming around Black Lazarus.

A murmur of discontent rose from the lips of the conjurers.

Mattie felt Geeta's tug at her arm as she whispered, "Mattie, look."

Mattie took a look around at the crowd of faces staring at them. They didn't look so happy. She took in the smoky room and saw that she, Geeta, and the Great Magician were up on a stage. Where were they anyway? In a quick movement, with loud shouts, the crowd of black spiritualists scrambled onto the circular stage, squeezing Fat Man to the edges.

Mattie and her companions stood at the center of the stage, surrounded by a closing circle of angry conjurers. Their shouts ricocheted up and moved in vibrations to stir the blue crystal wings, made from their magic, hovering uncertainly above within the dome. Their dark eyes shone with the frustration of ages of having what was rightly theirs stolen right from their hands. The crowd pushed closer toward Mattie, Geeta, and the Great Magician with menacing eyes and the rising sound of anger. The blue crystal wings flew uncertainly, high above the crowd, creating a small breeze like that of a ceiling fan.

"A devil child steals the spirit of Black Lazarus. See how she holds him in her hand!" they cried. "Let him through, let the reverend through!"

The crowd parted to make way for a stout, middle-aged, brown man with small features smashed together in the center of a hatchet-shaped face, his eyes lit with anger behind thick glasses. He was dressed in a black suit, shiny with age, that bore his rank of a respected preacher. He moved forward with authority. The reverend held his palms up like white flags, though it was not surrender that he was preaching.

He spoke in a deep, thunderous voice, "Magician, tell your demon child to give us the glass ball so that we may release the spirit of our brother, Black Lazarus."

The Great Magician felt the crowd's anger fall like a leaden blanket over the telepathic lines; it kept Bess from communicating with him. Again the Great Magician bemoaned his vigor in persuading Bess that there was no afterworld. She might never call him again, for ten tries was their agreement. The Great Magician shook his head in frustration; he had such little time to reunite with his beloved. He needed to hear her call again to him so he could move through the sound of her call to her.

"Give the crystal ball to them," the Great Magician commanded Mattie. "I will give you another one."

Mattie's eyes narrowed with offense, her frizzy red hair bristling with indignation to the sting of the Great Magician's comment. Like she was some little kid who could be tricked again! Her arm was thrust up, holding the crystal ball aloft.

"No," she said, a resolve growing. She tightened her grip on the crystal ball—it was the size of a softball and fit nicely in her palm. She knew she and Geeta needed it to find and rescue poor, confused Mr. Biddle. Mattie looked up at the ball; it glowed and felt hot in her hands. It looked like it wasn't a dud like the other crystal ball the man had given her in the alleyway.

The crowd pressed upon them, near but too leery to touch them. The reverend's teeth glinted as he spoke, his voice now menacing as he saw how the devil child held the crystal ball tightly, her arm stretched stubbornly upward. "Take heed, demon child, and let go of what belongs to us."

Someone in the crowd shouted, "It ain't yours to keep, demon child."

Others agreed, shouting, "That's right. That's right. Give it up, demon child. Give it up!"

Fat Man's drummer started playing. Again his hands were moving so fast that they were blurry. Those around him on the circular stage stamped their feet in rhythm.

The reverend thundered, "Demon child, seed of Satan! Surrender what is rightfully ours."

Those who crowded around the stage joined in the rhythm, clapping their hands. They sang:

O devil girl, thief you be.
Set Black Lazarus free!

A bitter bile rose within those gathered until it seemed as if that terrible yellowish-brown fluid ran through their veins as blood; it brought alive once more the memory of the riots that had raged in Harlem the year before at the rumor of a black child being beaten by the police for taking candy from a five and ten. It was an untrue rumor but one that spread like fire, lit their tinder-dry bitterness, and stoked the flames of rage for all the injustice they had borne. All this had happened last year, 1935, when business was bad anyway. Now it was worse, for white people no longer came up to the Harlem clubs to spend their cash. A sharp, metallic taste blanketed their tongues as the bearers of injustice year after year: how what was theirs had been stolen from them again and again; how it felt as if curses, rather than blessings, rained upon them generation after generation. "No weapon formed against us shall prosper," it was said in the Bible. Yes, but still, it was not forty years in the wilderness for them, away from the Promised Land, but always four hundred. Yes, rain fell on both the righteous and the unrighteous, but why the torrents upon them? This they'd had to endure too long. No more.

The reverend shouted, and soon the spiritualists joined in:

Set Brother Lazarus free!
O clap your hands, all ye people!
O stamp your feet!
Mine enemy doth not triumph over me!
O devil girl, thief you be.
Set Black Lazarus free!

Their hands shot up in the air, displaying knives that glinted threateningly.

Geeta's eyes widened.

The Great Magician wondered at the knives, for they glistened strangely. Suddenly he realized they weren't just knives but amulets against evil. He moved to launch himself out of this space, but his feet rocked as if glued to the stage. As his eyes moved back and forth, the anger and bitterness from the crowd rose and imprisoned him to this place more strongly than any chain ever bound him. The Great Magician—who, in his mortal form, had made unbelievable escapes from chains, from boxes that had coffined him, from the depths of waters as if he were not of body but spirit—was trapped. The curse of the mediums he had debunked was strong—that he would live eternity in a coffin unless called forth by his wife. Then he panicked: he was sure he felt Bess's skepticism rising. Did she firmly believe there was no spirit world, just as he had said in life? Had this been

proved to her, as he hadn't appearred to her on this final try?
What then would his fate be if he weren't reunited with Bess? A
wandering spirit, like a dead soul? Thrown back into the coffin
for eternity?

An ever-smaller doughnut of space was all that was left
between the furious crowd and the three figures. So close were
the conjurers that their breath fell like a warm wind upon the
three. The spiritualists' shouts were loud. The drumbeat grew
stronger, its vibrations moving through the crowd and into their
feet, where the rhythm of the beat hit the floor.

> *Set Brother Lazarus free!*
> *O clap your hands, all ye people!*
> *Mine enemy doth not triumph over me!*
> *O stamp your feet!*
> *Demon child, seed of Satan,*
> *give us what is ours and make retreat!*

The sharp points of the knives moved toward them like small
spears. Geeta's eyes grew with apprehension behind her black-
framed glasses. Next to her she felt the Great Magician squirm,
as if he were bound by chains, though none were upon him.
Geeta knew that her duty was to help Mattie fulfill her dharma—
after all, she was her guru—but no great wisdom came to her.

Geeta whispered to Mattie, "Perhaps it is wise to adhere to
their request."

Mattie ignored Geeta. The crowd's anger buzzed around
them. Who knew what would happen if she gave up the crystal
ball? Eddie wouldn't give it up; she was sure of that. They needed
to get out of this place. She moved her hand to her side, into
her pants pocket, to tug at the Card of Time, but it was lodged

tightly within. At Mattie's move, the conjurers instantly thrust their knives upward, the sharp points of their weapons glinting with hostility.

"Thus with violence shall you be thrown down and be no more!" The reverend's thunderous voice roared the Scripture above the beat of the drumming, the hands clapping, the feet pounding. "Demon spirits! Be cast down!"

𒁹𒀳𒌋 𒂍 𒁹𒀳 𒁹

Layard was kneeling next to the prone woman. She seemed to be in some sort of trance. Her body thrashed about; her eyes opened wide with fear and then closed. Her lips moved. *No... no...if God be for you.* Layard put his hand to her forehead to see if she was perhaps in a delirious fever.

Shaking one foot, Paddy strode in with the pitcher of water. *This fog is most annoying,* he thought, *so sticky and uncomfortable, but never mind. Dottie first, of course.* Then he saw Layard stroking Dottie's forehead. He rushed forward, barely avoiding colliding into George Smith.

Smith's arms were spread, his palms up, one frog leg up as if to kick. With snarled lips at the fog eddying about Paddy's feet, he proclaimed, "Spirits! Get back!"

As Paddy lost his balance, the water fell on Dottie's face and splattered Layard. "Good God, man!" Layard muttered as he flicked the water from his face. But Paddy had eyes only for his beloved.

Dottie's eyes opened. "Paddy..." she said weakly.

Paddy pushed Layard aside instantly. He knelt by Dottie and gently lifted her to a sitting position. She blinked again, her senses slowly returning as her eyes moved about the familiar room.

"Dr. Wigglesworth's office?" she asked, puzzled. "How? And… Mattie calls to me." Her breathing sounded wheezy.

Paddy interrupted, "Slowly, slowly, my beloved." The sticky fog curled up over his ankles.

Layard agreed. "You were in shock, my dear. You must acclimate yourself."

Paddy frowned at Layard in warning. *"My dear" indeed.* Dottie stared ahead, lifting her hands at something unseen. Paddy, Layard, and Smith looked up to see what appeared to be a small dark-brown bird flying down. It unfurled its wings to show that it wasn't a bird at all but a book's leather cover. It was facing the bookshelves, fluttering like a moth before a bright light. It flitted toward the shelf, where it stopped and pulled at something. The bookshelves trembled then glowed. Then a manuscript dropped down.

Smith caught it, his eyes wild as he scanned the title. "*Excursions under the Tunnels of Ashurnasirpal,* by A. H. Layard, Esq., DCL."

Layard's tan face turned white. He jumped up, his hands thrust at Smith. "Give that to me at once!" he commanded.

Smith laughed maniacally, jumping around the room with the manuscript held aloft, his head turned toward Layard. "You hypocrite!"

Layard moved menacingly toward him, flexing his muscular arms, his handsome face set in grim lines, "You lunatic! Give that to me at once!"

Smith read the first lines of the manuscript, his webbed feet suctioning the walls as he moved sideways. The words shot through the air like bullets, accentuated by his sardonic tone. "'During the last winds of the autumn of 1839 and before the winter rains, there was one spot that my very *being* was drawn to again and again: a mound of such great proportions that I could only behold it with *craven* eyes.'"

Paddy turned to Layard. "The forbidden mound? In Nineveh? But that was what Wigglesworth—"

Although Dottie's voice had been soft, her intellect was still sharp, so she hushed her husband. "Quiet, Paddy."

Her hand touched Paddy, cautioning him not to give voice to his thoughts, for they knew not what form of spirit this Layard was. *A fool speaks his feelings; a wise man keeps his own counsel.* Paddy felt the pressure of her touch and looked at her puzzled, for her words didn't penetrate his mind. Dottie, who had studied the excavations at Nineveh when she was a student at Columbia University, knew of Dr. Wigglesworth's dire fear of the unknown under the ruins, which lay like an atom unsplit, waiting for a touch to release utter destruction.

"Stop, you madman!" Layard shouted at Smith. "Hand that over at once."

Smith moved like a jackrabbit about the room, still reading aloud. "'Heretofore I had left the mound untrodden in deference to the *superstitious prejudices* of the inhabitants. Ultimately, however, the *lure* of what it held proved to be too much.'"

Smith laughed derisively. "I knew you excavated in the forbidden mound! I knew it!"

Layard stopped chasing after Smith. He would have to snare him like a rodent in a trap. Layard's eyes looked around the room for something that could function as a net. Wigglesworth had told him he had destroyed the manuscript, so how was it here? Never mind—the important thing was to take it from that crazed Smith and destroy it immediately.

Dottie now understood. The excavation of the mound was what Dr. Wigglesworth had feared, what he had warned her away from. She looked at Layard, contempt rising in her eyes, as she cited his words from the published *Discoveries of Nineveh*, the supposed account of his excursions. "You called it the *unexplored* mound that rose pyramidical in form. Deceitful man!"

But before Layard could defend himself, George Smith, with his suctioned frog feet on the ceiling walking in great galloping steps, asked sarcastically, "What did you write of these *unexplored mounds*, great sir? Let us take a peek, shall we?"

With a vengeance, Smith continued, "'This mound and its contents became the recurrent theme of my nightmares, where the vast ruins stood like a *taunt* before my eyes. A large stone rose like a great palm, stopping me from breaching the entrance. Wild beasts, serpents, and screams of agony rose from within in dire warning. I awoke from these dreams with my *desire* to breach the mound not thwarted but heightened. It was the *lure* of the forbidden fruit.'"

Dottie bitterly recalled how Dr. Wigglesworth and Herman Biddle had spent the time after Paddy's death protecting her from some unseen evil that had formed from that mound. This evil had taken Paddy's life and left her a widow with an infant child. So it was Layard, then, who had opened the Pandora's box that had caused so much agony. His actions had released the Spyglass into their world and plunged her child, Mattie, upon the dangerous Path of the Virtuous. Dottie's anger rose at the arrogance of Layard, who had risked the destiny of mortal man, releasing the power to destroy heaven, all because of an insatiable curiosity and reckless adventuring.

"Shame on you, falsehearted man," Dottie said, her eyes flashing in fury.

Layard shouted at Smith, who dangled above, "Stop you, crackbrained idiot! Give it to me before you cause more harm."

Smith snarled from the ceiling, his long wild hair swaying in triumph, as he moved waving the manuscript just out of the clasp of Layard. "Yes, I am *an idiot* indeed…for trusting you with my secret!"

Here Smith stopped and snorted, then continued reading. "'When only a sliver of the moon cut the relentless dark sky and the stars themselves were but pinpricks, I moved with a pick and shovel into the great vitrified brick mass, that tower of accumulated rubbish of the epochs.'"

Paddy's arms were about Dottie's waist, having lifted her to her feet. "A secret excavation at Nineveh?"

Dottie's voice held warning. "Paddy, no!"

The fog at Paddy's legs jutted up as if to give him the answer. Paddy shook his leg, ignoring Dottie. He was now taken with the contents of this cad's manuscript. "What is this all about, Layard?

Smith sneered, "About his pact with the Devil, you fool! What else?"

Layard retorted, "Ha. My pact? Which of us lives as a frog, mad as a hatter?"

Smith laughed, still dangling upside down from the ceiling. "Mad as a hatter, am I?" He continued to read. "'Recklessly, I sought what my nightmares warned against: the remains of the towers under the mounds; that which was buried by divine vengeance I sought to unearth. There I dug the tunnel deep and found subterranean passages upon whose walls were with an iron pen were etched: the *Eighth Tablet of Creation*.'"

Paddy gasped and turned to Layard, his eyes filled with admiration and envy. "The Eighth Tablet! You know its location? But why wasn't it unearthed?"

Dottie's heart now beat with trepidation. She knew the deadly fascination of the Eighth Tablet for Paddy; it had killed him once. "No, Paddy, it is best left alone!"

Layard shook his head as if to say, "What utter nonsense!" for he felt the poisonous longing for the forbidden knowledge rising in Paddy. "It is a complete fabrication by Smith, who speaks the words of the insane. See how his eyes dart with lunacy?"

Smith, above, laughed maniacally, giving credence to Layard's characterization. "A lunatic I might be now, but you wrote it yourself, Layard. You found it in the subterranean passages: the Eighth Tablet of Creation!"

The aching desire for the Eighth Tablet filled Paddy's body. His thoughts ran to 1938, when he had requested a sabbatical from his academic post at Columbia University to search for the Eighth Tablet of Creation in Nineveh in the kingdom of Iraq. Wigglesworth had pronounced it a fool's errand. Later Paddy's manuscript on that very subject contradicted the prevailing theories that seven tablets told the tale of creation by the ancient Babylonians—the Enuma Elish. His submitted paper, "The Eighth Tablet of Creation: Moving beyond the Hegemony of Layard and Smith," had been maligned, brutalized with an unrestrained red pen, summarily rejected by Wigglesworth himself, presiding mightily over the *JASA* as editor! Paddy instantly recalled that conversation held in this very room before he had embarked upon his sabbatical.

"*The Eighth Tablet?*" Wigglesworth's three chins had jiggled in astonishment when Paddy had told him about his quest and his need for a sabbatical. "Have you gone mad? There is no Eighth Tablet. The Seven Tablets tell the whole story! Seven, Paddy, a number that repeats itself in Genesis!" Wigglesworth had shaken a fat finger at Paddy as he quoted Genesis. "'And on the seventh day, God ended His work that He had done, and He rested on the seventh day.' *Seven*, Paddy," Wigglesworth had emphasized. "Not eight."

But Paddy had remained firm—he was a young academic, full of vigor, not like Wigglesworth, with dusty ideas petrified in the past. Yes, the Eighth Tablet, and he Paddy O'Reilly, was going to discover it. The cadence of the Old Testament flowed like a current rippling under the words of the Enuma Elish: "In the beginning God created the heavens and the earth. The earth was without form, and void; and darkness was on the face of the deep." That was written in Genesis, but the beginning was when the sky had no name. "And the Spirit of God was hovering over the face of the waters." The Spirit of God was there before the mingling of the waters, before Apsu and Tiamat. Paddy hadn't written of the biblical basis for the Eighth Tablet but had given voice to his inner belief: the Eighth Tablet would tell the tale of the *creation of the Creator*. What a find the Eighth Tablet would be!

Then, on excavation, under the hot desert sun near Mosul, where the dirt seemed to rise like a phantom mound at Nineveh, Paddy felt the missing Eighth Tablet beating faintly under the very earth he stood upon. He felt it as one feels a presence: it was somewhere under the earth, waiting for human eyes to light upon it. Paddy's mind was now a mist of recollections of the past of 1938, which was in reality the future, for he stood in L. Rufus Wigglesworth's office on October 31, 1936. He stood with his wife from the future; stood with Layard and Smith, who should have been long dead. None of this mattered, for Paddy was hypnotized by the manuscript that Smith was waving and the secrets that it held.

It was all in milliseconds that this occurred: the thoughts inter-woven with the longing. The fog eddying at his legs—that of the spirits of Peasely and the other two academics—was electrified by Paddy's longing; they moved up and lifted Paddy toward Smith. Deftly Paddy grabbed the manuscript. Faintly he heard the voices of the others: Smith yelling as the document left his fingers, Layard shouting for him to drop it, and Dottie calling to him not to fall to foolish longing. It was all too late, however, for Layard's manu-script, with its secrets, was in his chubby hands. He, Paddy O'Reilly, would unearth the Eighth Tablet of Creation, which was his destiny.

The office shook forcefully as the desire for the forbidden knowledge flowed through Paddy's hands into the manuscript and gave it life. Paddy felt himself moving into a hot wave, like radiant heat rising from a sunbaked land. He began to dissolve into small specks of color, dots of color disappearing fast. Layard's handsome face twisted in surprise and fear as his form moved from substance into spots then folded into the air. Smith's frog legs were now translucent, his wild eyes aglitter as he melted into specks of color into the air.

Dottie cried out, "No!" as Paddy, Layard, and Smith disap-peared right into the air.

Suddenly she was alone in Wigglesworth's office.

Then a vision formed before her: a dim alleyway in the city streets. There L. Rufus Wigglesworth wore the sacred shroud about his shoulders. Next to him stood another old man, balding and with a long white beard. His feet were bare, and he wore a bulky white shirt over cotton pants, secured with a black belt. His face appeared saintly but marked with worry. They were leaning over the fallen body of Herman Biddle, blanketed in the Cape of Light, which was now a flimsy purple-and pink-haze. Biddle's usually kind blue eyes were wide with madness.

Wigglesworth spoke through the vision to Dottie. "So the end has come, Dottie, for all that I have feared has happened. Biddle lies dying in lunacy, stung by the bitter poison of the Seven Widows. The White Book of Magic is as tattered as the cape that holds it. Chaos reigns, and darkness now cloaks the light."

Dottie's heart beat wildly, for the holds of her mortal life were strong. "I hear Mattie calling me. And Paddy? Where is he?"

"Go to Nineveh to stop him. The Eighth Tablet must not be unearthed," Wigglesworth said.

"Mattie is calling to me. We must protect her," Dottie beseeched him.

"Dottie, if Paddy does the unthinkable, there is no protection for anyone. You must go to Nineveh! Paddy must not unearth the tablet...Now go!"

"But how?" Dottie said desperately. "How?"

"Assume your powers, Dottie. It is time," Wigglesworth said, but his eyes were no longer upon Dottie, for on the ground Herman Biddle was racked with tremors. "Lev Nikolayevich," Wigglesworth said to the old man next to him in a panic, for Biddle was shuddering as if great bolts of electricity were jolting him. "Lev, we must take Biddle back to Yasnaya Polyana so that the spirit of light may restore him."

Lev Nikolayevich laid his hands upon the shaking Biddle. "Quickly, lay the ends of your shroud upon him and speak with me, for I feel the serpent rising." As he said this, Wigglesworth placed the ends of his cape upon Biddle. "Take us up hither, into the heavens, into the light, O Lord," the two men intoned.

Wigglesworth, Lev Nikolayevich, and Biddle were clothed in bright light before suddenly disappearing, leaving only the empty alleyway in Dottie's vision. Then what lay beneath the ground was revealed to her: a giant serpent moving underneath.

The alleyway shook as the serpent cracked the pavement, rising out, its great black wings piercing through its scales. Its yellow, black, and green tail shook. The snake's head was turned toward Dottie. It was Uri Gneezy, with one blue eye and one green eye, both glistening with evil. His forked tongue sprang out from his cobra head, which rested upon the shoulders and arms of a man.

The terrifying vision disappeared.

Dust motes floated where the vision had been.

In Wigglesworth's office, Dottie was alone, surrounded by the unreality of the reality.

The weight of her situation hit her: her husband had vanished; Mattie was in dire trouble, for the Snake was after her; no longer was Herman Biddle her daughter's protector, for he was in the throes of madness; and Dr. Wigglesworth also was gone.

Dottie steeled herself. Dr. Wigglesworth had told her to go to Nineveh. *Assume your powers, Dottie.* She looked around the office for a clue. *How?* she thought. *How?* She moved toward the bookshelf and looked helplessly at it, for it was haphazardly stuffed, bulging with academic tomes. She pulled out a textbook of excavation techniques from 1900. She put it back in frustration. *Useless, all of it,* she thought. Nothing to help her.

Tears stung Dottie's eyes as her lips formed words without sound: *My flesh and my heart faileth: but God is the strength of my heart.* But her love for Mattie, for Paddy, caused her to cry out, "O but Lord, you have put this destiny in me. Help me fulfill it!" Something fell off the bookshelf. Dottie bent down and picked it up; it was a flat, thin piece of wood the size and shape of a bookmark. She held it in front of her.

A smoky smell issued from it as a shimmering vision formed before her. Immediately Dottie recognized the object in the vision from its description in the Book of Exodus: *Overlay the top and all the sides and the horns with pure gold, and make a gold molding around it.*

It was the Golden Altar of Incense, where the holy incense burned: a box three feet tall—*Of shittim wood shalt thou make it,* she recalled—overlaid with gold and with a gold crown on top and a gold ring at each corner. The vision disappeared, but the room was filled with the familiar smell of the burnt offering of incense made of secret sweet spices*: the scent of the Lord of our tabernacle.*

Dottie reverently held the wooden bookmark; it was a piece of the Golden Altar, she realized. *Whatsoever toucheth the altar shall be holy.* She lifted the bookmark up to the light. The gold that overlaid it rose from the wood and transformed into a shiny, gossamer-thin piece of paper that was a creamy golden color. Then the shittim wood of the bookmark sprang from Dottie's fingers and turned into seven lines that engraved themselves onto the golden paper.

The golden page floated in front of her, light as goodness. The Small Book of Spells appeared and opened before Dottie. Then this golden gossamer paper—the hidden, last, and most potent incantation—flew into the Small Book of Spells. The cover of the Small Book of Spells turned into the creamy gold color of the last spell.

The Small Book of Spells flew into Dottie's hands. Her fingers felt how soft to the touch it was, like old leather that had been worn by loving use. Its softness was now like a whisper growing in her mind. It coursed through her thoughts and into her being. Then, like the wind, it swept away the detritus of her mortal life: the memories that had fallen like a blanket of dust, obscuring who she was. It blew away the surface persona of a wife, then a widow, a mother of an eleven-year-old, a saleswoman at Ladies' Hats and Accessories at Sears—all of that dissolved from her as she whispered the lessons taught to her by L. Rufus Wigglesworth and Herman Biddle in her dreams, if such a day as today were to happen.

Paddy had to be stopped.

Dottie felt the Mother's loving-kindness fill her as her many names flew through her mind, but it was the ancient trinity of the three mothers that rang now: *Tiamet, Tiamut, Tiamat.* She recalled how the Mother had been lost to time, defiled to irrelevance by the Master of Darkness as Tiamet, the mortal bodily form of a mother with no power, relegated to she who gives birth. But there was more, for the body that gave birth was first; then came the mind, which sought knowledge and gave birth to the wisdom; and then the spirit itself was reborn, the eternal flame that lived within, one small twinkle of light of the ever-shining light.

Dottie had sworn to help the Mother, for what was in the Eighth Tablet, if released, would destroy her. Dottie's memory formed that which she knew but did not know she knew. *Priestess of Light,* Dottie heard herself being called. She shut her eyes. Behind her eyelids, she saw an inky-black sky with pinpricks of silvery light. She traveled through her mind's eye into it. There, in the milky stars, she saw the forgotten Mother appear above her: she who was clothed by the sun, the moon under her feet, a crown of twelve stars upon her head.

Dottie bowed her head, her hands clasped in prayer. *Tiamat, O Most Holy Mother! I answer your call.*

The Mother lifted the crown of twelve stars from her head, and as she did, twelve teardrops fell from her eyes, for her powers were being swallowed as darkness rose in Chaos, as the Abyss split open to unleash the creatures of the underworld beneath the underworld. The Daughter had one more mortal life that had to be lived to be released.. But now the Hidden Daughter lay trapped as a spirit in the Abyss, where Tiamat could not penetrate her consciousness. And the Anza bird had shed two gold bands. Now the Eighth Tablet of Destruction was under threat of being unearthed.

The Mother's teardrops glittered and fell upon each star. From the twelve stars, the Mother took the point that held each teardrop to form a crown of light. She placed the crown upon Dottie's head.

The Mother spoke:

O Priestess of Light,
This crown of tears shall you wear.
Twelve points of stars,
Like wildflowers upon your hair.
Twelve teardrops
Are all that will shield you against despair.
Journey eastward into the land of the shadows,
Where gusty winds in breaths of fire and smoke rise,
Where misery and sorrow wrench the heart with their cries.
O Priestess, hear this warning well:
No matter the groans and sighs,
No matter what horror falls upon your eyes,
Remember the hot sands hold only lies.
O Priestess, hear this warning bell,
For in that land, your heart with woe will swell.
But not one tear must you shed.
If one droplet falls in that land of dread,
This crown of protection will vanish from your head.
Then upon your spirit, darkness will spread,
And prisoner you shall become of the reviled dead.

The Mother vanished.

Dottie opened her eyes. She looked around Dr. Wigglesworth's office, now with eyes that were bright like a new moon. The circlet of light sparkled upon her head.

She raised her arms, holding the Small Book of Spells aloft. She flung her head back, her blue eyes glittering, her silky blond hair moving like golden rays with her crown of light as she spoke. "And to the woman was given two wings of a great eagle that she might fly into the wilderness."

The Small Book of Spells instantly moved from Dottie's fingers and grew into two ivory-colored wings upon her back. Then she spoke the ancient words: "*E-nu-ma e-lish na-bu-u sa-ma mu sap-los am-ma-tim su-ma la za-rat!*"

The wings unfurled behind her, and she moved out of the space of time that was an office in 1936 in New York City. A searing heat enveloped her as the hot desert ground rose beneath her feet.

𒀭𒅗𒌋 𒂍 𒀭𒅗 𒁹

In a quick movement, the spiritualists' knives, dipped in potions of the dark roots, moved to stab the hearts of the demon child and the two other evil spirits. In the millisecond between when the knives were thrust toward them and Mattie's eyes caught their glint, she heard a voice so low that she couldn't understand it. Then it sharpened in her mind; a voice was guiding her, speaking the mysteries, the great truths into her soul: *Child, remember, greater is He that is in you than he that is in the world. If God be for you, who dare be against you?* Suddenly Mattie didn't see the knives thrusting toward her; all she saw was a gleam, a beautiful silvery gleam that formed into a shining Holy Cross.

Again she heard the voice speak to her soul: *He is your help and your shield.* Instinctively the great love of that sacrifice encased her. Mattie felt her soul stretch toward the shining cross. As she made the sign of the Holy Cross, a light filled her and embraced her in loving warmth.

Mattie felt the soft presence fall over her again, and the voice spoke through her. Although she heard herself say the words, she knew it wasn't her speaking but the gentle soul that was protecting her. "*But this I know, that thou favourest me, because mine enemy doth not triumph over me.*"

Some in that crowd would say they saw a shining light form around the red-haired child just as she made the sign of the Holy Cross; others would say they saw the light descend upon everyone present, like sunshine through stormy clouds. The arcs of the arms of the conjurers with the knives, thrust out to stab the three figures, froze. The drumming had stopped, and silence lay thick, hushing even the conjurers' thoughts. Then their hands fell to their sides, where the glistening knives dangled uncertainly. Now all eyes were turned to the reverend to guide them regarding what it meant that the girl had quoted Scripture. "*Mine enemy doth not triumph over me,*" they'd heard her say. She had made the sign of the Holy Cross and was bathed in a hallowed light. This child was surely not a devil.

"*All the paths of the Lord are mercy.*" A voice as sweet as a bell rang out over the crowd before the reverend could speak. It was the voice of the tiny old one, Seven Sista, whose misty eyes were clouded by age.

Many turned in surprise as they saw the bent figure, wearing a tattered, brown-checked, cloth coat several sizes too big, elbow her way through the crowd toward the stage.

"Seven Sista!" The surprised voices rose in murmuring waves as she moved past them with a speed that belied her many years.

How the Seven Sista was even here in the club was a mystery, for no one would have thought to bring such an old one out into the peril of the night of rising evil spirits. Some were surprised that Seven Sista was still alive. One hundred years old, many said she was. The reverend frowned at the intrusion, but his tongue, which sought to rebuke the old one, was silenced by an unseen hand. Seven Sista, who was born in the slave days, the seventh and only child in her family who had survived, had emerged into life with the caul, that light-blue veil of birth fluid upon her face, which shimmered underneath her still-smooth black skin. It was the sign of her connection to the divine, to the supernatural. The caul glistened under her silky skin, and the white cottony hair about her shrunken face almost seemed as if it were a halo—though her voice had grown lower and lower as each year passed, her eyes set into deeper and deeper hollows in her face as blindness had clouded them. Seven Sista's utterings, formed in her gummy mouth, had become more and more garbled and nonsensical; thus, she was relegated, as the old many times are by the young, to a place of condescension and irrelevance.

But here she was. Seven Sista, blind and barely able to walk, miraculously had appeared in the club, her elbows jutting out as she pushed herself through. She lifted herself unaided onto the stage then raised her bony hands toward the crowd, standing like a small beacon of protection in front of Mattie.

Seven Sista spoke in gentle chastisement, her unseeing eyes fixed on the reverend. Her words were neither garbled nor nonsensical. "*Who whet their tongue like a sword, who bent their bows to shoot their arrows, even bitter words.*"

The reverend felt the reproach strongly; he was vain, as his oratory powers were great. He was a *doctor* of theology, and to be lectured by an illiterate old woman from slave times, whose mind was addled, stung him. The reverend felt the eyes of the root doctors turn toward him, not in support but reproach.

Seven Sista's rheumy eyes gazed over the crowd, her voice shaking the room. "As false witnesses, you rose up, for with your eyes you did not see; with your ears you did not hear; but with evil minds you judged." Suddenly Seven Sista's eyes were no longer unfocused and rheumy but moving like lasers of reprimand over the conjurers. "Shall your tongues speak unrighteousness and *deviseth mischiefs like a sharp razor?* Shall your bitter words fatten the dead souls that rise this unholy night?"

The conjurers were chastened. Bitter words like arrows they had shot; their tongues had not spoken of righteousness and praise but instead words of the false judgment of the red-haired child and her companions.

"No, no," they replied, shamed. Seven Sista was right.

Seven Sista then said, her voice full with the power of the Psalms, "*I have been young and now am old; yet I have not seen the righteous forsaken, nor his seed begging bread.*"

Mattie felt the warm protection of Seven Sista as she spoke. Geeta's mind took in the power of the ancient one; it was like that of the *sanyasis* in the mountains, whose very beings were more spirit than body. Seven Sista, who was so tiny that the top of her cottony head was just a bit above Mattie's waist, turned toward her and lifted her old hands to reach up, her fingers splayed like dark twigs upon Mattie's face, cradling each side. As she looked into Mattie eyes, she spoke again in a clear voice. "*But thou hast saved us from our enemies, and hast put them to shame that hated us.*"

Mattie felt the brittle hands of the tiny old woman upon her and her eyes took in how beautiful she was, like a small angel. Her skin was so smooth and black, and her eyes shone so brightly now. The old woman was so familiar to her; her face was infused with such sweetness, such kindness that Mattie felt cocooned in love. The voice, Mattie recognized at once, was the one that had come to her, the voice that had spoken through her.

Agape. That word from long ago entered Geeta's mind. She saw how the old woman's face shone with enlightenment and how loving-kindness rose from her like the warmth of summer sunshine. *Avatar,* Geeta recognized—this was what ThaTha meant by a realized soul.

The Great Magician knew that the spirit power of the old woman was more potent than any trick he could ever devise.

The reverend bowed his head. Shame cut through his arrogance, for he was a good man who had just been derailed by vanity. Then he spoke for all, for even he, with his sharp hatchet face and accusing mind, knew that the old one had declared only what was true. "Seven Sista, we have ceased from anger, have forsaken wrath and the evil within us. Give us the blessing that our steps may once again be of the righteous."

Seven Sista lifted a small cross from her coat pocket. It was made of three kinds of holy wood: cypress, plane, and pine. As her small hand held the cross aloft, her palms were open and raised over the conjurers as she spoke these holy words: "*Create in me a clean heart, O God, and renew a right spirit within me. O send out thy light and thy truth.*"

The hands of the conjurers instantly shot up. The knives they held transformed into small crosses of silver light. Everywhere in the room, beams of light lifted the darkness of bitterness from those gathered. Those in that crowd felt the brightness first as a blinding light, and then they felt its heat. Divine light flowed through them as it cleansed them of the yellow poison that was the bile of unforgiveness; its venom no longer would be able to oppress their spirits. Geeta felt the spiritual strength of this small, ancient woman fill her. Beside her, even the Great Magician was speechless.

It might be that this is how the soul is awakened: when the heart grows into the truth and the lessons move from it like sunlight casting away the darkness of the lie. For the sight and the story that followed seared itself in those in that smoky basement club—not as facts but in the way you understand something with your heart and not your mind. For they—conjurers, root doctors, they who knew the power of the Psalms—had forgotten to see with their spirit eyes until Seven Sista had awakened that power within them. Seven Sista put the cross back in her tattered coat pocket and cupped her hands in front of Mattie, her gaze holding hers. She instantly placed the crystal ball in the old woman's hands.

"Please help us find Mr. Biddle," Mattie said.

In Seven Sista's hands, the crystal ball grew larger. In the small club, the only sound was that of the hushed breathing of the conjurers. Mattie and Geeta stared expectantly at the small woman.

Seven Sista's body rocked as she intoned:

Their beloveds' last garments tattered and bloodied
Seven Bitter Widows, their arms weak with sorrow, carried.
A spell they have laid upon this wizard,
Holder of the Cape of Light.
Tattered now is this magic cloak…dim, not bright.
Now his heart, like those of the Seven Bitter Widows, is broken and sore.
Like an arrow through his soul, it bore,
For he bears the Seven Bitter Widows' unrelenting sadness,
As its curse falls upon him and casts him into madness.

Mattie and Geeta said at once, "Please tell us how to save Mr. Biddle. Please."

Seven Sista's lips moved voicelessly. She was fading from this world. Taken by something unseen, she looked past Mattie, Geeta, and the Great Magician. Her eyes then turned upward into her head until only the whites could be seen. A small flame of silver shone at the third eye—that sacred space between the eyebrows— as her body collapsed to the floor. Instantly Seven Sista's tiny limp body, clad in a white shroud, lifted out of the oversize tattered coat and flew like a sparrow toward the blue crystal wings that hovered near the dome of the ceiling. The wings then clasped on to her back. Two feathers fell from the wings.

One feather floated and melted into Mattie's hand, leaving its imprint on her right palm. The other feather softly touched Geeta's right cheek, for her palms held the blue light of her life-line, and marked itself there.

The crystal wings flapped gently about the small, delicate body of Seven Sista to release a rain of blue crystal feathers upon the conjurers. They raised their right palms, and into each of them, a blue crystal mark imprinted itself; now they would have protection against the dead souls outside. Seven Sista's body was cast in a silvery light. The spiritualists held aloft their small silver crosses made of light beams and small light roots so Seven Sista's spirit would be guided upward. They swayed as their voices formed a song of farewell.

Travel fast into the heavens, Seven Sista,
For our days are but shadows that fall upon this earth.
Swiftly may the blue wings lift you into His sight.
May your spirit shine forever in His glorious light.

Mattie looked up to see a small flash of blue-and-silver light before Seven Sista disappeared. She then knelt by the old, brown-checked, cloth coat that was all that was left of Seven Sista. Tears flowed like a river from her eyes and down her chubby cheeks. She felt an emptiness like no other, as if a piece of her heart had been dug out. Mattie held Seven Sista's coat in her hands as she stood up. She put it on, and even on her, it was large; its tattered cloth felt like a soft blanket, and in it she felt Seven Sista's presence.

The crystal ball, floating like a balloon, began to glow.

Black Lazarus's panicked voice suddenly erupted from it: "A thousand years breaks. Satan is loosed out of his prison. The four winds of heaven scatter as the serpent rises strongly."

The conjurers were hushed. The Great Magician heard Black Lazarus and wondered again at his own foolishness, having spent so much time in his mortal life trying to debunk mediums.

A vision fell from the glowing ball: it revealed Herman Biddle, writhing upon the ground, his eyes crazed with lunacy, his gossamer-thin Cape of Light floating over him as a great serpent with large black wings erupted from the ground, its dragon mouth open and ready to devour him.

In unison, Mattie and Geeta screamed "No!" at this terrible vision. Then it disappeared.

The touch of Seven Sista's twiglike fingers stung Mattie's cheek as the old woman's words wove themselves into her soul. She felt them touching her, cloaking her, as if they made up the fabric of Seven Sista's brown cloth coat: *But thou hast saved us from our enemies, and hast put them to shame that hated us.*

Transformations come suddenly for some or are like a dawning light for others.

It was the latter for Mattie, upon whose ordinary shoulders first the journey of the Path of the Virtuous and then an extraordinary destiny had been placed: *Thou hast saved us from our enemies.*

But that destiny was a heavy burden indeed, for the lessons on the stones were brutal and real, not an imaginary journey like daydreams or even night dreams, but heartbreakingly real: where Mr. Biddle could become crazy, where Geeta could die, where Eddie could disappear—maybe forever—and her mother was just a voice in her head.

Then there was the Spyglass. "You must know good from evil, for you have become the Mistress of the Spyglass," Mr. Biddle had said. Everyone had told her to hold on to it, but they didn't know the Spyglass like she did, as the evil, double-crossing, selfish creature it was; thank goodness she had dropped it on the rooftop. Mattie's mind stretched as she tried to understand the meaning of the stones, of all the events that had transpired recently. Some she grasped; others were amorphous feelings that erupted as jolts in her heart. Again Seven Sista's words rang in her mind: *But thou hast saved us from our enemies, and hast put them to shame that hated us.*

The transformation of the soul is a journey that is not linear in strength or direction but one of fits and starts. Mattie felt a sort of desperation—the keenness of wanting to return to that innocent time, when everything seemed fun and different, when holding the Spyglass was something that was sort of like getting a magic wand.

An aching longing that things could go back to the way they were before hit her. She longed for Mr. Biddle to return to who he had been, not with crazy eyes but bright-blue kind ones—the Mr. Biddle who always listened to her, helped her with her homework down in the basement of Sears. When they had first escaped from Uri Gneezy and were hidden in the space-between-time,

Mr. Biddle's cape wasn't flimsy like the one in the vision but had an enchanted hue that seemed like a great ocean, turning color like the ocean waters might under a changing sky: first a steely gray, then greenish with specks of bright blue just underneath the surface, then a creamy purple. Mattie recalled how Mr. Biddle, with the Cards of Time, had taken them into New York City, where they had watched a parade celebrating the end of the war, and they had cookies and milk in a diner. In truth, for Mattie the First Stone seemed at first a sort of extended field trip with Mr. Biddle, Eddie, and Geeta. *As the serpent rises strongly.* The Snake had been their enemy from the start—way back when he first had shown up in Sears as an old man to take the Spyglass from her. Eddie's dad, Sergeant Petersen, had told them that a long time ago from the jungles of Vietnam, even before the First Stone. Eddie was a soldier, but who knew where he was and when Mattie would see him again?

The longing hit Mattie again: why couldn't it be like before? She knew that it couldn't ever be, and then her bitterness at that realization ebbed, growing into an acceptance of what was, rather than what she wanted. Mattie felt a blush of shame; she'd been acting like a kid. *I have to grow up.* She heard this thought in her mind, and she knew it to be true. She knew she was saying good-bye to a part of herself forever—for childhood lived and a childhood remembered are two very different things. It felt so sad, this loss of herself, yet it had to be.

Seven Sista's words came to Mattie again: *But thou hast saved us from our enemies, and hast put them to shame that hated us.* Mattie felt the words again in her heart and now *heard* them and understood. Seven Sista was telling her what she was supposed *to do*, not what she had already done: *Save us from our enemies.* The Snake Uri Gneezy was the first enemy, but the greater one was Marduk, the Dark Master. There was only one way to be saved. Mattie heard Seven Sista's sweet voice again: *I will guide thee, daughter. Raise your arms so that those gathered here will understand that you command.*

Mattie turned to Geeta. "Do what I do," she whispered.

Geeta's eyes had been upon Mattie and saw that her friend was changing, as she herself had changed in the cave where ThaTha had saved her life.

Mattie then turned to the conjurers. She lifted her arms, her palms up, the large sleeves of the brown cloth coat falling to her elbows. Geeta followed suit, raising her palms with their glowing blue lines.

As the crystal ball bounced above their heads, the Great Magician's eyes were fixed upon it. There was still a chance to find Bess. That crystal ball, he knew, had the power to lead him to her.

Mattie's eyes were burning, her body trembling. The conjurers knew why the red-haired one was shaking; she was falling to the visions.

Mattie spoke as if she were in a trance, directed by what she saw: Mother Tiamat, her face soft like light.

Her cloak is of the sun, the moon under her feet.
A crown of twelve stars rests upon her head.
She cries woe, woe, woe.
Broken are two bands of gold.
The Daughter writhes in the bottomless pit.
If she lives not her thousandth mortal hold,
Darkened forever will be the sun, blackness the face of the moon.
Seven heads of lies to devour the mind,
Seven horns of bitterness to pierce the heart,

Seven crowns of disease to eat the body,
For the red serpent dragon has been cast onto the earth
To deceiveth the world, to take from man his soul,
And to close forever the Book of Light.

Mattie then opened her eyes. The fierceness in her voice had spoken of her determination. The conjurers had heard the words and believed them to be those of Seven Sista.

Mattie then said in Seven Sista's voice, "The wicked have drawn out their sword and bent their bow, but their sword shall enter their own hearts. Will you stand still while goodness dies? Slay the demon, the serpent dragon." These last words came out softly, for Mattie was drained.

CHAPTER 14

the crown of disease

Fear resounded as a deep primeval note and rang through Eddie as the cave shook again. Then an image entered his mind: a pockmarked face that taunted him. But worse, Eddie felt Trina's spirit shaking in fright. *Oh, my love.* He thrust his soul, and it flew out of the light and toward the darkness to save her. Eddie's body arched back against the force of evil that relentlessly pressed against his soul. Then it was blackness. His next sensation was that he was crushed, broken. Eddie's eyes were shut tight against the pain. But then he felt a gentle, healing touch, and a warmth like sunshine fell over him. His eyes opened within the darkness. He looked up to see Nana, the wisewoman of Uruk, her black hair shot with crimson tied into a knot and her gentle face crisscrossed with lines. The flames of a fire at her side sent shadows of prophecy across her face. Eddie felt his spirit rise to sit by her. Nana turned toward him. She raised her hands to show him the lines of her palms, which revealed the coming fate of Gilgamesh: trapped forever in the darkness of the

Abyss, recoiling in agony, his tall blue frame bound in chains and slashed by the whips of the underworld demons.

Eddie's heart surged against the image. "No!"

Nana's dark eyes filled with sorrow as she spoke into his soul.

Muktablu, son of our son,
Culled by the point of Death's scythe,
Three drops of your heart's blood.
For though only seven there be,
Three drops must you give to set Gilgamesh free.

Eddie reached out and placed his palms flat upon hers, and then his lifelines touched those of the people of Uruk. Nana faded into the darkness.

Eddie opened his eyes. He was crouched on the cave floor. He stood up and saw that he was in his combat gear. The cave was the one that had shaken from the pounding feet above; the light of his warrior spear revealed the low rocky ceiling. The spear was in one hand, the scythe upon his back. He moved the spear to gather more intel. The flickering green light of the spear revealed a circle of stones scattered around him but not over him. It showed the wreckage after a storm; he had been in its eye but protected within the light of the spear. *Three drops of your heart's blood. For though only seven there be.*

Eddie didn't hesitate. He would never leave his brother behind. *Three drops of your heart's blood.* He placed the warrior spear flat on the cave floor. Then he removed the scythe from his back. It vibrated in ominous tones. He steadied himself, firmly placing his combat boots in place. The blue lines in the warrior spear shone in protest. *Muktablu!* Gilgamesh's voice, filled with alarm, shot through Eddie's mind. *No. Do not weaken yourself!*

The spear sprang up to thwart Eddie from stabbing the point of Death's scythe into his heart. But Eddie was deaf to its protest; his mission was clear. The spear fell to the ground at his feet. He flung his head back and plunged Death's scythe swiftly into his chest. Like a dark beam, the point went straight into his heart. He pushed the scythe's sharp point deep into his chest; he pushed it once, twice, thrice. The deadly poison of the scythe bore deep within him. It wrapped around the beats of his heart to still it.

"Stop! I am your master," Eddie shouted to the scythe, his eyes closing against its force.

It continued to move, unthwarted by his command. The scythe was an instrument of death, and just as a predator is designed to kill its prey, it moved to wring the mortal soul that touched its point and cull it for the underworld. Eddie fell to his knees, his head lowered in agony. Then he felt a warmth like the sudden sunburst that falls on one's face when all hope seems dead. The blue filament of Gilgamesh's one-quarter-mortal soul, wrapped within the iris in Eddie's eyes, pushed against the death force of the scythe. It moved with the will of the bravery of Eddie's heart. It beat the notes of courage and loyalty, of Eddie's love for his fellow warrior brother. The strength of generations of warriors who had given their lives for their fellow brothers moved through his veins. In his mind's eye, he saw a wondrous vision: the force of blinding light rising strongly. He felt victory being wrestled from the hands of evil. Against this force of goodness, the scythe's death hold wavered and reeled. Quickly the scythe gave way.

Gasping, Eddie pulled it out of his heart. He was crouched low on the ground. The point of the scythe shone brightly with three drops of blood. One by one, each drop of blood fell upon the warrior spear, which lay at his feet. The three drops of Eddie's blood moved into and through the blue veins of the spear. He fell on his haunches to stave off the dizziness that was enveloping him. He kept his head down and held the scythe by his side. On the ground, the spear glowed and pulsed. Then the blue line spun out of the spear, first as wisps of blue smoke then blue light. Eddie felt his heart beating stronger. He felt the warmth of the blue light. He looked up.

"Hello, King," Eddie said, smiling, as the blue light turned into his friend, his warrior brother, Gilgamesh.

The many splintered pieces of the *Condemned Ship of the Outlaws of Hell* fell like shards upon the rocky black shores of the island. The rocks were slippery with the sea's mist. From these pieces the ancient outlaw seafarers rose up first as thin tendrils of smoke, then into their forms, falling as their feet tried to gain footing on the slippery shore. Then appeared the Once-Noble One, his sword with its coral inlay clasped in his hand; his red-and-black robes fluttering against the wind, which rose as the waves of the Sea of Abyss hit the shores. His feet were apart, lodged between two rocks to steady him. He shuddered inwardly as he took in the great castle upon the mountain. He thought of the impossibility of escape from the Abyss. "Pla-toon," the young Ab-gal-lu, who had held his head with the proud spirit of a unsullied true warrior, had said as he had grouped them into three parts. *Ab-gal-lu. He Who Commands the Chariot of the Great Waters of the Underworld.* True, the young yellow-haired warrior held the noble spear, as well as Death's scythe. This Once-Noble One knew of the pure spirit, for he was of an ancient land with two rivers that crossed it and was born to royalty. Then he had betrayed his brother and ultimately was reduced in his mortal life to a scavenger of the sea. The Once-Noble One questioned the loyalty of the outlaws of the Sea of Abyss scrambling upon the shores. Thieves, liars, cheats, and killers they were. Could outlaws ever be trusted? Could he? "Leader" they might call you with their lips, while in their minds they plotted your overthrow. Though his sullied spirit was pierced by the pinprick of hope, the Once-Noble One felt the clutch of the doubt. He thought of the serpentine twists of how loyalty could turn to betrayal as it fell under the will of selfishness. Could the layers of deceit that lay upon a soul ever be cleansed?

The female seafarer of the Nile, her velvety black skin shining with drops of the sea's mist, called to those were in her charge to gather around her. She wore the red turban the Ab-gal-lu had placed upon her on the ship. "Pla-toon," the young Ab-gal-lu had called the group, but he was nowhere to be found. Those who were to follow the Ab-gal-lu looked to the One of the Nile with a question in their eyes and worse: fear of being captured by the creatures of the Abyss. Others circled around the Once-Noble One, in whose eyes the One from the Nile saw that his thoughts were troubled. Upon the slippery rocks behind the two, 150 of the outlaw seafarers stood, the salty mist of the Sea of Abyss filling the air, the sound of waves crashing against the black rocks beating the rhythm of their demise. The One of the Nile, with hazel eyes like those of a tiger, stared at the mountain where the castle stood.

She turned to the Once-Noble One and shook her black hair. It was fashioned in spikes, embedded with sapphire beads that rattled within the red turban. "Oh, Once-Noble One, where is the Ab-gal-lu?"

Her tone underscored the fear that perhaps the Ab-gal-lu had abandoned them to save himself. It was what the Once-Noble One himself felt, although he did not want to give that idea a voice.

"He will come," the Once-Noble One said with a certainty he did not possess.

The One of the Nile narrowed her eyes. In her mortal form, she had survived through thievery and the ever-changing faces from friend to scheming foe; therefore she trusted no one. But the Ab-gal-lu was a living soul in the land of the dead; stranger still, he had held the instrument of death and brandished the ancient warrior spear. The One of the Nile had felt hope pierce the thick blanket of desolation when the Ab-gal-lu had appeared upon the ship. But it was a beam of light in the darkness of her soul so small that it was almost invisible. Again she shook her red-turbaned head, and the sapphire beads rattled as if to oppose this impossibly childish wish to be rescued. *And what of the pla-toon?* she thought, as the thieves of the sea gathered about her, their eyes glimmering at once with loyalty and treachery. Would not their resolve to stand together fall away like water spilled upon the ground when the greatness of the enemy filled their vision?

With these thoughts in mind, she spoke to the Once-Noble One. "Yes, so you say. But what of them?" She pointed toward the road to the castle. "For surely we shall soon all be slaves of those creatures."

The Once-Noble One saw ahead that the road to the castle was teeming with the terrifying, formidable creatures of the Abyss.

It was what was beneath his feet, however, that he should have feared. A blotchy-gray, coppery-green slime floated upon the skin of the Sea of Abyss and moved upon the blacks sands of the shore. It moved as lava does, thick and relentless as it gathered momentum. A cloying stench of death filled the air. Soon the shores of the island of the Prince of Demons rang with the cries of the ancient outlaw seafarers as they were smothered beneath a blanket of slime.

𒀸𒅖𒌋𒁹𒀸𒅖𒌑

The murmurs of the thousands of creatures of the Abyss crowded within the great hall lifted and echoed with excitement as more and more of them pushed into the castle. Their voices reverberated from the stone floor to the walls, bouncing with their impatience to escape the Abyss, to break the skin of Kurnigi and pierce the land of the living. Stal remained unmoved; he let the creatures' words ebb and flow around him as he sat upon his throne, flanked by two advisors.

The one with the golden, blood-spattered mask stood to the right of Stal. He said softly to the prince, "Shall we not rise now and conquer Kurnigi?"

Stal did not respond. It was the pleasant weight of power in the form of the papal crown on his head that held his attention. Those who bowed to him would have to learn to wait, for he had been crowned their prince. Stal's eyes moved with a sudden thought. A royal wedding. Yes, he decided, he would take Trina as his bride, for that represented the fruition of his longings; he was in power now, and at his side would be the beauty who had been beyond his grasp when he was in his mortal form. Then they would move out of the Abyss. For it was he, and he alone, who held the secret dark power to escape this place. Stal's three-headed dragon steed, standing at wait to the side of the throne, flapped its great black wings, raised its heads, and spewed flames.

Stal turned, irritated at the interruption to his musings by a buzz-ing noise in his ear.

"Virtues and vices are twin brothers," the Counselor, at Stal's left side, whispered into the prince's ear. "Cruelty is paradoxi-cally the best virtue, for it produces peace, while kindness is a vice, for it is the breeding ground of discontent."

The whispers held the sibilant tones of a snake's hissing, for in truth the Counselor was as devious as the first serpent that had tempted mankind. It was important that this delicate beauty that the prince called his princess—who clearly had bewitched him—be removed from his sight so the Counselor could com-mand his full attention. As such, he had ordered, though with great tact so that the prince believed it to be his command, that the princess be taken to a room far from the great hall, to be placed high within a tower. The Counselor had commanded five female creatures of the Abyss, once devious handmaidens to mortal queens, to dress the princess. Here she would be bedecked with jewels and fine robes and then presented to the prince. All of this—the jewels and beautiful robes—were illu-sions of the Abyss, of course, but it was a desire of the prince, and this desire had to be fed so he could be controlled. Too, the Counselor was alarmed to have seen the man with the gold mask splattered with blood already at the prince's side when he had returned from the tower. Only he, the Counselor, should have the prince's ear.

The Counselor continued, "Cruelty administered swiftly and consistently will create stability and loyalty among the ruled."

Stal did not like the Counselor, this one with the brown robes of a monk, who had come to his side unasked. He had ordered the Counselor to bedeck Trina with jewels, as befitting his princess. Instead the monk had delegated the task to others and returned quickly to remain steadfastly at his side. Stal knew this Counselor well, though they had never met before, for he was like all the priests at the Georgian church school: pious in appearance, with humble monk robes serving as a thin covering for their true arrogant, greedy nature. The black and blue thumbs upon his hands shone. Stal itched to raise the Saber of Shadows and slash this Counselor's head right off. Instead he tightened his grip upon it. Not yet, he realized, for this fool's eyes showed that he held the secrets of the Unholy Trio—now Stal's enemies within the Abyss—who must be destroyed.

The Counselor continued, "To seize a state and to keep it are two different matters altogether."

Here the Counselor paused; he would subtly hint that the prince would one day too be overthrown, so he would have the seed of fear of losing control planted in his heart. Soon the prince would imagine others' plots to overthrow him. Then the prince would seek the Counselor's wit and wisdom, in desperation to keep his power from slipping through his hands like seafoam.

The Counselor's voice fell in soft, obsequious tones. "I speak only about that which I have observed: how the masses take up arms to overthrow and rule over another, only to repeat the pattern in endless cycles."

The Counselor's egg-shaped head, sprinkled with wispy brown hairs, wobbled. His dark eyes, barely hiding his contempt, looked with eagerness at the prince.

Stal's red eyes glared at the Counselor. "Are you warning me?" His tone was severe, for this court jester must know his place. "Take care, *Counselor.*"

The Counselor bowed his head low, too embroiled in his intrigue to see how the embers of evil glowed with displeasure within the prince's eyes.

The one with the blood-spattered mask heard the rising discontent of the creatures of the Abyss. He, whose face was a mask of gold—a punishment for his greed for riches as a mortal—understood their ache to be free. As a diplomat, a politician of old, he knew that the best tactic was to speak out of both sides of his mouth. For now his allegiance was to the prince. At their core, all the creatures of the Abyss were selfish, and their pledges to follow and obey were flimsy. Still, they needed the prince to break the black hold of the Abyss. He saw too that the Counselor's eyes blinked with plots and plans, but he was, in fact, a thorn to the prince. Above him, the masked man felt the cold gray breaths of the Unholy Trio as they moved invisibly within the black dome that now obscured the painted devils. They were waiting for the prince to reveal his weakness, for those high priests of the unrighteous were not so easily dismissed. *Now*, the one with the gold mask thought, *how powerful is the prince?* If one were to wrest from this prince the Saber of Shadows, slash the powerful black and blue thumbs from his hands, would he not too be prince? And why not him?

Stal rose from his throne; again he was aware of the murmurs of the creatures, and snatches of their chant—*Escape the Abyss*—ebbed and flow around him. In his role as prince, it was his prerogative to ignore it, for he was the ruler, not the ruled. These two self-appointed advisors at his side would learn who held power supreme. Stal had long resolved—having learned bitter lessons from his days under the brute force of his father's drunken blows, the pious beatings of his mother, and the taunts and kicks of the rich boys—that he would never be ruled by anyone again. *Never.* Too, strength was growing in his body; it fueled and honed a cruel streak. Stal reveled in delight at his ten feet of height. He flexed his muscular arms, and the shimmering silver scales that formed his tunic rustled. The black cloak upon his shoulders moved like a winter wind, and if one had stood still and close by Stal, its deadly chill would have cut through to the bone.

The Counselor, however, remained oblivious to the prince's display of his prowess, for he was gaining speed in his rhetoric. His tone was pedantic. "A newly risen prince, if prudent, treads the path of those who have excelled before him."

This was another hint for the prince to follow his wise counsel.

The Counselor's voice lifted, for here were the pearls of wisdom that, once they hit the prince's ears, would fill him with wonder at the cunning of his advisor. "He must, as the shrewd archer does, know the limitations of his bow and not strike so distant a mark as to fail," the Counselor continued. "Rather, the ambitious target is struck through the—"

"Bring me the princess!" Stal commanded, cutting short the Counselor's preaching.

Stal was tiring of the Counselor. It was time for Trina to see him in his full glory and for her to be presented to these creatures of the Abyss. Then she would become his bride.

The Counselor felt the sting of this order rise like a bile through his throat. But before he could respond, a great commotion rose. The creatures of the Abyss jumped back as a rippling movement formed underneath the red carpet that cut through the great hall. A dark, thick, slimy substance, mottled gray and coppery green, bubbled out. It filled the great hall with the humid stench of waste and decay. Those in the great hall uttered sounds of disgust, for the smell now permeated the castle, a smell as thick as fog. Then the slimy substance gathered in an arc and rose from the carpet, moving toward the prince like a storm cloud breathing a foul odor.

The prince's face contorted in disgust. The man with the blood-spattered gold mask saw with terror what rose. The Counselor held his thin hands over his face.

It darted downward now: a thick, scaly rope of mottled gray and coppery green. It slithered to the stone floor in serpentine movements to coil at the prince's feet.

"What is this foul substance that takes form at my feet?" the prince asked.

The one with the gold mask replied, "It is of the depths of the core of the Black Abyss. That is all I know, Your Highness."

The prince's face was slashed with revulsion as the thick, scaly rope uncoiled to circle the hem of his robes. But something kept him from striking it with his Saber of Shadows.

The Counselor shuddered at the slime and heard what the one with gold mask had said of this foulness that had risen. But he knew more. The Counselor had encountered its stench once, just as a whiff, while chained deep beneath the castle in one of the many wars between him and the Unholy Trio. It had emitted the scent of death by torture. He recognized it as an entity that he would not be able to control. Therefore it must not be allowed to stay. He fingered a small dagger he held within his robes, for he was always at the ready; its point contained a deadly poison culled from the black stones of the Abyss. He considered the possibilities: the poison was unlikely to quell the slime, as it was so large, and if he pulled out the dagger, his secret weapon would be revealed to the prince.

The Counselor's fingers moved away from the dagger.

The ropy form of the substance let out a screeching sound, as if it had heard the Counselor's thoughts. It uncoiled and sprang toward him as the wily one quickly stepped back behind the throne. He peered around and said, "You must destroy it, Your Highness, for see how it seeks to harm you!"

Stal ignored the Counselor. His black cloak, made of the weaving of the spider of death, rustled. The black and blue of his thumbs, which held the ancient souls culled by Abaddon in the throes of painful death, shone. Strangely the stench changed in his nostrils: it smelled of conquest. Revulsion gave way to an understanding that this was a spirit—or spirits—that brought terror.

The slimy, scaly rope had now uncoiled. Seven heads erupted from it. Each had great bloodshot yellow eyes and mouths that opened to reveal sharp teeth. Upon each head were yellow horns that bored through the forehead. The center head was the most gruesome, split as it was in two to reveal a gaping bloody wound, within which dirty white maggots wriggled. Then it healed whole and was again wounded and healed in an endless repetition; its punishment was the endless torture of the unhealed wound. This injured head hung low, weighted by its wound, and had upon it four horns, two on each side. This creature was a seven-headed beast with ten horns, each point ringed by a crown of furry yellowish fungus.

A body elongated from the slime: a body of a man but covered with mottled-gray and coppery-green scales; its two feet were like those of a crocodile, with claws upon them. Two long arms formed on each side, ending in filthy hands with curved black nails. The seven-headed creature with ten horns stood in its full form. It emitted an ever-stronger fetid odor of diseases that told the tale of how it once had ravaged the bodies of mortal man until they gave way to release their souls to it.

The creatures of the Abyss lowered their heads against the smell. Even they, denizens of the world of torture, recoiled against the stench of mercilessness that rose from the creature with the seven heads.

The one with the gold mask gave voice to their thoughts. "The Unclean One."

This Unclean One, ruthless and swollen with arrogance, had dared to blaspheme the Almighty himself—the Great Spirit of Darkness—and therefore had been condemned to the deepest cesspool of the underworld of the Black Abyss to live and be of filth.

Within the black domes that covered the great hall, a tremor of fear, envy, and awe rode across black eyes held in the gray forms of the Unholy Trio, those high priests for the unrighteous. "*Radix malorum cupiditas*: the root of evil is desire," they murmured hypocritically, for in truth, if they had possessed the power of the rotting disease to overcome mortal man, they too would have grown fat with power, like maggots feasting upon the carrion of souls. This seven-headed one had made its error by not using their evil skillfully, for they were blasphemers of the Great Spirit of Darkness, unlike the Unholy Trio, who had the misfortune to tangle unsuccessfully with the demon Marduk and always revered the Great Spirit of Darkness. Perhaps this Unclean One was here, they hoped, to destroy that pockmarked one, the false prophet.

The seven-headed creature with ten horns raised its two long arms and placed its filthy hands, with their curved black nails, in supplication. Its seven mouths sneered, "Heal us, if you be the true mighty Prince of Demons." Then, to the great hall, the creature's seven mouths roared, "If this prince be true, he will heal our wound. If he be false, our wound shall remain, and we shall devour him with disease."

Silence descended over the great hall. *If this prince be true, he will heal our wound.* The journey out of the Abyss was a maze of tests, and if the prince failed any, no movement out was possible.

Stal's red eyes drilled into the eyes of the seven-headed beast's center head. The bloody wound was ever healing and injured again and again. The insolence of the creature irked him. He would show this beast his might. He would heal the wound then slash the seven heads off.

Stal removed the Saber of Shadows from its sheath at his side and began to raise it but was stopped by a small whisper from the crafty Counselor at his side. "O Prince, you must show that you are both a fierce lion and a wily fox. Demand of this creature a payment for the healing: that which is his power."

The creature's voice held a taunt, and to the great hall, it uttered, "Heal us, if you can, O Prince."

"That I can," Stal said. "But upon the healing, you shall pay my price."

To this, the seven-headed creature's center head bowed in agreement, for it believed that this pockmarked one was not the true prince, and it had come to destroy him.

In a swift movement, Stal drove the blade of the Saber of Shadows into the gaping wound in the creature's center head. The wound began to close over the sword; Stal then pulled the sword out. Over its blade wriggled fat, dirty, white maggots that burned, turning into smoke that smelled of singed hair. The Unclean One's seven heads flung back as they roared in pain. The wound closed completely, and a scar, thick and green like bile, formed upon it then disappeared. The center head was now whole.

Within the great hall, the creatures of the Abyss murmured of this miracle, "The prince has healed the Unclean One."

Stal placed the Saber of Shadows in its sheath at his side. He stood, his legs apart, the black cape of the spider of death's weaving fluttering behind him, his papal crown gleaming with triumph upon his head. Again his red eyes drilled into the Unclean One. "Creature, I have healed you as you asked. Now you must pay my price: yield that which makes you fearsome."

The seven-headed creature nodded in assent. With its long arms, the Unclean One removed the yellow fungus that ringed the tips of its ten horns, placed the substance in its left hand, and closed that hand firmly. Then, with its right hand, the creature tore its horns off its seven heads. Ten yellow horns the creature threw into the air, and they transformed into a scroll. It unfurled and fell to the stone floor. Upon it were small slashes of writing of the souls whose faith had been broken by the Unclean One and who had sworn their souls to darkness for relief. The faces of these souls, ravaged by disease, floated from the scroll then moved back into the slashes. The scroll then curled and flew toward Stal, who grabbed it and placed in within his cape.

"Behold!" said the seven-headed creature with its seven tongues. "O Prince, we give you our Scroll of Death in gratitude."

Stal saw the Counselor's eyes dart toward the creature's left hand, which remained tightly shut.

The Counselor's eyes shone with greed. The wily one whispered, "Prince, this one cheats you."

It was then that Stal knew fully where the creature's true power lay: in the ten crowns of fungus that the Unclean One grasped in its left palm. Stal's long raven-colored hair rippled in recognition of this evil force. It penetrated into the deep well of his desire to stomp upon the necks of those who would dare oppose him, to have all who beheld him possess one impulse: utter obedience. *Beware the Unclean One, who opened its mouth to blaspheme His name.* The lessons of old from the Georgian school priests, which told of the Unclean One's blasphemy, rang in Stal's mind like church bells. *Plagues, dead bodies, and souls condemned to the bottomless pit. These are the things that come upon one who blasphemes Him.* But those stupid priests thought the Unclean One had cursed their meek and powerless god. *Seven heads and ten horns has this one, this unclean beast of the sea.* The priests had feared it and warned of the bottomless pit, of flames of torment that awaited those who blasphemed.

Stal's thoughts formed not from the goodness in the lessons and words the priests had taught him but rose perverted and bloated, like corpses that rise from the murky bottom to float upon still waters. These thoughts vibrated through him, his body shaking in tremors. *This creature's power resides in its filth, more poisonous than a viper's tongue. It dared to use its sorcery to rise against the Great Dark Spirit, to steal the Night Universe. For this it did not repent, and as its punishment, it lies for eternity as a slime at the bottom of the sea, sunk by its own Crown of Disease.*

But to these thoughts of Stal, the duplicitous seven-headed creature was deaf, for now that it had no wound to weigh it down with its torture, it could again rise to power. It was transforming, growing larger to fill the great hall with its form and stink, take back the scroll, and bend to submission this prince, who would lead it out of the Abyss.

Stal thrust the Saber of Shadows quickly and slashed off the Unclean One's left hand. The creature howled in surprise. The yellow fungus, the Crown of Disease, flew up from its fingers. Stal pierced the Crown of Disease with the blade's point, turning the sword to reveal his Sword of Deception. The Crown of Disease melted into threads of intricate patterns that embedded themselves into the blade of the sword. Powerless, the seven-headed creature fell to the stone floor. It transformed back into the mottled-gray and coppery-green substance until only the seven heads could be seen bobbing upon the slime, its mouths yelling curses at Stal as it became a foul vapor that disappeared.

The great hall was deathly silent. Even the Unholy Trio, above in the dome, were hushed to reverence, for the prince had felled the Unclean One and taken its power, the deadly Crown of Disease.

"Fortune bestows greatness upon a new prince through his enemies." The Counselor's sibilant tones rose in praise, falling pleasantly within Stal's ears.

Stal's shimmering tunic of silver scales glimmered. The current of the power of the Crown of Disease pulsed from the blade into him. Now Stal vibrated with these thoughts: *The Unclean One blasphemed the Great Spirit of Darkness himself. Who would dare curse the all-powerful Dark Spirit but one who held the secret to overthrow him?*

Stal's pockmarked face shone with a new realization. He now held the Crown of Disease. A sneer formed on his lips, framed by his pointed beard. Why should he settle at overthrowing Marduk, who only held the puny dark underworld of human souls? Then only Kurnigi would be at his command, with smaller demons ever nibbling at his feet to overthrow him. His destiny was greater: to conquer the Creator of Darkness himself, to shut out Light, and to become the All-Powerful Spirit of the Universe.

𒀭𒁉𒂍𒀭𒐊

Though his heart was heavy, Gilgamesh returned the young *muktablu*'s smile. Even he, though he was Gilgamesh, the seventh king of Uruk, was daunted by the weight of the Abyss above. Though his head was covered with a golden, turban-shaped, peaked helmet, nonetheless he felt oppressed by the lowness of the cave's ceiling, for the cavern's darkness surrounded him like a blanket of bleakness. As Gilgamesh moved, his rope-like black hair collected the dirt that fell from the ceiling of the cave, and his many-braided beard was covered with a thin film of gray dust.

Eddie stood up. His heart was light with joy. The king was here! He lifted the warrior spear. Its green flame let off a translucent glow that cast shadows upon Gilgamesh's solemn face. He was puzzled by the king's silence and more so the sad smile and the even sadder thoughts he suspected were behind it. The king's blue face was wreathed with worry and ran in contrast to his gear: the golden armor and long blue tunic that fell to his knees, the gold bands upon his strong arms and wrists, all of which cried of his warrior strength and resolve.

Still, Eddie dismissed the emotions that flitted across Gilgamesh's face. He knew the king was a worrier. He smiled broadly, for it was good to see his brother warrior. "Take your weapon, King."

Gilgamesh stared wordlessly at the warrior spear. How did the *muktablu* hold it with such strong hands and the brave heart of a man? He smiled at the memory of long ago, within the bowels of the museum that had imprisoned him, when the *muktablu* had fallen upon his buttocks while trying to lift the spear.

"How strong you have become, *muktablu*," Gilgamesh said at last.

"Your weapon," Eddie said, holding out the spear. Still, Gilgamesh did not take it. Eddie looked quizzically at him. "What's going on, King?"

Gilgamesh kept his arms at his side, as if to refuse the weapon. He could not speak the words. He thought of how the *muktablu* had pierced his own heart to give him three drops of blood in order to save him. Gilgamesh felt the nobleness of those three drops of blood given without hesitation. But the *muktablu* was weakened by that sacrifice. He wished desperately that the *muktablu* had ignored Nana's counsel.

Gilgamesh was weakened, with a form that was just three-quarters in strength—divine, true, but one-quarter empty—and that gap was a vulnerability that could be entered by the dark spirits to take possession of him. He looked into the *muktablu*'s eyes and saw his own one-quarter-mortal soul glinting within the young warrior's eyes. He saw now how it was woven tightly into the young warrior's spirit. If he took it back, the *muktablu* surely would perish. The king of Uruk never would risk that. The Black Abyss, was a trap that ensnared one deeper and deeper the more one struggled against its hold with sacrifices and battle.

The spear's green light flickered upon his troubled blue face. Gilgamesh was ten feet in height but felt small next to the *muktablu*, whose thoughts were not weighted by anguish and doubt, but who moved with the strong and certain steps of a true warrior. Gilgamesh again felt the smallness of his spirit. Doubt had led him to lose his warrior brother, Enkidu, to the dark underworld those many eons ago at the threshold of the forest of Humawa. Doubt had kept him from finding Utnaspishtim and the eternal leaf. Doubt had kept him from saving his people from the death winds that had turned them to dust and plunged them into the Land of Darkness. Doubt had left him trapped within the Seven Tablets in the bowels of the British Museum. Doubt now kept him from his destiny: to restore the truth of the sacred tablets. Here Gilgamesh bent his head lower, weighed down even more by his thoughts. And though he had plunged into the Abyss to save the *muktablu*, though he had given his one-quarter-mortal soul so the young warrior might live, he knew that bravery was not his first impulse. Gilgamesh lowered his head further, his great shoulders slumped.

I am not worthy of this spear, he thought. Then he said, "*Muktablu*, you have shown valor worthy of this noble weapon. Keep it. It is yours."

Gilgamesh's mortal soul glistened within Eddie's eyes. Though he didn't realize he held one-quarter of his brother warrior within him, he felt in a wordless manner the deepness of the bond; he sensed the doleful drumbeat of doubt that sounded within the king, rattling his courage.

"Brother warrior," Eddie said softly, "I've only guarded your weapon. It's not mine."

Eddie then forcefully placed the weapon in Gilgamesh's hand. The spear's golden staff glowed in response to the king's touch.

Eddie felt the king's spirit burdened by some secret knowledge, something he would not speak out loud. The king held the spear tentatively, as if it were new to him and not his weapon.

As Gilgamesh held the spear, the ancient strength of its warrior lineage vibrated through his body. The will and strength of six kings of Uruk before him—and still more warriors of old—filled him and lifted his hope. After all, was he not three-quarters divine? The spear would serve as protection to keep the evil spirits from penetrating the hole in his being, where the one-quarter-mortal soul once resided. Too, if the muktablu hoped for any chance of escape from this black hell beneath hell, he needed help, and for that Gilgamesh had to be strong and armed. Two weapons would only weigh down the *muktablu*.

Gilgamesh struggled in thought. Still, the *muktablu* must be warned; what if the dark forces overcame the power of the spear? He had to tell the *muktablu* what to do if the spear failed to protect him: that he must destroy him at the first sign that darkness was entering to overtake him, before the first flicker of evil rose in his eyes.

The king finally spoke, his dark eyes intent upon Eddie. "I will keep the spear, but only if you promise me this, *muktablu*:

if ever the blue of my skin begins to fade, cut me down with Death's scythe and take the spear for yourself. Plunge the spear's tip into my forehead until there is nothing left but dust."

Eddie smelled the stink of fear rising from the king. He pushed down the impulse to ask the king what it was he feared. *Speaking of weakness only feeds it*, he remembered his dad saying. It didn't matter anyway; they would battle whatever it was together.

Eddie shook his head firmly. "No."

Gilgamesh thrust the spear back toward Eddie. "Then you must be the holder of the spear."

Eddie stood back, his arms folded. "No, King."

Gilagmesh cried out in frustration, holding the spear out. "*Muktablu*! You do not understand!"

"I do understand. Know this, King: I'll *never* make that promise." Eddie arched his head up. "Something's happening. Get down!"

The cave convulsed in tremors. Eddie crouched low and pressed himself against the side of the cave. Gilgamesh held the flame of his spear down so as not to light the cave, his heart and thoughts still troubled.

Death's scythe by Eddie's side vibrated, and through it the power of nocturnal vision filled him. For death moved in the darkness, and its master had to see the shadows of the rising dead so he might capture it. Eddie's eyes were like those of a cat now, adjusting quickly to the darkness. In the highest part of the cave's ceiling, he detected a small movement. Then three large coppery-green, mottled-gray drops fell. They had a slick, slimy, iridescent, silvery glow. As they fell, the cave shook, and the drops, seedlike in shape, fell and then coalesced into a coppery greenish-gray translucent globe. It then split into a cluster of three smaller forms the size of small bird's eggs. Inside each one were larvae-shaped forms that moved restlessly.

The tremors stopped. There was a deathly silence. The cluster hung from the cave's ceiling, pulsating in a greenish-gray glow. Gilgamesh moved closer to Eddie's side, his words of caution stilled only by the fear of what the sound of his voice might awaken. Gilgamesh lifted his spear to light the cave. Now, with the spear's illumination, they could more clearly see the cluster of three grape-shaped sacs hanging from the ceiling. Each sac was transparent, and within each sac were smaller sacs with delicate crisscrossing veins that formed around tiny dark blobs that moved as if breathing. Although they were small, Gilgamesh instinctively felt that the dark spirits within were strong, and their size was no indication of how much destruction they could wreak.

"Let us move away from this thing that breathes death," Gilgamesh whispered.

Eddie stood right underneath the cluster; it was just a foot or so above him. Something was calling to him—something that vibrated within two of the sacs. He heard it faintly, a plaintive sound that rang in his mind and stung his conscience as he tried to move away as the king had instructed. He moved back. Now he heard it clearly: it was a cry for help. Eddie raised the scythe and used the tip to touch the two sacs.

"*Muktablu!* Beware this thing of darkness," Gilgamesh whispered again fervently, for although his head was lowered, it touched the ceiling of the cave, and he felt the strength of the spirits in the cluster.

The two sacs swayed at the touch of the scythe's tip. The surface of the cluster was beginning to solidify from its rubbery form. After a few moments, it was hard as glass. The tip of scythe, however, had pricked two small holes into two of the sacs. Two dark streaks poured out like a vapor before the pinpricks closed.

The vapor had the smell of sickness; it grew and arced toward Eddie.

"*Muktablu!*" Gilgamesh cried out in alarm, for the vapor had rapidly encircled Eddie. This smell the king knew well. It was the death sickness, carried in the wind, that had lodged into the people of Uruk until their bodies had withered and darkness had taken their spirits.

Eddie stood in the center of the dark vapor, and though the smell was horrific, he pulled back the scythe to his side and waited. He saw Gilgamesh through the vapor, preparing to strike it with the spear's flame.

"No, King!" he shouted. "Don't use the spear."

Something told Eddie not to be afraid. Then this vapor, this miasma of sickness, moved down to his feet. In a flash, it swirled in dark waves upon the cave's ground until the smoke of illness disappeared. Then two sets of hands formed and rose.

One pair of hands was the color of the night; the other was the color of almonds, the color of the skin that held the blood of those who were once mighty. Then the rest of their bodies appeared. The first one had black skin, hazel tiger eyes, and hair in spikes embedded with sapphire beads, capped by a red turban. The other was bareheaded, with an almond-colored face and the bearing of the royalty of ancient noble Egyptian seafarers in the Red Sea. Both were upon their knees, their heads lowered.

Eddie moved Death's scythe to his back. "At ease," he said to the bowed figures.

The Once-Noble One rose. Then too followed the One of the Nile, her black-velvet skin glistening.

The Once-Noble One, the sword with the coral inlay at his side, in his red-and-black robes, said, "Ab-gal-lu, we praise you for our rescue, for we have been held by the slime of the Unclean One."

As Eddie had asked, Gilgamesh hadn't used his spear's flame, and a great unease settled upon him. The *muktablu* was too trusting. He thrust his spear toward the Once-Noble One and the One of the Nile, his face fierce, for he knew these to be the sea thieves from the *Condemned Ship of the Outlaws of Hell* when he had been trapped within the body of the spear.

"*Muktablu*," Gilgamesh said, his eyes narrowed, "these creatures are outlaws, thieves, and criminals, even to the treacherous creatures of the Abyss."

Gilgamesh knew that deceit fell from their lips, sweet like honey at first but then quickly bitter and stinging when the listener was caught in the trap of the lies—as was the *muktablu* now.

"King," Eddie said, "put the spear down. They're not enemy combatants." Not heeding him, Gilgamesh kept the flame of his spear pointed at the Once-Noble One and the One of the Nile.

"Where are the platoons?" Eddie asked them.

The Once-Noble One, keeping his gaze upon the king of Uruk's spear, replied, "They are held by the spell of the Unclean One, trapped there." He pointed to the ceiling while his mind asked the question, *Why does the Ab-gal-lu not hold the sacred spear? And who is this great blue giant with the golden armor and eyes fierce with suspicion?*

Eddie cut off each sac from the ceiling with the scythe's blade. He caught all three in one hand. They were small glass-like eggs with dark, moving larvae inside. Two had tiny pinpricks dimpling the top. "The platoons are in here?"

The One of the Nile spoke. She too was puzzled that the Ab-gal-lu would allow this great blue warrior to hold the sacred spear. "Yes, Ab-gal-lu," she said. "The *pla-toons* lay trapped in the prison of the slime of the Unclean One."

Eddie handed one pinpricked egg to the Once-Noble One and the other to the One of the Nile. The third he put in his flak jacket. Gilgamesh shook his head, his ropes of black hair swaying in disapproval.

"We'll figure out a way to get them out," Eddie said. "Let's move out before this cave collapses."

Gilgamesh saw the calculating eyes of the sea thieves upon him. How soon would they discover his weakness and try to overtake him? If they did, they could hold the warrior spear and kill the *muktablu*. How could Gilgamesh protect the *muktablu*? He knew he couldn't share the secret of his weakness; if he did, the *muktablu* would risk sacrificing himself to return his one-quarter-mortal soul to him. It had be done quickly, Gilgamesh decided. With lightning speed he slashed the flame's tip at the two sea thieves. The flame touched and lit the robes of the Once-Noble One and the red turban of the One of the Nile. They cried out in pain as the green flame began to engulf them.

"King!" Gilgamesh heard Eddie's shouts. "Put out the flame!"

The king did not move, for he was heartened that the spear's flame could envelop them. "They are evil spirits, *muktablu*!"

Eddie jumped toward the burning sea thieves, swinging his scythe to put out the flames. The spear's flame caught his flak jacket. Gilgamesh saw with horror that the *muktablu* would soon be engulfed in fire. The king of Uruk cried out in agony, for the spear's light he could not quell. Why was it that everything he touched seemed destined for destruction? Gilgamesh sprang toward the flames to divert them onto him, but the warrior spear lifted him up and hurled him against the side of the cave.

Within the green flame, Eddie felt no heat. He swung his scythe like an ax through the green licks of flames around the Once-Noble One and the One of the Nile. But it wasn't the scythe but Eddie's warrior bravery that shone from his soul and fell like water upon the green flames, which instantly disappeared. All three of them stood unscathed.

The Once-Noble One and the One of the Nile stood silent and in awe that the *Ab-gal-lu* had overcome the great spear's flame, but most amazing of all was that he had risked *himself* to save *them*. Of this pureness of warrior spirit, of loyalty and trueness of one's word, they had heard, but it was a faint voice from long, long ago. But now the voice grew louder in their ears, and they felt the lifting of the many encrusted layers of deceit that lay upon their spirits. Hope the size of a mustard seed it had been, but now it grew to circle their spirits. To be truly cleansed, however, they knew required more, and this they were willing to do.

Gilgamesh, who had been thrown to the side of the cave by the spear, rose up, hitting his head on the ceiling. His dark eyes, empty of the spiral of his one-quarter soul, brimmed with regret. He thought now, though he did not say it, *I must leave the mukta-blu, for I am a danger to him. I will find a way and also leave him the warrior spear so he can defend himself.*

Although Eddie didn't hear these thoughts, the anguish in Gilgamesh's heart was too loud for him to hide from his warrior brother. He didn't know what was bothering the king, but it needed to be put aside—look at how it almost had destroyed them.

Before Eddie could speak, the Once-Noble One did. His eyes had been upon the troubled blue warrior.

He quickly moved toward Gilgamesh. After bowing, he looked up at the giant, blue, kingly warrior. "You rightly feared us, O mighty warrior of old. You, whom I see are a king and the son of kings and true of form, acted as I once would have before I threw away my honor for gold."

The king of Uruk looked down warily at this Once-Noble One, whose robes of red and black showed that he had held a high rank in some ancient time.

Then the Once-Noble One took his sword, the one with the coral inlay, and lifted it up to the king. "This weapon of mine, forged with gold and coral culled from the seas as they ran red with blood, was once given by a mighty pharaoh of old to my father as a weapon for his honor in battle, and then it was given to me. This I give you as a token of my pledge of peace and good-will toward you."

The king said nothing. Though his mind put forth a thou-sand reasons against trusting this outlaw spirit, it was his heart that pushed his hands forward to take the sword. His heart moved him, as the words of the Once-Noble One rang with honor; Gilgamesh knew that the giving of this weapon of his family was no trick.

The king of Uruk spoke from his heart, his words surprising even him, for they came from the ancient tongue forged by war-rior trust. "In peace I stand with you, brother." He then placed the sword back in the hands of the Once-Noble One. "You shall hold this weapon for me so that we may together battle those who come against us."

"So it shall be, brother," the Once-Noble One replied, his voice broken by emotion, for never had he thought it possible to walk once again in honor. He quickly bowed his head to hide his face as he took the sword from the king.

With surprise, Gilgamesh saw that tears fell down the seafar-er's cheeks and that his own heart was filled with emotion.

Eddie breathed a sigh of relief. Okay, maybe now they could move forward. He looked at the One of the Nile and noticed that her face was somber, that her eyes also were fixed upon Gilgamesh and the Once-Noble One.

The eyes of the One of the Nile were filled with an incredible sight: warriors of old—one a mighty king, the other a sea thief—forging a peaceful alliance and calling each other "brother." *So, it is true,* she thought, her mind whispering the prophecy of redemption. *When the sea of change comes upon the spirit, when the thief turns to honor, when greed his heart does not heed, then it will be that the tarnished souls of old the Sea of Abyss no longer can hold.*

𒁹𒇹𒁹𒁹𒇹𒁹

Stal jumped upon his three-headed dragon steed to gallop it across the red carpet. He flashed the Saber of Shadows and then the side of the Sword of Deception, both showing the intricate patterns of the Crown of Disease. His eyes blazed red; he threw back his raven head, flames spewing from his mouth. Then he hit the flanks of this three-headed dragon beast, which unfurled its wings and flew up.

Stal circled the heads of the creatures of the Abyss, his words cutting sharply into the stunned silence of those within the great hall. "Behold! From the breath of death, I rise, for I am the Spirit of Darkness, to whom you *shall* bow."

The castle's floors shook as the creatures stamped their feet and shouted their assent.

𒁹𒇹𒁹𒁹𒇹𒁹

The ceiling of the cave trembled. Then words resounded, falling first as sounds then forming sentences that echoed through the cave. It was a voice that sent tremors of terror through the Once-Noble One and into the One of the Nile, as notes of pure evil filled the cave. "Behold! From the breath of death, I rise, for I am the Spirit of Darkness, to whom you *shall* bow." Even Gilgamesh shuddered; the Prince of Demons had risen.

CHAPTER 15

ðemon nuptialis

The small, windowless tower chamber of the Castle of the Abyss held a prisoner: Trina. A large mirror, cracked and blackened with age, leaning against the wall, reflected her face back in pieces. A dank smell rose from the walls. At her feet, Trina felt the rippled wooden-planked floor. Close upon her, and holding Trina tightly, were five female creatures. Their long fingers, with pointed black nails, savagely grabbed her hair, braiding it into a thick rope. Then they yanked it and wound that thick braid upon her head. These vicious hands belonged to the handmaidens of long-dead queens of the ages when Christendom's notes were first rung against the gods of old. They wore their servitude poorly, for their bitterness at their stature ate at them: lowly in mortal life, lowly in the spirit world. Oh, how the souls they had sold to the Dark Master had been for naught: no great reward did they see in mortal form, and even less so in Kurnigi, and then, punished for their plots, they had been trapped in the very walls of the Castle of the Abyss until now. The faces and bodies of these five handmaidens bore the traces of their malicious mortal lives. Though their gowns were tattered, their eyes glistened with crisp plots. Three among them had been great beauties in their mortal forms, with long blond tresses that fell like a river of gold upon their shoulders. Their faces held remnants of this beauty, like a marred painting, for their eyes were bloodshot; their lips were torn; and upon their cheeks were long scars made by the mortal queens they had served, so as not to bewitch their kings. One was a gnome, her head too large for her body, with a forehead that bulged and held a mind stuffed with trickery. The last was a horse-faced one, she who had been the workhorse for her mortal queen; for her imperious ways and her revulsion of her feet touching the ground, her horse face was her beast of burden, carrying her hither and thither. The handmaidens' critical eyes turned upon Trina as they murmured their assessment in their tongue: "She is ugly. Look at her dark hair; it is like dead wood. Look at her eyes, like muddy water with green moss. And her form: thin like a stick, the skin so pale." Each one thought, *I would be the better consort for the Prince of Demons.* This last thought shot through their fingers and moved about their forms to wrap each handmaiden in sour discontent.

"Princess of Demons," began the one with the horse face, her teeth yellow kernels of corn that rattled in her mouth. Each word brought with it puffs of breath that smelled of stagnant ponds. "Your bridal gown awaits."

Trina said nothing, for her heart was in agony. She sensed the *muktablu's* presence; now she knew with certainty that he had followed her into the Black Abyss. Somehow she had to warn him away from Iosif. No, not *Iosif.* She must not think of him by that name, for he no longer was that poor Georgian boy with the pockmarked face she had once pitied. She had to remember that—he was the *Devil* himself, a satanic being that would destroy her beloved. Her eyes bore deeply through the walls: sometimes she could see into the beyond. But not now, for the stone walls remained solid and unmoving to her will to see where the *mukta-blu* was within the castle.

She stilled her heart. The impossible was possible only with a calm mind. When she had been taken into Kurnigi and had found the wandering spirit children, she had suffered great difficulty and danger. The journey of the Seven Tears was arduous indeed, for the way out of darkness was not meant to be easy. In Kurnigi, Trina had sought ways, tricks to protect the children's spirits: small amulets found that had traces of magic to protect against creatures who wished to overcome them; twigs and stones that, upon her touch, would glow and shine and tell her the path to follow. Then there were the other experiences: those of a gleaming light, of starlight that pierced the inky-black sky and the memory of being cocooned within that light. Trina understood those experiences in an intuitive way but could not give them words. Always she felt a deep sorrow for her: a mother's sorrow, but vast, like the universe—something that was of the beyond.

Trina remembered how her mortal parents had worshiped in the temple in Gori, for they had been Jews, Ashkenazi, who had come from Russia. Her father had been a merchant, wealthy but fair and generous too. The Georgians—who held on to their culture fiercely and felt the oppressive breath of Russian imperialism upon their necks—made no difference between Christian and Jew, for the Jews of the mountain had been there for hundreds of years. "Trina, these Georgian mountain Jews are not us," her parents had cautioned her, lest she become too comfortable, for always their history was of a welcome that was woven from flimsy cloth, disintegrating into persecution in the blink of an eye—this they knew well, as they were Russian Jews.

She remembered the nightly teachings, secretly given to her by her mother, from the Book of Creation, the Sefer Yetzirah, also known as the Book of Formation. The mystical traditions it detailed were frowned upon by her father, whose worship was more for secular than spiritual drives. Her mother saw in Trina's eyes the beyond and stroked her head as she lay in bed. "Daughter, who passed through my womb, precious one," she would say, "thirty-two paths of mystical wisdom are engraved by the king of the universe, high and exalted." Trina recalled the softness of her mother's words; they fell like kisses upon her as her eyelids became heavy with sleep. "It is written in the Book of Creation that the High and Holy engraved His name by three seraphim: numbers, letters, and sound." Then the words came into her sleeping mind and formed an understanding that she could not speak. "Ten Sephirot of Nothingness: their measure is ten, which have no end: there is a depth of beginning, a depth of end, a depth of good, a depth of evil….All things then come from the Three and how He sealed the universe in six directions."

Eventually Trina's soul had been pulled by an evil female spirit who took her body, and she was thrown into limbo and downward into Kurnigi, where glimmers of awareness of another presence sought to protect her: *the light that is bright in the skies but also of the Three Mothers, who hold the mystery sealed in six rings: of fire, water, and air and in three sounds.* Her mortal mother's words moved in her and spoke, *Ten Sephirot: ten vast, boundless regions with no end, an abyss of good and ill.*

In the Land of Darkness, Kurnigi, she had found the wandering spirit children—who, like her, had fallen into limbo then darkness—and felt her heart pierced with pain for them. She had learned of the journey of the Seven Tears they had embarked upon. Then they had been trapped until the *muktablu* had come, with his yellow hair and his fierce love for her. Trina and the *muktablu* suddenly had grown, and now she was a woman, as it seemed she always had been—a woman whose fate seemed to be heartbreak over losing her beloved again and again.

The melancholy song of her lost love filled her heart with sadness.

Muktablu... O my precious warrior,
Ever seared within my soul.
Eyes that brim with courage, brave against the darkness, shining like
the sun.
A tale of love that fate has spun forever destined to die
Like the tender green stalks of an early spring
Against the crafty winter's last stormy sting.

Trina was jolted from her thoughts by hands that pulled at her clothes. The plain dress that she wore fell away from her, and the bridal gown of death came upon her. She shuddered as it moved to clothe her: a bridal gown made of the crushed spirits of brides, for everything in the Abyss was just essence—from rock to dirt, from plant to water, so too was this gown, soft as velvet and a plummy purple so deep that it was almost black. Trina felt the brides' heartbreak. The gown formed to show a wide neck that bared Trina's shoulders. It quickly hugged her torso through the hips then flared down in organza folds of purple that were shot with silver that glittered—for they were the teardrops shed by the sorrowful brides. Then the gown flowed to the ground. The arms were three-quarters in length and then at the midway point flared out; large organza sleeves fell beyond her hands. Silver ropes, slashes, were around the hips and silver beads around the neckline. Upon her feet were satin shoes of silver that cut her feet with sharp bolts of pain. On her hands she felt long gloves grow and move like pythons over her elbows. She couldn't resist any of it, for she was a prisoner of the Abyss, and the bridal gown fell around her like the prison cell that it was.

"Your veil," said one handmaiden, the eyes in her gnome-like face bulging with envy. Oh, the life she would have had as the consort of the prince! But it was, like everything else in her world, withheld from her—she, who in her hands held secrets and spells that rightly made her suitable to be at the side of the Prince of Demons. This girl was not worthy of him—she was shallow in power; one could readily see that. A flimsy spirit.

The veil fell heavily upon Trina's head. The deep-purple gauzy material was almost black. A circlet of silver and pearls formed a headband embroidered with silver threads running around its edges like small needles. The bridal gown of death rustled around her like a coffin, the circlet tightening around her head. Trina looked through the veil; her vision was cloudy, as if she had been plunged into murky waters. The sorrowful dirge of the dead brides moved through her, but it was her own song, of her lost love, her *muktablu,* that went through her.

One thousands deaths. One thousand lives.
One thousand times wrenched from your arms,
With every step fearing death's alarms.
For you alone have ever held my heart,
Though time and distance have held us apart.
O my noble warrior!
O my beloved muktablu!
My heart flutters in crushing anguish,

for your presence in this Abyss do I feel.
Tortured am I that your spirit this darkness will crush and steal.

A small deep-purple droplet—one tear that held lifetimes of sorrow—ran down Trina's cheek but was unseen by the handmaidens, for the veil obscured her face.

Trina's tear touched the veil, instantly awakening the dead brides' stories. In the gauzy vision, she saw the tales of the dead brides form before her eyes: how when their true loves, warriors all, were off in foreign lands, they were pledged by their greedy families to marry men of wealth—some lecherous and old, others who were young but whose faces were ugly and their ways cruel. The anguish was too much; the unwanted touches of the grooms had been like fire upon their skin. On their wedding nights, they had plunged knives into the necks of their sleeping grooms and felt the warm blood spurt upon their hands and heard the gurgles of their deaths. Then they plunged the sharp knives into their own hearts as they cried out their true loves' names and fell upon the floor in bloody heaps.

Murderesses they were called and buried not with the holy rites but thrown into dirt pits as one might bury waste. Their true loves had returned to find them dead, reviled, and into madness some of them fell; into their own deaths fell others. Seven murderous brides they were; seven stories of heartbreak were their song. For their punishment, they were plunged into the Abyss, where forever more their spirits would rustle in the bridal death gown. In the Castle of the Abyss, in the bridal tower, they had remained.

Now they felt Trina's cry of love for the *muktablu*, of her anguish like their own. The circlet around her head loosened. The gown itself shifted gently now. Then their spirits gathered around her tenderly. Their ghostly, bloodied hands reached toward her and stroked her cheek. *Sister,* they said, for as they had been, this bride they clothed with their bitterness was to be wrenched from her true love and given over to he whom she reviled.

The dead brides' thoughts, which rose from the bridal grown, were like the rustle of a gentle wind among new autumn leaves. So it was that the jealous handmaidens surrounding Trina did not hear it.

The handmaidens' faces twisted in jealousy, for this Trina was beautiful. The bridal gown of death did not squeeze her in a tomblike hold, as they had hoped. In fact, it fit her slender figure well; virginal innocence rose from her like the clean scent of pine forests after a spring rain. The handmaidens' hands pulled at the fabric with their razor-sharp nails to defile the gown. The spirits of the dead brides repelled them with jagged bolts of pain that moved through the handmaiden's fingers as they touched the grown and they recoiled back. The handmaidens faces revealed their contempt for Trina.

𒀭𒈗 𒂍 𒈗 𒀸

Stal jumped triumphantly off his three-headed dragon steed and landed in front of his throne, his feet apart, the Sword of Deception held with both hands and raised high. His shimmering tunic of silver scales glimmered like a shark swimming beneath a deep-gray sea. He cut the air with the Sword of Deception and turned it to reveal its other side as the Saber of Shadows. He felt the power of the Crown of Disease move down the blade, through the handle, and into the black and blue thumb that encircled it. The roars of adulation of the creatures of the Abyss echoed within the great hall of the castle, another set of vibrations that coursed through him.

Two deceptive creatures flanked the throne: on one side stood the one with the blood-spattered gold mask, still seeking to be a favorite of the Prince of Demons. Although the one with the gold mask knew the prince was powerful, his thoughts still ran to wrestling from this prince the Saber of Shadows and slashing the thumbs of Abaddon from his hands to seize power. But first he would have to do away with this rival, the crafty Counselor, who stood at the other side.

Stal felt the aphrodisiac of power. His lips formed an arrogant smile, framed by the pointed beard like a vessel that held it. His raven-black locks shook with glee: yes, he, once a poor Georgian boy, was destined to rule not over just man but over *all* spirits as the All-Powerful Spirit of the Universe.

From the painted dome above, the Unholy Trio looked on and heard Stal's thoughts—*All-Powerful Spirit of the Universe*—for his thoughts rose visibly to the Unholy Trio like tendrils of smoke.

The Counselor's monk face wore the veneer of the meek, his head bowed. It was the Counselor whose sharp ears heard Stal's thoughts, for the Prince of Demons hadn't taken care to guard his inner wishes; he must be taught to do so.

"O Principe," the Counselor whispered, as he fluttered his fingers to make a rustling sound like that of dead leaves lifted by the wind, so his message would be covered, his eyes lifted up toward the dome. "Guard your thoughts that the Unholy Trio who are hidden within the dome know not your path."

Stal's irritation rose at the intrusion of the Counselor, but he took heed.

The one with the gold mask looked toward the Counselor, who was whispering something into the prince's ear, but all he heard were the sounds of the rustling of dead leaves.

"Appear! Now!" the Prince of Demons roared, and pointed his great Sword of Deception toward the dome. Stal willed them to appear before him, for though he disavowed the pious murmurings of the priests, he yearned for the sanctification of his union with Trina. It was critical that Trina be branded *his*. *His*. That was a mortal longing of the poor Georgian boy that had to be satisfied: to have as his bride the wealthy merchant's daughter. This son of the maid who, upon her knees, had scrubbed their floors clean would hold as his own the rich girl. With Trina at his side, he would move out of the Abyss and into Kurnigi to overtake Marduk and all those who held allegiance to him, including the Snake.

The Counselor was alarmed that the prince had called for the Unholy Trio. It was best and most prudent that the Unholy Trio, powerful enemies, be left here deep in the Abyss, for in calling them the prince was allowing their release from the hell below hell. Had they not just tried to destroy the prince? But the Counselor stayed his thoughts, as he knew that which is unsaid can always be said, and folly is the end of he who has an unbridled tongue. In the deep recesses of his locked, guarded mind, the Counselor resolved this: he would need to break the weak female's spirit, for she held too much power over the prince.

The Unholy Trio stirred with displeasure in the dome. This pockmarked cockroach was commanding them, the arbiters of the unrighteous, who read the Unholy Rites, as if they were servants. "*Radix malorum cupiditas*: the root of evil is desire," they had preached. Too, they who knew that for evil to flourish so must desire in mortal man's heart: to overcome, overpower, control, and step upon the necks of their fellow man to rise higher, as it was that this pockmarked one strove to do. "False prophet," they had called him, and asked that the creatures of the Abyss crush him. But they had lost, for this creature was the Fallen One, who came to them from the skin of the living land. Chaos had splintered the land of light and darkness into anarchy, where there no longer was a divide between Kurnigi and the Abyss, between the land of the living and dead. Yes, all this, the Unholy Trio knew, had occurred as prophesized in the Dark Revelations.

"Down, I command you, as your prince!" they heard the pockmarked one shout.

The Unholy Trio stayed within the dome—yes, the prince's call would have to be obeyed, but it would be in their time not his. For they were high priests of the unrighteous, not dogs to be shouted at to come. How was it that this one, this unworthy commoner of a mortal world, had been chosen? How was it that the Asuru-alim-nuna had given this pockmarked one the powerful Sword of Deception? Were not they, the Unholy Trio, destined to overcome Marduk? Hadn't they defied the Dark Master not for their glory but for the Great Spirit of Darkness? But they were hypocrites, in death as they had been in life, in their pious verbalizations: their desire to be all-powerful pounded strongly. "Savior of the Unrighteous," they were to crown the prince at the Altar of Misery, but so they, the Trio of Tarnished Knights, could once again rule. This pockmarked one, however, had slashed the crown of the Unholy One with *his* desire. He had overcome the Unclean One and now had the Crown of Disease upon his sword. The prince called for them again, now the third time, and they could no longer ignore him, for his anger rose and formed before them in gusts that pulled them out of the dome.

The Unholy Trio of Tarnished Knights appeared before the pockmarked prince, who stood mightily and arrogantly in front of them at the throne. He loomed over them, as he had great height now. The Unholy Trio saw the smallness of his spirit and how he was brushed with insecurity born of shortness, of poverty, and of bitterness from the beatings at the hands of his oppressors. The Unholy Trio saw, rising like a stink about the Prince of Demons, that his heart had been steeped with desire: to wreak revenge on those who had oppressed him, to taunt them with his wealth and power, and to beat those who had seen him as less than them with an iron fist. Most of all, the pockmarked one was to overcome Marduk, yes, but they also saw, rising like a dust storm, the incredible hubris of this newly risen dead soul to overcome and become the Great Spirit of Darkness.

Stal reveled in his height, for he estimated that he was easily more than nine feet tall, perhaps even ten feet. What mattered was that he *towered* over the Unholy Trio. He sneered, his words speaking of deference, his tone clearly not. "O most unholy ones, this marriage you will sanctify, as I, your prince, humbly command."

The Unholy Trio bowed their heads deep within their hooded gray robes, their mummified faces leeched pale by their false austerities but also bearing the marks of their sins. These faces hid the smiles that were manifested from the knowledge of the Book of the Enemies. "Pride cometh before the fall," the book of their enemies had said, but in the Unholy Book of the Brethren of Satan, they knew pride leadeth to dust. Their cloaks moved in unison as a dark storm cloud moves over the land before it strikes, revealing glimpses of the black tunics underneath, upon which were embroidered in red letters "*Radix malorum cupiditas*" (the root of evil is desire). Desire and pride were two routes to dust. And dust would this pockmarked one soon be—but first they would indulge him: allow him to marry the weak female spirit then lead them out of the Abyss to seize Kurnigi. Then the Sword of Deception, which now held the Crown of Disease, would be turned against this pompous pockmarked demon, and dust would he become. So, to serve the Spirit of Darkness, the Unholy Trio would ascend, as was their right, to overcome Marduk, for he no longer was fit to be the Dark Master.

Thin arms shot out from the folds of the Unholy Trio's cloaks and were raised toward the dome. The Unholy Trio fluttered their bony fingers. Then, from the painted dome, threads fell, which swarmed together like locusts to form a mantle. This loose sleeveless cloak was long, its color blacker than black. As it fell, it appeared deceptively velvety in texture, for in truth there was nothing soft about it.

"For Your Highness, the groom's wedding cape," the Unholy Trio said in unison.

As the cape fell, the throne moved so that it rested against the back wall of the great hall.

Now the Prince of Demons was on a dais, flanked by the Counselor and the one with the blood-spattered gold mask.

Before him stood the Unholy Trio.

The great hall was instantly filled with pews, an anti-church for the creatures of the Abyss, who sat or stood with their terrible forms, bloody and broken—forms of animals, sea creatures, hideous beasts. "Demon Nuptialis," they whispered, and their whispers formed a sound like a rushing river that echoed up to the painted devils within the domed ceiling, transforming it into great stained-glass panes. The stories in the stained glass told of the torture of reluctant brides, how the grooms had taken them by force, and how the brides had killed the grooms in their sleep—their fists bloody, holding the hearts of the grooms they had murdered. To this story that formed above him, Stal, the Prince of Demons, was blind, for all he heard were the hushed whispers of the creatures of the Abyss expressing their awe at the splendor of his nuptials.

The groom's wedding cape fell like a mantle over the prince's shoulders, covering his cloak made of the black-silk weaving of the spider of death, which covered his tunic of silver scales.

The one with the gold mask felt the cold gray fog of the Unholy Trio and knew that this mantle, formed for the prince, was to be feared. He saw the story of the murder of the grooms forming in the stained-glass plates above.

The Demon Nuptialis was indeed a feared ritual. For the groom to survive, he must kill the bride, though the story was written such that it was the bride who overcame him. The one with the gold mask did not understand why the prince would foolishly call forth such a deadly ritual and concluded that it must be through ignorance. The one with the gold mask moved so that the folds of the deadly groom's wedding mantle did not touch him. The prince's weakness was revealed; it was his desire for the spirit female.

The Counselor's shrewd eyes darted about in his monk face as he immediately noted that this mantle was not made of fabric but of ill will gathered and woven to fall upon the Prince of Demons until such time as it could strangle him into submission. To the prince was his allegiance. The Unholy Trio had long been his enemies; only a fool believed that a foe could turn to friend. They would make the prince a prisoner, chained within a dungeon of the castle as they left the Abyss. The Counselor noted a small movement from the one with the blood-spattered gold mask. He kept this counsel to himself; when the time came, he would be the one to rescue the prince from the mantle's deadly clasp and make certain it was the bride who was destroyed and not the prince, thereby solidifying his influence over him.

The wedding mantle fell upon Stal soft as an embrace before a knife is thrust into one's side. His red eyes were now brimming with power. The crown upon his head gleamed. *Prince of Demons.* His days of being a puny, pockmarked beggar were indeed over.

The prince thundered his command. "My bride I will take this night!"

In the tower, the five handmaidens instantly obeyed the words of the Prince of Demons. They held hands to form a tight circle around Trina.

The words of the Prince of Demons echoed again and again: "My bride I will take this night!" They rang loudly, with lascivious intent, crushing the very walls of the tower where Trina stood within the circle of the vicious handmaidens and pulling them all into a black hole.

Trina shuddered within the circle of the malevolence of the handmaidens. The words of the prince laying his claim to her echoed about her in hot drafts and blanketed her in darkness.

Then the blackness receded.

Trina now stood in the great hall of the Castle of the Abyss. Her five attendants, the treacherous handmaidens, were just behind her, like wardens of their prisoner. The great hall arched up eight floors or more to a domed stained-glass ceiling. They were on the dais, and behind them were the endless pews filled with the creatures of the Abyss.

Cold drafts moved above, and Trina knew this was the evil breathing of the creatures of the Abyss, whose presence she felt pressing around her. She was veiled and clothed in the dead brides' gown. Through the veil she saw three thin, hooded figures in gray cloaks; behind them stood an enormous throne. From her peripheral vision, she saw Stal at her side, toweringly tall and fearsome and wearing a shining crown and a black cape that moved about him like the promise of despair. Next to him was a small monk wearing a brown robe and a creature whose face was covered by a blood-spattered gold mask.

A black mist shaped like a crescent moon appeared. It took form into the Book of the Unholy: *Spiritus Non Sancti.* It floated before the Unholy Trio and opened to yellowed pages.

The Unholy Trio chanted, "*Per ipsum, et cum ipso! Nupitarum Principe daemoniorum!*"

"Enough!" Stal shouted, interrupting the ritutal. That was the language of the Georgian Orthodox Church, the language of the weak, who spoke the words of the beaten: of mercy, of turning the other cheek.

The prince's fingers were upon the Sword of Deception. He made a slight movement, intent on cutting off the heads of the Unholy Trio to demonstrate his displeasure. The prince's impulse was stopped, however, by the rising cries of protest by the creatures of the Abyss: "Demon Nuptialis! Demon Nuptialis!"

Then the Counselor's soft, sibliant whisper moved into his ears. "Principe, rebuke them not, for they are the Priests of the Abyss, and the creatures here hold them in great regard. They speak through the Great Unholy One, in the *Spiritus Non Sancti,* of Darkness, of the unsanctified and unpurified."

The prince therefore kept silent, though his fingers encircled the handle of the sword at his side. Then he turned, and his eyes were met with a soothing sight—the trembling figure of his bride next to him—and her fear quelled his heart. That she should be fearful was good, and soon she would hold him in such fearful respect.

All around, a lugubrious dirge rose from the lips of the creatures of the Abyss, their chants resounding ominously through the great hall.

Sanctificaret! Trium corporum in mortis!
Calicem Nupitas
Spiritus Non Sancti
Tenebris, Malum O Principe Daemonirum
Satanam Diaboli Daemonium
Satanas Diabulus Antitheus
Archangelus Diaboli
Unum in malo maledicta

These vibrations portended evil; they moved through Trina in notes that evoked a primal terror.

Sister, fear not, for we know your plight, the dead brides within sang to Trina. *We will protect you.*

But it was not for herself that Trina feared, for she sensed her love was nearby. *O muktablu,* her heart cried out. *O my precious warrior.*

𒀭𒆷𒁹 𒂍 𒀭𒆷 𒁹

Beneath the great hall, within the bowels of the Castle of the Abyss, Eddie heard Trina's anguished voice calling him: *O muktablu. O my precious warrior.* His eyes glimmered with the blue strands of Gilgamesh's one-quarter-mortal soul. The cave shook again as dirt and small rocks rained upon the four. The Once-Noble One's red robes were coated in a sheen of fine dust, and pebbles were lodged within his great mane of black hair. The One of the Nile also was covered with dust; she shook her head and body to clean herself.

Gilgamesh, the giant blue king, lowered his head so it wouldn't hit the ceiling. He held aloft the sacred spear, which shone a green light over them. The voice of the Prince of Demons echoed in his mind. As the Abyss was filled with terror, and the *muktablu's* youth made him rash and impervious to danger, the king feared for his young brother warrior.

Eddie heard his father's voice. *Caves and tunnels are coffins. Move out quickly or they will crush and kill you.*

"Take cover!" Eddie yelled to his three comrades. The floor trembled, and they were hurled against the side of the cave. In the middle of the cave, a large hole was forming, as if someone were shoveling from underneath, for rocks and dirt were spewing out.

"Weapons!" Eddie said, as he thrust the scythe toward it. Something was emerging from the hole.

At once, Gilgamesh, who had fallen upon his haunches, stood up to look intimidating, though the cave's low ceiling forced him to bend at the knees. He snarled and menacingly pointed his spear toward the hole. The Once-Noble One immediately thrust his sword toward the opening. The One of the Nile threw off the red headdress upon her head; two sapphire beads fell into her hands and immediately grew and transformed into two sharp daggers that glinted, one in each hand.

In a flash, out of the hole, flinging a shovel to one side, emerged a lanky young man. He was wearing dusty army fatigues; his head was helmeted, and ammunition was strung across his chest. He scanned the cave, which was still cast in green light from the king's spear. The young man pointed his M-16 rifle at the figures around him, who had surrounded him with their weapons.

Eddie couldn't believe what he was seeing: the guy was carrying an M-16, the rifle used in Vietnam, and wore regulation US Army fatigues.

"Ab-gal-lu, I shall kill him!" said the One of the Nile, as she made a move to spring forward and plunge her weapon into the man's neck.

Eddie stopped her in her path. "Wait." But he kept the scythe pointed toward the man. "Drop your weapon now!"

The young man smiled a toothy grin when he spotted Eddie. He immediately put his M-16 to the side and held his hands up to show he meant no harm. He threw his head back toward the hole and shouted, "Found him, Sarge!"

Gilgamesh knew that the Abyss was full of illusions. "Beware, *muktablu*, this is a spirit of the Abyss come to trick us."

The toothy young man smiled again. "No, Blue King, you got that wrong." Then he nodded at the scythe and winked. "Your weapon's not regulation, Eddie. Sarge'll straighten you out."

As he said this, six other men, one after another, wearing dusty camouflage, scrambled out of the hole, their M-16s pointed. They formed a semicircle around the toothy young man.

Eddie took in the king's caution not to believe what he saw, but his heart brimmed with emotion and propelled him forward. He slid the scythe to his side and moved toward the tallest figure, the last to come out of the hole—the one whose handsome face, though streaked with dirt, bore a striking similarity to his.

"Dad!" Eddie said, as he embraced his father, whose eyes were pooling with tears.

Sergeant Petersen's platoon moved back to give him room. Of Eddie they had heard much—of how the sarge had led an old wizard, Mattie, Geeta, and Eddie to find the Golden Path of the eight stones with the Buddhas. How he had fallen from it. How his son and his companions had traveled the path and moved on to battle the evil that was rising and growing so that soon all of mankind would lie under its dark grip. How their military occupational specialty, their MOS, was meant for this battle, not the one of the mortal land. So they had moved deep into the jungles of Vietnam to find the path between the living and dead, and when they did had crossed it.

They had traveled downward into blackness, holding seven grenades aloft, each one made of light. These they had been given when the earth had split and the Buddhas had appeared. They couldn't understand any of it with their minds, only with their souls.

But that was the way of the jungle, and each soldier had experienced its mystic hold in one way or another. And if you had asked them, "Are you alive or did you die? Are you dreaming? Is this real?" they all would have answered, "It doesn't matter. It's all the same." They had moved to the sounds of a voice that the sergeant said was that of his son, Eddie: once a boy, now a young man. In a deep pool, they had seen a vision of a giant blue-skinned warrior of old, wearing gold armor and a helmet, with great black ropes of hair and with a beard that was bound like twine—a gentle, anguished warrior who called the sarge "brother." This one, the Blue King, as they called him, they could track. They had followed his footprints into a black slash that fell beneath them, a terrible gash that breathed evil.

The sergeant loosened Eddie's clasp upon him and turned to Gilgamesh. "Brother, thank you for protecting my son."

Eddie wondered at this, for how would the king know his father?

The Once-Noble One and the One of the Nile took in this communication—*father of Ab-gal-lu*—and looked with admiration at this warrior of new. His garb was not of the seafarers or of the ancient warriors, though his face was streaked with dirt, and his hands were bloody and bruised. They knew at once that this mortal man was a warrior of consequence.

Gilgamesh had immediately recognized the voice of his warrior brother, the father of the *muktablu*. He shook his head, and his hair and beard swayed with the regret that had risen in his heart. This heart pain was an ache that coursed through him as pangs of shame—the old hurt of having let Enkidu fall into the Land of Darkness and the new hurt that he hadn't kept the *muktablu* safe.

"I wish that were so, brother, for see where we are: buried deep within the Abyss of Blackness."

"That's why we're here. My platoon will guide you out," Sergeant Petersen said, his square jaw set in certainty. The six men behind him stood with determination, a collection of faces of different hues and colors.

The One of the Nile placed her daggers in her hair. She pulled out the small egg Eddie had given her and held it between two fingers. The Once-Noble One followed, sheathing his sword and pulling out his egg from beneath his red-and-black robes.

"Father of Ab-gal-lu, we too have pla-toon," said the One of the Nile, for the seven mortal men seemed not much of a force.

Sergeant Petersen quizzically looked at the One of the Nile and the Once-Noble One and the eggs they showed him. "Is this the size of your force?"

Eddie's emotions were still running high. He had to swallow his feelings at seeing his father. So many emotions tumbled against one another: of safety, of love, of fear for his dad.

He pulled out the small egg from his flak jacket. "There's one hundred and fifty total that can be released from these three eggs. Not sure how, but we'll figure it out."

"Ancient seafarers," Gilgamesh said, then added, "Brother warrior, beware, for those trapped within these eggs are sea thieves who have been condemned to the Sea of Abyss for their evil deeds." It was best that the brother warrior know what the *muktablu* would not acknowledge.

The Once-Noble One bowed his head in shame, and the One of the Nile followed suit, for the ancient king of Uruk spoke the truth of their dishonor.

Gilgamesh felt a pang of guilt, for he knew these two had moved toward honor. Still, caution was advised until they proved they could be trusted.

Eddie immediately felt irritated at what the king had said. It destroyed morale. "No, King. That was what they *were*. Now we're all one team." He turned to his father and added, "The mission is to rescue someone. Her name is Trina. She's being held prisoner in the castle above."

Gilgamesh quickly glanced at the sergeant and spoke in his mind this time, *Brother, this girl has bewitched your son. She is a spirit from the Land of Darkness. The muktablu heeds not my warnings about this spirit girl.*

The sergeant turned his eyes toward his son. Eddie's face told the story of his heart. The sergeant knew at once that Eddie was in love, and his own heart pounded in anxiety for his son, for the most dangerous of all weapons was the necklace of love.

� cuneiform symbols

The floating Black Book of the Unholy appeared before the Tarnished Knight who was in the middle of the trio of Unholy Ones. Two hands shot out of the recesses of his gray robe as the skeletal face within shone and the chant escaped as a hiss: "Demon Nupitalis!"

A chalice moved out of the pages, forming first as a shadow then transforming into a golden tulip-shaped goblet. Within it sloshed a red liquid that emitted a sharp metallic odor.

The Unholy Trio began the *Cantus Toni Demon Nuptialis*, the Chant of the Demon Wedding.

> *O Princeps Demonum! Mortua mille garcionibus*
> *vetus eorum sanguinis per gladium pleam calicem auri.*

The creatures of the Abyss were hushed. Drinking the blood of the murdered grooms meant destruction to the one whose lips the potion crossed. But this was the mighty Prince of Demons who had felled the Unclean Ones. This prince would only grow strong from the potion, they concluded.

The creatures of the Abyss echoed the words of the Unholy Trio. "O Prince of Demons! A thousand dead grooms of old, their blood drawn by swords, fill this chalice of gold!"

> *Mortale sanguine quo mille semel puer*
> *et fortis et corda tenens susurrat*
> *de tristitia cecinit per vidui nuptae.*

The creatures of the Abyss cried out, "Mortal blood of a thousand warriors, once young and strong, their hearts holding whispers of sorrow at their sides, sung by their treacherous widowed brides."

"*O Princeps Demonum*," said the Tarnished Knight in the middle, who now held the chalice toward the Prince of Demons. "*Hic calix Domini repletus est sanguine acutae cum agasonibus et cruciatus in cor confractus qui olim. Potum ad strengten ut amantes, sponsa autem occiderit te in nocte.*"

Stal's red eyes bore into this Unholy One, though his mummified face was hidden deep within the hood of his robe. He felt a mocking in the tone of the Unholy One. Stal's mortal study of Latin had been sparse, and though the Georgian priests in the church school in Gori had provided an excellent education in Latin, that was reserved for students whose families were wealthy. As Stal had been a poor boy, his questions were left unanswered, and he had struggled alone, his sharp intellect his only guide in the mysteries of the Latin texts. Now the words reached his mind in pieces of comprehension: *drink…blood…grooms…bride.*

Here the one with the gold mask glanced and saw that the arrogant face of the Prince of Demons revealed his ignorance of the Unholy One's words. He smiled inwardly. The Unholy Trio would be the winners. He deftly switched his allegiance. He turned to the prince and translated the words: "This chalice is filled with the sharp blood of grooms of old who died in heartbreak and torment. Drink of it to strengthen yourself so that your bride does not kill you in the night."

The Counselor's eyes twitched at what the one with the gold mask had said. He felt the eyes of the Unholy Trio upon him and knew all of his thoughts were being read. Quickly he stilled mind; deep in its recesses, however, the Counselor's thoughts churned. *The chalice traditionally holds the blood of murdered grooms, and one sip means the same fate for all whose lips it crosses. How to warn the prince?*

The groom's wedding mantle, woven of ill will, moved with deceptive gentleness over Stal's shoulders and back. It swayed to the words of the Unholy Trio in small movements, as imperceptibly as the stealth of a deadly serpent uncoiling.

The red eyes of the Prince of Demons glowered in displeasure. "I am too great to be killed by my bride," he snarled. "Beware, Unholy Trio, that you take care to celebrate my strength."

The Unholy Trio did not respond to this. They raised their voices in a terrible acapella that filled the great hall. "*Adiuro Tenebris bibite ex eo onnes dolore Spiritus mali in corde tuo ut tollam!*"

And the creatures of the Abyss too sang out, "*Adiuro Tenebris bibite ex eo onnes dolore Spiritus mali in corde tuo ut tollam!* O Prince of Demons! Drink from it, Dark Groom of the Spirit of Evil, that you take the blood of these grooms' sorrow into your heart!"

The Unholy Trio took in how the pockmarked one's eyes warily glanced at the chalice. Too, they saw how his desire was greedy for the adulation and approval of the creatures of the Abyss.

Still, the prince did not move to grasp the chalice. A hush fell over the great hall. Stal's pockmarked face indeed showed suspicion; these Tarnished Knights were duplicitous and riddled with hypocrisy and bent upon destroying him. Even so, he wanted the authority and sanctification they possessed. He grumbled at the doleful chants of the Unholy Trio, too reminiscent of the priests of the Georgian Orthodox Church.

The chant of the creatures of the Abyss rose and moved in echoes through the great hall. "*Adiuro Tenebris bibite ex eo onnes dolore Spiritus mali in corde tuo ut tollam!* O Prince of Demons! Drink from it, Dark Groom of the Spirit of Evil, that you take the blood of these grooms' sorrow into your heart!"

The Counselor's face was still. From his peripheral vision, he felt the cloaked eyes of the Unholy Trio upon him. The Counselor kept his focus on the chalice and lowered his head, as if in reverence. In his mortal form, he had lost to those who controlled a great royal family and, as a result, had suffered unspeakable tortures. The physical tortures he could have endured, but to have been cast to irrelevancy was unbearable. Hence, he had poured his words of wisdom into a text of beseechment to the prince of that great family, but it had gone unread, unheeded. But now... now was different. This Prince of Demons he would mold and control. All these thoughts the Counselor held deep within the nooks and crannies of his brain. He was well disciplined in the art of emptying the surface of his mind; the ears of the Unholy Trio were sharp, even to unspoken thoughts.

The Unholy Trio said in unison, in voices that echoed from within the deep hoods of their robes, "O Highness, these are the rites of the *Cantus Toni Demon Nuptialis.* You must take the chalice for the wedding to proceed, for only if the blood of the dead grooms crosses your lips can we call the *Magno Spiritus Tenebrarum,* the Great Spirit of Darkness, to sanctify the union."

The Prince of Demons snarled again at the Unholy Trio and whispered, "Take care, Unholy Ones, for your tricks are known to me."

The Unholy Trio's skeletal faces, hidden deep within their hoods, held smiles at the conceit of this stupid demon; however, they remained silent.

The sanctification of the Great Spirit of Darkness upon this union was what the prince deeply desired. It would bind Trina to him irrevocably. And Trina he must possess. That mortal desire was too strong and lived too robustly in his demon form to remain unfulfilled. The Unholy Trio would be punished for their insolence after the ceremony; he would slash them to shreds with the Sword of Deception and leave them to rot in the Castle of Abyss.

Stal moved one hand from the handle of the Sword of Deception, which hung at his side. Both hands reached for the chalice; he would encircle it with his two large black and blue thumbs, and any evil spell against him surely would be absorbed by those thumbs. Indeed, as soon as the black and blue thumbs touched the chalice's gold skin, they pulsed: it was evil hitting evil.

The voices of the creatures of the Abyss rose as the chalice moved toward the prince's lips. "*Adiuro Tenebris bibite ex eo omnes dolore Spiritus mali in corde tuo ut tollam!*"

𒀭𒆳𒄀 𒁹 𒀭𒆳 𒀸

The cave shook fiercely. Sergeant Petersen turned toward his platoon and was about to shout the orders.

Eddie preempted him just as the cave began to collapse and called, "Move out!"

The cave rained rocks and dust. Eddie wielded the scythe to form some protection for the group. He swung its blade against the deadly rain of rocks and dirt as if they were great swaths of wheat.

Suddenly an unseen force moved like a whip, grabbing the group and swinging them out of the torrent of rocks and dirt. They were held within the force of this whip then tossed down through the collapsing floor of the cave.

Eddie's boots sunk into soft, wet ground as he held Death's scythe aloft. They were in a dungeon dug out of the sides of the mountain, deep within its center. The dungeon was dank, and its smell carried the sharpness of blood, the stench of burning flesh. Eddie's eyes adjusted to the new surroundings quickly, for as master of Death's scythe, he saw the unseen: the wisps of dead souls recoiling at the sight of the scythe, which had once culled them out of their mortal bodies.

After taking a moment to gather their bearings, Sergeant Petersen's platoon moved as one. They formed a protective circle around Eddie, their backs to one another, their weapons up. Outside this circle, Gilgamesh stood with the One of the Nile and the Once-Noble One. The roof of the dungeon was high and domed; the flame at his spear's tip showed its horror, which moved in shadows about the wall. Small licks of flame then sprang from the wall, revealing that the dungeon held no prisoners. Instruments of torture were scattered about: wrenches; daggers; a large chair made raw wood, old and grayed, blood staining its grooves. Eddie saw the ghostly outline of a form in monk's robes that once had lain there.

"Ab-gal-lu," said the Once-Noble One, his eyes taking in the horror. "This is the Dungeon of Terror, where the devious one was held."

"He who calls himself the Counselor," added the One of the Nile, shuddering at the memory of that false monk, whose lies had led her and the others to be buried in the sands of the Sea of Abyss when they had fallen for his false promises. The Counselor wore a red collar that ringed the neck. His dark robes, wisps of mouse-colored hair: meek, it all said, but deadly was what it was, for those ferret eyes blinked with his greed for power. "He has escaped."

Sergeant Petersen and his platoon already had assessed the dungeon by the light of the flickering flames on the wall and the green light cast by the Blue King's spear.

"One exit, Sarge," one of his men said.

The sergeant nodded. Just beyond them was an opening that showed a rusty metal gate that had been flung open. What lay beyond it was cloaked in drafts of cold darkness.

"Guard your minds!" Sergeant Petersen shouted.

But his platoon knew this well, for the jungle had taught them that fear opened the mind's gates. As with all things of the Abyss, the dungeon was a place of retribution, and the terror one experienced was created by the mind. This the sergeant knew as soon as the first whiff of the dungeon had moved through his nostrils.

Gilgamesh moved the warrior spear against the evil in the dungeon. The tip's light served only to reveal more clearly the details of this tableau of horror. On one side of the wall of broken stones, empty hand and leg manacles were lodged, telling the silent tale of the torture of the captured soul. Around the manacles were streaks of dried blood.

The sergeant's platoon remained like a fixed wall of protection around Eddie; their eyes were flat and still. They saw at once that terror was the weapon of this bloody dungeon.

Then the wisps of blood moved off the wall to become bloody fingers. They sprang to grab the faces of those closest to them. Immediately Gilgamesh thrust his warrior spear to thwart these bloody fingers. Repelled by the spear, the gruesome fingers moved away from him. Then, in a flash, they leaped toward the One of the Nile and the Once-Noble One. Though their weapons were up, their eyes reflected fear, for their minds played the images of the terrible tortures of this dungeon, which were in the consciousness of all who inhabited the Abyss. The bloody fingers suddenly elongated and wound themselves around the One of the Nile and the Once-Noble One. The One of the Nile felt the sting of these bloody fingers as they grabbed her neck. Suddenly her anguish rose, her cry piercing through those in the dungeon like a blade.

Eddie jumped and thrust Death's scythe up. It lifted him in the air, catapulting him over the circle of protection of his father's platoon. He ignored his dad's cry for him to remain within the circle. He felt the platoon reach up to hold him down, but Eddie wouldn't leave one of his own unprotected. From his throat sprang a primeval cry; it was Death's Song, for the scythe vibrated through him as it chopped the bloody fingers into pieces. The scythe was a force of death that the bloody fingers could not overcome. Soft hisses formed from their nails as they released the One of the Nile from their grasp and moved away from the Once-Noble One, forming again on the wall as bloody slashes.

The dungeon walls began to move toward them—if not by bloody strangulation, the dungeon would crush the creatures within. The walls on each side moved in to sandwich the group.

"Now!" Sergeant Petersen shouted. "Jump!" He pointed toward what was now a black hole, but the sergeant knew it was the location of the dungeon's gate, which they had spotted before.

The group swiftly shot out just as the walls behind them completely closed in. The space they were now in was claustrophobic; the ceiling was low, the flickering of Gilgamesh's spear the only light. It showed that they were at the bottom of a narrow stairway.

"*Dolore Spiritus mali in corde tuo ut tollam!*" The chant of the creatures of the Abyss echoed down the twisted stairway. A stench rose, dense and terrible, even greater than that of the bloody fingers. It prophesized a terrifying fate and moved into their mouths and noses like a poisonous gas.

Eddie sprang forward and moved rapidly up the crooked stone steps, propelled by what he feared: Trina's fate. These stairs led up to the castle, where she was being held. He felt her presence strongly, felt her shaking at the chants, which now echoed down the staircase; whatever they forewarned was about to happen. Whatever it was, he had to stop it. He smelled the Counselor's stink and saw the bloody footprints on the mossy, jagged, slippery stairs, those stone platforms that confirmed that he was on the right path. "*Dolore Spiritus mali in corde tuo ut tollam!*" The words resounded down the stairway.

"Eddie! Stop! Let me recon it!" he heard his father's shouts far below him.

King, Eddie spoke to Gilgamesh in his mind, *stay back. Protect my father and his platoon. I'll let you know when it's safe to come.*

Behind Eddie, the One of the Nile whispered, as the Once-Noble One followed her, "We will stay with you, Ab-gal-lu."

Eddie swiftly moved up the narrow stairway, followed closely by the One of the Nile and the Once-Noble One. As his feet hit the wedged stone steps with lightness, he swung the scythe, slashing any spirit that might have been on the staircase. He heard small hisses and sparks as the scythe's blade struck the dank air. The One of the Nile and the Once-Noble One struggled to keep up, for the Ab-gal-lu possessed a speed and sureness of footing that they did not have.

As the Counselor had traversed these stairs, so did Eddie. But unlike the Counselor, who knew the unpredictable slashes and hairpin turns that could plunge one downward, back into the bowels of the mountain, Eddie moved without deliberation or care, for his eyes cast a light upon the dark blindness. This light came from love and guided his feet. Eddie's soul was mesmerized by the unseen, for he felt Trina's spirit. The memory of who she was flooded his eyes: she who had been clad in a flowing gown of golden light, made of the threads of rays of sunshine. She had risen from the water, slender as a reed, her long hair the color of sunbeams, her face the light green of a new leaf, her eyes the purple of amethyst. Of course, this was not as he knew her now in his mortal form, but his heart was imprinted with the memory of her.

Sergeant Petersen moved quickly when he saw that Eddie wasn't going to heed him. He saw his son leap impulsively onto the spiral staircase, followed by his two strange comrades, and then almost instantly disappear into its darkness. The sergeant saw every twist of the stairway as a sign that he and his platoon were moving fast into the enemy's trap.

"Sarge!" one of his men said behind him. "I'll go first." It was the voice of the toothy soldier who had first come upon the cave; they called him "Gopher," for he was small and lithe and dug through tunnels like a rodent.

"*Dolore Spiritus mali in corde tuo ut tollam!*" The chant of the creatures of the Abyss echoed down the staircase.

Sergeant Petersen called back, "I'll take this one." He wouldn't endanger his men. He stopped at a wedged stone. He called back down to his platoon, "Narrow stairs turn to wedged stone steps. Watch out for the hairpin turns."

As the sergeant climbed the dangerous steps, he heard his men's boots move quickly behind him. They would follow him as he forged ahead of them on this crooked, slippery path of death. The sarge had always had their backs: from mortal battles in Vietnam—where the enemy had hurled grenades and fired a rain of bullets upon them—to the ones they had faced traversing downward into hell. And to him they gave their full allegiance. The platoon had maneuvered the narrowness of the stairway as they moved upward, confronted the wedged stone steps that swung in hairpin turns, and unlike Eddie, moved cautiously. Soon they were standing on a precarious, narrow stone ledge. Beneath their feet they saw that one misstep meant a plunge into the deadly Abyss.

Gilgamesh had been the last to enter the narrow opening into the staircase. *Stay back,* he had heard the *muktablu* say. *Protect my father and his warriors.* The staircase was oppressive in its tightness. It was formed by walls of crumbling stones on each side and slippery, mossy stone wedges that served as steps—a serpentine, circular staircase of medieval vintage. It was especially confining for someone of Gilgamesh's height and girth. Also, it was difficult for him to maneuver his long warrior spear in the tight corners and twists of the winding staircase. He stopped, unable to move upward.

Gilgamesh's words moved up the stairs. "Brother, I move slowly in this prison of stone walls. Take my spear so you may protect the *muktablu*."

The last man in the sergeant's platoon turned and saw that the giant Blue King was struggling far below them to move up the narrow passageway. His warrior spear's green flame showed that he was holding the weapon at an angle.

"Sarge," the soldier called up. "Blue King looks stuck. I'm going back to help him."

The sergeant agreed. The soldier was lanky, his brown face streaked with dirt protruded in determination under his helmet. Although he was young—like the sergeant's entire platoon—the hollows of his face revealed a sinewy spirit grooved by combat. He moved quickly back down the stone wedges, having learned their weaving way on the way up. Then he proceeded back down the narrow spiral portion of the staircase and was fast by Gilgamesh. Quickly he pulled out his combat knife, a KA-BAR given to him by a marine. It had a seven-inch blade and was about a foot long, deadly and sharp. The knife was strong now, like all of the sarge's platoon and their weapons, forged as they were by the mystic cries and spirits that lived in the jungle. This was the power that had allowed them to bore into the Abyss through a tunnel that was dense with evil in order to find Eddie. Swiftly the soldier loosened a few stones in the wall with the point of the KA-BAR. They fell, allowing just enough room for the king's shoulder to be dislodged. Gilgamesh nodded his thanks.

The soldier smiled in return as he jumped up the stairway. "I'll cut a path for you. Follow me. Be careful, Blue King. It opens up fast into stone steps, and then there's a ledge."

The sergeant's platoon was behind him, each man standing with his back to the wall on the slippery stone ledge. Gilgamesh followed the last soldier, feeling the precariousness of their perch most keenly, as his large feet were almost over the stone ledge upon which he stood. Beyond them was a gap that had to be jumped to reach another set of zigzagging stones. The sergeant heard the echoes made by Eddie's boots upon them. The sarge's profile showed his clenched square jaw—a sign, his platoon knew, that he was angry. In truth, Sergeant Peterson had gone beyond anger; his son's impulsiveness frightened him. Eddie was untrained; he had suddenly grown from a boy to man, with no maturity and wisdom. Plunging into the stairway with no recon was a violation of every impulse the sergeant had, for there had been no assessment of the terrain. Even if it could not be known by reason, it could be seen and tracked by his sixth sense.

To continue up onto the zigzagging stairway would surely mean capture by whomever controlled the creatures whose chants rang in their ears. They were being lured right into the jaws of the enemy. But the necklace of love, the sergeant now knew, was quickly strangling his son. Eddie would not be deterred. The sergeant wondered how his son's heart could have been captivated so quickly by a spirit of the underworld. What poison had this Trina shot into his heart? How could it be leeched out?

The narrow confines of the staircase were like a coffin. This could be their last mission. Quickly the sergeant dismissed that thought. That kind of defeatism wasn't the thinking of battle hardened soldiers, as they were, for look how far they had come—the path downward into the Abyss had been just as unknown as this one when he and his platoon had moved into it.

The devious stone path moved under Eddie's feet. Indeed it deliberately twisted here and there, seeking to hurl him into the

Abyss. Eddie, however, was oblivious to it, for his feet moved to follow the chants of the creatures above; they marked the path and pulled him upward. Behind him, he only felt rather than saw the others, propelled as he was toward Trina. Suddenly he was at the last step, where he peered through a barred opening in a wall; it was a glimpse of the great hall, massive in its size. The One of the Nile and the Once-Noble One moved up behind him, for as the Ab-gal-lu protected them, so too would they protect him. Eddie looked out through the bars, which curved out of a tower wall of the castle; he was just beyond where the great throne had been thrust back when the Demon Nuptialis had begun. At his angle, Eddie saw the backs of the Unholy Trio in their gray robes facing a group, but he couldn't see who they were, only a veiled figure in a long gown closest to him. Throughout the hall, the chants of the creatures of the Abyss echoed. *"Dolore Spiritus mali in corde tuo ut tollam!"* they cried. Where was Trina? Then his heart stopped, for his eyes penetrated the veil. It was Trina.

From behind the veil formed by the dead brides, Trina felt Eddie's presence. She turned her head to the side and saw his handsome face at the bottom of the curved wall, hidden behind the bars. She let out a small gasp. *Muktablu, no. Go back!* Eddie's eyes locked on to hers. *My love!* his heart called to her.

In that same moment, the seven murderous brides shivered with awareness. *Sister, your beloved has come! Your true love will be yours. Mourn not, sister!*

𒐖𒌋𒐊𒐖𒐊𒐊

Through the hoods of their robes, the Unholy Trio watched the pockmarked demon closely. His hands were upon the chalice, the thumbs of Abaddon encircling it. The Sword of Deception hung at his side, unprotected. In anticipation of the prince's sipping of the blood of the murdered grooms, the voices of the creatures of the Abyss rose yet again: "*Dolore Spiritus mali in corde tuo ut tollam!*" Now they would act to unleash the creature Abaddon. He who had been upon the pockmarked demon when he first had appeared on the castle grounds. They also knew that though Abaddon had fallen underneath the hooves of the demon prince's dragon steed, no creature in the Abyss could be destroyed; only imprisoned. So Abaddon had been plunged deep into dungeons beneath the Castle.

In unison the Unholy Trio hid their call under the rising chant. "Abaddon! Abaddon!" they commanded. "Claim that which is yours!"

The Counselor's keen ears burned, for he heard the Unholy Trio's hidden call to Abaddon. He moved his fingers in front of his face; the dust of black magic fell from his fingertips; and his rodent form developed under the folds of his monk cloak. His sharp, hairless tail shot out from his robes. The snout of a rat protruded from his face, and whiskers that could feel the unseen twitched as the form of the mild monk disappeared.

The Prince of Demons did not hear the hidden call of the Unholy Trio, for as the chants rose, the chalice suddenly thrust itself at him, striking his mouth. Although no blood crossed his lips, he scowled at the prick of pain as a small cut formed.

𒀭𒉿𒁹𒀭𒉿𒄑

On the ledge where Gilgamesh stood, the green-tipped flame of his warrior spear wavered in a wind made by a shadowy figure that flew past him. *What creature is this?* Gilgamesh wondered. But that thought lasted just a fraction of a second, for the creature moved silently past him and through the next set of zigzagging steps beyond. It was only its stink of death, like a foul gas, that gave notice that something was about.

Within one of the many dungeons of the Castle, Abaddon felt the hold upon his wings pinned to walls loosen. Swiftly, Abaddon had flown up towards the sound of the Unholy Trio; His black bat wings stretched and silently flapped. His body was small and bony; his oily gray face held the sharp features of a rodent, with eyes that were dark-yellow slits, shifting about, alert and scheming. His teeth, crisscrossed webs of deceit, were another curse he suffered, for his words came out garbled instead of in the smooth voice he had possessed in his mortal form. His black hair rose like broom bristles upon his head. He scratched the air with his hands, which ended in talon-like black nails and were missing their thumbs. As a mortal sorcerer, Abaddon had secreted into the thumbs demonic magic given to him as payment by the Dark Master for turning souls to the darkness. As the thumbs had grown, they had turned blue and black, only to be slashed from his hands long ago by the Beast, when he was the mortal King Ashurnasirpal. Then Marduk had punished Abaddon for his arrogance in demanding that he be the wielder of Death's scythe; instead he became a prisoner held within the Grim Reaper's robes. There Abaddon had been imprisoned through the ages, looking out through the hollow orbs of the Reaper—powerless, never once the holder of the scythe. When the yellow-haired mortal male had taken the scythe from the Reaper, he inadvertently had freed Abaddon, whose malevolent spirit rose from the black dust, which was all that remained of the robes of the Reaper. The yellow-haired mortal held Death's scythe, but all that would change once Abaddon seized his thumbs from the pockmarked demon, another thief in a long line of thieves of what was his. All of this moved through the bat creature Abaddon's mind as rapidly as bitterness rises like bile in those who believe themselves victims of injustice.

Abaddon flapped his wings silently as he moved behind Eddie's head, wishing him ill. The four fingers of his right hand moved toward the scythe, even though he knew that without his thumbs, he could not hold the weapon for long. The One of the Nile and the Once-Noble One thrust their blades at the flying creature of the night. Death's scythe vibrated in warning then threw sparks to repel the flying creature, who hissed. Eddie swung the scythe back mechanically. His eyes were locked on Trina; she was all that formed his awareness. The scythe glanced off the wing of Abaddon, and the creature moved away.

Then a set of events quickly played out: Abaddon's wings struck the bars, and they instantly exploded at the touch of evil and formed a gaping hole in the tower's wall. Eddie leaped out toward Trina, who stood upon the dais with her five handmaidens. The Once-Noble One and the One of the Nile were hurled into the great hall.

Abaddon swooped down toward the Prince of Demons, his wings flapping silently as his sharp fingernails elongated into blades. In an instant he had sliced off the thumbs that encircled the chalice.

The chalice tumbled from the hands of the Prince of Demons, who howled in pain as the thumbs fell. These black and blue thumbs hovered in the air like small bullets, unsure of their target. They moved toward Stal as Abaddon flew to grasp them, his eight fingers, with their long black nails, scratching the air.

The wedding mantle, which lay upon Stal's shoulders, moved to crush him. As he flung his arms to escape its hold, he hit the falling chalice. Its contents—the blood of the murdered grooms—splashed like teardrops upon him. They splattered upon the wedding mantle, and in an instant, it disintegrated at the touch of the grooms' sorrow.

The Counselor had made his move as soon as his rodent whiskers had caught the scent of the Abaddon. Quickly he had sprung off the dais onto the prince's fearsome three-headed dragon standing at the side. This steed roared flames as the Counselor's rodent feet pierced its sides. He and the prince would escape the Abyss before the Unholy Trio felled them.

The fearsome steed unfurled its great wings and, carrying the Counselor, flew toward the prince.

The Unholy Trio saw their chance: the pockmarked one's hands, where once there had been thumbs, were helplessly attempting to remove the Sword of the Deception from his side.

The Unholy Trio sprang out of their gray monk robes. Now they showed themselves as the Tarnished Knights of Old, clad in armor pitted with age, armed with long spears—pikes fitted with the head of an ax—their heads in peaked helmets. These deadly weapons they thrust toward the prince to lop his body in half and take from him the Sword of Deception. As the ax-topped pikes moved to slash the Prince of Demons in two, the hooves of the multiheaded dragon steed struck the Unholy Trio's heads. The knights' heads toppled off their necks and fell to the floor, rolling down the red carpet of the great hall.

Then the Counselor moved in close with the dragon steed so Stal could jump on. The steed bowed low to allow its master to mount it, its black wings unfurled.

Stal's red eyes were daggers of fury, aimed at the Unholy Trio below him. He looked mighty upon the steed and crowned in his *magna coronat*, with its inscription, "*Prince of Demons*," aglow.

The Unholy Trio had retrieved their rolling heads. They leaped up, guided by the eyes in the heads they now grasped under their arms, their weapons striking the hooves of the prince's great steed. The steed stumbled a bit then began to fly up.

Stal knew he dared not unsheathe the Sword of Deception, which would surely slip from his four-fingered hand. He rode toward the flying black and blue thumbs.

Abaddon flew about the great hall as the thumbs darted here and there.

"The prince escapes the Abyss!" The cries rose like a great wave through the hall as the Prince of Demons rode the flying dragon steed. It triggered an exodus. The pandemonium then broke out.

"Exodus!" The word thundered inside the castle hall and outside its gates like the pounding of a thousand drums. Everywhere upon the island of the Abyss, the words rang out. "The prince escapes the Abyss!" The time had come. The lucky creatures within the great hall were in the best position of all the creatures of the Abyss to try to climb onto the prince's steed as he moved out of the horrible hell beneath hell.

It was a dance of survival, in which each creature sought its escape from the Abyss. They moved in their bloody and broken forms: some half beast, half man; others torn, headless, limbless; others with bones only; still others with the faces of fish, as they had escaped the waters of the Sea of Abyss and had been lucky enough to enter the castle. Others were birds of prey in form; some had snouts with large sharp teeth; others had burned faces. Some wore the ropes that had hanged them or had knives protruding from their sides. Their bodies reflected the Abyss's torture. Some of the creatures could fly, and in their frenzy to be upon the prince's steed, they struck the black and blue thumbs and flung Abaddon away. A tumult of confusion rose and filled the air like a storm of locusts.

Eddie rushed against the movement of the sea of creatures, who came toward him in the thousands—not for him but to grab on to the fleeing Prince of Demons before he left the Abyss. Eddie wielded his scythe to form a pathway to Trina. The blood from the chalice of the murdered grooms had splashed onto her veil. It fell away to reveal the face he so loved. He moved toward her, her beautiful face before him, shining, waving as leaves do in a breeze under a bright sun.

Flying above the storm of creatures to retrieve his black and blue thumbs, Stal spied the yellow-haired mortal moving swiftly toward *his* bride, Trina. He pulled the reins and turned the steed downward to grab his bride beneath him.

Panicking at the prince's move, the Counselor whispered, "We must leave this spirit bride. There will be others more beautiful for you to take."

It was a move that the beheaded Unholy Trio had hoped for. They struck the side of the dragon steed with their weapons. As the dragon stumbled and fell down, the flames from its three mouths seared the creatures flying beneath it.

Stal did not hear the Counselor's whispers behind him as the dragon steed tumbled downward. He only felt the sting of defeat each time his thumbless hands pulsed, bringing to the forefront of his mind all the humiliation he had suffered as a mortal when he was nothing but a poor, small, beaten boy.

It incensed him. He was Stal, Prince of Demons, mighty, not a poor washerwoman's son. Trina was his. He would not lose her to a puny mortal. Enraged, he dug the heels of his boots against the dragon steed's side; its hooves flung up then hit the beheaded Unholy Trio of Tarnished Knights just as they swung their deadly spiked poles at him. The dragon's wings flapped wildly, lifting Stal and the Counselor into the air.

Trina felt a great desperation, for the *muktablu* could not overcome the Prince of Demons, even with Death's scythe. She knew his love for her would lead him to sacrifice himself in order to save her. *Please, muktablu,* she pleaded to his mind. *My love, I beg you, make your escape from this place.*

Eddie was deaf to her plea as he jumped onto the dais that held Trina. All he could see was her, his heart beating the sounds of the voice of his many lifetimes: *My love, my love.* As he moved to grasp her, the five ugly handmaidens, whose mortal beauty had been marred by bitterness and jealousy, blocked Trina from Eddie's grasp. Why should the female spirit have her true love? She was nothing. The horse-faced one pushed her head as though she were a bull, charging at him. Eddie slashed Death's scythe; its point fell on this handmaiden's head and pushed her back. The gnome-faced one, bearing her yellow teeth, lunged at Eddie, who spun to strike her with the blade of the scythe.

The bloody teardrops had splattered from the chalice onto Trina's wedding gown. They now bore holes into the fabric, breaking the vengeful spell of the murdered grooms.

Instantly a mist formed around Trina. Her wedding gown dissolved, leaving her clad in the simple undergarment of a white cotton gown. The seven murderous brides now appeared around Trina, each wearing their wedding gowns of light and dark purples, with ballooning sleeves. The folds were wet with blood, and their faces were glimpsed through diaphanous veils. Each revealed their once-mortal beauty: long tresses fell in silky waves;

their eyes were large, with long lashes; and their faces showed an ethereal loveliness. For in their mortal forms, it was their beauty that had enchanted the greedy grooms to take them when they knew the brides had been pledged to other suitors.

The ugly handmaidens lurched back at the sight of the seven murderous brides. Then two of the handmaidens reached for the chalice, intent on throwing any remaining contents at Trina so that they might mar her face. Instead, the seven pairs of hands of the murderous brides moved upon the chalice to turn its contents upon the treacherous handmaidens.

The blood of murdered grooms moved like maggots boring into the ugly handmaidens' face. Curses to destroy Trina sprang from their lips for making them uglier than they already were. Then their eyes moved to the sides of their heads and bulged out; dragonfly wings sprang from their backs as they metamorphisized into giant insects. They flew up into the tail of the prince's flying steed. Their bug faces sneered as the steed flew upward. They would escape the Abyss. Each one vowed that she would find a way betwitch the prince and become his bride.

The seven murderous brides quickly moved to protect Trina and Eddie, their hands holding the very daggers they had plunged into the hearts of their unwanted grooms. They snarled as the creatures of the Abyss moved over them.

The seven brides looked upon Trina with kind eyes. *Sister, you and your true love will be reunited, as we never were with ours!*

The brides' bitterness for their lost loves melted within their hearts, for what they couldn't have themselves, they could at least vicariously experience through the joy of their sister. Within the protective circle of the seven murderous brides, Eddie and Trina spoke to each other through their hearts. Their foreheads touched, and their eyes locked on to one another.

O song of my heart,
I stumble, searching, searching.
Ribbons of your love
Rise in my memory like a mist,
Only to fall away.
Hues imprinted in my soul,
Cycles of love found and lost.
O Song of my Heart,
In life after life, only your face
Is the beacon of all my hopes.

Trina's eyes brimmed with infinite love. As she gazed at the *muktablu,* her heart was wrapped in a blanket of pain and love. *O mortal man, why do you die?* The old question rang in her ears, although what it meant she did not know. Her mind could not tell her why, but she knew she had led him into peril again and again, in lifetime after lifetime, and now into the Abyss itself. This time she had to find a way for him to escape and be free in a place where his heart would be emptied of his love for her. It would be the only way that he would live.

Eddie raised Death's scythe. "Hold on tight," he said. As the scythe lifted them up, a great wind created by the creatures of the Abyss who were flying up pulled Trina away from Eddie. As Trina fell onto the dais, the seven murderous brides quickly and protectively surrounded her.

Eddie was pulled up toward the great hall's dome. The scythe was drawn toward the flying black and blue thumbs like a magnet, for in its memory it saw the thousands of souls it had reaped and deposited into those thumbs. Struggling against the energy of Death's scythe, Eddie fought to move down to Trina.

Muktablu, Trina cried to him through her heart. *Save yourself. Do not seek to rescue me.*

The Counselor again whispered to Stal, "We must escape now!" For the Counselor had added in the cost of taking the thumbs back; it meant being sealed in the Abyss, to be under the torturous grip of the Unholy Trio, for the prince would fall here, with his weak grasp upon the Saber of Shadows.

The prince ignored the Counselor. The yellow-haired mortal flew up, holding Death's scythe, intent upon seizing the black and blue thumbs. Stal would not be defeated. He was the mighty Prince of Demons, and the thumbs, which the Crone had given him, would be his. No mortal would possess them. Beneath him, the creatures of the Abyss jumped and flew to grab the dragon steed. Amid this pandemonium, the prince flew. He would break the yellow-haired mortal with the kick of his steed, and the thumbs would fly back to him, their master.

Eddie was under the control of Death's scythe. *Trina,* he called to her mind. *Stay. I'll come get you.* The scythe followed the path of the flying black and blue thumbs. Close upon them was Abaddon, his bat wings flapping vigorously but silently. Hissing sounds issued from his mouth.

Above Eddie, the stained-glass ceiling of the castle's dome broke, releasing the forms it held. They rained down upon the creatures of the Abyss, toward Stal.

The collision was slow, yet it was the occurrence of an instant. In that movement of the stained-glass creatures falling toward Stal, a wind was created. It flung Eddie right toward the black and blue thumbs and flung Abaddon away.

The thumbs moved, drawn to the scythe, and fell like a glove onto Eddie's thumbs. His head lurched back in pain as the malicious evil of the thumbs surged through him. Then the contagion of the Crown of Disease, which had moved through the Saber of Shadows into the prince's hands and then into the black and blue thumbs, coursed through Eddie. His face turned the ashy gray of the disease. Death's scythe vibrated in his hand as his eyes turned backward until the helix of the entwined mortal souls moved back and only a mossy white showed. He cried out in agony as boils burst out all over his face and body.

The Prince of Demons, riding the dragon steed with the Counselor upon it, collided with Abaddon. The rodent creature flew, his teeth bared, ready to bite the prince, but the hooves of the steed struck his head, and Abaddon toppled down, landing under the stampeding feet of thousands of creatures of the Abyss. Stal was caught in a web of movement: creatures flying up toward him, painted ones flying down. Beneath him the Unholy Trio, headless in their armor, walked across the heads of the creatures as if they were stepping-stones. Under one arm they held their decapitated heads, eyes glowing, directing their bodies. These headless knights grasped and pulled themselves up onto the flying creatures, hoping they would move them up toward the falling prince. They swung their ax-topped spears and hit the dragon steed, gashing it this time.

The prince was defenseless. The Saber of Shadows hung at his side as he tried unsuccessfully to pull it out with four fingers. His face showed the frustration and fury he felt at his position as his raven-black hair moved across his face like whips. The Tarnished Knights knew they were close to overcoming the pockmarked one. In unison they fell onto the body of a giant flying insect creature and rode it like a horse, moving it into position so they could thrust their lethal poles straight into the prince's body.

The Counselor hadn't lived in the Abyss without having learned some lessons. His rodent eyes had rolled back when he had witnessed the first gash upon the steed. He frantically moved himself into a hypnotic state so he might see a way out. A vision formed: that of the prince's averted mortal fate. A cold land appeared before him, thousands cheering in adulation to a balding man whose face was bearded with deadly ambition—not the prince but someone else. *This one would be killed, and the prince would take his throne.* The pockmarked one's mortal life—the one not lived—was the way out of the Abyss, for its desires rang strongly in the spirit of the Prince of Demons.

The Counselor fluttered his fingers, which were dusted with black magic, and touched the four-fingered hand of the Prince of Demons as it struggled to pull out the Saber of Shadows. The Counselor whispered incantations, for he was a necromancer, to strengthen the prince's fingers so they would grasp the talisman of the sword tightly. The black magic moved over Stal's fingers, and a tar-like substance dripped onto his hand and glued his fingers to the Saber of Shadows as he pulled it out. The blade struck the decapitated Unholy Trio; in one fell swoop, the Tarnished Knights clattered through the air, falling upon the hordes of creatures.

The Counselor's eyes lit the path. *Let us go toward this man of the cold lands, whose breath says peace but means death.*

The prince's thoughts were upon revenge, but that would come to fruition in time; he still held the Saber of Shadows. Upon the dragon steed, he and the Counselor leaped onto a gleaming black path. Behind them, throngs of creatures jumped onto the path to escape the Abyss as well.

Eddie struggled against the overpowering disease of the Unclean One as a vortex of energy moved him directly onto the black path forged by the Counselor.

Trina cried out loud, for her heart was breaking. Her beloved *muktablu* was being drawn into Stal's black path. She had glimpsed the gray in his face as the disease of the Unclean One had moved into him, and now his body was covered in boils and welts. She heard his moans of pain in her mind. Her beloved would soon be overcome. Trina desperately searched her heart for a spell to protect the *muktablu.*

The seven murderous brides continued to stand in a protective circle around Trina. All around them, creatures were stampeding and flying, all moving in desperation to set foot upon the path out of the Abyss. The brides' hearts beat with torment, for they felt not only Trina's loss but also their own.

The words came to Trina's mind, long ago whispered to her by her mortal mother—words from the Sefer Yetzirah, the Book of Formation. *A depth of beginning…a depth of evil…a depth of above…Ten Sephirot of Nothingness…three mothers.*

As these words formed in her mind, the seven murderous brides ripped their veils from their heads and threw them over Trina, forming a net around her. Then each bride pulled the mesh, which now encased Trina, and flung it upon a flying creature of the Abyss as it leaped onto the path out of the Abyss.

Sister, the seven murderous brides called to Trina's mind, *this veil holds our magic. Travel fast to your love and save him.*

𒀭𒌓 𒂍 𒀭𒌓 𒁹

The Once-Noble One and the One of the Nile had followed the Ab-gal-lu toward the female spirit he sought. As chaos had broken out, they were separated from the Ab-gal-lu. They saw him spirited up and fall victim to the disease of the Unclean One as the black and blue thumbs fell onto his hands. Then, as Death's scythe moved the Ab-gal-lu into the black path of the

Prince of Demons, they had mounted two of the flying creatures of the Abyss that were seeking escape from the Abyss. These large birds of prey had human faces and long poisonous tongues. They hissed and snarled and shook, feeling the weight of their unwanted passengers. The One of the Nile and the Once-Noble One held tightly as these flying creatures of the Abyss flew onto the black path, close behind Eddie. Though this path led out of the Abyss, they knew it meant their destruction, for the creatures of the Abyss knew them as outlaws, and if the One of the Nile and the Once-Noble One were caught, it wasn't freedom from the Abyss they would have but eternal imprisonment in whatever hell the prince and the creatures of the Abyss could create. None of this mattered, though. They would not leave the Ab-gal-lu without his pla-toon.

𒀭𒊑𒌋𒁹

On the ledge in the dungeon below, in an instant before the zigzagging stairs leading to the tower collapsed, the sergeant and his platoon, followed by Gilgamesh, leaped onto the stairway.. They had moved as quickly as the treacherous turns of the stairs would allow. When they arrived at the tower wall, it already had exploded. They moved swiftly onto the great hall's floor, buffeted about by the stampeding creatures of the Abyss. The sergeant and his platoon arrived just as the current of energy was pulling Eddie onto the black path of the pockmarked prince.

The sergeant and his platoon immediately jumped upon a swarm of huge dragonfly creatures to move onto the path. Gilgamesh followed. They struggled to hold on to the bodies of these creatures. These beasts were long tailed, with heads that held sharp teeth. These winged creatures morphed from man to bird to insect as they flew toward the prince, shaking their bodies to rid themselves of their riders.

Gilgamesh thrust his spear to hit the flying creature that the sergeant rode so that it would move faster. *Brother,* he called to the sergeant's mind, *move quickly before your son is lost!*

Then, just as Sergeant Petersen and his platoon were nearing the black path, it closed and disappeared.

CHAPTER 16

prima donna assoluta

The seats began to fill in the gargantuan auditorium of the Hippodrome Theatre. The lights brightly sparkled to reveal the interior in all its glory: an elaborate homage to the Roman Colosseum, with a semicircle of multilevel stadium seating that fronted the enormous stage. Everything about the Hippodrome was meant to be larger than life; the dome itself was reputed to cover an acre. Grandeur and exotic elegance were recurrent themes, what with the theater's marble floors, ivory accents, rich red-velvet draperies shot with threads of real gold and silver, seats covered in the same red-velvet upholstery, and elaborate tapestries. Its 22,000 electric lights required almost a hundred stagehands to operate, and it even had a stage that could be moved up and down.

The Muhra's borrowed eyes took it all in: the Hippodrome was shabby, true—the tapestries were moth-eaten; the upholstery on the seats was now threadbare. The gold and silver were all but gone, the ivory hidden under the grime of neglect.

Still, it was *the Hippodrome*! Those seated, those who would be the audience, were dazzled. Not all of the Muhra could be the actors; some had to be in the audience. Those who had been bit players when they were mortals were relegated to this duty by the Muhra who were higher in the dead-soul chain. Those in the audience carried out this duty resentfully, for every one of the Muhra itched to be on the stage—especially this one, in New York's Hippodrome. Each longed to be the ones with adoring eyes upon them.

But as always, it was the senior Muhra who would take the stage, and among them, the most admired (and resented) one, the Great Diva, was to star. "*Aida...*" They heard the murmurs as they were ushered into their seats. The Great Diva had willed this, and she would be playing the starring role of Aida. Snickers rose from the audience as they waited for the pageant to take place. Catty remarks—so emblematic of the theatrical world—swirled amid the buzz of the excitement of being at opening night. *Aida*, the great love story of a beautiful Ethiopian princess (how much makeup would need to be caked on that one for her to look the part of a young innocent? What about her large beaked nose? What wig would fit upon that bald Great Diva so she could play this part?), captured by the Egyptians (so many roles to be filled, allowing many Muhra to take the stage—ah, that they could be one!) and enslaved as a handmaiden to Amneris, the jealous daughter of the pharaoh (only some mousy, nondescript Muhra who wasn't going to upstage the Great Diva would be cast in this role), who knows that her betrothed, the Egyptian captain of the guard, Radames, loves Aida (who could convincingly play a lover to the Great Diva with her donkey teeth, not to mention the breath that went with it? That would be a performance indeed!). Still those who were assigned to the audience grudgingly acknowledged that Verdi's *Aida* was the perfect choice for the Hippodrome stage, which was reputed to be able to hold a thousand performers.

So many, many roles: slaves and prisoners, the priests, the priestesses, soldiers, Egyptian ministers, officials, the common folk, the Ethiopians, the chorus, the animals that would be ridden to and fro as the great story of a love triangle, of war and glory rose and filled the Hippodrome!

Rapidly all 5,300 seats of the theater were occupied by dead souls encased in their newly found bodies. They stared through eyes that no longer saw, waiting for the performance to begin. Most of the occupied bodies, when alive, never had been in the Hippodrome, never had seen an opera, though a very few of the dead souls had once glinted and gleamed, as they belonged to the city's rich and powerful and were nabbed by the Muhra while they were on their way home or, truth be told, to a night of debauchery. The Muhra looked out as the Hippodrome stage transformed while the stagehands moved to turn it into ancient Egypt, replete with golden pyramids and a sphinx.

Some eyes zigzagged out of habit, as they belonged to those of lunatics; many were those of the drunks and other wayward denizens of the city's night world who called the streets their homes. The Muhra audience wore the newly dead bodies tentatively, as one might a new tuxedo or gown. Soon the audience was a pageant of movement. Hands and feet thrust out suddenly; bodies bounced up out of their seats then crashed down. The Muhra moved their new bodies like jumping beans, not in restlessness but just to relish the feel of form and to stave off the inevitable rigor mortis. Yes, most of the bodies had been worn down by the mean streets of the Depression, but they were forms nonetheless.

𒀭𒁺 𒂗 𒀭𒁺 𒀸

The Beast and the Brotherhood of Evil lay trapped within the yellow light of pain formed by the primordial serpent-shark demons. Soon they would be crushed into oblivion. The Beast moved his tongue to feel the Droplet; it was still there, which meant he hadn't been crushed just yet. The Prince of Wallachia's signature foppish red-velvet hat bobbed with the vibrations of his pain. Trapped too were Khan of the Huns, with his sallow face and protruding, almond-shaped eyes, which appeared even more askew under his cap of bloody leaves. Beyond Khan the aristocratic Grand Duke of Muscovy, the first tsar of Russia, had his eyes closed in agony.

The serpent-shark gods did not care about the Brotherhood of Evil. They had merely entered the trap set for the Beast. The yellow light was the mark of destruction, for it signaled that the Beast's form would soon be obliterated into dust, and all that would remain would be the Droplet, plucked up to be theirs. These demons, those ancient gods of the underworld waters who evoked a primeval fear in man, had been relegated to irrelevance for eons by Marduk. Now they would hold the Droplet, which held the secret of the Great Master's demise. The thought of such triumph over one who had held them in bondage for so long led to a foolish movement: an irrepressible triumphant laugh.

It was then that their jaws opened—just for the smallest of seconds—to reveal the soft, vulnerable roofs of their mouths beyond their fearsome teeth. Instantly the Prince of Wallachia shook his head. Out of his jeweled red-velvet hat sprang the small, sharp, deadly blades that adorned it and that had earned him his mortal name for his many atrocities, not the least of which was a killing field in a terrible battle against the Ottomans, demonstrating his signature method, impaling. So it was that he was called Vlad the Impaler, although in the underworld had insisted upon the title of "prince," which he had recovered only just before being killed in battle. These blades shot straight into the weak spot of the serpent-shark gods: their mouths. They stung them and stunned them, loosening their grip upon the Brotherhood of Evil. Their excruciating pain stopped. The yellow light disappeared. Instantly they were back within the basement of the Hippodrome. The net of scales fell away, and the Brotherhood of Evil leaped out of the serpent-shark gods' hold.

The demons' bodies writhed in serpentine movements in the air, as if it were water. The Beast, Khan, and the duke scrambled to their feet. The tips of the blades, now lodged within the demons' mouths, had been dipped into the necks of those who, in their death throes, had pledged allegiance to Vlad. The blades' tips contained their agony, their despair, and the dominance the prince wielded over their souls. Although these tips could destroy lesser spirits, they merely stunned these sea-serpent demons. The Prince of Wallachia knew that the blades' effect would dissipate quickly and that the demon pythons would instantly recapture them. They had to escape.

The prince differed from Khan, the duke, and the Beast now that they were out of Kurnigi. They had no spirits under their control in the land of the living. But he, as Vlad, had cultivated a following. Though he had been dead for many centuries and buried in the bowels of Kurnigi, he remained a prophet of cruelty to many. In this way, those who were bloodthirsty for wealth, power, and domination over others would call upon Vlad in the night for eternal mortal life. It was Vlad who harnessed blood power—the ability to keep a corpse alive long after its mortal end—for which these creatures readily exchanged their souls. He had become the master of the unliving—a great collection of men and women who lived unnaturally long lives in their mortal bodies, who held in their greedy palms riches, who manipulated fortune so it was they who held it and preyed upon those who did not. They became creatures who left in the night as the living and entered the day as the dead—nocturnal beings who plunged their fangs into the necks of the living to suck their blood and who rested in the day, entombed peacefully in their mansions. It was these creatures of the night who had brought on the Great Depression, indeed a movable feast of pleasures created with the ingredients of mortal despair. The night held endless prey for them and for their master, Vlad. But the price for such fortune was steep: they owed full allegiance to Vlad as Master Sanguis Draco. They called themselves the members of the Ordinem Sanguis Draco, the Order of the Blood Dragon.

"Ordinem Sanguis Draco!" The Prince of Wallachia shook his long black hair, his narrow face set in a fierce countenance, his brows knit together.

The walls of the basement of the Hippodrome shook as numerous elegant figures appeared, pale with the greenish sheen of their master and dressed in fancy evening wear: glittering gowns that clung tightly to the women's figures or flowed in vast swaths of silk, tuxedos black as the night with long tails upon the men.

"Master Vlad!" came their surprised cries, for the master previously had come to them only through visions. Drops of blood dripped from their lips, as they had been amid a feast when they were called. It was All Hallows' Eve, a night of celebration.

"Take us from here!" Master Vlad ordered.

The nocturnal creatures pressed in closely upon the Brotherhood of Evil. The sea-salt smell of fresh blood rose from their breaths and covered the four in a vapor.

"Ordinem Sanguis Draco!" the bloodthirsty creatures said.

In an instant they all vanished.

The sea demons snarled at the escape of the Beast and the rest of the Brotherhood of Evil. Vlad's poisonous hold on them was slowly receding. Onto the floor of the Hippodrome's basement clattered Vlad's deadly blades from their mouths. The demons stirred as shadows of fear do, traveling in tendrils of terror upward into the Hippodrome's auditorium.

𒀭𒌋𒁀𒀭𒁹

The shoebox-shaped, smoke-filled tenement club in Harlem trembled as the crystal ball came shooting down. This time the Great Magician was quick, deftly moving in front of Mattie to catch it.

As soon as the Great Magician touched the crystal ball, Fat Man's body swung back as if jolted by an electric bolt. The drummer began drumming, and the piano and trumpet players sounded. The drumbeat moved faster and faster.

Fat Man was again in a hypnotic state, his eyes shut tightly, his dark-brown face beaded with sweat as his massive body shook to the beat.

Lalalaaaaaalalalaaaaalalalaarrrarrrra!
Dodododdoddodo!
Oooooooooooooooowhooawhoaaa!

The spiritualists swayed to the beat, their palms shimmering with the blue crystal feather, their protection against the rising dead souls. The conjurers' faces were a quilt of blacks, milky light browns, and dark browns. They sang to release Black Lazarus from the crystal ball.

Son of Moses, son of Moses!
Brother Lazarus, rise, we say, rise!

Fat Man was lost to his music.

Datdatdatdatdatdap!
A voice comes floating in sweet notes in the air,
Reminding me of my darlin', her face set in prayer.

Large musical notes formed on the small stage. They swirled about as the beat grew louder and stronger.

One note pierced the crystal ball held by the Great Magician. It pulled out a hand then a whole body.

It was Black Lazarus, lifted out by the notes of the song with which he once had opened his act. He landed on his feet on the stage.

The large black musical notes now plunged like spears, snaring the performers and audience as easily as fish in a shallow pool. Everyone in the Harlem club was caught. The conjurers were the first to disappear into the black notes.

Black Lazarus was not exempt, as he fell prey to a note, as did the Great Magician, even though it was he who held the crystal ball. Mattie yelped as a note grabbed her. The last thing she saw before blackness descended was Geeta's black braids wound in a musical note that was reeling her into it.

𒀭𒊏 𒆠 𒀭𒊏 𒉌

Time was of the essence; the buzz rose in the Hippodrome like a chant. Backstage, the performers moved hurriedly to be outfitted in their costumes. Others, who had been in life the makeup artists, the assistants to actors, also were in a hurry. For these performers and stagehands knew that the bodies they inhabited would soon decay. The stiffness of rigor mortis would come in just a few hours, and though the stiffness would later lift, the bodies would be no good by then. Drunks, thieves, those debauched by the night, the former denizens of the Dorothea Dix Insane Asylum, cab drivers, restaurant workers, nightclub patrons—the scattering of the wealthy set who were out this Halloween night of 1936—these were the bodies that the Muhra occupied.

In droves they moved into the theater in their new bodies— in jumping, jolting movements, true, for the fluidity that comes naturally from having form was now new to them. Oh, the sheer freedom of moving in an individual form, not to be clumped together with egos pushing against egos. Backstage some moved to open trunks to pull out costumes, others to open the fitting rooms. Others stretched their dead limbs, preparing to perform, calling out notes, moving the vocal chords of the possessed bodies to spew out operatic sounds. It didn't matter that these bodies weren't as they once had been, for now they were on stage.

The Great Diva cooed happily at herself, seated in her dressing room backstage, gazing at an enormous mirror over the vanity. Yes, she was pleased with her reflection in the large mirror. She saw her face shining and glimmering like a shark under the waitress' skin. The Great Diva had appropriated for herself the biggest dressing room, as naturally befitting the star. The theater's days of glory were in evidence in this room, with its deep plush carpeting, though it was worn and stained now. The Great Diva had pushed herself—that inflated, bombastic, breathtakingly self-centered spirit—into the small frame of the waitress. It was a bad fit, like a sweater three sizes too small for the wearer, stretched beyond recognition. But the Great Diva saw none of that; her vision in death, as in life, was sharpened through the prism of her all-encompassing narcissism.

The dressing room was crowded with the Great Diva's assistants and abuzz with activity. Several of these assistants gathered fussily about her, bringing her costume after costume. The Muhra wardrobe workers rolled in several large clothes racks crammed with costumes. Some held in their arms heaps of gowns that they presented to the Great Diva.

"No!" the Great Diva said in her high-handed manner to one after another. "No! No!"

All were too obvious: red gowns that flared out with low, seductive necklines; green silk numbers with embroidered borders that were fussy and overwrought; blue dresses that garishly shimmered.

"My Aida is pure! Bring me something virginal…something Madonna-esque!" the Great Diva demanded.

At last a pale silk gown the color of inner corn tassels was found. This gown would drape the curves of her body to show the simplicity yet nobility of Aida.

The Great Diva stood as hands ripped off the meager skirt and blouse of the dead waitress. She moved the arms through, and her assistants fastened the gown at the front. If nothing else, the Great Diva's instincts about what was faithful to a character were unerring. These sycophants murmured how the body captured by the Great Diva was the perfect vessel to play Aida. The Ethiopian princess in Verdi's great opera had never been so well cast, they cried. All felt honored to have this great privilege of getting the Great Diva ready for the opera, they exclaimed.

The Great Diva twirled and then fixed her bulging eyes greedily and admiringly upon her reflection within a full mirror. The she then dramatically threw out her arms and tried out an aria:

AaaaAaaaAaaaAaaa!

All the Muhra clapped dutifully.

The Great Diva gave a small conceited bow; her voice had moved through the dead waitress's vocal chords unimpaired. She sat down in front of the vanity and snapped her fingers.

"Hair! Face!" she commanded. "And someone, do *something* with these hands."

The Great Diva held out the waitress's hands. They weren't in good shape, having been worn by dishwashing and floor scrubbing. Quickly the assistants went to work, their dirt-encrusted fingers aflutter. They delicately handled the Great Diva's calloused hands and massaged them with creams.

Other makeup artists, bums with the bulbous red noses of the long drunk, now focused in concentration and flitted about the Great Diva with powder puffs and brushes. Their movements with the makeup brushes were dainty and delicate. These effete motions were feminine strains running paradoxical to the sausage-shaped hobo fingers that held them. They delicately lined the Diva's fish mouth with an intense, vibrant red as it protruded and overcame the dead waitress's rosebud lips; they applied a dark bronze to give her complexion the darkness of an Ethiopian princess. Others with fingers worn by sickness and starvation, veined and pale, ran combs and brushes through the hair upon the body's head.

Yes, the delicate innocence needed for the ingenue was there—provided one kept one's gaze to the neck down.

For there was *that* problem: the Great Diva's ego. So strong was it that it stretched the skin on the dead waitress's face, ballooning it out until the inner Great Diva's face insistently took its shape: the beaked nose, the moon-shaped forehead, the flat flounder lips over the donkey teeth. This was intentional. The Great Diva resolved it was imperative that it was *her* face (and not the face of some worthless waitress) that everyone saw perform *Aida*.

A Muhra hairdresser let out a yelp. The dead girl's hair was falling out in clumps as the Great Diva's scalp, nubby with gray bristles, poked through.

"Quickly! A wig!" she whispered, panicked, to the Muhra next to her, who was fearful of angering the Great Diva. "I need a long black wig!" The costume designer gasped. The Great Diva's borrowed body was already displaying ominous signs of stiffness. "And stand-ins! Get at least four ingenue bodies!"

𒀭𒁀𒌋 𒂍 𒀭𒁀 𒀸

Aida had begun. The Muhra audience felt the exhilaration of a performance unfolding. The music played by the hidden Muhra orchestra started. Oh, how long it had been since they had *felt* anything! Yes, these forms were not ideal; yes, they were in the audience, but the thrill of opening night was still that. And it was that grand opera *Aida*: that majestic story of the love triangle of the royal Ethiopian Princess Aida, the enemy Egyptian commander Radames, and the jealous pharoah's daughter,

Amneris, to whom he is pledged. On the stage was a giant background that depicted pyramids and enormous columns with Egyptian symbols of birds of prey. From backstage the players streamed out: the bodies of men and women, looking zombified but moving. The women wore simple sleeveless white wraps to depict Egyptian handmaidens. They had a circle of white flowers about their heads, and their waists were draped with a swash of deep-red cloth; some carried palm fronds that they waved in rhythm. The men were bare chested, some of them emaciated, as many of the bodies available to the Muhra had belonged to those sleeping in alleyways. They wore white cloths, longer than loincloths, with white sashes about their foreheads. Some wore mustard-colored gowns; others wore red turbans. Some wore helmets and brandished swords. Still others held large spears with tribal faces painted upon them; others waved white flags.

A shiver went through the borrowed Muhra bodies: of course *Aida* would have to be abbreviated; the bodies would last only so long, and all would leave to get more. How brilliant of the Great Diva to begin with the emblematic scene of triumph in Act Two, at the grand gate of the city of Thebes, where Radames makes his return to Egypt after his victory on the battlefield. Next Radames would be reunited with Aida, an Ethiopian princess captured and brought to Egypt. Ah, yes.

Carried onto the stage, high upon a red-carpeted dais, by ten Ethiopian slaves, five on each side, was the triumphant Radames, strong and majestic in his white royal robes and peaked helmet and bearing the spear of victory (this took some imagination, for the body taken for Radames had a decidedly bookish, peevish aspect that contradicted the valor and soldierly manliness that the part called for). As well, the Ethiopian slaves had the darting eyes of the insane (for they had once been residents of the Dorothea Dix Insane Asylum). But no matter, the audience thought. There was more than enough pomp and splendor in the 1908 Hippodrome sets to convey the glamour.

Then, from behind Radames on the dais, a vibrant aria suddenly rang out:

Aaaaaaaaaa! Mi dolce Radames!

It was the Great Diva as Aida. The Muhra audience clapped, surprised that the Great Diva would so break the classic opera with her appearance, for Aida was not in this scene at all. Perhaps it would be a quick move into Act Four, the imprisonment of Radames and Aida, the touching scene of love requited?

The Great Diva now inhabited a new body—as the waitress's had fallen apart—but still this one conveyed litheness. It was perhaps a bit emaciated, as the Muhra had retrieved her from a tuberculosis ward, and "ingenue" was a stretch, as the body was in middle years rather than youth. Still, the Great Diva had wrapped the body in the gentle folds of the virginal silk gown the color of inner corn tassels.

The Great Diva's moon head and beaked nose ballooned out of the dead woman's face. Suddenly she pulled out a large sword from the folds of her gown and plunged it straight into Radames's chest. The bewildered Muhra playing Radames toppled off the platform.

The Muhra audience gasped. Many had been in *Aida* themselves, not just once but many times. They stirred at the audacity, the shocking and absolute conceit of the Great Diva to tamper with Verdi! The Diva had commandeered a classic!

The orchestra played on. Rules were for others, not the Great Diva. This was her opening night—who cared about the story?

She took the best scene for herself. After all, *she* was what mattered. The Great Diva would demonstrate how, even though she had been dead so long, even though her arias moved through the vocal chords of a corpse, she was still *prima donna assoluta*!

The flounder lips parted to tell the story of her beauty:

Aaaaaaaaaa!
O mio amore ora così morto
Lei non potrà mai vedere la mia bella faccia
Le mie labbra come boccioli di rosa
I miei occhi che brillano come diamanti abbagliante.
Aaaaaaaaaa!

The platform shook; the Muhra playing Ethiopian slaves were falling prey to rigor mortis, their bodies stiffening. The Muhra inhabiting these bodies moved out; they needed new forms. The dais tilted then collapsed. The Great Diva yelped as she slid down. Her long, dark wig flew off. The body she had taken was bald, and the Great Diva's gray bristles were pushing up the scalp.

Then there was a thump.

Fat Man and his band fell onto the stage. The Muhra *Aida* players scrambled away as quickly as their bodies would allow.

Fat Man's eyes were shut. The fact that he was no longer in the smoky environs of the shabby club was unknown to him, as he sang from a mesmerized state.

The drummer beat the drums; the piano notes rang out; and the trumpet sang its song. They drowned out the Muhra orchestra.

Bababarrarum babarararum!
I say it right now…the heartbeat goes crazy
Whenever I see you, darlin'.

My mind goes hazy
As I fall under your spell.

The Muhra spectators were very puzzled. Who were these players? Their noses sniffed—some of these intruders were alive.

Fat Man sang:

O R-R-R-R-Rosabelle...O R-R-R-R-Rosabelle!
Wanna be, wanna be, wanna be, wanna be, wanna be
With a you, with a you, my sweet baaaaybee.
With a you, with a you, with a you, my sweet baaaaybeee.
I walk in love...I walk in love...I walk...in laaaoove...can't you see?
Because you, my darlin', you my darlin',
You got me under your spell,
O dark-eyed, sweet O R-R-R-R-Rosabelle.

It was the hardness of the Hippodrome's stage that Mattie felt even before the heat or the brightness of the stage lights. Instinctively she pulled Seven Sista's brown-checked cloth coat around her, as if for protection. She was overwhelmed by the noise, the colors, and the evil that surrounded them, for beyond the stage she felt an audience made of thousands of eyes staring right at them. She and Geeta were in the center. At the side stood Fat Man and his band, along with the Great Magician, Black Lazarus, and a circle of conjurers.

"Geeta," Mattie whispered about the chaotic scene. Something about the eyes around them was very familiar, but she couldn't place it.

The audience was stiffening. Some Muhra had left their bodies already; others were readying to do so.

Mattie saw the Great Diva, with her beaked nose, moon-shaped forehead, and bulging eyes, move toward her. *It's them, from the rooftop!*

Indeed, the Great Diva had immediately recognized Mattie as the one who held the Spyglass. She pounced forward to take the body of the red-haired child, then the amulet. How triumphant would she be now, as holder of that powerful talisman? Then she could command as many bodies as she needed, firm and young ones, at will.

Mattie gasped and pushed Geeta behind her. "It's those nasty ghosts in the fog who tried to kill you. Stay back."

Geeta shivered. *They didn't try to kill me—they did kill me.* Then the thought struck her: *Am I now a spirit rather than a body?* She looked at the restored lifeline on her right palm, which pulsed bright blue.

The Great Magician's eyes scanned the Hippodrome. *From the basement to the theater. Could Bess be here?* He looked into the crystal ball and saw the swimming figures of the Phantom Magicians trapped inside. A bell chimed. The midnight hour was over. Then the image cleared in the crystal ball. He saw his beloved Bess in her bedroom. From her end table, she picked up a picture of the Great Magician.

His heart plunged. "No! Bess, please don't."

Bess turned it facedown. She blew out a small candle and turned off the lamp. The crystal ball cleared. The trapped Phantom Magicians swam, their lips moving, pleading to the Great Magician to release them. But the Great Magician heard only the sounds of his heartbreak.

The Muhra onstage smelled the odor of the living. New fresh bodies. They moved toward the conjurers and the band.

Black Lazarus cried out in warning, "Souls from hell!" for he too feared the Muhra. Even in spirit form, they could pull him into their lair of darkness.

The conjurers raised their palms, and the blue-feather imprint lifted from their skin to turn into blue bottles again. They raised these toward the approaching Muhra to trap them. The Muhra instinctively moved back as the conjurers shook the blue bottles to ward them off.

The Great Diva's possessed body was lurching now, as rigor mortis quickly moved through her. Suddenly she fell, right onto Mattie. Geeta and Mattie screamed in unison, though it was lost in the unending song of Fat Man's band. The Great Diva's Muhra spirit rose like a fog. A face broke out of that fog, with bulging eyes that looked familiarly at Mattie and Geeta. The white moon of a forehead appeared, and then below it emerged eyeglasses over a beaked nose and prim expression. She said in a reprimanding tone, "I warned you: trick-or-treating can be dangerous."

Mattie and Geeta shouted in terror, "It's Mrs. Elmwood's ghost!"

But it was the Great Diva's trick to frighten them. Suddenly her arms reached out to grab Mattie. *Raise your palm!* she heard Seven Sista in her mind. Mattie raised her right palm to reveal the blue crystal imprint. The Great Diva fell back, her donkey teeth clattering.

Mattie's heart pounded. Geeta looked terrified. They had no magic, no Mr. Biddle, no way to thwart this evil. Mattie turned to the Great Magician and tugged his coat, for he seemed in a daze. They needed that crystal ball to escape; they had to leave this place.

When she touched the Great Magician's coat, her speech became garbled as the bitterness of his heartbreak moved through her. Mattie's eyes were fixed on the unseen. A doleful song fell in bitter droplets from her mouth, heard only in the Great Magician's ears.

O my lost love!
Weep do I for you!
Not for us is sunshine.
O my lost love!
Not for us are the singing pines
Or the soft green meadows,
For our loves are lost and beaten,
Taken from our bosoms,
Taken from our sides.

The Hippodrome Theatre was now a cacophony of noises: Muhra screeching as they left their stiff bodies, the sounds of the conjurers driving back the Muhra, the endless notes of Fat Man's band, and the song of the Seven Bitter Widows. The Great Magician was lost in sorrow, holding the crystal ball to his chest.

Then the Seven Bitter Widows appeared above in a semicircle, with faces of the tilled earth, the pale moon, the sand of redrock mountains, the black pebbles of the stream, and the yellow of a fading sun. To Mattie and Geeta they spoke.

But cry alone we must.
You have not tried to beg or borrow
One way to mend our endless sorrow.
Not one tear did you shed for love lost,
Nor did you care of our heartbreak's cost.
Cared not did you for our aching hearts' wails.
Cared not did you for their bitter tales.

Now you will pay for your sneers,
As you move from this tale of tears
To ever-greater fears.

From the Hippodrome's vaulted ceiling, hundreds of Buddhas in saffron robes, translucent in form, appeared. Some had rolls of fat, so corpulent were they; others were gaunt, with ribs that protruded from their sides, their eyes hollow. Some were male, some female; some were chalk white, others black as obsidian. Others bore the brown color of tilled soil; still others were pale yellow, and still others had a rusty reddish tint. All were suspended in meditative poses as they chanted:

Eight precious stones,
Eight matters of the soul,
Rise like the wind of wrath.
Eight stones of suffering:
Fear, hate, anger, bitterness, envy, duplicity, greed, and despair.

Four stones remain.
If you can cross them,
You will find the Seer of Truth.

The Buddhas enveloped a circle of few on the stage. Their hands pulled the Great Magician and Black Lazarus up, followed by Mattie and Geeta, and then they vanished into a harsh green light.

The alleyway behind the Hippodrome shook. The cement rippled and broke, and from it emerged a black stink. Then the stink turned into great black wings that pierced through the scaled body of a giant serpent with the tail of dragonfly: yellow, black, and green. The tail tightly clasped the Iron Knight, his ruddy face bathed in sweat. The huge cobra head wobbled, and the blue and green eyes of the Snake glistened in triumph as he flapped his enormous wings against the walls of the Hippodrome, ready to strike and kill.

The Snake lifted his head and scanned the empty alleyway. He had seen Biddle writhing here in his vision, with two old men kneeling at his side, their eyes wide with fear as he, Uri Gneezy, formed into a fearsome serpent before them. Saghulhaza, the upholder of evil, the Sebitti, those seven guardians of Marduk, had called him when he had overcome the vulture. Gneezy was much more than the possessor of the Black Book of Magic. He would finally be able to destroy Biddle and take from him the White Book of Magic and, most important, seize from the red-haired child the Spyglass with all its powers.

The emptiness of the alleyway mocked these thoughts. Disappointment then anger shook his serpentine body. His forked tongue shot out and stung the air. Yes, Biddle had been here, for he felt the residuals of his spirit. The Snake's body moved again. The great black wings flapped forward and backward, their tips scraping the walls that formed the alleyway. His tail flicked to release the Iron Knight, clean-shaven, ruddy faced, blond, and pudgy; his eyes flashed with arrogance and conceit in death, as they had in life. He fell ungracefully onto the ground, his stomach protruding in bulges above and under the broad black belt that cinched his middle. The gray dust of Kurnigi covered the Iron Knight. The Snake's tail flicked again. The

Reichsmarschall's baton appeared in the Iron Knight's hand: that long tube of ivory, covered with gold and silver blades, embedded with gold snakes and scorpions, and inlaid with rubies, emeralds, and diamonds—a nod to the Iron Knight's egotism. On each end of this baton was a black snake, entwined to form the symbol of the swastika but now changing. For that was an old master, and the Iron Knight now swore allegiance to the Snake. Each black snake around his arms now had two eyes that glittered blue and green. He stood in sturdy, knee-high black boots.

Gneezy flung his head back to release the Black Book of Magic to guide him to Biddle but was stopped by a rise of ominous sounds. They were the beats of a death drum, rising in a dense fog in the alleyway. They enveloped the Snake, shaking his body. Then within the fog the chants of the seven guardians of Marduk formed. They heralded the coming of the Master of Darkness.

Devel, Deofol, Ha-satan-ba-al devar, Iblis!
Azazel, Baphomet, Ba'al-zevuv, Beliar, Bheliar!

Marduk appeared within the fog before the writhing Snake in the Goliath form of a man. Narrow red eyes sat above an aristocratic aquiline nose. His face was gray and green at once, his hair and beard made of writhing black-and-orange vipers. Adorning his head was a crown of daggers encircled by a silvery-gray band. Ram's horns sprouted from his head, ending in sharp points. He wore silver armor upon his torso, and on his breast the Tablet of Destiny of Darkness glowed. Marduk unfurled great black wings behind him. His muscular arms were encircled with straps of silver with incantations upon them; his wrists bore broad black bands that moved and showed themselves to be creatures of the night: a circle of bats flying closely upon one another.

Marduk's eyes glowered, angry and red, in his devil face. They turned upon the Snake, who was slithering on the pavement. Great lashes of heat struck the reptile; the pain rolled in waves through the Snake's body as his tongue struck the air. The Iron Knight, at the Snake's side, raised and dropped his gaze as he shuddered in fear at the might of Marduk. Then light shot from the Dark Master's eyes, laser beams that struck only the Snake. The Snake's cobra head shook, and he kept back a hiss of pain. Gneezy felt the Dark Master's unhappiness that he had survived. It was clear that the vulture creature that the Snake had fought and killed in Kurnigi had been the Sebitti's anointed one, meant to destroy him and capture the Black Book of Magic.

Marduk spoke:

Snake, winner of the battle and Saghulhaza may you be,
But loser to the forces of our enemies,
For see how it lies in Kurnigi:
The gates of hell now open wide, souls captured turned to dust.
Holder of the Black Book you remain, but capture the traitor you must.

The sound of the giant hands of the Sebitti striking their thighs in a foreboding drumbeat rose around the Dark Master. Gneezy slithered uneasily on the ground, the wings of the vulture creature melting into his scaled body.

The drumbeat of the Sebitti and the words of the Dark Master sent shivers of fear through his cold, bloodless form. The Snake's body turned blood red.

Marduk's order rang out:

Portals dark! Shadows fall!
Harken, Snake, to this call.

In the land of the living you are now, where capture you must the Beast.
Find him among those for whom the gushing blood of mortals is their
ghoulish feast:
Creatures of the dead, their fangs bloody, their bellies well fed.
Overcome that evil trio who lie with the Beast in a traitorous bed,
Crush must you these enemies of your master.
Imprison must you this Beast.
Speaker of falsehoods, keeper of secrets, holder of lore,
This treacherous Beast must be no more.

The Dark Master brandished a scepter inlaid with lapis lazuli
that blazed an intense blue. From the top of this staff sprang four
dark ropes with beads of silver that he swung in the air. He threw
down the scepter to the Snake, who caught it in his bony hands.

This mighty weapon, forged in the battle with the demon gods of old,
Formed when the story of the Dark Book was told,
To the Saghulhaza, it is given to hold.
Bind must you the Beast's hairy form with dread.
To do so, these four bands of silver beads
Must be embedded deep within his head.
Then will this scepter, with its lapis lazuli,
Glow black then blue and shine anew.
Then your deed will be done.
Then your battle will be won.

Marduk vanished with his seven guardians.
Silence followed.
The Iron Knight stood with his ruddy face bathed in sweat.
Circles of wetness seeped under his arms through his dust-cov-
ered gray uniform. His master, the dark-red giant serpent, with

his cobra head and a body from which two arms sprang out—
one holding the staff with the beads of silver—hissed.

The long forked tongue hit the air.

The Snake raised his hand to show the imprint of the Spyglass.
"Crone!" he said. "Bring it."

End of Book Three

Gratitude

I am profoundly grateful to Bob Newlon for his support of my journey in and through the Mattie series. I remain in awe of the artistry of Dan Ungureanu so beautifully in evidence in the cover illustrations of all three of the Mattie books. I am thankful to Dan Smee for his counsel by word and deed of the warrior ethos. Lastly, I am deeply appreciative of my editor Angela Brown for her thoughtful and careful review of the manuscript and her delicate wielding of "Occam's razor" when needed to excise the fat.

about the author

Shoba Sreenivasan holds a Ph.D from UCLA in clinical psychology. She has worked as a VA psychologist and a forensic psychologist for much of her career, has published scholarly articles, and also holds an academic appointment at the University of Southern California.

www.ingramcontent.com/pod-product-compliance
Lightning Source LLC
Chambersburg PA
CBHW071630260626
47170CB00001B/37